Praise for Elaine Everest

'A warm tale of friendship and romance'
My Weekly

'Captures the spirit of wartime'
Woman's Weekly

'One of the most iconic stores comes back to life
in this heartwarming tale'
Woman's Own

'Elaine brings the heyday of the iconic high-street
giant to life in her charming novel'
S Magazine

A Christmas Wish at Woolworths

Elaine Everest, author of bestselling novels *The Wool-worths Girls*, *The Butlins Girls*, *Christmas at Woolworths* and *The Teashop Girls*, was born and brought up in north-west Kent, where many of her books are set. She has been a freelance writer for twenty-five years and has written widely for women's magazines and national newspapers, both short stories and features. Her non-fiction books for dog owners have been very popular and led to her broadcasting on the radio about our four-legged friends. Elaine has also been heard discussing many other topics on the airwaves, from her Kent-based novels to living with a husband under her feet when redundancy looms.

Also by Elaine Everest

The Woolworths Girls series
The Woolworths Girls
Carols at Woolworths (ebook novella)
Christmas at Woolworths
Wartime at Woolworths
A Gift from Woolworths
Wedding Bells for Woolworths
A Mother Forever
The Woolworths Saturday Girls
The Woolworths Girl's Promise
Celebrations for the Woolworths Girls
A Christmas Wish at Woolworths

The Teashop Girls series
The Teashop Girls
Christmas with the Teashop Girls
The Teashop Girls at War

Standalone novels
Gracie's War
The Butlins Girls
The Patchwork Girls

Elaine Everest

A Christmas Wish at Woolworths

PAN BOOKS

First published 2024 by Macmillan

an imprint of Pan Macmillan
The Smithson, 6 Briset Street, London EC1M 5NR
EU representative: Macmillan Publishers Ireland Ltd, 1st Floor,
The Liffey Trust Centre, 117–126 Sheriff Street Upper,
Dublin 1, D01 YC43
Associated companies throughout the world
www.panmacmillan.com

ISBN 978-1-0350-2068-3

3 5 7 9 8 6 4 2

A CIP catalogue record for this book is available from the British Library.

Typeset by Palimpsest Book Production Ltd, Falkirk, Stirlingshire
Printed and bound by CPI Group (UK) Ltd, Croydon, CR0 4YY

Visit www.panmacmillan.com to read more about all our books
and to buy them. You will also find features, author interviews and
news of any author events, and you can sign up for e-newsletters
so that you're always first to hear about our new releases.

To my fellow 'boomers', born December 1953.
Happy seventieth birthday x

Prologue

Sunday, 6 September 1953

Maisie stretched her long, sun-kissed legs and sighed as she relaxed in the red and white striped deckchair in her back garden. 'It's good to have a day off once in a while and be able to enjoy the sun on my body.'

'You've got enough of it on show,' Claudette laughed. It was true as the yellow seersucker sunsuit barely covered Maisie's legs and left little to the imagination further up. Even though she was well into her thirties, she looked as youthful as Bessie and Claudette and as glamorous as she had the day she walked into the Woolworths store in 1938, her blonde locks just as stylish and not a worry line on her face.

'As you well know, this was one of our best-selling summer lines. It far outsold what the pair of you are wearing,' she snorted, while still admiring the seersucker frocks with matching boleros her two stepdaughters were wearing. 'I think I'll start taking more days off now we have this garden to enjoy, before the autumn arrives and then winter,' she groaned.

1

'Then it will be Christmas,' Bessie said, 'and I can't wait. It will be wonderful celebrating it here in our new home. However, today is Sunday; you should start taking at least one day off each week. It's not right working on the sabbath.' She was sitting on the lawn next to Maisie, watching her young daughter run around in the long grass. 'Mind you, this all needs mowing and the flower borders are out of control.'

'Blimey, have you caught a dose of religion?' Maisie mocked the girl before looking serious. 'But you are right, we do need to make time for family and friends and with the business being closed on a Sunday, it's the ideal time. In fact, I'm one step ahead of you as I've invited Sarah, Freda and the gang over for tea this afternoon. It's about time we showed the place off.'

Claudette jumped to her feet. 'I'll make a cake. I take it Nanny Ruby and Bob are also invited? I want to show her a recipe I found in *The People's Friend*.'

'We've got enough food in the pantry to feed an army, but if you want to make a cake, I'll not argue. What doesn't get eaten I can give to the team tomorrow when they come over to work in my bridal studio; I'm looking forward to seeing ladies working on the gowns in the room I've designed especially for them.'

'That sounds a bit posh. We've never had a studio before,' Bessie chuckled. 'Next we'll be having an *orangery* like next door,' she went on, overemphasizing the word as Claudette joined in with the laughter, pointing out that their neighbour's orangery was nothing more than a lean-to with a glass window and a few pot plants.

'Shh, stop it, we may be overheard,' Maisie hissed,

although she was finding it hard not to join in with the laughter. 'I read how all the best dress shops have bridal studios and thought how nice it would be to have one for Maisie's Modes. It will attract the right kind of clients if we plan to go upmarket and they can come here to try on their gowns.'

Bessie nodded her head although she looked serious. 'Don't forget your roots, Mum, as the people of Erith supported you when you started out.'

'I'll never do that, my love. In fact, I have a few more plans,' Maisie replied as she pulled her straw sun hat over her face and leant back in the deckchair. 'I'll just have a little snooze then pop in and see how lunch is doing . . .'

Claudette nodded to Bessie and the two sisters crept away, leaving Maisie to rest.

Bessie lifted her daughter, Jenny, perching her on one hip as the two sisters walked towards the house. 'I still find it hard to believe we live here,' she said, shading her eyes with one hand as they looked up at the four-storey house.

'And we have a servant,' Claudette giggled. 'I'll never get used to that.'

'I don't think Mrs Ince can be classed as a servant. She told me she prefers to be called a "woman what does" as she does anything she is called upon to do. I think she's a marvel and Mum loves having her about the place. Do you know she offered to clean my rooms and do Jenny's ironing? Of course, I refused, but for a moment I waivered . . .'

'She's a diamond, as Nanny Ruby would say. I know I'm aware when she's working about the house and keep my own room clean. I'd be embarrassed to have her tidy up after me.'

'And that is why we will always be working class and proud of it,' Bessie laughed as she opened the door to the ground-floor rooms where she lived with Jenny. 'Posh folk would have Mrs Ince running after them and never even give a thank you. I reckon her next door would be like that. She's so stuck up; she caught me the other day as I was taking Jenny to the park and casually mentioned that she hasn't seen my husband about.'

'What a cheek,' Claudette fumed. 'Whatever did you say to her?'

'I put on a sad face and said how he was lost to me,' Bessie giggled. 'I'm pretty sure she thought my imaginary husband had passed away. Thank goodness I kept wearing this ring from Woolies.'

'Even if it turns your finger green. Perhaps it's time you found someone to put a proper one on your finger?'

'Why, Claudette Carlisle, I'm surprised at you,' Bessie said, half in jest. 'I would never seek someone to marry just to be respectable, especially for nosy old biddies like her next door. I made a mistake, but look at what I have now,' she said, gazing lovingly at her daughter who was now sitting on a colourful rag rug brushing her dolly's hair.

'Perhaps one day you will find your prince charming,' Claudette said as she started to dance around the room, causing Jenny to giggle.

'Not everything in life is like your pantomime, Cinders,' Bessie said, referring to the role her sister had just been cast in for the Erith amateur dramatics group's proposed Christmas extravaganza. She couldn't help thinking how well suited Claudette would be to the star part of Cinderella; she had started to slim down, losing her childhood puppy fat, and although Claudette would never agree, she was beginning to look like a beautiful young woman. 'Here, look at this,' Bessie said as she peered from behind the blue floral curtains.

Claudette hurried over and looked towards what her sister was pointing at. 'Why, the nosy old—' Bessie nudged her before she finished her sentence.

'Little ears,' she whispered, looking past Claudette to where Jenny was oblivious to her mother and aunt and in a world of her own.

'But they are spying on Mum,' Claudette hissed as they watched their neighbour, along with another woman, peering through a hedge that bordered their property. Maisie, who was still sunbathing with her sun hat over her face, was unaware she was being watched, let alone being talked about.

Bessie frowned as she observed the women. She was tempted to tap on the window to show them they had been noticed, but felt it wasn't enough. Putting a finger to her lips to stop her sister commenting, she crept from the room and went outside once more, to where a hosepipe lay close to the back of the house. Taking one end, she aimed it towards the women and nodded to Claudette to turn on the tap.

'Gosh, these plants look as though they are wilting. Let's give them a good soaking,' she said loudly as Claudette agreed.

Maisie leapt to her feet, startled awake by the shrieks from the two elderly women as the jet of water hit them through the hedge, which they'd parted to gain a better view of their new neighbour. 'What the bloody hell?' she shouted as she shook droplets of water from the short skirt of her sunsuit. She waved a finger at the women, not noticing their bedraggled appearance. 'Are you responsible for this?'

The woman Maisie recognized as her neighbour had turned red as her usually perfectly coiffed hair dripped around her face. 'What? You think I did this to myself and my friend? Madam – and I use the term lightly – look to your offspring, as they are the miscreants. When two ladies are accosted by a hosepipe while spending a peaceful Sunday in the garden, one must question what kind of riff-raff has moved into this prestigious road.'

Maisie was dumbstruck. She had meant to visit her next-door neighbour and introduce herself properly, perhaps with a homemade cake, although that may have started relations off on the wrong foot as her baking wasn't up to much. However, what with getting their home straight and the business taking over her life, her plans had run amok.

Her hackles raised, she stepped closer to where the women stood looking through the gap in the hedge. 'Riff-raff, you say? What right have you got to call my family such a thing? I'll 'ave you know, madam, that me and my 'usband are respectable business owners and our kids are decent human beings.' Even as she spoke, she could feel herself falling back to the Maisie of old with her dropped aitches and fiery temper.

'Mum, it's all right. We apologize,' Bessie said as the two girls stood beside Maisie.

'It's just that they've had their beaks through the gap for ages watching and talking about you and as we started to

6

water the garden . . .' Claudette stopped speaking as she wasn't one to tell lies.

'We gave them a good dousing – they deserved it,' Bessie said, not being one to hold back. 'Nice neighbours don't spy on people,' she hissed, causing the women to take a step back as she started to raise the hosepipe.

Maisie took the hosepipe from Bessie knowing it wouldn't help matters to soak the women for a second time.

The friend of her neighbour looked down her beaky nose and spoke with some disdain. 'Nice neighbours aren't unmarried mothers,' she sneered. 'We know your type and you aren't welcome around here.'

Bessie looked between the two women and, before Maisie could utter a word, she had run back towards the house sobbing her heart out.

'Now, you look here, you nosy old cow. No one speaks to my girls like that,' she said through gritted teeth as she stepped closer to the hedge. 'You know nothing about me or my family and I'll ask politely for you to apologize for your unkind words.'

Both women crossed their arms across their chests, making Maisie think they looked like a pair of fisherwives. They turned to walk away, with one saying out loud, 'How someone who worked in Woolworths has gone downmarket working in a factory I don't know – no doubt her money comes from illegal means. I mean, look at the way she's dressed. No wonder her daughters have children out of wedlock.'

Maisie growled out loud as she leant through the gap in the hedge and aimed the hosepipe at the women's backs. 'Turn the tap on full power, Claudette,' she said as she kept aiming at the squawking women. 'Don't you ever make assumptions about my children,' she yelled as loud as she could. 'Say what you like about me, but not my kids or you'll have me to answer to . . .'

She turned to walk back towards the house, throwing the hosepipe to the ground as she did so, calling out to Claudette who stood with her hand on the tap. 'Leave it running as who knows when we will need to use it urgently.' She was rewarded with another small shriek from next door before they quickly hurried inside, slamming the door shut behind them. She laughed out loud until a cough from the back door announced her husband David was home and looking none too pleased.

*

'I'll leave you to it if there's nothing else you need?' Mrs Ince said as she looked with pride at the perfectly roasted leg of lamb she'd placed in the middle of the dining table. Next to it were bowls of roast potatoes and vegetables. 'The apple pie's in the oven keeping warm and the custard just needs heating,' she added.

'Mrs Ince, you are a marvel. My family would starve if it weren't for you.' Maisie reached into her pocket and pulled out an envelope. 'There's a little something extra in there for all the help you've been to me this week,' she smiled, as the older woman blushed and the children clapped.

'I'm just doing my job,' she said as she looked around the table at the Carlisle family. 'Enjoy your meal and I'll see you in the morning. Don't worry about the washing-up; leave it stacked in the sink. Oh, and I've made the sandwiches for your guests and put them in the pantry,' she added before leaving them to their lunch.

'She's a goddess, a blooming goddess!' Maisie declared before noticing David's stern look as he started to carve the joint of meat.

'That keeps her safe from having a hosepipe turned on her,' he said, glancing at his wife and eldest daughters, who didn't help by starting to giggle.

'Dad, the two women were asking for it snooping as they did on Mum, and it's not the first time.' Bessie tied a bib around Jenny's neck and pulled her highchair closer. 'I saw her the other day leaning so far between those bushes she was almost in our garden. Why are people like that and what have we done to deserve her looking down her nose at us?'

The tension David had felt since spotting his wife and eldest daughters showering their new neighbours dropped from his shoulders. He had a good family, and he knew it would take a while for them to fit in with the people living in Avenue Road, just as the neighbours would have to learn to accept his family. They were all hardworking and affable women so it shouldn't take too long for those living either side of the house to understand that.

'Is Bob coming to tea this afternoon?' he asked Maisie as she started to pass dinner plates to him while he continued to carve. 'I thought I'd have a word with him on how to add to the hedging.'

Maisie tried not to grin at the older girls as she replied. 'Yes, Sarah and Alan are picking Ruby and Bob up, so they don't have to walk up the avenue; it's rather warm for them to walk far. Now, our Ruby, can you be a good girl and eat properly or I will have to put you in a highchair and feed you with a spoon, just like your niece, Jenny.'

Maisie and David's youngest two children started to laugh and nudged each other. 'You tell her.'

'No, you do it.'

A stern look crossed Maisie's face as she looked between the twins. 'Well, spit it out before our food gets cold. You know I don't stand for bad manners at the dinner table.'

David stopped carving and looked at his nine-year-olds, Toby and Mabel. 'Come on, you heard your mother.'

Toby turned to his sister and nodded for her to speak. 'Ruby doesn't want to be called Ruby any more. She says it's an old lady's name.'

'I reckon our Ruby can speak for herself,' David said, looking at the child. She may have been older than the twins but she was overshadowed by her boisterous siblings. 'Is this true?'

Ruby started to sniff as large tears ran down her face. She wouldn't look up at her father but kept her gaze on her lap.

Maisie knew they'd get no sense from the shy child. 'I tell you what, let's get on with our meal and we can have a chat while we do the washing-up, eh?'

The twins started to protest. 'Mrs Ince said to leave it,' Mabel said.

'That's right, she did,' Toby added, supporting his sister.

'I don't want our visitors seeing I have a messy kitchen, so wash up we will and you three are going to help me. Have you got that? Now, Ruby, why don't you pass around the mint sauce? Is that right you helped Mrs Ince to pick the mint from the garden?'

Ruby nodded and opened her mouth to speak but she was too slow, and the twins spoke for her.

'She did, but we had to stop her picking the nettles.'

Ruby sighed and looked back down at her lap.

Maisie was thoughtful as she helped David pass the plates around the table, encouraging the children to add vegetables to their plates. He gave her a concerned look. 'Are you thinking what I'm thinking?' he whispered.

'Yes, I believe I am, but don't worry, I'll get to the bottom of it. Although God knows how.'

Maisie stroked her daughter's golden hair as she passed behind her seat, and Ruby looked up at her with a timid smile. Maisie was struck by a memory as she smiled back, leaning over to kiss her cheek. 'Now, eat up as we have a busy afternoon ahead of us.'

*

Maisie filled the large butler sink with hot water and dripped in a little Quix soap. 'You know, Ruby, there was a time when I had to boil a kettle before I could do the washing-up and we would grate soap or use soap flakes in the water. You have no idea how my life is so much easier these days, especially as we have hot water that comes out of a tap. So many people aren't as lucky as us.' She started to wash the plates knowing she had her daughter's attention. Through the window she could keep an eye on the twins who'd been sent out to tidy away toys and put cushions on seats before their guests arrived. Claudette was tidying the front room while Bessie put Jenny down for her nap. 'I used to bath you in a sink smaller than this one.'

Ruby giggled as she leant against the wooden draining board. 'How did you do the washing?'

'Why, I took it down to the riverbank and bashed it with

11

a big rock,' she jested while dabbing soap on her daughter's nose.

'Really?'

'Blimey, kid, I'm not that old. We had a copper and a mangle, but it was back-breaking work. You should ask Nanny Ruby what it was like when she was a young woman, and her George and Pat were children.' She knew she'd hit a raw nerve as a cloud fell over the girl's face. 'Do you know who you reminded me of?'

'Nanny Ruby?' the girl asked, looking miserable.

'No, not for one moment. After all, we aren't blood-related to the Caseltons – that was Nanny Ruby's first married name as Bob is her second husband. We all think of her as one of our family as she is such a wonderful person; that's why I named you after her.'

'It's an old person's name,' Ruby said.

Ah, so that's what is eating her up, Maisie thought as she turned away to reach for more crockery to dunk into the hot water.

'An honourable name all the same. No, you remind me of my little sister.'

'I didn't know you had a little sister. Why don't you talk about your family?'

'One day I'll tell you, but for now let's just say they caused me a lot of hurt when I was much younger than I am now. Sheila didn't, and that's why your second name is for me to remember her. She died when she was younger than you.'

'That's a shame,' Ruby said, slipping her hand into Maisie's. 'Perhaps sometime you could tell me about her? It is such a pretty name. I wish it had been my first name. Ruby is nice but . . .'

'But it's an old lady's name and you are growing up in the shadow of a woman everyone knows and loves who has the same name. I can see why it upsets you.' They were both silent as Maisie washed and Ruby dried.

'How would you like to be called Sheila? I'm sure Nanny Ruby would understand?' Maisie asked, knowing the name spoken in everyday conversation would bring back memories she'd wished to bury, but for her daughter's happiness she could cope with it.

Ruby beamed. 'I'd like that very much, but how can we tell everyone?'

'Leave it with me, Miss Sheila Carlisle,' she said, kneeling down and hugging the child. She would move heaven and earth to have her child happy even if she had failed to save her sister's life. 'Now, pop out and help your brother and sister. They seem to be fighting each other with the cushions rather than tidying up.'

Ruby hurried out of the room as Maisie went to the door and called for Claudette to join her. 'There's something I need you to do before our guests turn up.'

*

'Thank you for showing me about,' Ruby Jackson said as she followed Maisie into a long bay-fronted room that stretched from the front to the back of the house. 'I must say, this is an extraordinary room,' she exclaimed as Maisie led her to a velvet-covered chaise longue set at an angle to an ornate fireplace.

'This is going to be my workroom and where some of my ladies will also work on the more delicate fabrics. The cutting table is down at the far end and these cupboards will hold embroidery silks.'

'You've really thought things out, haven't you?' Ruby said as she ran her hand over the deep red velvet. 'I take it the children won't be allowed in here?'

'God forbid,' Maisie chuckled. 'Although our Claudette and Bessie can work here if they aren't at the factory. Remind me to tell Bessie to show you her rooms at the bottom of the house. I almost commandeered them for myself just to escape everyone.'

'That would be wonderful,' Ruby chuckled. 'I could do with my own room at times even though it's just me and Bob living at number thirteen these days.'

Maisie looked at Ruby with fondness. In the fourteen years she'd known her she thought how little the older woman had changed. There might be a few more laughter lines but Ruby's hair still had the golden threads from her younger days and her figure was as trim as it had been in 1938, although Ruby complained of her matronly figure and a few aches and pains. 'You are welcome to come here whenever you like. Which reminds me,' she said, going to a door set between shelves on the wall opposite the fireplace and pulling it open. 'This is my office.'

Ruby looked around the small room holding an oak desk and matching chair with wooden filing cabinets along one wall.

'This is mine alone and I will keep it locked,' Maisie said with a grin. 'As much as I love my family and my staff, I need somewhere to be alone to think. I thought it would happen in the factory, but no such luck. I've given our Claudette the room at the factory where she can design to her heart's content.'

'She's a clever girl. Do you think the younger ones will follow in her footsteps?'

'The twins aren't interested, but Ruby has a talent for drawing, so who knows?'

Ruby nodded approvingly as she looked around the room.

'Actually, there's something I wanted to tell you about our Ruby . . .'

Ruby placed her hand to her chest. 'She's not ill, is she?'

'No, she's fighting fit, but I wanted to run this by you as it affects you in a way. She is going to change her name to Sheila, and I wanted to tell you in case you thought it was personal. Sheila is her second name.'

'After your little sister, isn't it?'

Maisie walked to her desk and picked up a small gilt frame, handing it to Ruby. 'Yes. There's quite a likeness and I only noticed recently.'

'Sheila does suit her, and Ruby is quite an old-fashioned name. I'm honoured you named her after me, but I'd not want to saddle the girl with a name her granny should have. Sheila Ruby Carlisle sounds just as good, if not better.'

'Thank you so much for being so understanding. We are going to announce it later while we are having tea.'

'Just don't let nosy Mrs Bennett overhear as she may make more of it than what there is. You've no need to look so surprised, the twins told me all about her before I'd taken my coat off. Now, let's go and join the others, and perhaps you'd point out where that hosepipe is as I'll be the first one to use it if she appears.'

'You are a bad influence on my children.' Maisie snorted with laughter as she took Ruby's arm, and they headed out into the garden.

*

'What I'm thinking is to plant more hedging to strengthen what is already there,' David Carlisle said to Bob Jackson as they strolled down the long length of garden with Alan Gilbert following to get out of the hearing range of the youngsters. 'The problem is, I have no idea about gardening and wouldn't know a weed from a rose.'

Alan, sandy-haired and serious-looking, was thoughtful as he stepped closer to the hedge and peered through the gaps before ducking back quickly as he spotted the troublesome neighbour. 'What I'd do is build a bloody great wall the length of the garden. That would save all problems in the future. What are the neighbours like on the other side?'

'We haven't got to know them yet, but they seem nice; we'd hardly moved in before the husband and wife knocked on the door to welcome us to the street with a cake and bags of sweets for the kiddies. Maisie recognized her as one of her customers at the Dartford shop from when Maisie advised the elder daughter on a wedding gown.'

'So, you'd not be interested in putting a wall up both sides?' Alan asked.

'A wall would be worth doing,' Bob said as he sat down on an old bench set under an apple tree. His breathing was still laboured since his spell in hospital and a convalescence home several months ago. 'If you plan to live here for a few years, it would be money well spent and save you having to maintain a hedge.'

David rubbed his chin thoughtfully as he observed Bob. His illness had taken a lot out of him and he'd still not regained the weight he'd lost while in hospital. Consequently, his suit looked a little large, making him appear to be a shadow of what he'd been. He thought about what Bob and Alan had said. 'I'll have a word with Maisie. I reckon she'd agree, although we'd only need a wall along this side. It's Mr and Mrs Arndt's boundary fence; that showed up in the land deeds when we bought the house. Mind you, if they'd like a wall, I'd not mind paying so we have it match both sides. But first I need to speak to the boss to see what she has to say about it. There is one problem: I heard that there is still a shortage of bricks due to the post-war housebuilding. I would think houses would come before garden walls.'

'Not if you use reclaimed bricks. There's a yard down the lane towards the marshes where they sell them. The owner came into my shop last week to purchase a television set and we got chatting like you do,' Alan said, pulling a small black notebook from his back pocket. 'Here's his phone number, I'll write it down for you before we go home.'

'I know a couple of retired brickies who do the odd job for cash in hand,' Bob added. 'This could all be done in a week or so if you get everything organized and find yourself a decent builder. A wall built properly will last as long as the house. Now, what about the garden? It's starting to look the worse for wear. I could sort it out for you if you like?'

'Oh no,' both David and Alan said at the same time.

'It's very good of you, Bob, but Ruby will have my guts

17

for garters if she finds out. I thought I'd ask around for a young man just setting up in a gardening business who might like to take it on. There must be a fair few around who've not long been demobbed.'

'You could put an advert in the *Erith Observer*,' Alan suggested as they were interrupted by a loud voice from the other side of the hedge.

'That's him, Gordon. That's the man who was spying on me through the hedge.'

Alan groaned. It was foolhardy of him to look so far through the hedge as he had been spotted. He apologized to David before the three men went to where the woman could be seen alongside a pompous-looking man.

'I'm sorry, I was checking the hedging,' he started to explain before being talked over by the man.

'Now, look here, my good chap, you cannot go frightening ladies in the privacy of their own homes. I could have you arrested as a peeping tom.'

'I believe you will find your wife has done more than peep through a hole in the hedge,' David started to say, at the same time trying not to lose his temper, not wishing to cause problems for his friends.

There was a short silence as the man sized up David Carlisle. 'You must be the husband of the woman who attacked my wife this afternoon. I plan to report her as well,' he said, looking down his nose at the three men.

Bob pushed David aside. 'Now, look here, you have no grounds to be reporting people to the police as it is a blatant waste of their time.'

'What would you know?' he sniffed at Bob before pushing the branches of the hedge together. 'Come along, Daphne, we will go inside away from this riff-raff. I don't know what the area is coming to.'

Bob opened his mouth to inform the man he knew the law being a retired copper, but David held him back. 'Don't waste your breath, Bob. I'll be getting that wall built as soon as I possibly can.'

'What's that about a wall?' Maisie asked from where she was sitting in a deckchair chatting with Sarah Gilbert and Ruby, who were on garden seats padded with colourful cushions Claudette had made from offcuts of cotton fabrics, which were being much admired.

David knelt close to Maisie, and in a low voice explained what had just happened, along with Alan and Bob's suggestion that they should have a brick wall. He also put his finger to his lips and nodded towards the Bennetts' garden, making it clear they could be listening.

'It seems to be for the best, but aren't there rules about how high a wall can be built? Perhaps George can find out from the council?' Ruby suggested.

Bob walked over to the hedge and turned to wink at the group of friends. 'A nice ten-foot wall along here will be just the ticket,' he said in a loud voice before returning to them with a broad grin on his face. 'That'll teach her a lesson for snooping; I spotted the woman peering through that gap while you were talking in a low voice.'

Ruby scolded her husband. 'Bob, you shouldn't stir the pot. Maisie and David have enough on their hands with the miserable woman without you adding to it,' before speaking in a loud voice herself. 'Maisie, I'd be tempted to add some more bolts on your doors as there's something not quite right with a woman who snoops like that. I reckon she's not all there and may break in and murder you all in your beds,' she said seriously before passing her empty cup to Claudette. 'Any chance of another cuppa, love?'

Sarah looked at Maisie and they both fell into a fit of giggles while the youngsters watched open-mouthed. It was always the same when their mum got together with her friends. They looked as alike as chalk and cheese with Maisie being tall and blonde, Sarah slightly shorter with chestnut wavy hair and Freda, who was yet to arrive, shorter still with darker hair cut short.

Claudette shook her head at her sister Bessie. 'Honestly, the old folk tell us how to behave, and just listen to them! You couldn't make it up,' she added, imitating Ruby.

'I still say that girl should be on the stage,' Ruby said good-naturedly as she waved her furled umbrella at Claudette.

'I'll never allow her to leave Maisie's Modes, even if it means chaining her to her desk; she's an asset to the business,' Maisie said as she watched the girl walk slowly over the uneven grass holding a laden tea tray. 'She still works the odd day at Woolworths as well, as she reckons she'd miss her mates too much if she gave up working there.'

'She is also an asset to Woolies,' Sarah said as she wriggled to get comfortable. 'I'll be glad when my little asset is born – roll on Christmas.'

'When do you pack up work? It can't be long now,' Maisie asked as the men wandered away, not wanting to listen to baby talk.

'I'll stay as long as I possibly can. Betty is only allowing me to sit at my desk and says she will give me the sack if she finds me working on the shop floor.'

'And I hope you've given up working at Alan's shop?'

Maisie said in a loud voice so Alan could hear from across the garden.

'Don't worry, he's banned me from entering the premises, which is a shame as now he sells more household goods I'm happy to be there.' Sarah grinned. 'He brings the books home for me to go over and point out his mistakes. However, I love working at home now we rent your old house.'

'And I can keep an eye on her as she's just up the road,' Ruby chipped in as she unfurled her umbrella and gave it to her granddaughter to shade her from the sun.

'Just like I walk down to check on you, and pop over the road to see Freda,' Sarah said, adding, 'It's lovely that we all live so close to each other. Speaking of which, shouldn't Freda be here by now?'

'She's probably been held up getting those kiddies ready. I still can't believe our Freda is a mum with three little ones,' Maisie said. 'It doesn't seem that long since she was a young scrap of a thing without a bean to her name.'

'We were all rather naive and a lot younger back then,' Sarah reminded her. 'Although you never looked it. That is, I still remember you walking into Woolworths dressed up to the nines and asking for a job. I thought you were a Hollywood film star.'

'I too didn't have a bean to my name, but I hid it well. Living with Joe's mum was hell. She was a right pain in the neck. I'd have worked in an abattoir to stay away from her house.'

They fell silent thinking of Maisie's first husband, who had died during the early days of the war.

'Here they are,' Ruby called out, glad to be able to break the silence.

'The twins are here,' Maisie's twins called out in unison, racing over to help Freda with the double pram while her husband, Tony, followed behind with their older brother, William, in his arms.

'It has taken us an hour to get here,' Freda declared as she kissed and hugged her friends. 'We changed four lots of nappies before it was safe to leave the house. It is never-ending!'

'Oh, I should have stopped by and helped you, only our Buster fell over and grazed his knees, and I was fussing over him and stopping the tears. Although he wouldn't thank me to tell you that, not now he's a prize boxer,' Sarah said, glowing with pride, her son having recently won a medal at his boxing club. 'As much as I'm looking forward to the arrival of this little one, I'm not so sure about all those dirty nappies,' she said as she placed a hand on her stomach protectively.

'It'll be a doddle for you this time round. Not only will you have Georgina and Buster to help you, but you have that super-duper twin tub for your washing.'

'I am lucky to have the twin tub; perhaps you should ask Tony to buy you one? You certainly need help with three little ones under two years of age.'

Freda looked over her shoulder to where her Tony had joined the other men. 'I'm working on it.' She winked.

'I'll make sure Alan plays his part in encouraging Tony to agree,' Sarah laughed. 'In the meantime, please do bring the nappies up to me and we can have a cup of tea and a natter while they wash.'

Freda thought of the back-breaking work filling the copper each time she wanted to do a wash and nodded her head enthusiastically. 'I'll take you up on that, thank you. Oh, what's happening?' she asked as Claudette walked from the house carrying a large tray while the twins danced around her excitedly.

'We have a special surprise for everyone, but especially our darling daughter ... Sheila!' Maisie announced, removing a napkin that was covering a beautifully iced cake.

'Who is Sheila?' Freda whispered to Sarah, who shrugged her shoulders and looked around her to see where this new daughter could be. At the same time Ruby Senior got to her feet and hugged her namesake, whose cheeks had turned pink.

'You'd best explain,' she urged the child.

'From now on I am to be called by my second name, which is Sheila. This is to remember Mum's young sister who died when she was a little girl, but also because there is only room in this family for one Ruby.' She grinned before kissing Ruby's cheek and moving to stand by her mum. 'Thanks for the cake,' she whispered.

'Thank Claudette. She's a dab hand with an icing bag and we already had the cake made for our tea.'

'It's like a birthday,' Georgina piped up before everyone started to sing '*Happy birthday, dear Sheila*' at the top of their voices.

Bessie started to bring out plates of sandwiches followed by David with plates and napkins. 'Time for tea,' she announced.

The friends and family settled down to enjoy the spread with Maisie, Sarah and Freda going to and fro topping up three teapots with fresh tea and making squash for the youngsters. After demolishing the cake, they all sat back in the garden chairs and on blankets spread on the grass, too full to say very much at all until Ruby spoke out.

'I meant to ask you, Claudette, how are the rehearsals going for the next show with your amateur dramatics group? Don't forget Bob and I will want tickets.'

'I won't forget,' Claudette said as she brushed cake crumbs from the front of her dress. 'It is getting busy as not only will *The Student Prince* be performed in a couple of weeks, but we are already in rehearsals for the Christmas pantomime. It's to be Cinderella this year.'

'Claudette has the starring role,' Maisie said proudly.

'And Alan is going to be Buttons.' Sarah grinned as the men started to josh their friend.

'He has the best singing voice,' Claudette scolded them.

'Sing us something, Alan,' Ruby said. 'What's that song about drinking?'

Alan didn't need any bidding and stood in the middle of the group to sing to Ruby.

'*Drink, drink, drink, to eyes that are bright as stars when they're shining on me . . .*'

Ruby pretended to fan her face as everyone clapped loudly at the end and Alan took a bow. 'Oh my, that was wonderful. What about another? Claudette, why don't you sing with Alan? Give us a song from the pantomime.'

Claudette whispered in Alan's ear, and they broke into a rendition of 'If You Were the Only Girl In the World'.

'I know this one,' Ruby said as she joined in and encouraged everyone to sing along, with them all cheering loudly at the end.

They never noticed the face peering from behind the hedge before she rushed back indoors.

*

Sergeant Mike Jackson walked up the imposing drive towards the detached Victorian house. It crossed his mind that his friends, the Carlisle family, had moved to the same road; he and Gwyneth should pay them a visit. He ran his finger under the band of his policeman's helmet; it was too warm a day to be in uniform. There would usually have been a constable undertaking this duty, but with no one available at Erith police station he'd offered to visit the householder himself on his way home at the end of his shift. He'd been lucky to receive a lift by one of the police drivers and could easily walk home after chatting with the homeowner. Checking the name on a slip of paper, he raised the brass knocker and let it drop before repeating the process, sending a reverberating echo through the large house. He nervously cleared his throat as footsteps approached and wouldn't have been surprised if a butler had answered the door. As it was, it was a slim elderly woman who did so, pointedly checking her watch.

'I expected you before now,' she sniffed as she held the door open for him to enter. 'I reported the noise over an hour ago. At one point I could hear singing, and so many children you wouldn't believe . . .'

'I'm sorry, Mrs Bennett, it is a Sunday, we are short staffed,' he said, giving her a charming smile that would normally melt the hearts of many elderly ladies, resulting in the offer of a cup of tea and a slice of cake. Mrs Bennett sniffed again and led him through to her back garden.

'It seems to have fallen quiet, but I can assure you the

people who live in the house are quite uncouth and not the kind of people we usually encourage in Avenue Road. We are professional people with some standing in the community. Raucous parties are unacceptable.'

Mike tried to bring to mind a polite reply, thinking how grateful he was not to have a neighbour like Mrs Bennett. Most people in Alexandra Road where he lived were the salt of the earth. 'I'm afraid there is little we can do. Perhaps if it was late at night we could knock on their door and ask them to be quiet, but a get-together on a Sunday afternoon in the garden is not the same thing at all.'

She frowned for a moment and gradually her face screwed up until she resembled a shrew. 'Young man, I'll have you know I socialize with your chief inspector, and I'm most certain he would not approve of you failing in your duty to protect a vulnerable lady.'

Mike gulped. Here he was thinking he was making a simple courtesy call to a worried neighbour before he could head home to where his wife, Gwyneth, would have his Sunday roast dinner keeping warm. His mind wandered for a moment as he thought about Gwyneth's fluffy Yorkshire puddings. For a Welsh woman, hers were the fluffiest he'd ever tasted.

'Are you listening to me?'

'I'm sorry, I was thinking . . .' he blustered. 'I would advise that you keep a diary of anything untoward that happens and notify us if the situation doesn't improve. However, there must be some give and take as you must learn to live with your neighbours and you don't want to encourage a hostile situation because of a concern about noise.'

Mrs Bennett's eyes opened wide at his words. 'Do you not consider the woman and her daughter attacking me a cause for concern?'

Mike frowned. This was a different kettle of fish, he thought as he opened his official notebook. 'Please tell me more.'

Mrs Bennett went into graphic detail about the drenching both she and her friend had received, conveniently forgetting to say how they'd been poking their heads through the gap in the hedging.

'This does show the incident in another light. However, if you and your friend were not hurt, I would still advise you to keep a diary and put through a telephone call to the station if things start to progress. I will leave you to enjoy what is left of your Sunday,' he said, snapping closed his pocket-sized notebook and bidding her farewell.

Mrs Bennett pursed her lips as she watched him walk down the tree-lined drive and disappear onto the avenue. She would not wait for anything else to happen, she thought. It was time she progressed matters herself. It was time these new neighbours toed the line and learnt that there were standards to achieve if they wished to continue living here. If not, God save them from her vengeance.

1

Wednesday, 25 November 1953

Betty Billington looked across her desk at the young woman sitting opposite. Even though her reference letters were impeccable, and the application form and test put her in the top ten per cent of her staff, she couldn't help but feel worried. There was something about her that didn't ring true. 'As I explained to you, our personnel manager, Mrs Gilbert, is not on duty today otherwise you would have been interviewed by her.'

'I've not got to come back again, have I?' the woman said, frowning, before Betty could finish speaking.

She counted to ten and smiled. 'I can assure you, Gloria, I have the experience to interview staff,' she said, taking a quick glance at the brass name plate on her desk that declared her to be the store manager.

The woman thought for a moment before looking apologetic. 'I'm sorry, it's just that I'm keen to start work as soon as possible. Things haven't been easy lately since . . . since my husband's illness,' she added, lowering her face towards her lap and giving a delicate sniff. 'I find it hard to talk about it.'

Betty's heart melted. No wonder the woman wasn't relaxed or able to talk properly – and there was her thinking the worst. She felt terrible; after all, anyone could have to seek work while caring for an ailing husband. She silently thanked God her Douglas was well and in work. 'I'm sorry, I didn't spot any mention of your husband on your application form.'

'Like I said, it's not something I like to talk about as it upsets me so.'

Betty nodded her head, choosing not to ask another question. 'As I explained earlier, the position I'm hoping to fill is in the staff canteen under Mrs Maureen Caselton. She has overseen the cooking and feeding of our staff for many years, but I am reorganizing the staff in that department and the position I have to offer is of assistant to Maureen. There is another young lady who does odd jobs as well as cleaning and washing-up. I see from your application that you worked as a shop supervisor. We are a smaller store and don't have any supervisor openings as we usually promote in store; that is why I would like to offer you the position in the staff canteen. That's if you don't mind working behind the scenes? Many of our ladies prefer working on the counters.'

'I'm happy to be behind the scenes as you put it,' Gloria replied quickly, causing Betty to raise her eyebrows.

Gloria noticed and added, 'It's my first job since my Eric took poorly and, to be honest, I'd rather keep myself to myself and just work to bring home a pay packet. Perhaps later I'd be up to working in the public eye – that's if you wouldn't mind?'

'My staff are always invited to apply for different positions if they become available; you will see cards pinned to the noticeboard in the staff room. Now, let me take you through to meet Maureen and Dora, and if you are agreeable, you could start tomorrow morning.'

As Betty led Gloria from the office she stopped for a moment and placed her hand on the woman's arm. 'There is one thing about your husband . . .'

Gloria spun round, her auburn hair shaking around her shoulders. 'What about him?'

'Oh, it's nothing to worry about. I was simply wondering who would care for him while you were at work. I'd hate to think of him alone at home on his own.'

Gloria smiled and shrugged her shoulders. 'There's no need to worry about him as there are many people to keep an eye on him.'

Betty directed her towards the canteen. 'Family and friends can be such a help at times like this. It must be a relief to you?'

Gloria looked away while giving a small smile. 'You could say that.'

*

'What do you think of our set-up in here?' Maureen asked as she carefully lowered herself into a seat to join Gloria and Dora. It had been a long day, and her leg was aching. It had been damaged at the end of the war when she'd been a victim of the V2 rocket disaster at the New Cross branch of Woolworths.

'I can see a few changes that need to be made, but all in all it looks good,' Gloria said as she stirred her tea. 'I'd have thought you'd have retired before now?'

Cheeky mare, Maureen thought to herself but she held back her comments. She was grateful to at long last have a second assistant. Dora was a good girl but in a world of her own most of the time, and only good for pushing a broom, wiping down tables and washing up. 'What would you change?' Maureen asked as she slid a plate of biscuits across the table. 'These were homemade this morning.'

Gloria examined a biscuit before biting into it. 'For one thing I'd stop making biscuits when you can get them for nothing from downstairs. Broken ones are good enough for staff. Then there are the tables and chairs; they've seen better days,' she added, picking at the cracked Formica top of the table where they sat.

'I like the tables. They remind me of home,' Dora said as she helped herself to another biscuit.

'God knows what kind of home you live in if you like these,' Gloria sniffed before slapping Dora on the back of her hand as she reached for a third biscuit. 'You'll never get rid of those spots if you keep eating biscuits. So, when are you retiring?' she asked, turning to Maureen, whose mouth had dropped open at the way Gloria had treated Dora. She'd have to keep an eye on that one!

'Who said I was retiring? I just need more help now we have more staff working downstairs. I'm in charge so don't you forget it,' she said, getting to her feet after collecting their cups. 'Ouch!' she exclaimed as she stumbled over Gloria's foot.

'Mind yourself or you'll have two gammy legs,' Gloria laughed. Dora joined in although she had little idea what she was laughing at.

'Get on with the washing-up, Dora, or you'll be late

getting home,' she snapped at the younger mousey-haired girl. 'I'll see you at seven thirty sharp,' she said to Gloria.

'That's a bit early. No one told me there'd be early shifts.'

'There's plenty to do; we have meals to prepare for lunchtime and cakes and biscuits to bake and sandwiches and rolls to fill for tea breaks. Oh, and get that muck off your fingernails before tomorrow morning,' she added, nodding to Gloria's red fingernails. 'I'll find a cap for you to wear, so that hair doesn't get into people's food,' she sniffed.

Dora giggled then gave a yelp as Gloria pinched her arm. A glare from the new woman stopped her from saying anything. Dora knew people laughed at her and poked fun; she'd long ago stopped answering back.

'I'll see you both bright and early,' Gloria said, giving the young girl a wink as she left the canteen with a spring in her step.

Maureen watched her go. She was in no doubt Gloria would be a hard worker; she had seen that in the couple of hours she'd been here and had told Betty as much when the manageress had popped into the staff room for a confidential word and to sound out Maureen's opinion on the new employee. However, she'd have to watch Gloria. There was something about her . . .

*

Councillor George Caselton sat down in the worn but comfortable armchair. When he'd first become a local town councillor and found residents wanted to speak to him about their problems, he knew he had to be not only accessible to the people of Erith, but also not sit behind a desk looking pompous like some of the others who worked for Erith Urban Council. After speaking to the vicar of Christ Church about this, he was offered a small room off the church hall. They came to an understanding whereby George furnished the room, and the reverend Cedric Jewell was able to use it if his parishioners needed privacy to chat about their spiritual needs.

He had just settled down and taken a sip of his tea when an irate woman pushed her way through the door. George took a second look at his list as the first appointment should have been with a man who wanted help with a persistent blocked drain problem.

'I'm so sorry,' Mrs Jewell, the vicar's wife, said, her head bobbing over the shoulder of the woman. 'I did try to explain there was a list of names . . .'

George gave her a gentle smile. It had been so good of her to act as his receptionist until such time as he got himself organized. She also supplied tea, biscuits and the occasional sandwich when he'd left home without packing up what Maureen had left out for him, which was most welcome. 'Yes, we do have a list, but I'm sure we can give you five minutes, Mrs . . . ?'

'Mrs Bennett. Mrs Gordon Bennett.'

The vicar's wife backed out of the room with a hand over her mouth as she tried not to laugh. George felt his cheeks start to twitch and quickly took a mouthful of tea while waving at the other armchair for her to be seated. Such an unfortunate name, but it would have been quite unprofessional of him to show mirth. 'Now, how can I help you?' he asked, replacing his cup in the saucer and pulling the cap from his fountain pen.

'It is my neighbours; they are most antisocial They are

34

noisy, there are too many goings-on for my liking and a few weeks ago they attacked me with a hosepipe.'

'Attacking you is more a case for the police. Tell me, were you injured?'

'I was soaked to the skin, as was my dear friend who was visiting at the time. I pray she doesn't tell anyone about this as I could be the laughing stock of the upper echelon of Erith.'

George, who had been brought up in Erith from the age of five, had never heard of an upper echelon of townsfolk. If it existed, he no doubt was blackballed. 'Oh dear, we can't have that now, can we?' he sympathized. 'Why would you like my help?'

'To send them packing, of course! I doubt they can afford to live in such a grand house, not with all those children and her doing what she does, the brazen hussy. There's even talk her daughter . . . well, her daughter is an unmarried mother.'

George raised his eyebrows at the picture painted by the woman. 'To be honest, Mrs Bennett, there's little I can do and if they have broken the law, then the police should be called. Can you at least try to get along with them?' He did feel as though he was passing the buck, but feared if he didn't nip Mrs Bennett and her complaints in the bud, she would be a regular visitor to his surgery, what with Avenue Road being only a street away from the church hall where he now sat.

'I called the police, and the sergeant who visited couldn't have cared less. He was only in my home for ten minutes and I doubt he even followed up on my complaint as I've not seen another policeman near nor by since then. I do wonder if this Sergeant Jackson was even a proper policeman,' she sniffed as she tightly clasped her handbag in her lap. 'I hope you intend to do more?'

George froze in his seat. Mike Jackson was a good friend, and also a relative with Mike's father having married his mother at the end of the war, but he dared not say that to Mrs Bennett as it was almost a conflict of interest. 'Let me take some notes,' he said, checking his watch as she started to talk. He would have a word with Mike when he next saw him.

A tap on the door and the vicar's wife looked in. 'I'm sorry to bother you, but there's quite a queue waiting outside,' she said as Mrs Bennett tutted at being interrupted.

'We'd best leave this here,' George said as he turned over another page covered in notes. 'If you think of anything else, please put it in a letter and I'll add it to the file.'

'There is something else,' she said quickly as George got to his feet to see her to the door. 'They are building a high wall between our properties and haven't consulted me or my husband – I feel it is against building regulations.'

George sighed, hoping this wasn't a proper grievance as she would see it as a victory and most likely make life hell for her neighbours. He felt sorry for the family, and he'd not even met them. 'I'll make a note and speak to the building regulation office. Can you give me their house number?'

'The house is called Sunrise and the family name is Carlisle.'

George groaned out loud before covering it with a cough. This made things very sticky, but he didn't believe Maisie and David Carlisle would have done half of what Mrs

Bennett stated. At this precise moment he felt sorry for the Carlisles as this woman was like a terrier with a bone – she'd not let go.

The morning shot by as he talked to residents about a plethora of problems and left the small room just after midday with Reverend Jewell's praise ringing in his ears for the help he'd given the parishioners. He stopped outside the church wondering whether to walk down to Alexandra Road to see his mum, Ruby, or to head home for a late lunch. Both were equal distances from where he stood, albeit it in different directions. Then he thought of Mrs Bennett and the Carlisle family, and without overthinking what he intended to do, he crossed the road to the street where they lived and strolled up the tree-lined avenue. There was a time when he was married to his first wife, Irene, the mother of his daughter, Sarah, that he had a hankering to move 'up the avenue', as locals called the posh street in Erith. The tall Victorian properties appealed to him, as did the large gardens. Irene had been keen as it would have moved them up the social ladder. He laughed to himself as he thought how well she'd have got on with Mrs Bennett. Maureen, his current wife and the love of his life, would have protested loudly to living there; she certainly kept his feet on the ground. He walked on past the bowls club and the entrance to the park, commonly known as 'the rec' by locals, and about ten houses up he spotted Maisie's van she used for her work parked in the drive along with two others he didn't recognize. As he knocked at the door, he spotted net curtains twitching from next door's bay window and turned his back, pulling his hat down over his eyes in case Mrs Bennett recognized him. At that moment, he was thankful he didn't stand out in a crowd, being of average age and build and wearing a dark suit.

'We're round the back,' a familiar voice called out.

George followed a narrow path to the side of the house and met Maisie, who was coming the other way. She looked like her younger self, dressed in a siren suit she used to wear in the air-raid shelters during the war, with her blonde hair tied up in a bright red scarf.

'Don't you look a sight for sore eyes,' he said as he hugged her close.

'Get away with you! I've been supervising the lads out the back garden, so they don't put up our brick wall in the wrong place. It's taken ages for the council to say we could build it as high as we want. Silly me thought when we decided to have a wall built back in September it would have been done and dusted by now, but it wasn't as straight-forward as we thought, finding a builder who was available, so now we are in a rush to get it finished before the bad weather really sets in. I've ended up stacking bricks myself,' she said, checking her fingernails with a sigh. 'I don't know what my ladies are going to say.'

'Ladies?' George asked as he followed her to the garden to see a hive of activity as two young men were mixing cement ready to pour into a long trench that ran the length of the garden. From where he stood, he caught sight of Mrs Bennett watching the proceedings from her back door and turned his back. The woman terrified him; she must be spending her days dashing from the window at the front of her house to the back garden to keep up with the move-ments of the Carlisle family. At least he knew Maisie's build complied with regulations and wouldn't fall foul of Mrs Bennett. He would write her a letter to say all was in order. That was one item he could tick off the list of Mrs Bennett's demands.

'I have two brides coming here tomorrow to be measured for their bridal gowns. They will take one look at my fingernails and run for the hills.'

'Why here and not at one of your shops?' he asked, admiring the size of the garden.

'I've turned some of the rooms on the first floor into a place to sew. I plan to keep it for the more delicate dress-making and embroidery. I'll take you up there in a moment, let me just have a word with the lads. I want to know when this wall will be finished.'

George watched Maisie head off to where the builders were stacking bricks ready for when the footings had set firm enough to start building. He thought it would be more than a day or two. Turning to look up at the back of the house, he couldn't help comparing the businesswoman Maisie with the younger Maisie he'd first met at his mum's house in Alexandra Road just before the start of war. She was a glamorous woman with a heart of gold, but under the make-up and fashionable clothes there was somebody determined to succeed in her own business. No wonder she only lasted a few years working in Woolworths, he thought to himself. 'It sounds like you have everything planned out,' he said as she joined him, looping her arm through his.

'Oh, I've got lots of ideas, but I'm mentioning them slowly to my David, so he doesn't object too much.' She grinned. 'There's one fly in the ointment, though . . .'

George quickly looked around him in case Mrs Bennett was eavesdropping as they were walking close to her property. 'Would it have anything to do with your Bessie chatting to the brickie?' he asked as he spotted her in deep conversation with one of the workers, rather than asking about the nosy neighbour.

Maisie frowned for a moment before grinning. 'Oh no, a young lad doesn't worry me. Come to that, our Bessie won't be taken for a ride a second time,' she said, referring to her eldest daughter's short romance resulting in the birth of her first grandchild. 'She learnt her lesson. No, let's get inside and I'll tell you all about it.'

George took a deep sigh as he followed her into the house and up a side staircase to the first floor. It would be good to hear Maisie's version of events, not that he would favour the young woman. For the first time ever, he regretted his work as a local town councillor.

'You certainly have a problem,' he said when she finished explaining about her next-door neighbour. 'I suggest you have a word with your girls and do your utmost to steer clear of the woman. Once your brick wall is built you may find the extra privacy helps. Now, tell me more about your plans to work from the house,' he asked as Maisie started to point out where her ladies would work and how she planned to expand the bridal department.

'Ah, George, I heard you were here. I wonder if you could spare me five minutes?' David Carlisle said as George followed Maisie downstairs to the kitchen.

George shook David's hand. 'By all means.'

'You'll find it more peaceful in the front room. I'll bring your tea through,' Maisie said.

George headed through the door she had indicated and gave the room an appreciative look. 'You've done well here in such a short time.'

'I can't accept your praise as this is all down to Maisie. She recovered the sofas and made the matching curtains. Oh, and the rugs,' David said, pointing to the brightly coloured rag rugs scattered on the varnished wooden floorboards. 'There was very little else needed doing in this room as the previous owners left it in good order. We've been very lucky.'

'You both worked hard for your good luck,' George corrected him as he sat down in one of the comfortable sofas while David took a nearby armchair. 'Now, what was this word you wanted?'

David was silent for a moment as he picked the right words. 'You know me, I'm not one for gossip, but I've heard this news from a few different sources.'

George raised his eyebrows but said nothing.

'I thought you might know if there is any truth in the rumours that part of the town is to be bulldozed and that it could affect the High Street and Pier Road?'

There was a cough from the doorway as Maisie entered with a laden tea tray. 'I thought you'd like a slice or two of cake. Claudette has been in the kitchen taking lessons from Mrs Ince; she's not bad, not bad at all,' she said, looking between the two men as she lay the tray on a coffee table before standing with her hands on her hips waiting for one of them to talk. 'Well, come on, you both know I was listening at the door so cough up and tell me if this is true. It can affect our businesses as well as Woolworths.'

2
~

Maisie peered into the ornate mirror set on her dressing table furiously rubbing cold cream into her forehead and cheeks. David thought she'd never looked so adorable in her peach-coloured negligee, her blonde hair tied back from her face with a matching chiffon scarf.

She looked up and caught his gaze in the reflection as he watched her. She scowled. 'When were you going to tell me, David?'

David ran his hand through his greying hair, not sure how to word his answer. 'To be honest, it's all hearsay at the moment, Maisie . . .'

'But it worried you enough to want to speak to George rather than me?' she said, pulling off the scarf and dragging a silver-backed hairbrush through her hair before retying it.

'But darling, it wasn't like that . . .' he pleaded. 'I was concerned for the business.' He froze on the spot, realizing what he'd said. 'What I mean is—'

'What you meant was that my business is not as important as yours. Maisie's Modes, my first shop, is next door to your funeral business in the High Street and if the area is demolished then we will both suffer financially. What about Alan Gilbert's shop up the road? He has a family to support, and Sarah expecting a baby; shouldn't he be worried about what could happen?' she spat at him, unable to stop her thoughts from tumbling out. 'Come to that, what about Woolworths in Pier Road? Why, everyone we know could suffer. God knows what will happen to the town's tradespeople. I take it Douglas Billington knows? After all, he is your business partner. I wonder if he has told Betty . . . ?' As she stopped to draw breath, she noticed David's face had turned bright red before he stared down at the carpet.

'I've only . . .'

Maisie frowned. 'You've not told Douglas or me, but you spoke to George?'

'Alan knows; he was in The Prince of Wales with me when we overheard two men talking about it. They looked like surveyors. Alan shrugged it off as he was busy telling me about a new portable gramophone player he'd ordered for his shop, but I was worried enough to decide to speak to George as he may have heard something at the council.'

'But not worried enough to confide in me?' she said, looking sad. 'Oh, David, I thought we shared everything.'

David reached out and pulled her close. 'Let's not worry until we know more. George said it could be something and nothing.'

'Promise me you won't keep any secrets from me, or I'll swear you'll be sleeping in the spare room,' she said, looking him square in the eye. 'If anything happens to our town, it could have devastating effects for us all – and yes, I will worry, if you don't mind.'

'I promise,' he said as he kissed her forehead, wincing at the flavour of her face cream.

As Maisie snuggled close to David, she decided she'd have a word with her friends. She doubted it was nothing as there was never smoke without fire. Besides, her gut was telling her they were in for a fight.

*

'Whatever is the problem?' Betty asked when Maisie hurried into her office all hot and bothered. She'd been going through stock records and signing them off before starting to sort out her files that were heaped on the edge of her desk. The office with its tall windows overlooking busy Pier Road was lined with shelves containing ledgers. Usually from her small oak desk she could look around and know where everything was kept, but at the moment she had fallen behind and wasn't looking forward to filing paperwork and catching up on a multitude of small tasks.

'I have an hour before my next client arrives at the house and I need to speak to you and Sarah, if she is here,' Maisie said, looking around the office in surprise.

Betty frowned. 'Why couldn't you use the telephone if you have clients due?'

'I didn't want anyone to hear what I'm about to tell you,' she gasped, holding on to the back of a chair as she tried to breathe. 'God, I'm getting old. Those stairs nearly killed me . . .'

'Whatever is all this commotion?' Sarah asked as she joined them. 'I could hardly hear myself berating one of the storemen for his continual lateness. It doesn't set a good example when the store manager's office sounds like all hell's been let loose. I lost every ounce of authority when he started laughing at the hullaballoo.'

'It's only Maisie,' Betty said as she hurried to pull out a seat for Sarah to sit down, completely ignoring Maisie who was finally bringing her breathing under control. She had told Sarah a hundred times to take time off now she was expecting.

'We all need to calm down. Why, even *my* heart is beating ten to the dozen. I'll pop out to the staff canteen and arrange for a tea tray to be sent in.'

'One of Maureen's sticky buns would be nice. I missed breakfast as I was too nervous to eat,' Maisie said as she sat down in the chair Betty had just vacated.

Sarah and Betty frowned at each other. 'Things must be serious if you missed your breakfast,' Betty said before hurrying from the room.

'You look as though you ran all the way here from your home,' Sarah said as she dipped into her handbag and pulled out a hairbrush to give to Maisie. 'I was going off for my lunch break with Freda once I'd seen what all the commotion was about in here. I don't usually carry my handbag about while I'm working,' she said, seeing Maisie's questioning expression. 'May I ask why you are wearing a row of pins on the lapel of your jacket?'

Maisie ran her hand down her jacket and swore as one of the pearl-headed pins caught her finger. 'Bugger,' she said, sucking her finger to stop it bleeding. 'For your information I didn't run here, I used David's car and parked it in front of the store. Thanks,' she said as she took the brush and attacked her unruly curls.

'Don't say you've parked a hearse in front of the store. That'll frighten off some of our customers.'

Maisie burst out laughing. 'David doesn't bring his work home, so we don't tend to have his vehicles in the drive. Ha, that would annoy the nosy old biddy next door. I used our family car,' she said as she removed the pins before they did any more damage to her fingers. 'I have a bride coming to the house at two o'clock and can't bleed on the fabric while she's having a fitting.'

Sarah found the first aid tin Betty kept in a filing cabinet and took out a roll of sticking plaster and some cotton wool. 'Hold your finger there while I cover the wound,' she instructed. 'There you go, that'll help until you get yourself home, although you ought to change it and wash your finger before your client arrives. Now, what's your neighbour been up to?'

Maisie then explained how Mrs Bennett seemed to spend every waking hour spying on her family and on the brickies who were building the wall between their properties.

'If it's any consolation, she won't be able to watch you for much longer, and it'll be nice when it's finished,' Sarah assured her, hoping Maisie didn't decide to move back to her old house in Alexandra Road as it would put her and Alan in a spot of bother, what with them renting it.

There was a tap on the door and Freda walked in, followed by Betty. 'I thought I spotted the old gang,' she grinned. 'It's not often we all get together in the same room without having children and husbands with us.'

'It would be divine if it wasn't for the news about the town and how it could affect us all. That's the reason I came rushing down here.'

Silence fell as three pairs of eyes stared at Maisie waiting for her to explain.

Sarah's stomach rumbled, breaking the silence. 'Hurry up and explain yourself as I'm starving,' she said.

Maisie took a deep breath. 'My David overheard two men talking in the Prince of Wales. It seems there are plans to demolish much of the housing around Cross Street and down towards the river.'

Betty frowned. 'My first home in this area was in Cross Street; it was so convenient for this store. I only needed to cross the road into Pier Road . . .' She stopped speaking as a thought crossed her mind. 'Would this affect the businesses in Pier Road, do you think?'

'What about the High Street?' Sarah asked. 'It's only a hop, skip and a jump from Cross Street. Three of us have businesses that could suffer. Alan would be devastated.'

Maisie looked at her friend's flushed cheeks. She couldn't tell her that Alan already knew and had dismissed it as nothing. 'David spoke to your dad yesterday afternoon and he promised to find out what's going on,' she said, giving her friend's hand a squeeze. 'Don't worry yourself unduly.' She turned to look at Betty who was busy writing down what had been said. 'Do you think head office would know anything about this, what with Woolworths being one of the largest businesses in town?'

Betty pursed her lips. 'This afternoon I will place a few telephone calls to people I hold in high regard at head office. I pray there is no substance to this news, but I fear the worst. Ah,' she said, looking up at a red-headed young woman standing by the door. 'Thank you for bringing in our tea, Gloria. You can put it down on my desk,' she said, moving a couple of buff-coloured files before turning back to her friends. 'I don't know about you, ladies, but I could

47

do with something stronger after Maisie's news. How about we all decamp to Hedley Mitchell's tea room for an early lunch and a glass of sherry? It will be my treat.'

Gloria watched as the women left Betty's office with the tea and buns she'd prepared left untouched. She shrugged her shoulders and sat down in the manager's vacated chair, pulling off the ungainly cap Maureen made her wear and shaking her shoulder-length auburn hair free of its confines. 'Waste not, want not,' she muttered aloud before picking up one of the iced buns and taking a large bite out of it and then pouring herself a cup of tea, stirring two heaped spoonfuls of sugar into the cup. She leant back in the seat to enjoy the treat, thinking how angry Maureen would be at the amount of sugar she'd used. The daft bat couldn't understand that rationing was almost over. Pulling open a desk drawer, she took out a brown paper bag and placed the remaining buns inside. 'Perhaps there are some perks here after all,' she grinned, thinking she'd have a second cup of tea before she went back to the staff canteen to help serve lunch. She looked around the room wondering if there was anything of interest. Some buff-coloured files caught her eye, but there was nothing in them but stock forms and lists of orders. A wire basket labelled 'pending' looked more interesting and she flicked through the contents until she came across her application form with a note pinned to the front: *Contact the Maidstone branch and enquire about the applicant* was all it said. Picking up the paperwork, she lifted her white work overall and tucked it into the waistband of her skirt. With luck, Betty Billington would forget about this pending item. Thank goodness she'd been too busy to complete the task, she thought to herself, before jumping as the office door started opening. As quick as a flash she picked up the tea tray, placing her cup and saucer on top of the unused crockery, making it look as though she was about to leave the room.

'Why are you here alone?' Maureen asked, giving Gloria a sharp look.

'Mrs Billington asked me to tidy up before she went out to lunch with her friends,' Gloria said, starting to line up the files while balancing the tea tray with one hand and hoping Maureen didn't notice the bulging pocket of her overall where she'd stuffed the bag of buns. 'I'll get on now,' she said, pushing past Maureen. 'I can see there's a queue stretching out the door for lunch and dozy Dora can't be trusted to serve the shepherd's pie on her own.'

Maureen muttered something unpleasant under her breath as she closed the door and followed Gloria the short distance down the corridor to where hungry staff were waiting for their hot meal and starting to complain.

*

'I shouldn't have had that second sherry,' Maisie said as she fanned herself with one hand before checking her wristwatch. 'I'm not sure I'm up to meeting a new bride this afternoon to decide on her wedding gown, let alone driving back to the house. I know it's only a few streets away, but I feel quite light-headed.'

'I'll drive you home as I'm not working this afternoon,' Freda told her. 'I have another hour before I must relieve the marvellous Sadie from caring for my three little ones. I love them all dearly, but it's a joy to be able to work a few hours each day and feel human.'

'I'd offer, but you all know I can't drive from one end of Alexandra Road to the other without hitting something,' Sarah said, giving a deep sigh. 'Goodness knows I've tried . . .'

The girls chuckled. Sarah was far too nervous to be behind the wheel of a car.

'We can't all be drivers,' Freda consoled her. 'Look at how good you are at your knitting, and as for organizing paperwork . . . why, I'm amazed. You leave me standing.'

Betty agreed. 'I'm not keen on driving these days, there seems to be so much more traffic on the road. Nine times out of ten I travel in with Douglas. It won't be that long before your Georgie and Buster are old enough to drive and they can chauffeur you,' she chuckled.

Sarah gasped, raising her hands in horror. 'I can't imagine my Buster driving a car as he is such a tearaway; I never know what he is getting up to as it is. I have a good few years before I must worry about him driving on the roads of Erith. Thank goodness I can walk to work and once I have this little one, I'll have a pram to push.' She smiled as she gently stroked her stomach. 'I shouldn't wish away my life, but I can't help wishing it were Christmas and he or she was here with us.'

'It will be a joyous day as Christmas babies seem extra special in my eyes,' Betty said as she looked around the table at her three chums. 'It's been a while since we've all sat down together for a meal. I've missed you all,' she said, giving an overbright smile. 'I know we celebrated the coronation together, but there were so many people that we hardly had time for more than a quick chat – and now what has brought us together? Concerns for the store. I can't believe we may lose it. Erith wouldn't be the same without a Woolworths.'

Maisie looked sad. 'I hate to say it, but if they knock down the two main roads in the town, will they even contemplate rebuilding a new branch of Woolies?'

Sarah chewed her fingernail as she thought about the situation. 'When you think the houses in Cross Street and the others around them are so close to the heart of this old town, it will leave a large gash across it. Granted, the houses are old and there is also bomb damage, but it won't be the same. We'd probably be able to see down to the Thames from the store, that's if they don't decide to demolish the shops as well, as most are the same age as the houses in Cross Street.'

Freda looked at Betty, who seemed a little down in the dumps. 'Chin up, Betty, it may all be gossip. It is down to us to find out all we can and then we start to fight back.'

'You're right. Why be glum when we don't have any proper news? Now, who would like sponge pudding and custard? Then you can come back to the store, Maisie, and enjoy a cup of coffee with me until you feel fit to drive home.'

'I'll do that,' Maisie agreed. 'If you don't mind me using your telephone, I'll contact Bessie and Claudette and have them help with the bride's fitting. They are of a closer age so will have more in common. Claudette has an eye for design. In fact, she has come up with some splendid sketches.'

'I can see that before too long I'm going to lose her working part time for Woolworths,' Betty said. 'But I'd not want to hold her back when she has such a talent.'

Freda agreed. 'I feel tired just thinking about the hours she puts in working at Woolies and for Maisie's Modes. Even when I was her age, I didn't have that much energy.'

'It was a different time,' Sarah said as she waved her hand to get the attention of a waitress. 'For one thing we had the war to contend with.'

'And for another, we didn't have mothers who indulged us,' Maisie added as the girls all fell silent thinking of their own mothers.

Freda was the first to speak. 'I was wondering, but it may not be the right time to mention it . . .'

Maisie nudged her arm. 'Spit it out, you can't keep quiet now.'

'Well, it has been an age since we had a Woolworths staff outing. I wondered if we could arrange something for Christmas – perhaps a trip to London to see the shops and festive lights? It's a shame we didn't think of it for the August bank holiday although I'd have hated a trip on the Thames like the old days.' She shuddered, recalling her disastrous wedding reception on the Thames.

Betty beamed. 'I remember with fondness trips I've enjoyed to the coast on charabancs.'

'That's a word I've not heard for a few years,' Sarah grinned. 'We call them coaches these days. Margot's are a local company; I could check to see if they have any available for December.'

'Book an extra coach and I'll treat my staff and their families,' Maisie said. 'If there is any truth in the rumours about the town being flattened, then we deserve something to cheer us all up.'

'Goodness, I pray it doesn't come to that. Just as Sarah

is wishing for Christmas to arrive, I too am wishing for a favourable outcome to this awful news about decimating our lovely town,' Betty said. 'Now, look snappy and finish your meal as we have work to do,' she said with an encouraging grin.

3

'I thought you'd like this,' Bessie said shyly as she placed a mug of strong tea close to where the fair-haired young man was mixing cement with a shovel in the back garden of the Carlisle family's new home.

He grinned as he leant his shovel against a nearby apple tree and wiped his hands down his overalls. 'Thanks, I could do with that.'

Bessie looked at the wall now three feet high after only a couple of days' work. 'It'll look nice when it's finished; we will have so much privacy,' she added as she spotted movement behind the hedge that ran the length of the garden between them and the Bennetts' house.

'It will, and I can see why it's needed. What with the boss and her next door I feel as though I'm under supervision all the time. Why don't you join me for a little while? I'm due a break and the boss is off somewhere pricing up another job.'

'Thank you, I'll just get . . . I'll just get my tea and some biscuits,' she said, hurrying back to her garden flat where Jenny was in her playpen cuddling her favourite toy. 'Would you like to come out into the garden with me?' she asked.

The child didn't need asking twice as she threw down her doll and raised her arms to be lifted out. 'You will have to walk with me as I have to carry a tea tray,' she instructed her daughter, who nodded her head solemnly before heading to the open door. 'Wait for me,' Bessie called after her as she quickly picked up a knitted blanket and a tray emblazoned with the face of the young Queen Elizabeth. She added her own mug of tea along with some ginger biscuits and Jenny's bottle containing cool milky tea. Her daughter was fussy and wanted to eat and drink whatever her mother was having. Rather than put up a fight, Bessie simply agreed with the child who loved a drink of tea. Glancing at a mirror hanging next to the door, she wished she had time to run a comb through her hair or at least pull on a clean blouse that didn't have a smattering of Jenny's soup she had for lunch down the front when she fought to feed herself. 'Why am I kidding myself? No lad is going to give me a second look when they know I have a daughter,' she muttered before hurrying after Jenny, who was toddling up the garden arms open wide as if to balance herself. Even so, she landed heavily on her padded bottom before climbing to her feet and staggering on. She looked back at Bessie and shrieked with laughter as Bessie almost caught up with the child.

'Slow down or you will hurt yourself,' Bessie called after her as the little girl made a beeline for the young brickie. He bent down and picked her up, swinging the child above his head. Jenny screamed in delight.

'Aren't you a beauty,' he said as he set her down on the blanket Bessie had shaken out on the grass. He watched Jenny for a moment, checking she didn't fall over. 'I have a sister about her age, but she isn't dressed so prettily. Our Aggie is usually in hand-me-downs and making mud pies in the garden.'

Bessie thought before she spoke. Did he think Jenny was her sister? What would he think if he knew the truth? She sipped her hot tea, wondering why she cared what he thought. 'It's one of our sample dresses from the factory. Jenny is often a model for the baby clothes. Mum's very good handing around stuff that doesn't pass her strict inspection as she won't have seconds going into the shops. If you like, I can give you some bits and pieces for . . . Aggie, did you say?'

'That's very generous of you. I know my mum won't refuse something for the kids. Aggie is the youngest in the family, so she doesn't get many new clothes.' He started to laugh until he saw her puzzled look. 'Here I am talking about my youngest sister, and I haven't even told you my name. I'm Jake – Jake Brown.'

'I'm Bessie Carlisle,' she said, shaking the hand he held out to her.

'I know,' he said, before looking embarrassed. 'The boss told me the name of the family who are hiring us to build the wall.'

Bessie offered him a biscuit. 'They are freshly made; Mrs Ince baked a batch this morning. They won't last long in this house,' she grinned.

'Mrs Ince?'

'She's our housekeeper. If it wasn't for her, we'd more than likely starve and end up with no clean clothes, what with Mum being so busy and Dad working all hours. Not that he cooks,' she chuckled before seeing him grit his teeth and look away. 'Oh, please don't get the impression we are landed gentry or anything. Before we moved here, we all mucked in and Mum's friend, Sadie, would help look after the younger ones while Mum was at one of our shops or the factory.'

'I'd best get back to work,' he said, handing her his mug and refusing a biscuit.

Bessie frowned. 'Jake, have I said something to upset you? Or perhaps the tea wasn't to your liking . . . ?'

He stopped and turned to face her. How could he tell her he liked the way she smiled and how she didn't worry when her blonde hair fell from the combs that held it in place when she played with her little sister? But knowing they had servants and that, to his knowledge, she didn't have to work for a living, as she was always around the house when he was working there, put a different slant on things. He could never be like her, and if he should show her how interested he had been in her from the moment he'd set eyes on her, how would it end? The likes of him didn't mix with people like her. He was kidding himself even speaking to her. There again, she was very friendly towards him and didn't appear to be a snob like some who lived up the avenue . . .

'Jake . . . ?'

He turned slowly. Even though his brain was telling him to walk away, his heart told him otherwise. He was searching for something to say when Jenny tugged at his overalls then raised her arms, wanting him to lift her up as he had before, which broke the ice. He bent to pick her up. 'You can't come with me, young lady. It's very mucky over there and we don't want your big sister telling us off if your pretty

57

dress is spoilt.' He carried her over to the blanket and handed her to Bessie, whose cheeks had turned bright red.

'You are mistaken,' she said quietly. 'Jenny is my daughter.'

He shrugged his shoulders. 'My mistake,' he said, glancing down at Bessie's ringless left hand; she'd removed the cheap wedding band purchased from Woolworths when she was expecting Jenny, as it had started to irritate her finger just the day before.

She bristled as she took Jenny from him. 'If you'll excuse me, I have work to be getting on with,' she said, getting to her feet and going back to the house carrying the tea tray in one hand and the protesting Jenny under her arm.

'Oh, there you are, lovie, you are needed upstairs. I'll take the little one off your hands; you can help me roll out some pastry.' Mrs Ince beamed as she took Jenny, whose eyes lit up. 'Don't worry, no one will have to eat it.' She winked at Bessie before disappearing up a flight of stairs to the kitchen.

Bessie tidied her hair and checked herself in the small mirror on the wall, trying not to glance up the garden. However much she tried, she couldn't help having a quick look. Jake was at the fence talking to Mrs Bennett from next door. 'No doubt dishing the dirt on me. Who the hell does he think he is?' she huffed out loud before hurrying upstairs to the workroom.

'I'm glad you're here,' Miss Trott, Maisie's head seamstress, whispered as Bessie entered the workroom on the first floor of the house. 'Our young bride is having problems with her mother. With you being a similar age, you may be able to calm troubled waters. I had hoped your mother would be here by now, but it must be something important for her to be late.'

Bessie nodded as she glanced over Miss Trott's shoulder to where the pouting bride-to-be sat on the edge of Maisie's best velvet-covered sofa looking as though she would burst into tears at any minute while her stern-faced mother held court telling Miss Trott's assistant how her own wedding had been a society event and she'd wanted for nothing.

'Mum will be here as soon as she possibly can. Where is Claudette? I thought she was helping you?'

'I sent her to the kitchen to ask Mrs Ince for a tray of tea as I thought it would soothe nerves.'

'Good thinking,' Bessie said as she patted the older woman's arm. Although her sister was a gifted designer and an asset to their mother's business she would have been seen as too young in the eyes of the mother of the bride. 'I meant to ask if you like working here?' she said, giving Miss Trott a smile.

'It makes a change from working out of the Bexleyheath shop or, come to that, going to the factory. My bus stops on the corner of the road, and I can be home in half the time.'

'I'll see if we can keep you here on a permanent basis rather than have you travel back and forth. I'll have a word with Mum. Now, let me see what I can do for this poor bride.'

Bessie walked calmly over to where the mother and daughter sat, and introduced herself. 'I'm sorry my mother has been held up. She's been detained on important business,' she added, hoping she sounded sincere.

'That's all right.' The girl smiled at Bessie although her

eyes were full of unshed tears. 'I don't know if you remember me. We were at school at the same time although I was several years ahead of you. Petronella Wilson, although my friends all call me Nella.'

Bessie felt the muscles in her stomach clench as she recalled who this was. She remembered nothing but kindness from the older girl, although she feared Nella had heard about Bessie's child and her being unmarried. 'Of course, now you mention it I do remember you being captain of the netball team,' she said, forcing a smile onto her face. 'You must be very proud of your daughter, Mrs Wilson.'

The thin-faced woman sniffed at Bessie. 'Aren't you rather young to be working as a couturière?'

Bessie nodded politely at the woman even though it went against the grain. 'I assist my mother and she is happy with my work. Now, Petronella, would you like to come with me, and you can try on a few gowns before you make your decision on the style you prefer?'

Mrs Wilson went to stand as her daughter got to her feet, giving a look of thanks to Bessie.

'If you don't mind, I'd like to work with just your daughter for now. Perhaps Miss Trott could show you some designs we have made for the most important guest . . . ?'

'Most important?' Mrs Wilson frowned.

'She means the mother of the bride,' Nella said before following Bessie to a side room where the door was firmly closed to keep out prying eyes.

Nella collapsed into a velvet-covered chair set in the small bay window while Bessie perched on a stool used by seamstresses to pin and tack hems. 'Thank you for rescuing me,' she said, giving a big sigh. 'This wedding is driving me up the wall.'

'Weddings can be extremely stressful,' Bessie sympathized.

Nella bit her lip and gave Bessie a worried look. 'I've let my mother down and she keeps reminding me of the fact.'

Bessie could see that would be a problem. In the short time since meeting Nella's mother, she knew the woman was not one to cross. 'May I ask why?'

'I really didn't want a big wedding with a white dress, but she insisted and started planning it as soon as my father summoned Geoffrey to his study.' Her voice cracked as the emotion got the better of her. 'Daddy didn't have a shotgun, but he made his wishes known loud and clear.'

Bessie hurried to her side and put an arm around the girl as she sobbed into her handkerchief. 'Am I right to think you and Geoffrey are to expect a happy event before too long?'

Nella nodded her head in agreement as she composed herself. 'You must think so badly of me?'

Bessie gave her an understanding smile and held out her hand for the girl to follow her. They stood at the window and watched as Mrs Ince hurried after little Jenny as she ran up the garden squealing in delight after having spotted Jake who was now back at work. 'That's my daughter and whatever the world says about me, I adore her and would go through everything again.'

Nella's eyes opened wide. 'Your . . . ? But you are only . . . ?'

'I'm eighteen. I was sixteen when Jenny was born.'

'Is that her father?' she asked, nodding to where Jake had put down his trowel and was bending down to talk to the child.

'My goodness, no! Jake is here to work on our new wall. I have no contact with her father. He was a bad lot, but it took me ages to realize. I was young and extremely gullible.'

Nella sniffed into her handkerchief. 'We are a right pair, aren't we?' she said, giving a small giggle. 'Will you help me find a suitable gown? I don't want people pointing the finger and laughing at me on what should be the happiest day of my life.'

Bessie put her arm around Nella's shoulders and gave her a squeeze. 'It would be my honour. I'll enjoy every minute of it. In fact, I have an idea. Stay there, I will only be two ticks,' she said before leaving the room.

Out in the main workroom Claudette was handing out tea using Maisie's best tea set.

'Claudette, would you be able to assist me for a little while?' she asked politely as she gave Mrs Wilson a smile. 'We won't be long,' she assured her before picking up a fabric sample book and Claudette's sketchbook then returning to the small room where Nella was waiting. Claudette was hot on her heels carrying a tray of refreshments.

'I know Mum will frown at us having food close to where we are working, but by the look on your face you may need it. That mother looks a bit of a tyrant,' she said as they entered the room. 'Oops!'

Nella chuckled as Claudette looked mortified.

'I'm so sorry.' Claudette blushed as she put the tea tray down on an ornate side table. 'Mum tells us how we must be professional at all times in front of clients, and I put my big foot straight in it before we've been properly introduced.'

'Please, there's no need to apologize,' Nella begged. 'It's not as if we don't know each other.'

Claudette frowned as she looked between her sister and Nella. 'Do we?'

It was Bessie's turn to laugh. 'Claudette, this is Petronella Wilson. She was a few years ahead of you in school. You must remember her; she was really good at netball.'

'Gosh, it's been a while since we were at school, but now you come to mention it, you do look familiar – and you are getting married?'

'She needs our help,' Bessie said. 'Can you work your magic and design a dress that will cover her . . . ?' She looked at Nella for help.

'I'm going to have a baby and I'm so happy about it, but my parents aren't so happy and want to rush me down the aisle with the full works. My fear is I will look a complete fool. Mother thinks I can hold a large bouquet in front of my stomach, and no one will guess.'

The three girls giggled as Nella pretended to hold a bouquet while looking angelic.

'Of course I can help you, but best not to tell your mother it will be my design as she is sure to think I'm just a child who isn't capable of such a task.'

'I can imagine that would not impress her, and there is something else . . .' Nella looked embarrassed.

'You can tell us, I promise it will go no further,' Bessie prompted her.

'Can we keep it a secret about your daughter? She has

some strange notions about having babies out of wedlock and will straight away insist we can't be friends. We are friends, aren't we? I so desperately need friends,' she pleaded, looking between the two sisters.

Both girls stepped forward and hugged Nella. Bessie picked up a cup of the cooling tea and offered it to her. 'Now, sit yourself down and drink this while we show you some of Claudette's designs. We must have our new friend looking perfect on her special day.'

4

'Gosh, I do feel perhaps we shouldn't partake of alcohol at lunchtime,' Betty said as she sat down hard on her office chair before putting her head into her hands. 'I'm too old for drink.'

Sarah chuckled. 'It wasn't exactly hard liquor! We had three small glasses of sherry while eating. I feel fine.'

Maisie perched herself on the edge of Betty's desk and nodded to Sarah to take the spare seat. 'You are drinking for two,' she laughed.

Freda, who had made one glass last throughout their meal, looked serious. 'I read somewhere that expectant and nursing mothers shouldn't drink as it may harm the baby,' she said, raising her eyebrows at Sarah as if she should know better before sitting on the wide window ledge of the first-floor office.

Sarah slapped a hand to her mouth in horror. 'My God, I never thought of the baby! I'm such a bad mother. What if I've hurt him or her?'

Betty looked sympathetic. 'A few glasses of sherry occasionally won't hurt, surely?

Perhaps we should ask Maureen as she is the fount of all knowledge?'

'What is it you wish to know?' Maureen asked as she appeared at the office door pushing a tea trolley. 'I thought you'd all like something to perk you up after your liquid lunch,' she grinned.

Freda hurried over to relieve her of the trolley. 'We had a sherry or two with our lunch in Mitchell's cafe. Will it hurt Sarah's baby?'

'Of course not,' Maureen scoffed.

Sarah gave a sigh of relief. 'Thank goodness for that. By the way, was someone spying on us?'

'Hmm, you could say that. My new assistant – and I use the word loosely – spotted you all. I caught her regaling staff in the canteen about your debauchery,' she said, trying to look serious until a belly laugh escaped and the girls joined in with her.

'Next, you'll be telling us we were spotted carrying Betty back to work as she belted out a rendition of "Roll Out the Barrel",' Maisie giggled.

'The problem is gossip can get out of control and it can damage reputations. It is best we nip this in the bud as soon as possible,' Betty said thoughtfully. 'I know what to do. Freda, you and I will make a tour of the store asking who would like to put their name down for our coach trip to London.'

'Make sure you start in the canteen so Gloria can see you aren't drunk,' Maureen said as she started to pour out their tea from a large Brown Betty teapot.

'In that case I'd better take mine into my office and ring the coach company and book a coach or we will look daft with a group of eager trippers and no way of transporting them to London. I'd hate to herd a large group on the train and Underground,' Sarah said.

'Don't forget to add a coach for my crowd,' Maisie reminded her. 'Try Margot's as they are the best around and never let people down.'

'I've already made a note of that. It is going to be such fun!' Sarah replied before taking her tea from Maureen, along with a slice of bread pudding. 'Why not hold off from telling the staff until I've made a booking? I'll be back in two ticks,' she said as she left the office already biting into the pudding.

'Sit down and take the weight off your feet,' Betty said to Maureen. 'There's something I'd like to ask you. Stay where you are, you two,' she added as Maisie and Freda went to leave the room. 'Maureen, you seem to know what is being talked about both in the canteen and in the store. Has there been much chatter about the demolition of Cross Street and possibly other roads? I intend to put a call through to head office and ask those who may have news of this store, but it doesn't hurt to enquire of people who may have heard something.'

Maureen gave a sigh as she sat down, taking the weight off her bad leg. 'That's better. Well, I know my George has spoken to your David,' she said, looking towards Maisie, 'and I'm afraid he isn't saying much until there is more concrete news. He is as concerned as you are that the shops and businesses in Pier Road and the High Street will be affected and if the future becomes bleak, he'll be fighting it all the way.'

'I'm worried about everyone's jobs if this store closes,'

Freda said as the office door started to open. It was Gloria who peered through the gap.

'Sorry to bother you, but I wondered if I could take the tea trolley away?' she asked, looking at each of the women.

Freda frowned. 'I'll help Maureen bring it back so you can go about your duties and not worry.'

Maisie went to the door and checked Gloria was not loitering outside. 'That one's too nosy by half if you ask me,' she said, and Maureen agreed.

'To answer your question, Freda, do you recall when the Bexleyheath store was damaged by an oil bomb back in the early days of the war?'

'That was an awful to-do,' Freda said, thinking of how Betty was visiting the store that day and was injured.

'Apart from the casualties, not one staff member lost their job. Some worked here for a while, while others were distributed elsewhere. The powers-that-be made sure not one staff member was inconvenienced.'

'So, if push comes to shove, I feel it will be the same here,' Maureen said. 'However, it will be a right shame if we ever close. I know I for one will take that as a nod to retire. I'm too old to start at another store after all these years.'

'You aren't that old,' Freda said. 'How long have you worked for Woolies?'

Maureen thought for a moment. 'It must be getting on for twenty years, and that's long enough. Mind you, I'm still up for a fight if the council decided to pull down this place. You'll find me at the front of any protest march waving my banner. Now, I'd best get back to work and see what those two girls are up to; they are forever squabbling. I could bang their heads together at times.'

'Leave the tea trolley, I'll bring it through shortly,' Freda said as she held the door open for Maureen.

'You're a good lass. I'll keep my ear to the ground about Cross Street and don't forget to put mine and George's names down for the trip. I could just do with getting dressed up and enjoying myself.'

Maureen headed back along the corridor to the staff canteen. She was deep in thought as she approached the double doors. She would have to speak to George to find out more about what was going on in the town. She loved the streets of old houses and the many shops in the High Street and Pier Road and couldn't imagine the bustling town without them. Why, there'd be hardly any shops left it that was to occur; a few corner shops and some in West Street. It didn't bear thinking about. In her heart of hearts she knew something needed to be done about Cross Street as many of the houses were empty due to bomb damage as well as old age. There were also those homes that were well loved and perfectly good for another fifty years. What a problem. She didn't envy her husband helping residents and fighting right from wrong with the planning departments. If it should happen and the powers-that-be decided it was time to tear down the shops in Pier Road and the High Street, perhaps she could convince George they should retire to the seaside? She fancied Ramsgate where they'd spent happy times staying at Flora Neville's guest house. She closed her eyes and imagined herself back there . . . So deep in thought was she that she didn't hear the raised voices until she pushed open the doors to the canteen.

'It's rubbish! We'd have been told if we were to lose our jobs,' one irate storeroom lad was shouting.

'I tell you management all know about it. By this time next year there won't be a Woolworths in Erith,' Gloria told those at the early afternoon tea break from where she stood in front of the serving counter. 'Why would I lie to you?' she added with a toss of her head and a smirk.

'Because you want to cause mischief?' Maureen said as she faced her assistant. 'Now, get back to your work. As for you lot' – she turned to look at the staff sitting around tables looking either worried or indignant – 'there's nothing to worry about yet. Mrs Billington is making enquiries, and you will hear as soon as she does. She's a decent boss and cares for us all, whatever new staff like to say,' she said, glaring at Gloria. 'For now, if any of you are worried, come and speak to me and let Mrs Billington do her work. Talking of work, if you all don't finish your tea and food, the bell will be ringing for the end of your break.'

As Maureen finished speaking a bell could be heard ringing through the store. Staff quickly gulped down their drinks and stuffed food into their mouths as they hurried out of the room, some still discussing what they'd heard.

'Now, what's started all this?' she demanded, turning to Gloria. 'You had no right to stir up the staff like that. I suggest you clear the tables and give them a wipe over before the next lot start their breaks, then you can help Dora with the washing-up.'

Gloria pouted. 'It's the employees' right to know if they are going to lose their jobs. Perhaps management shouldn't talk so loudly if they don't want us to hear.'

Maureen gave the girl a withering look and chose not

to reply. The nosy so-and-so must have been listening at the door; she'd keep a closer eye on her in future. That one looked like trouble.

*

'That was quick,' Betty beamed as Sarah joined the friends in the manageress's office. 'I take it by the smile on your face you were successful?'

'Yes, I've reserved three coaches for the seventeenth of December until I've spoken to you. They'll be outside at two o'clock sharp to take us to London for afternoon tea at the Lyon's Corner House in Marble Arch, then on a tour to see the Christmas tree in Trafalgar Square and the decorated shops and lights in Regent and Oxford Streets. They will bring us back in the evening after we take in a show. You'd best get cracking and fill those seats as we will have to pay for the coaches in a few days. It seems they had a cancellation so are wanting the money upfront.'

'We need to book seats for a show as well,' Betty said, reaching for a newspaper and turning to the page that listed all the London shows. 'There is such a choice. Oh, I would adore to see *The King and I* at the Theatre Royal Drury Lane. What do you all think? The star is Gertrude Lawrence, and the male lead is someone called Yul Brynner.'

'The film was dreamy,' Freda sighed, looking star-struck.

'I would love to see the musical as long as the theatre has adequate toilet facilities; you know what my bladder is like at the moment,' Sarah added.

'Then let's get cracking,' Betty said, reaching for her trusty clipboard and a clean sheet of paper. 'Thank goodness we have a half-day in which to organize our trip. Sarah, can you arrange for the coaches to be booked and paid for? Tell them I can drop the money off to them tomorrow.'

'I can give you a cheque right now if you wish?' Maisie said, reaching for her handbag. 'I'll make it out to the coach company, so you don't have to mess about cashing it through the Woolworths account. Mine will be a treat for my staff and I will also pay you when you know the price of the theatre tickets, but what will you be charging your staff?' she asked Betty.

Betty had taken a small cash book from her desk drawer and was running a finger down a column of figures, before referring to a note Sarah had placed in front of her. 'With what we have in our social club account I reckon we can charge sixpence per person as I intend to cover the cost of the show tickets as my treat to the staff, but that won't include tipping the drivers.'

'We always pass the hat around on the way home and give the contents to the driver as a thank you,' Freda said, 'so there's no need to worry about that.'

'In that case I suggest we start to collect names. As I said earlier, I will walk around the shop floor with Freda right now.'

'I'll put a sheet up on the staff room noticeboard,' Sarah added. 'Then I need to get off home as my shift has ended.'

'Me too,' Maisie said. 'I was supposed to be fitting a bride this afternoon. I just hope my staff have coped without me. I'll have to love you and leave you,' she said, giving each of her friends a hug. 'Keep in touch over you know what,' she said as she nodded towards the closed door. 'Just remember, walls have ears.'

'Take care,' Betty called after Maisie. 'Do you think she is all right to walk back to her house? She was quite wobbly on her feet when we crossed the road from Mitchell's.'

Freda peered out of the large window that looked out from the front of the store until she spotted Maisie. 'I reckon she is fine. Now, shall we go down to the shop floor and chat with the staff? I need to be heading home in half an hour,' she said, shrugging on her supervisor overall she'd left in the office before lunch.

'I shall say you have been helping me with the Christmas project, which is true to some extent.'

As they left the office, Sarah to collect her coat to go home and Betty and Freda to go to the shop floor, they spotted Maureen looking through the open door of the canteen. She hurried out and led them further away from the canteen before explaining what she'd walked into as she'd gone back to her work.

'Oh my, I thought we'd have a little longer before the news came out. Let's hope our trip to London will help to soothe the savage beast while we find out more about what is happening to our lovely town,' Betty said, giving a sigh.

'I'm that angry I could have sacked her on the spot,' Maureen said, her face turning red with anger.

'I do agree with you,' Betty added, 'but it would be unheard of to give someone their cards just for gossiping.'

'It was more than that. She was winding up the staff and, above everything else, she was enjoying it. Well, I've left her washing up. Let's see if she enjoys that as much,' Maureen huffed.

Betty looked to where Freda was waiting for her, aware

that once they had walked around the shop floor chatting to staff about the trip and starting to collect names Freda would want to be off home to her young family. 'I suggest that for the moment let sleeping dogs lie. Perhaps it will all blow over once she settles in more. However, before I go home today, I will be speaking to a contact at head office to see if they've heard anything.'

Maureen thought for a moment before agreeing. 'You are right, I shouldn't let her get under my skin. It is just that there's something about her I don't like, but I can't put my finger on it. Anyway, on to more important matters, when I get home this evening, I'll have that word with George and make him tell me all he knows. Why have a husband in local politics and not make use of him, eh?' she said, giving a wry grin.

Betty patted her arm. 'That's the spirit. We are all upset about the rumours and once we have more concrete information, hopefully we can share the news with the staff and that will stop the gossiping.'

'You are right, I was overreacting. I'll leave you to collect your names. At least we have our trip to look forward to, even if it's the last outing for this store,' Maureen said before returning to the canteen.

Betty stood watching her go before joining Freda. She hoped it was just rumours, but it wasn't like Maureen to act out of character, and she felt there were dark days ahead for the store.

5

Sarah let herself into her house and stopped for a moment to soak in the silence. Her dad, George, was collecting the children from school and taking them back to his house for their tea. She'd been so grateful when he told her it would be his contribution to help her take things easy while she was expecting his third grandchild. Her husband, Alan, had laughed at the time and suggested instead that he visit their new home at the top of Alexandra Road and deal with the mounting pile of ironing and sorting out the garden. Instead, George had reminded Alan that he should be helping with those chores and more by passing some of the responsibilities of his own business to his staff, then at least he'd be home on time for his dinner and to see his children before they went to bed. Sarah had laughed until she had a stitch in her side and waited for Alan to heed his father-in-law's words. She was still waiting. As much as she loved her husband, she did wish he spent more time at home, but then the business was important to their family's future. Perhaps when he had a chain of shops, they too could move up Avenue Road and live in a large house just like Maisie. She sighed, not with sadness but with delight as she thought how lucky she was to now live in the house they rented from Maisie and her husband, David, and how they in turn rented their home to Betty Billington's daughter, Clemmie, and her new husband. Everything had worked out for the best, she thought as she hung her coat up and walked into the kitchen to put her shopping away and make a hot drink. It had been nice to be able to pop into a few shops on the way home without having to worry about collecting Georgina and Buster. Perhaps she would sit and read her *People's Friend* magazine for a little while before she set about her chores, she thought as she went to the stone pantry to fetch milk, just as the telephone started to ring, causing her to jolt upright as fear ran through her. Who was ringing at this time of the day? Was there something wrong? Were the children all right? Or perhaps it was her nan . . . ?

'Pull yourself together,' she said out loud as she hurried into the hall where the telephone was situated on a shelf. 'Erith 349 . . .' she said as she held the receiver to her ear, dreading what she would hear.

'Sarah, it's Freda,' she heard her friend's voice. 'I wondered if you'd like to come down to mine for a while? I have some news for you.'

'Goodness, don't say you are expecting again,' Sarah laughed, relieved that it wasn't bad news. 'I had a Nanny Ruby moment and feared the worst.'

Freda started to laugh. 'Oh, Sarah, next you will have a crocheted mat for the telephone to sit on and be telling it not to ring. Then we will know you've turned into Ruby.'

They both loved Ruby very much, but she had such a strange relationship with the telephone at number thirteen that it had become a family joke even the elderly woman took with good grace, laughing at herself.

'I do have some ironing to do, but that can wait. Put the kettle on and I'll be down in two ticks,' Sarah said before replacing the receiver and going into the kitchen to take the kettle from the hob and put her cup and saucer back into the cabinet. Relaxing even for an hour would be delightful, and if the twins were awake, she'd be able to have a cuddle of her favourite little people.

Sarah closed the front door behind her and walked slowly down the long road, admiring the neat rows of bay-fronted terraced houses that faced each other.

As she approached number thirteen, she spotted her nan standing in the small front garden with a broom in her hand. 'You put me to shame,' she called out while still a few yards away.

'By rights, Bob should be out here sweeping our path as he made the mess. He only had a little weeding to do, and I told him not to overstretch himself,' she said, seeing Sarah frown. 'He decided to pull up the old privet hedge between us and number eleven and just look at the mess!'

Sarah had to admit there was almost more soil on the path than in the small patch of garden. 'Here, let me do it,' she said, taking the broom from Ruby and ignoring her protests. 'It's not going to hurt the baby,' she smiled as she briskly brushed the soil back into the garden. 'There you go, all spick and span again.'

'Bless you, love. Was you coming down to see me?'

'No, Freda rang and asked me to pop down for a cuppa. Why don't you come over with me?'

Ruby beamed. 'Let me pop inside and tell Bob and collect

a knitting pattern Freda asked to borrow. I'll be two ticks,' she said, hurrying inside to return a minute later with a wide grin on her face. 'It's a good job I went in when I did as he'd fallen asleep holding his cup of tea. That little gardening job tired him out. And there's no need to look at me like that; he had a thorough check-up just the other day and he's as well as he can be for a man his age. He just needs to slow down and regain his strength. I'll make sure he does,' she said as she took Sarah's arm to cross the road to number fourteen.

As they approached Freda's front door, they were welcomed by the sound of three screaming babies. 'Thank goodness you are here! They all woke up at the same time,' a flustered Freda said as she opened the door holding William, the eldest, under one arm. He wriggled and complained while continuing to wail.

'Here, let me take him,' Ruby said before they'd even stepped over the threshold. 'Come to Nanny Ruby,' she cooed as she rocked the child in her arms.

'That leaves one each for us,' Sarah grinned as she took a twin from Freda who'd lifted them from the twin pram parked in the hall.

'Come through to the kitchen while I make tea. We won't be long, Ruby,' she called back to where Ruby was watching out from the bay window while soothing young William.

'Don't worry about me and the little man. I swear you can see more of the road from your window than mine,' she called back.

Sarah laughed as she followed Freda. 'Of course, it has nothing to do with Nan's aspidistra and the heavy lace

78

curtains at her window,' she said. 'Not that I'd change a thing if I lived at Nan's house.'

'Neither would I. In fact, Tony suggested we too had an aspidistra plant just like Ruby's, but we've yet to find one as lovely as hers. She must have had it for years.'

'I recall it being in that same spot when I visited as a child. Nan told me it had survived since she moved to Alexandra Road when Dad was only five years old.'

'Fancy that,' Freda said as she passed baby Bertie to Sarah, who held a baby in each arm while Freda put the kettle on the hob and reached into the cupboard for her cups. 'I do like to use my best china when Ruby visits.'

'She deserves to be treated like a queen,' Sarah smiled as she bent her head to put a light kiss on the two babies' cheeks. 'I'm so pleased she managed to see the royal family when they visited the area after the floods.'

Freda chuckled. 'Let's face it, she wasn't going to let a crowd get in the way of her speaking to the Queen.'

'She's the Queen Mother now. Nan will never forget that day even though so many people were without homes and had lost all their possessions. The icing on the cake was her photo in *The Erith Observer* as she curtsied to the royal family even though Bob had to grab her elbow to help her up,' Sarah said fondly.

Freda poured some of the boiling water into a teapot and swirled it around before tipping the water into the sink and adding four spoonfuls of tea leaves, followed by the boiling water. Once she put the lid onto the teapot, she covered it with a knitted tea cosy. 'I do worry about Bob. He seems to be so frail since the floods and his illness. I pray nothing happens to him . . .' Freda said as her chin started to wobble and she pulled a handkerchief from the cuff of her cardigan.

'Don't say any more,' Sarah whispered, looking towards the door. 'Nan's hearing is still sharp, and she'd hate to think we were worrying. I'll put these two in their pram,' she said, looking at the now sleeping babies, 'and we can take the tea tray into the front room; it's not often Margaret Rose sleeps at the same time as her brother Bertie.'

'Before you go, there's something I want to tell you,' Freda said. 'I'd prefer Ruby not to hear for now.'

Sarah quickly put the sleeping twins into their pram that was still in the hall and pulled the door to, so the girls had some privacy. 'What is it?'

Freda sat down at the dining table. Her house was the same as Ruby's with a kitchen at the back and a bay-windowed front room and a dining room. Unlike Ruby, she used both rooms rather than keep the front room for best. Sarah sat down opposite. 'You know when you left work I was helping Betty take names from the counter staff?'

'It couldn't have been more than two hours ago so I'm unlikely to have forgotten,' Sarah grinned. 'Did many staff members sign up? I must say, I'm looking forward to the trip.'

'Yes, but that's not what I want to tell you,' Freda said impatiently, looking towards the closed door. 'As I was assisting Betty on the shop floor, I spotted that Gloria who helps Maureen leaving the store. There was a chap waiting for her outside. He looked so familiar I told Betty I needed to go as my shift had finished. I quickly grabbed my things from my locker and hurried into Pier Road just as they turned into the High Street.'

Sarah frowned. 'There's nothing wrong with that. Perhaps it's her husband or a boyfriend, or even a relative?'

'They'd stopped to talk and rather than stand and listen I went into Alan's shop to look about; he had the door open, so it was easy to listen to them.'

'Gosh, you'd make an excellent spy.'

Freda flapped her hand at the comment and looked serious. 'She was telling him how we were all going on a coach trip in a couple of weeks.'

'Ooh, perhaps she is going to have a romantic liaison with him . . .'

'No, my gut tells me there is more to this. I can't help thinking I've seen him before and it may have been at my wedding reception on the *Kentish Queen*. I have a feeling he is one of the Unthank family . . .'

Sarah looked troubled, falling silent as she digested what Freda had told her.

'I caught a few words . . . He told her she'd done well. Why would he say such a thing?'

'But we all gave evidence after what happened at your wedding and in the days leading up to it; surely he's not going to cause trouble for all of us, is he?'

'I wouldn't put it past him as his dad passed away while behind bars, so he's bound to be bitter. There's something else . . .'

'Spit it out,' Sarah hissed as they heard Ruby's footsteps in the hall.

'As he walked away, he stopped to look in the window of Alan's shop and held his hand up as if he was pointing a gun towards Alan, who was serving a customer, and pretended to fire it before grinning and walking away.'

81

Sarah froze. 'We have to do something.'

'For a start you can pour the tea before it gets stone cold, then you can tell me what the pair of you are whispering about,' Ruby said as she walked into the room with a grizzling William in her arms.

6

'Let me put William in his cot. He's just tired,' Freda said, reaching out to Ruby.

'I'll do that while the pair of you work out what you intend to tell me,' Ruby grimaced before taking the child upstairs.

'We can't get Nan involved, she has enough to worry about with Bob being poorly,' Sarah said as she carried the tea tray into the front room and started to pour out their tea.

Freda followed, carrying the biscuit barrel and stopping to check the pram where Bertie and Margaret Rose were sleeping soundly. 'We have to tell her, or she won't give us a moment's peace until she knows everything,' she said as they heard the floorboards of the bedroom above creaking. 'If we tell her we are treating her and Bob to a trip to London, it may help take her mind off our problem.'

'We don't know yet if there is a problem, or just you putting two and two together and making five,' Sarah whispered.

'If you'd been there, you'd have felt the same as me. Besides, even Maureen isn't keen on the new canteen assistant.'

'That's true . . .'

'So, what's this all about?' Ruby asked as she sat down in an armchair by the fireside and Sarah passed her tea with a biscuit on the saucer.

Freda explained what she'd seen that afternoon while Sarah added how Maureen had misgivings about the new staff member who was doing nothing to endear herself to her colleagues in the store.

'She doesn't sound pleasant. Why did you employ her?'

Sarah shrugged her shoulders. 'It was Betty who took her on; I was off that day. She knew Maureen was struggling to cope and needed more help.'

Ruby shook her head. 'What a pickle. I'd like to say we should ignore it all and that what you saw was innocent. However, my gut is telling me otherwise. Those Unthanks are bad news for our family. What with some of them getting locked up and their father passing away, I have the feeling they may be out for revenge.'

'That would make sense after what happened on the day of my wedding . . .' Freda added as she gulped her tea, trying to steady the nerves that fought to overcome her as she thought of the terrible incident on board the *Kentish Queen* and the people who died or were injured, including some of the Unthank clan.

'Bob reckons they don't forget anyone who slighted them and that includes him and Mike. He said they keep a list of names . . .'

Sarah was aghast. 'Mike's a police sergeant; I'd think they don't like any coppers, but Bob?'

Freda butted in. 'Bob helped rescue me from the Unthanks' office when I was caught up in something they were up to not long before my wedding. Besides, the older members of that family will recall Bob being a policeman years ago, so no love lost there.'

'God, what a mess,' Sarah groaned. 'Nan, what can we do?' she asked, forgetting she didn't want Ruby involved.

'First you can put the kettle on again while I think about this. However, we are not to tell Bob; you know what he's like, he will get involved and his health isn't up to it. It could be the death of him.'

Freda and Sarah sighed with relief and quickly agreed with Ruby before hurrying to replenish their cups.

'I'd like to see this Gloria so I can check her out. I'll pop in to see Maureen tomorrow morning. Betty won't mind, will she?'

'Not at all. In fact, you can come in to find out more about the trip to London. I've added yours and Bob's names to the list. It'll be our treat,' Sarah said before Ruby asked.

'We've not done that for a few years,' Ruby said, her face lighting up at the thought. 'It reminds me of when we had trips to Margate and sat on the beach before going for fish and chips and a visit to Dreamland. We should do that next summer. I hope the weather holds up and there's no snow when we go to London.'

The girls agreed. 'What will you do after that?' Freda asked.

'Fall into my bed dog tired, I'd think.'

'No, I mean after you've seen Maureen in the staff canteen,' Freda chuckled.

'We need someone to follow Gloria when she leaves work to see what she gets up to. If she meets that Unthank chap, they can find out where the pair live so we can help the police if push comes to shove. I'll see if I can follow her when I leave the store.'

'I agree, we need to know where this chap is staying and have him watched. If he's up to anything, we can ask Mike for help, but you must be careful, Nan.'

Ruby slapped her hands on her knees before getting to her feet. 'I'd best get back to Bob and have his tea started or he'll give me merry hell and raid the cake tin. He has no idea food is still in short supply. As far as he's concerned, when the war ended the pantry magically filled up,' she chuckled.

Freda saw Ruby to the door and kissed her cheek. 'Thank you for your help. I'm working tomorrow, so I'll look out for you,' she said. She waved her goodbye then watched to see Ruby cross the road safely before closing the door. 'Thank goodness that worked out well,' she said, collapsing into the armchair Ruby had just vacated.

'I'm still worried,' Sarah said. 'What if Nan is spotted following them? She's no spring chicken and may get hurt.'

'What can we do? It's not as if we can follow Ruby while she follows Gloria and Unthank.'

Sarah chuckled as she imagined the scene.

'Hmm, perhaps you should let Betty in on our concerns?'

Sarah shook her head as she disagreed. 'No, we really ought not to tell too many people until we are sure what is happening. Then we speak to Mike Jackson; he will know what to do.'

'Then that's how we should proceed,' Freda said before she started to giggle. 'This is rather like one of the Clive Danvers spy films where he follows the guilty party; I did enjoy them,' she sighed, thinking of the handsome actor, Johnny Johnson, who was now married to her friend Molly.

Sarah sighed. 'You are right, Clive Danvers would have been ideal for this task, but he is just a character in the movies and what Ruby is about to do is real. I pray she isn't spotted as the Unthanks are a nasty bunch of villains.'

'She will be all right. Ruby is sensible and won't come to any harm.'

'I'll make sure she doesn't. Now, I must get home and start dinner, or I'll have a grumpy husband on my hands,' she grinned, standing up to hug Freda. 'Let's see if we can take our tea breaks together when Nan arrives at the store tomorrow so we can observe Gloria.'

'Good idea,' Freda agreed. 'Now, get off home and stop worrying, things will be fine.'

*

Nella Wilson watched as Claudette skilfully sketched an outline of a Grecian-style wedding gown after asking numerous questions of the bride-to-be. She thought of how Nella's body shape would change in the coming weeks by the time of her church wedding, before considering the way the gown would drape and flow around the girl's body.

'It is rather daring and not at all what brides of today are wearing.' Nella sighed with delight. 'Mother would have me trussed up in heavy satin carrying that large bouquet to hide any suggestion that she would soon be a grandmother. I'm not sure if she would approve . . .'

Bessie bent over her sister's shoulder to obtain a clearer view of the sketch. 'Perhaps raise the neckline a little, and what about embroidery in silver thread at the hem and scattered across the skirt? Silver lily of the valley would look pretty.'

'Oh, I'd adore that! Can it be done?'

Claudette chewed her lip thoughtfully as she added floral details to her design. 'What do you think of this?'

Nella clapped her hands together. 'Perfect! Would you be able to design something for my two bridesmaids? They are my two colleagues from the dance school. We are similar in size and age.'

'Yes, how about a similar design in crepe de chine, but without the silver embroidery? Do you have a favourite colour?'

'A pale green would be lovely if you can find the fabric. The wedding is to be in three weeks. Can this be completed by then?'

'Of course, although you will have to come in for a few fittings,' Claudette said, trying not to appear shocked at the time frame; it would certainly be a speedy job. 'If you would excuse me for a moment, I will fetch our fabric samples so you are able to choose the right colour for your bridesmaids,' she said, hurriedly leaving the room.

Nella ran her finger over the page of sketches. 'Your sister is so talented for one so . . .'

'Young?' Bessie grinned as she finished Nella's sentence for her.

'I feel embarrassed for mentioning such a thing. My only worry is Mother may bring up the subject of someone so young overseeing my special dress.' She looked up as the door opened, expecting to see Claudette. Instead it was Maisie who entered.

'I'm so sorry I wasn't here to welcome you,' she said as she shook Nella's hand.

Nella smiled. 'I have been looked after very well by Bessie and Claudette. I hope my mother has not . . .'

'Miss Trott has been caring for your mother. They have fashion magazines spread out on the work table discussing gowns, but I see Claudette has been busy,' she said as she picked up the sketchbook and studied the design. 'I can see how the books she has been reading on ancient Greece have influenced this design. I like it very much.'

'I simply adore it, but Mother may have other ideas.' Nella stood up to look closer at the design as Maisie held it next to the girl, studying her height and how gracefully she moved. 'I'm expecting a baby, so Mother is rather in a stew over the whole wedding thing. My fiancé and I had thought of scuttling off to Gretna Green to save her being embarrassed by the whole sorry situation,' she said, looking embarrassed herself.

Maisie couldn't help but give the girl a hug. 'You are not to scuttle off anywhere! We are here to help you, so relax and enjoy the experience. There is one thing, though.'

Nella and Bessie frowned, waiting for Maisie to explain, as Claudette returned struggling with several fabric sample books in her arms. 'Mum, you are not to change my design,' she said, winking at Nella. 'Honestly, you'd think she owned this business the way she interferes!'

'Mind how you speak in front of a client, or I will give you your cards and you will have to go back to Woolworths full time,' Maisie said, wagging her finger at Claudette who just laughed.

'Then who would design your frocks?' Bessie chipped in.

'Mrs Carlisle was about to make a suggestion,' Nella said, slightly shocked at the banter between mother and daughter.

'Go ahead, Mum,' Claudette said as she placed the samples on a vacant side table and sat down next to Nella, waiting to hear what Maisie had to say.

'I do wonder if white chiffon is right for the gown?'

'Chiffon is perfect, and it will float around Nella's frame from the high waistband . . .'

'And disguise any sign of a baby,' Nella finished for her.

Maisie smiled, noticing the bond between the girls. 'I'm not disputing that chiffon is the right fabric, but white . . . ? Under the circumstances it may not be the right colour as guests may notice; not that you should be ashamed.'

'I'm not.' Nella jutted her chin out, looking defiant. 'However, you are right. As much as I adore the idea of white with silver embroidery, it may not be the correct colour.'

Maisie picked up one of the sample books. 'How about this with gold thread?' she asked, pointing to a rich cream chiffon. 'We could have the same embroidery, but in a gold thread.'

Nella felt the fabric between her fingers. 'This would be perfect.'

'We can manage that,' Maisie said as she jotted a few notes next to the design. 'Now, shall we go into the work-room and show your mother?'

Nella turned pale and looked towards Bessie and Claudette for help.

'Mum, please don't tell Mrs Wilson that Claudette designed the dress as she may not approve,' Bessie pleaded.

'Leave it with me,' Maisie said as she ushered them out of the room.

*

'Your mum is wonderful,' Nella said as she walked with the girls towards the front gate. 'She worked wonders with my mother and had her eating out of her hand, especially after she told her the gown was to be designed by an up-and-coming dress designer. I wish I could have stayed longer but as it is, I must hurry to get to work on time.'

'I would adore to dance for a living,' Claudette said as she gave a twirl.

'What, and give up your designing career?' Nella laughed. 'I only work at Erith Dance Studios because, quite honestly, I'm no good at anything else. Not that I don't enjoy dancing. In fact, I met my husband-to-be at one of their tea dances. He asked me to dance and trod all over my feet. It was so romantic,' she sighed.

'What I wouldn't give for some romance in my life,' Bessie said as she opened the gate.

'Me too,' Claudette grinned. 'And there's no need to look at me like that, Bessie Carlisle. I'm old enough to have a beau and go dancing.'

'I have an idea, why don't you both come along to tomorrow evening's classes for beginners? We have a good mix of male and female dancers, and you may just meet a lad or two.'

The sisters looked at each other before agreeing.

'I have a shift at Woolies tomorrow, so can bring a dress and go straight there,' Claudette said as Bessie agreed to join her so they could walk there together and get changed in the ladies' cloakroom at the studio.

Nella was shocked. 'However do you find time to do two jobs? I'd have thought working for your mother's business took up all your time.'

'I love working at Woolworths and would miss all my friends if I left. Besides, I don't have a boyfriend so have time on my hands,' she grinned.

'What's all this about boys?' a friendly voice asked as George Caselton arrived, accompanied by Alan Gilbert.

'I thought you were promised to me?' Alan grinned at Claudette, who he'd known since she was a young child.

Claudette and Bessie burst out laughing and hugged the two men, unaware their next-door neighbour was in her front garden pottering about.

'Is your dad home yet? We wanted a word about the goings-on in the town,' Alan said as he shook Nella's hand after being introduced.

Bessie checked her wristwatch. 'He will be home very soon. Why don't you go up to the salon? Mum will be pleased to see you both.'

'I'll do just that. I need to avail myself of her services,' George said as he and Alan left them to go into the house.

'And I must be on my way,' Nella said, kissing both the girls' cheeks. 'I will see you tomorrow evening and I promise there will be lots of male escorts for you,' she said, causing the girls to giggle as they waved her goodbye and followed the men into the house.

Next door Mrs Bennett rushed into the living room while her husband was having a quiet snooze. 'Gordon, Gordon, wake up this instant!' she shrieked, shaking him roughly by the sleeve of his jumper. 'I knew I was right, there is something going on next door. Why, that awful

Carlisle woman is running a brothel! There are men going in and out of the house and there's a woman standing at the gate planning to find male escorts. I wouldn't have believed it if I hadn't heard it with my own ears. We need to be rid of that family before they bring the whole avenue into disrepute.'

7

Claudette glanced up at the large clock on the wall of the Erith store. As much as she loved her Saturday job and refused to give it up, while holding down a full-time position with her mum, she was keen to get away on time as she wanted to get to the Erith Dance Studios to dance – and possibly meet a boy. She had never told a soul that she longed to have a boyfriend, but who would look at a plain Jane when her sister, Bessie, was the beauty in the family? Perhaps tonight would be the night it happened and it would not be for want of preparation. She'd stayed up late finishing a buttercup-yellow poplin dress and making a headband to match. Cinched in at the waist and flaring over her hips, the dress did a lot to hide her dumpy frame. As much as Maisie told her she was growing out of her puppy fat and blossoming, she was fed up with waiting.

'Why, girl, you look as though you are miles away. I could have slipped this in my pocket and legged it down Pier Road,' Ruby said, standing the other side of the polished wooden counter holding out a can opener. 'Bob bent ours, and I thought it was time to buy another.'

Claudette jumped at the sound of Ruby's voice. 'I'm so

sorry, Nanny Ruby. Here, let me put this in a paper bag for you,' she said with a beaming smile.

'Perhaps take my money first,' Ruby laughed, 'unless Woolies are giving things away today and that would be a first.'

Claudette giggled as her cheeks turned pink. 'Oh goodness, I'll be getting the sack if I don't concentrate,' she said as she took the one-pound note and went to the till. Holding the note above her head, she called out, 'One pound!', and was given a nod by a passing supervisor. Although all staff had to do the same when given paper money to pay for a purchase, she still felt daft doing it. Counting the change into Ruby's hand and watching as she put it away safely in her purse, she felt she should explain why her head had been in the clouds. 'Bessie is coming to meet me, and we are going dancing,' she explained, again feeling the thrill of the evening ahead rippling through her.

'I hope you both enjoy yourselves,' Ruby said as she placed her purchase into her shopping bag. 'You work too hard, young lady, and should be out enjoying yourself more with people of your own age. I used to enjoy dancing, but my old knees won't allow me to do much more than walk to the shops these days.'

Claudette felt sad for Nanny Ruby. 'It must be awful to be old. I couldn't imagine not being able to do everything I wanted to do.'

Ruby chuckled. 'Less of the old. My bones may protest but I'm just as bright up here,' she said, tapping her head. 'Watching you young people enjoy yourselves is good enough for me. Are you going on the charabanc trip to London?'

'I wouldn't miss it for the world! Can I sit with you?'

'What, and miss being with your friends?'

Claudette wrinkled her nose. 'I'll leave the socializing to our Bessie; she's the pretty one.'

Ruby cocked her head to one side and looked at the young girl. 'Don't put yourself down, love. There's many a person who would dream of having a smile like yours and your happy disposition. Now, I must go upstairs and see Maureen, so I'll wish you a happy evening dancing,' she said, giving Claudette a warm smile and a wave as she headed towards the staff door and started to climb the stairs to the offices and canteen.

'Hello, Ruby,' Betty said as she came out of her office and spotted her at the top of the staircase.

'Hello, love. I hope you don't mind but I've popped in to see our Maureen. I won't stop her working.'

Betty adored Ruby, who had always included her in the Caselton family. 'Go on in, there's bound to be a kettle on the boil and perhaps even a sticky bun; we had a fresh supply today. It is long past the last staff tea break so the canteen staff will be clearing up.'

'Thanks, love,' Ruby smiled.

'Before you go . . .'

Ruby stopped in her tracks. 'Is there something wrong?'

'I wondered if you'd heard anything about the proposed demolition of Cross Street?'

Ruby grimaced. 'I have and I'm not happy about it. Some of those houses may be a bit run-down, but local families have turned them into homes to be proud of. Where will the council house them? I told George to do all he could to stop it all.'

Betty could imagine Ruby telling off her middle-aged son; George would have had a right flea in his ear from his mother. However, she felt guilty as she'd given no thought to the families who would have to find somewhere to live. She'd owned her own little house in Cross Street when she first moved to Erith and looked back with great affection to her time living there before she met and married her Douglas. 'I hope something can be done for the families if the demolition goes ahead. I was also wondering if the news was true about the demolition including Pier Road and the High Street. It would affect so many small businesses, as well as the families who live over their shops.'

'I've heard that rumour and told George to get to the bottom of it. Maureen is also nagging him to do all he can.' She started to chuckle. 'That'll teach him to get mixed up in local politics. He thought he was going into it to help people and all he's getting is a lot of grief.'

'George is doing a very good job. I've heard great things about him,' Betty said, thinking Ruby was being a little harsh, or was she joshing?

'He has one of his surgeries tomorrow at the church hall. He gets to meet lots of locals. I just hope they don't all want to talk about the demolition plans rather than the state of their drains and housing problems.'

Betty grimaced. 'I wouldn't do his job for a million pounds; there will be so many disappointed people in the months to come.'

'It'll all come out in the wash,' Ruby said as she left Betty to her thoughts.

Ruby tapped on the door of the staff canteen before walking in to see Maureen berating her two helpers.

Standing in front of them with her hands on her hips, she was giving them what for. 'If you think leaving smears and spills on the tables is your way of cleaning up, you've got another think coming. Rinse out the cleaning cloths and go over them again – and don't flick bits onto the floor as you'll be mopping it again,' she said, wagging a finger at someone Ruby hadn't met before.

Maureen kissed her mother-in-law's cheek and led her to a table that looked cleaner than the rest. 'Honestly, Ruby, I need eyes in the back of my head with that pair. Dora is a good kid but doesn't have much idea. The new girl is insolent and picks at Dora all the time. I've given her more than one warning. I don't think she'll be here for long,' she said before going to the counter and pouring out two steaming cups of tea. 'I'll put two iced buns in a bag for you to take home.'

'Thanks, love. Bob will enjoy them with his tea,' Ruby said, trying hard not to lick her lips. She was partial to something sweet and even though rationing was all but over she found herself still being careful when she did her shopping. As Maureen joined her, groaning a little as she stretched her aching leg, Ruby leant close. 'Who is this new girl they've taken on?'

Maureen sighed. 'Betty meant well, and took her on to help me out, but I can't take to her. She won't take orders from me without a lot of fuss and arguing and isn't very nice to poor Dora. She has a sly way about her. I don't know why she works here when she doesn't like me. Granted, she can work hard at times but . . .'

'Perhaps she needs the money. Do you know much about her?'

'No, I didn't get to see her application form and she doesn't speak about her circumstances even when I ask in a friendly way. When I think of all the people who'd like a job here it annoys me that I'm lumbered with her. Why, I'd rather take on an older person for a few hours a day; at least they know how to graft.'

Ruby was thoughtful as she sipped her tea and watched the girl half-heartedly go about her work. After chatting about the trip to the theatre and agreeing that she and Bob would sit with Maureen and George on the coach, she made her goodbyes. It was close to closing time and she wanted to be on the pavement outside the store when the girl left so she could keep an eye out for the man Freda had mentioned.

As she passed the open door of the manager's office, she could see her talking on the telephone. She had never seen Betty look so serious. Raising a hand and mouthing goodbye, she was pleased to see a smile cross the woman's face as she waved back.

'Hello, Nanny Ruby,' Bessie said as she caught up with Ruby on the staircase. 'I was just collecting Claudette's bag so we could dash off once the closing bell sounds. Thankfully I know her supervisor from when I worked here, and she said I could come upstairs.'

Ruby held her arm as they negotiated the steep stairs. 'Do you miss working here?' she asked.

'I'll always have a soft spot for good old Woolies, but Mum needs me more now and working at home gives me more time with Jenny.'

'You are a very lucky young lady as things could have turned out so differently,' she said, alluding to when Bessie

99

ran away from home when she found herself in the family way.

Bessie stopped as they reached the bottom of the stairs and turned to Ruby. 'A day doesn't go past when I don't think of what could have happened to me,' she said, looking Ruby straight in the eye. 'I intend to work hard to give my daughter a good life.'

'I know you do, ducks, but you have to enjoy yourself sometimes, so off you go and have a lovely time dancing,' Ruby said as they entered through the staff door to the shop floor.

'Hang on a minute,' Claudette called out as she finished straightening the cotton sheeting they used to cover the counters for the night. 'We can walk down the road with you.'

As much as Ruby loved the company of Maisie's eldest girls, she groaned inside. How could she follow Gloria when they were with her? 'Come along then, I must get these iced buns home to Bob,' she said, opening her shopping bag to show the girls the bag inside.

'I had one in my tea break to keep my energy up for the dancing,' Claudette said as Bessie raised her eyebrows. Her sister was always encouraging her to curb her appetite.

'You'd better do a few quicksteps to work the bun off,' Bessie said although she had a twinkle in her eye as they left the building, calling goodnight to the supervisor who stood by the door holding a large bunch of keys.

'Hold on, I think I left my gloves behind,' Claudette said as she stopped suddenly, checking the pockets of her best coat she'd worn to look presentable when they arrived at the studio.

'Mind where you're going,' a female voice hissed as she shoved Claudette to the side of the pavement and walked past her.

'Sorry . . .' Claudette started to say before Bessie stopped her.

'There's no need to be rude,' Bessie called after her as the woman gave her a hard stare and carried on walking, before stopping at the end of the Woolworths building and checking her watch. She looked impatiently up and down the road before lighting a cigarette.

'That's the new woman who is working in the canteen with Maureen,' Claudette whispered to Bessie and Ruby. 'She's not very nice. I find it best to steer clear of her when I take my breaks.'

Bessie was thoughtful. 'I'm sure I've seen her somewhere before . . . It'll come to me,' she said, looking over her shoulder with no luck as the woman had her back to them.

Ruby's ears pricked up. She'd not recognized her dressed in a thick coat and woolly hat and looked again as they passed her on their way to the end of the road. 'This is where I leave you.' Ruby gave each girl a kiss on the cheek. 'I want to catch the greengrocer before he closes as I'm short on greens. Now, you both have a lovely time and make sure to pop in and tell me and Bob all about it,' she said before waving them goodbye as they crossed the road to the dance studio that was positioned on two floors above Burton's, the tailor's shop.

Bessie waved back from the other side of the road before they walked down a side turning to the entrance of the studio. 'That's strange. I thought Nanny Ruby would have had enough vegetables with them having the allotment.'

101

Ruby waited until the girls had entered the building and walked back to the corner to see if Gloria was still there. She felt uncomfortable standing in front of the bank in case she was thought to be a lookout for bank robbers. The thought made her titter, causing a passing couple to stare and give her a wide berth. She shifted from foot to foot, hoping she didn't have to wait too long as her feet were starting to ache. Peering around the corner a second time, she was pleased to see Gloria was talking to a scruffy-looking man. There seemed to be much waving of arms by the woman while the man pushed his hands into his pockets and shrugged a lot before they started to walk in her direction. She delved into her bag as if searching for something until they'd gone past, then she followed. They kept up a brisk pace as they walked the length of the High Street, crossing the road in front of the Odeon cinema and starting to walk away from the town up Crayford Road. They stopped at the entrance to the cinder path that followed the railway line towards Slades Green. Ruby stopped by a post box and pretended to be posting a letter. I hope they aren't going down to the green otherwise I'll never get home, she thought.

As she stopped to make a show of checking the post times and tightening her scarf around her neck, she heard them talking.

'The whole store is off to London to see a show, even the security man. I asked him when I gave him an extra slice of pie with his lunch. He likes his food,' Gloria scoffed.

Ruby frowned. Why was she telling him this? She started to follow them, hell-bent on hearing more, as they turned and walked over Britannia Bridge and into the small estate of prefabs. Once she had memorized the number of the property, she turned back and headed down Alexandra Road and home. She wasn't sure if she should tell Betty Billington what she'd overheard or keep it to herself for now. After all, it wasn't exactly incriminating evidence. She at least knew she couldn't share what she'd heard with Bob, or he would fuss and worry and that could reverse his recovery. No, she'd ponder on this for a while.

8

'I'm so pleased you could come,' Nella said, giving the girls a hug as they entered the first-floor ballroom of Erith Dance Studios. 'The dancing doesn't start for an hour, so you have plenty of time to get ready. Come with me and I'll show you around,' she said, holding out her hand to Claudette. 'I'll take you upstairs first as that's where we give most of our dancing lessons.'

Bessie looked around at the large expanse of polished wood floor surrounded by seating. She walked over to the tall windows and looked out. 'You have such a lovely view of the town from here. I can see straight up Pier Road to Woolworths,' she said, pointing to show Claudette.

'There is a ladies' cloakroom here where you can change; it's a little tidier than the one downstairs. You can leave your things in there when you are dressed as it's only we staff members who use it.'

Once they were alone Claudette slipped out of her Woolworths overall and quickly washed her face in the small wash basin before stepping into her new frock and brushing her hair. 'What do you think?' she asked as she placed the matching headband above her fringe and gave a twirl.

'You look so pretty in your new dress; you are so clever. Every lad will want to dance with you. Here, you need a dab of perfume.' Bessie dipped into her handbag and handed her a small phial of Evening in Paris. 'You can use my lipstick too, but only a little or you will look like a painted doll. Let me do it,' she said as she added a little colour to her sister's lips. 'Perfect.'

Claudette peered into a small mirror over the sink, pursing her lips and checking the colour wasn't on her teeth. 'I do wish I was a redhead like Nella,' she said, securing her headband then looking left and right checking it was straight. 'Here, you use the mirror while I pack my things way.' She took her dancing shoes from the bag and put her overall and work shoes away.

Bessie opened her make-up bag and checked her face before adding a little more lipstick and powder. 'To be honest, I wouldn't like to have red hair as it can be hard to wear the right coloured clothes. Fancy not being able to wear red as it would clash horribly. Imagine if she worked at Woolies and had to wear the uniform!'

'I don't know, I think it looks stylish. Are you ready yet?'

After running a comb through her hair, Bessie gave a nod of approval. 'That'll do. Come on, let's go downstairs before everyone arrives and we can't find a seat.'

Claudette followed Bessie down the flight of stairs, thinking how light she was on her feet and how she was as pretty as a picture in her pale blue dress that swirled around her legs as she almost skipped along. 'If you had a decent partner, you could enter ballroom competitions; you'd look lovely in one of those ballroom dresses with the full skirts. I could help you stitch on the sequins.'

'I can just about shuffle along to a foxtrot, so I'm not sure where you get your strange ideas from,' Bessie replied as she reached the last step.

'I just think it would be nice if you had a hobby and met a lad and—'

'And married and lived happily ever after, you mean?' Bessie said ruefully. 'I'm afraid that boat's long sailed. No lad wants to take on a wife and another man's child. Besides, I'm more than happy living in my little flat at home and working with Mum. Come on, let's have some fun,' she said, entering the ballroom and heading over to where Nella was talking to two young women.

Nella introduced the women, who were to be her bridesmaids, and they spent a few minutes planning for them to visit the house to be measured for their gowns.

'Let me show you the rest of the place,' Nella said as she led them to the corner of the room. 'This is our coffee bar where we play the dance records. We also lay on refreshments when we have dance nights.'

'What's this if it isn't a dance night?' Claudette asked with a puzzled look on her face.

'Oh, this is a get-together for the adult students where they can practise their steps in more of a social atmosphere than classes.'

'But we don't have partners. Will we have to dance with each other?' Bessie said, thinking back to when they went to a holiday camp, and she danced with her female friends.

Nella chuckled. 'No, the lads will be along soon. You won't be short of partners.'

'We haven't danced much,' Claudette said, feeling as though she wanted to turn around and go home.

'We give short displays before each dance so you should get the hang of the basic steps. I promise you will enjoy yourselves,' Nella assured them before showing them the rest of the large ballroom and the impressive array of trophies arranged on shelves at one end. 'Who knows, if you both enjoy dancing, you can join our classes and one day soon, you'll be winning trophies.'

Claudette and Bessie burst out laughing at the thought as they heard laughter and footsteps coming up the staircase.

'Let the evening commence,' Nella said as she went to greet her students.

'Oh, my goodness,' Bessie gasped as she turned away from the people entering the room. 'I really don't want to be here right now.'

Claudette looked at her sister, who had turned deathly pale. 'Are you feeling ill?' she asked, taking her arm in case Bessie fainted.

'Be discreet and look at who has just come into the room,' she hissed.

Claudette peered over Bessie's shoulder and checked out the many people pouring in. 'I don't know what or who I'm looking at. Can you give me a hint.'

Bessie sighed. 'It's Jake.'

'Jake?'

'The Jake who is building our garden wall.'

'Oh, good. He looks different out of his work clothes. At least we know someone.' Claudette grinned as she spotted the young man and started to wave.

'Don't do that,' Bessie groaned as Claudette beckoned him over.

'Why not? He seems a decent sort,' she asked, thinking how she'd seen Jake watching her sister on more than one occasion.

'He doesn't approve of me; we had words earlier. I don't think he approves of me being an unmarried mother. I also spotted him talking with Mrs Bennett next door so goodness knows what he was saying about us. The woman doesn't like us living there and he seems to think the same.'

'Oh, goodness, I think you've got him all wrong. Look out, here he is with his mates. Hello, Jake, I had no idea you were a dancer,' Claudette said, giving him a wide grin before looking shyly at his friends.

'This is Richard and Nigel,' he said as the two men shook hands with the girls.

'I'm Claudette and this is my sister Bessie,' she explained. 'We've not been here before. Is it your first time?'

'No, we've been having lessons for a couple of months,' Jake said, trying not to look at Bessie.

'Yes, ever since we got out of—' Richard was silenced by an elbow in the ribs from Jake. 'Yes, a couple of months.'

Bessie frowned. Where had Jake been? He seemed embarrassed and she wondered why. They were spared from the stilted conversation by Nella, who was clapping her hands for their attention.

'I want to start with a waltz so can the gentlemen choose a partner, please? Stop your giggling,' she called to a group of young lads. 'For our new members I will choose your partners,' she said, glancing to where Bessie and Claudette were watching and looking nervous. 'You aren't to worry as I will go over the steps first before we put on the record.'

'Thank goodness for that,' Bessie whispered to her sister. 'I can't remember a waltz from a quickstep.'

'I hope she doesn't put us with those silly young boys,' Claudette said, giving them a disparaging look. 'Two of them work in the stockroom at Woolies.'

'Now, there's no need to look nervous,' Nella said as she joined them. 'I want you to be able to dance enough to enjoy my wedding reception.'

The two girls looked puzzled. 'I beg your pardon,' Claudette said.

'I want you at my big day to show the guests who made my gown. Besides, I need as many friends as possible at the wedding to help placate my mother,' she grinned. 'As far as she is concerned no one is good enough for her little girl, especially not my intended's family.'

'Crikey, what's wrong with them?' Bessie asked.

Nella gave a look of despair. 'They are greengrocers, which in Mother's eyes is below her as they are in trade.'

'I suppose our family is also trade,' Bessie said as she shook her head, wondering why anyone would be such a snob. 'Surely holding down a job is better in anyone's eyes than queueing at the labour exchange?'

'Mother is impressed with Maisie's Modes as your mum is a couturière. In her book that counts for something.'

'But Dad is an undertaker,' Bessie said.

'He is a director in a chain of funeral establishments,' Claudette chipped in with a grin as she clocked on to Mrs Bennett's way of bragging.

'Perhaps we won't mention that,' Nella laughed before taking Bessie by the hand and leading her to where Jake stood. 'You make a fine-looking couple,' she said before turning to his friend, Richard. 'You can dance with Claudette and the rest of you can follow me,' she said to the few boys without partners, leading them to the other side of the room where a group of wallflowers sat together looking nervous. 'Gentlemen, take your partners in hold,' she said loudly. 'I shall be the woman and Sharon here will take the man's part,' Nella continued as one of her brides-maids joined her. 'These are the steps we will start with.' The pair demonstrated several moves before encouraging the students to do likewise. Once she was happy they under-stood, after correcting a few holds and foot positions she went to the coffee bar to put on a record.

Bessie stared at Jake's tie, not being able to look at his face. She didn't want to be his partner and felt he really didn't want to be there. His arms were rigid as they stood waiting for Nella's instructions.

'I didn't ask Nella for you to be my partner,' she said in case he thought otherwise.

'We have to dance with someone,' he replied, giving her hand a squeeze. 'We are here to learn. Just don't step on my foot.'

Bessie felt the tension drop from her shoulders even though she was angry with the way he'd acted that after-noon. Perhaps she could enjoy the evening and not think about his impression of her being single with a child. 'I'll try not to,' she said, taking a deep breath as the first bars of Mantovani's Orchestra playing the heart-wrenching 'Charmaine' started.

'Ready, everyone . . . One, two, three, one, two, three,' Nella called out above the violins. 'Head up, Bessie. Stop looking at your feet. Jake, hold your partner closer; I could cycle my bike between you both. Claudette, stop singing and concentrate on your feet.'

Bessie gave a nervous laugh as Nella placed a hand on her back and the other on Jake before pushing them closer together. 'Much better,' she said after putting a finger under Bessie's chin to raise her face towards her partner. They continued to follow the steps until the record stopped, whereupon they sprang apart.

Bessie was trembling as she turned away from Jake. Why did he make her feel like this when it was obvious from the way he spoke to her today that he did not approve of her? She wondered what he had said to their odious next-door neighbour. She would have to ask him, or not knowing would eat her up inside.

She turned to face him, noticing he'd not moved and was watching her with a frown on his face. 'I saw you this afternoon when I looked out of the workroom window.'

'You knew I was working in the garden.'

'Yes. What I mean is I saw you talking to Mrs Bennett from next door.'

'That's right. Is that a problem?'

'You must be aware she doesn't like us living there. Was she asking questions?'

He shrugged his shoulders. 'Nothing I couldn't answer . . .'

Bessie waited for him to continue and raised an eyebrow when he didn't. 'And . . .'

He looked into her eyes for a second before turning and walking away.

'Hmm, that spoke volumes,' she said without thinking who could hear her.

'What did you say?' Nella asked as she joined her.

'Nothing, I was thinking out loud. I wonder, could I have another partner for the next dance?'

'By all means,' Nella replied. 'I like you all to work with different partners, although swapping after one dance is a little quick. I detected a frosty atmosphere as I came over. Is there a problem?'

'Perhaps we could chat about it when you aren't so busy?' Bessie said as she worried someone might overhear her talk about her private life.

'Let's do it over our coffee break,' Nella said as she squeezed Bessie's arm. 'Now, I have the perfect partner for you. Come and meet Jeremy. He is training to teach dance and helps me out when we are busy, like this evening.'

Bessie liked Jeremy as soon as he started to talk about his love of dancing and teaching. She was surprised a young man was so committed to what she'd always thought of as a woman's occupation, but decided it took all sorts to make the world go round. He was encouraging and gentle as he taught her the fundamentals of the quickstep, followed by the foxtrot. As their coffee break was announced he twirled her once more around the dance floor before delivering her to where Claudette was sitting as she did her utmost to ignore the sniggers of some of the young men who'd been told off earlier for chatting.

'You looked good together,' Claudette said as they watched Jeremy hurry back to the counter to help serve drinks. 'I just wish people could be kinder.'

'What do you mean?' Bessie asked as she fanned her hot face with her hand.

'He's a . . . you know . . .'

'A very good dancer?'

'A homosexual. Why do you think those lads were laughing at him?'

'Because they are childish and have got nothing better to do? How do you know such things?' Bessie asked. She was shocked that Claudette knew things like that about men at her age. She just about knew about men who preferred male company.

'At the amateur dramatics group. Uncle Alan told me.'

Bessie shook her head in disbelief. 'Why would Uncle Alan say such things?'

'It seems it is common in the theatrical world, and he was explaining why I may find some people a little different to us. He was being kind and wasn't mocking like those lads,' she said, nodding across to where the lads had become bored with poking fun at Jeremy and were now play fighting.

'Here we are,' Nella said as she joined them with a tray of coffee and a selection of biscuits on a saucer. The sisters budged up to make room for Nella and helped themselves to their drinks. 'Are you enjoying yourselves?'

'Very much so. Jeremy is a great dancer,' Bessie enthused.

'You did look good together. Did he tell you he is looking for a partner for competitions?'

'What, me?' Bessie spluttered into her coffee. 'I've only done three dances since we arrived. I'm not sure I'm competition material,' she joked.

'We have classes that could help you learn with a partner. Erith Dance Studios prides itself in turning out competition winners. You could do a lot worse than partner Jeremy,' Nella said.

'Now, what was it that upset you earlier?'

Claudette looked worried. 'I didn't know you were upset. Is that why you changed partners?'

Nella gave her an apologetic look. 'Sorry, I should have thought before I opened my big mouth.'

Bessie was quick to stop her concern. 'No, Claudette knows I saw Jake talking to our neighbour. He acted so cold towards me I wondered if the old witch had been stirring her cauldron.' Bessie sighed as the two girls filled Nella in on what had happened since they'd moved into the house.

'Jake seems a nice enough lad from what I've learnt since he joined my classes. He had a rough time in the army and since he was demobbed, he's had to start a new life.'

Bessie couldn't believe what she was hearing. To think she was so caught up in her own selfish thoughts she'd never given a thought to Jake having his own problems . . .

'Anyway, I want you to have a think about dancing with Jeremy. You could always take a few lessons with him and decide after that. What do you say?' Nella looked at her hopefully.

'I'd quite like to have some lessons with Jeremy. Even if I decided not to take up dancing competitively, it wouldn't hurt to learn a little more.'

A delighted Nella kissed her cheek. 'There's a competition at Christmas that would be perfect for you to begin with,' she smiled before leaving them to start the second half of the evening.

Claudette leant over to whisper in her ear. 'You'd best have a word with Nanny Ruby.'

'Why do I need to do that?' Bessie sighed as she stood up to shake out the skirt of her dress.

'Uncle Alan told me if I wanted to know more about the men at our club, she would be the one to explain things. I don't need to know, but I think you do if you are going to couple up with Jeremy.'

9

Betty Billington sunk her head into her hands as she sat at her desk giving a deep sigh. In front of her lay three letters informing her the writers were giving notice of their intention to leave the employ of F. W. Woolworths at the end of the following week. She placed them in a tray for Sarah to process in her position as staff supervisor; that made seven letters in three days, ranging from counter assistants to cleaners and one stockroom worker. Whatever was she to do? As each staff member had approached her, she had asked that they withdrew their resignations until such time that they had more concrete news.

'But my old man says if I don't act now and find a new situation, there could be hundreds of people after employment, what with Pier Road and the High Street being flattened,' one of the cleaners had said.

Betty couldn't argue with that, even though nothing was yet confirmed.

She was still deep in thought as Maureen knocked on the door and walked in without invitation. 'I'm sorry, Betty, but I can't put up with it any more. Those wretched girls are driving me up the wall with all their bickering,' she all but cried, collapsing into the seat facing Betty's desk and reaching for a handkerchief in the pocket of her voluminous white apron.

Betty put her own worries aside as she looked at Maureen's stricken face. 'My goodness, whatever's happened?'

Maureen sniffed into her handkerchief before wiping her eyes. 'I caught Gloria taking the mickey out of me and all the staff were laughing at her, or should I say they were laughing at her impersonating me and my bad leg. You know how I need my walking stick when my leg is playing up? Well, she was using a furled umbrella and leaning heavily on it just as I do while muttering about the dirty tables and the washing-up piling up in the sink. I might have joined in with the laughter if I hadn't seen the look on her face. Not happy with that, she egged on Dora to copy her. Honestly, that girl would not have done that kind of thing without Gloria pushing her.'

Betty left her seat and went round the table to bend down next to Maureen, placing her arm around the woman. 'Why, Maureen, you're shaking! It's not like you to be so upset. Why have you let her get under your skin like this?'

'It's every day, non-stop, Betty. She has a sly look on her face all the time and I swear she hates me. I have no idea why; she can work hard when she wants to. I'm at my wits' end.'

Betty knew this situation couldn't continue. Maureen was a good worker and was valued for the way she looked after all the staff in their tea and lunch breaks. Throughout the war she'd managed to make nutritious meals and have a little spare for the mothers to take home for their children. Even when she'd injured her leg after the Deptford branch of Woolworths had been bombed, she insisted on being back at work before she'd fully recovered. 'I promise you I'll have a word with her,' she said, standing up and wincing as her own knees creaked before returning to her seat.

'I'd hoped you'd give the girl her cards and send her packing,' Maureen said, looking hurt. 'I'm not sure I can keep working with her as I feel she is undermining my position as staff canteen manager. She makes me look a fool.'

Betty picked up the seven envelopes from the basket and spread them across the desk. 'I'd like nothing more than to take her by the scruff of the neck and deposit her on the pavement outside this store; you know I value you too much as a staff member and a good friend to allow you to be upset like this. But at the moment, with seven staff leaving within the week, we are going to be so low on staff I'll be donning an overall and working on a counter myself before too long. In fact, with the loss of a cleaner I'll be in early scrubbing the floors as well. It was my first job when I was taken on at the Woolwich store, so I know the ropes,' she said as Maureen looked astonished.

'I knew you'd worked at Woolworths for a long time, but I had no idea . . .'

Betty gave a small laugh. 'As a manager I've always said I'd not give someone a job that I hadn't done myself, although I'm not much of a cook . . .'

'My job's safe then,' Maureen said as she brightened up, joining in with the laughter. 'But seriously, Betty, what's to be done? You can't keep losing staff or the store will have to close.'

'Before it is pulled down, do you mean?' Betty's laughing

face was suddenly serious. 'Head office have not returned my calls so I'm none the wiser about the future of the store. I shall put on my best suit and head to London to enquire what is going on; it looks as though Muhammad will have to go to the mountain. As for Gloria, I'm going to have a word with her and move her so that half her working time is in another department to give you some peace.'

Maureen's chin almost hit the ground before she stopped to think. 'I suppose you are right; I'd hate the store to be even more understaffed. I can't say I'm happy about it, but there's not much more to be done right now.'

'Staff should expect to be moved between departments if they don't have any skills; she can work in the stockroom just as I did at one time.' She watched Maureen, waiting for the penny to drop.

'You mean, she may knuckle under working elsewhere?'

'She may start to learn she cannot treat people as she has treated you. If we are wrong and she knuckles under, then I will have to reconsider. However, my feelings are that she will walk out and if she does, then so be it. Maureen, we are so short staffed, and it is going to get worse . . .'

Maureen thought over what Betty had decided before speaking. 'If it helps, I won't require a replacement for her. Me and Dora coped perfectly well on our own. She may be a little slow on the uptake, but the staff love her, and she follows my instructions and is a hard worker. Sadly, she's been at the sharp end of Gloria's tongue a few times even though I've reprimanded the girl; as I've already told you, she is a law unto herself. When will you tell her?'

Betty looked at the calendar on the wall. It was one of Woolworths' finest that had been on sale last Christmas.

'Someone working in the stockroom leaves on Saturday so it will work out nicely. I'll move her there then.'

Maureen nodded her head, giving a satisfied smile. 'I can put up with her for a little longer, knowing she will soon be out of my hair, but what if she tells you what to do with the stockroom job and leaves, making you short staffed?'

'We will just have to cope.'

Once Maureen left the office after reminding Betty she was still working on her husband, George, to find out all he could about the plans for the town, Betty headed down the corridor to Sarah's office. She knocked on the door before entering.

Sarah and Clemmie looked up from where they were poring over a set of ledgers. Betty was thankful that Sarah was still coming into the store two days a week even though she should have taken maternity leave weeks ago. 'Hello, Betty, you look hot and bothered,' Sarah said as she noticed her boss's harassed appearance.

'You do, Mum. Is there anything we can do to help you?' Clemmie, Betty's eldest daughter, asked as she stood to give up her seat.

'I'm just a little flustered,' she said as she watched Clemmie open one of the tall sash windows that looked out over the busy road below full of shoppers enjoying the bright day.

Sarah gave her a stern look. 'It's more than that. Come on, Betty, get it off your chest.'

Betty handed her the envelopes containing staff resignations. 'We now have seven and I feel there will be more once the gossip spreads.'

Clemmie groaned. 'I had no idea it was this bad. I've heard the odd whispers on the shop floor when I've been collecting takings from the tills, but the staff tend to go quiet when they see me approaching.'

'You can blame me for that; being the daughter of the store manageress sets you apart from many of the staff who believe you would come to me with what you've heard,' Betty said apologetically. 'If they knew you better, they'd know you are a kind and fair person.'

'As are you,' Sarah added. 'Shall I start to process the paperwork for the leavers, Betty? This can be your first lesson in how we prepare payroll information, Clemmie. I'm so relieved to be leaving my job in safe hands when I have my baby.'

Betty watched the interaction between two of her favourite people. It wouldn't be the same when Sarah left work completely, but she knew her eldest stepdaughter would cope admirably, taking on both the personnel manager's job as well as being a cashier. She foresaw promotion for the girl soon. 'Perhaps you should. I fear these won't be the last to hand in their notice. Although it will leave us even more understaffed, I can't blame any of them for seeking fresh employment when the news is so worrying.'

Clemmie looked between the two women. 'I can't believe you are giving up so easily; it is so unlike the pair of you. Mother, why are you giving up without a fight? You've not even had concrete news from head office as to whether this store is to be demolished, unless there is something you haven't told us?'

Sarah looked to Betty with enquiring eyes. 'Clemmie

does have a point. Have you heard anything from the powers-that-be?'

Betty shook her head. 'I've lost count of the times I've rung and held on while a telephonist tries to put me through. I'm beginning to think they don't want to talk to me, which can only mean one thing. It is bad news, and they aren't ready to put plans to close the store into operation.'

The three women sat looking glum. 'There must be something we can do,' Sarah said. 'Erith wouldn't be the same without a Woolies.'

'If there isn't a Woolworths store, chances are there won't be any other shops either as the two streets will be bulldozed to the ground,' Clemmie said.

Betty felt tears welling. She'd hardly ever cried in front of staff or friends. 'It just doesn't bear thinking about . . .'

'That's why you are going to put your best suit and hat on, and we will both pay a visit to head office tomorrow,' Clemmie said with a look of determination. 'If they don't know we are arriving, they can't ignore us when we walk into the building.'

Betty gulped. Clemmie was right. Why had she not thought of that? 'Are you sure you want to come with me?'

'I wouldn't miss it for the world.'

Sarah grinned at the two women. 'That's a splendid plan! I'll come into work for a few hours tomorrow to cover your duties, Clemmie. I do wonder if we need to arrange more staff events, so if the store does close, we can take some happy memories with us.'

'What do you suggest?' Betty asked as she warmed to the idea.

'We need a big Christmas staff party, but also something for the retired members. We've had them in the past.'

'We also used to entertain the old soldiers, as well as old boys from the Royal Alfred Seafarers' home. We should think of doing something else along those lines.'

Sarah grinned. 'I loved it when we used to entertain the old folk. Once you get back from head office let's put our heads together and see what we can come up with.'

Betty felt much happier now that something was being done to fight for the store. 'For the first time in a while I'm beginning to look forward to Christmas. My one wish is that it will be full of happy people looking towards the future with hope in their hearts.'

10

~

Bessie knocked on Nanny Ruby's front door and for the umpteenth time thought about what she was going to ask the wise old lady. Although Ruby wasn't her real grandmother she was as good, if not better, than a relative who they all relied on for her words of wisdom.

'Why, Bessie, how lovely to see you! Come on in,' Ruby said as she peered over the girl's shoulder. 'Where is the little one?'

'I left her at home with Mrs Ince as I have some errands to run,' she replied, following Ruby into the living room and putting a paper bag on the table. 'Mum said these are the buttons you were looking for to finish Bob's cardigan,' she said, tipping out the leather buttons that looked like footballs. 'By the way, where is he?'

'Thank you, lovie, these are perfect for the cardigan I'm knitting him for Christmas. I know there's plenty of time still, but I can only work on it while he is out of the house, or it will spoil the surprise. Did you want him for something?' she asked, seeing Bessie look around her. 'Only he's over at Mike's house helping him distemper their kitchen walls. I've warned Mike not to overwork him

124

as I don't want Bob back in hospital,' she said, looking worried.

'Mike won't allow him to do much,' Bessie said, thinking of Bob's police officer son who was such a gentle person. 'It was you I wanted to speak to on your own, if you can spare me ten minutes?'

'I'm all yours,' Ruby said as she nodded for Bessie to sit down. 'Would you like a drink before you start?'

'No, I'm fine, thank you. Perhaps afterwards. I've been invited to have dancing lessons at the dance studio, and perhaps enter competitions. Nella – that's a girl we're making a bridal gown for – works there, and she introduced me to a young man who is keen to compete and make it his work to teach people to dance.'

'And you want to ask me if you should change your career to dance with him? What does your mum say?'

'No, it's not that at all. It would be a hobby for me, and Mum says I can do as I please and she will help make my dancing frocks. Oh, and Claudette told me she would stitch on the sequins,' she chuckled. 'In fact, it was Claudette who advised me to speak to you . . .'

'I'm not much good at hand stitching, what with my eyesight these days, but I'll do what I can.'

Bessie felt frustrated. She needed to find the right words before she chickened out. 'No, I mean, it is very nice of you to offer but it is more about the lad I will be partnering. He's a bit different to the normal lads who go dancing and Claudette told me that Uncle Alan told her . . .' She sighed, trying to explain her predicament.

Ruby gave a small smile. 'You mean, he's not interested

in girls? Claudette is right, I can give you advice, but she seems a little young to know such things.'

'She wasn't being nosy, it was more that she'd met a similar lad at her amateur dramatics and Uncle Alan had told her you once had a friend . . .' Bessie was glad she'd got her words out in the open, but sad as she saw a shadow cross Nanny Ruby's face.

Ruby held her hand to her heart. 'My love, I knew such a man many years ago; he used to live over the road with his parents and two brothers, where Freda lives now. I first met him forty-eight years ago when I moved into Alexandra Road.' She gazed away, deep in thought. 'It was a lifetime ago, and then again it feels like yesterday.'

Bessie fell silent, waiting until Ruby spoke again. She'd no idea Nanny Ruby had lived in this house for so long. How the world must have changed in all that time.

'He was a gentle soul, and it caused a problem with his family as he didn't want to fight in the war – that's the First World War, the war to end all wars, but it didn't,' she snorted angrily. 'That's how he came to live here with me for a while.' She gave a harsh laugh. 'He even helped me out by pretending to be my husband for a while. That put the cat among the pigeons I can tell you . . .' She fell silent again, lost in her memories. 'Well, as I said before, he wasn't interested in women.'

It was then that the penny dropped with Bessie. She turned bright red. 'I didn't really know what it meant.'

'I don't know about that, but all I can say is that we are all the same under the skin and if your dance partner is that way inclined, he will need a good friend and you might just fit the bill. At least there won't be any more little ones coming along,' she chuckled.

Bessie felt uncomfortable. 'Oh, Nanny Ruby, now you are embarrassing me. Thank you for putting me straight. I'll put this all behind me and concentrate on dancing. Shall I put the kettle on now?'

'You do that, love. Now it's my turn to ask you a question.'

'Fire away,' Bessie said as she went to the kitchen and filled the kettle before returning to sit down.

'The girl that works in Woolworths in the staff canteen . . . you saw her when you walked out of the store with me. What did you think of her?'

Bessie shrugged her shoulders. 'I thought she was a bit rude the way she bumped into Claudette, but apart from that I did recognize her from a few years ago. It was playing on my mind until I remembered. It was when I used to meet Jenny's dad outside his factory down West Street. She was one of the girls hanging about for her boyfriend to finish his shift. He got the sack not long after for pinching stock. He wasn't very nice; one of the Unthank family from what I can remember, and they've got a bit of a reputation for being a rough lot.'

The kettle started to whistle as Ruby wondered what one of the Unthanks' girlfriends was doing working at Woolworths. Bessie, being younger, wouldn't have known about all the ins and outs surrounding the time of Freda and Tony's wedding. She just hoped the past had not come back to haunt them.

*

George gave a long yawn and stretched his arms above his head. It had been non-stop ever since he arrived at the church hall for his weekly clinic. Even though the vicar's wife, Audrey, had kept order and served tea while constituents waited in the hall in an orderly queue, sorting out urgent appointments, handing out leaflets to those with minor queries, there was still a good dozen people left to see before he could head for home. He browsed through his notes, sipping the tea Audrey had provided even though it was now stone cold – something he had become used to. He nodded to her as she asked if he was ready for the next person.

He tried not to laugh out loud as his stepfather, Bob Jackson, walked in. 'Why, Bob, it is good to see you, but you do know if you have a problem, you don't have to visit my weekly surgery?'

Bob sat down and gave a small groan, something George had found himself doing as he'd got older. 'This is business so to speak and I didn't want your mum getting het up over it. We have a problem up at the allotments: a few sheds have been broken into and we think someone has been kipping up there overnight. As chair of the allotment society, I said we should hide away and nab the blighter, but most of the others are against doing that. You'd hardly think it's only eight years since we were up in arms fighting the enemy. These days men are turning their backs on any form of conflict and want an easy life.'

George grimaced. Even with Bob's failing health he was up for a fight. 'Perhaps they are right as the last thing you need is to be injured, then what would Mum have to say about it?' Especially if she was aware I'd known about this, he thought to himself. 'Have you mentioned it to the police?'

Bob rubbed his chin thoughtfully. 'I didn't want to make it official just in case it is some poor soul down on their luck. You must agree it is unfair for someone to have their collar felt when they are probably trying to survive. That's why I came to you for help.'

'I'm sure there is nothing in my local councillor handbook that advises me on such a thing.'

Bob's eyes lit up. 'They give you a handbook! I'd like to see that.'

'I was jesting. What is it you want me to do?'

'I want you to come up to the allotments tonight and help me catch the blighter. You can also be my alibi as Ruby will want to know why I'm out all night.'

'So will my Maureen,' George said, thinking how he just wanted to have a good dinner and sit down in front of his television set this evening, even if he would nod off soon after.

'You are taking me night fishing on the Thames, we are fishing for eels,' Bob explained.

'That's feasible, but better if we take along a couple of mates . . .'

'I'm impressed you are thinking this through. I can buy a couple of eels at the fishmonger's shop before they close as we can't go home empty-handed.'

George knew when he was defeated. 'I'd prefer we have a couple more chaps with us. Mum will think it strange if it is just the two of us when we usually go fishing with a larger group.'

'You've got a point there,' Bob said as he rubbed his

hands together in anticipation of the night's catch. 'Who do you suggest?'

'Leave it with me,' said George, nodding to Audrey who poked her head around the door to check if they were nearly finished. 'We are winding up here, so please send in the next person.'

Bob got to his feet. 'I take it the crowd out there are worried about what's going to happen to the town?'

'It's giving me a headache as I can't find out much. I don't want to promise the townsfolk something that won't materialize.'

Bob stopped with his hand on the door handle. 'Speak to that Norman Dodds; he's our member of parliament and even if we don't support his politics, it is him that should be doing the worrying and not you. He gets paid to represent the town so let him get on the job.'

George was thoughtful as he waved goodbye to his stepfather, who was heading back to help distemper Mike's kitchen walls; he was always on the move helping his family. Bob did have a point. He gazed over to the telephone on his desk as the next person walked in already complaining about the drains in his road. Perhaps it was a telephone call to make at home when it was quiet.

The day continued with George not even having time to stop to eat the sandwiches Audrey had provided. When she walked in and spotted them starting to curl up at the corners, she put her foot down. 'I'll not allow another person in until I see that plate empty. Sit down and start eating. I'll make a fresh brew and be right back.'

George was grateful for her intervention and with a sandwich in one hand he delved into his briefcase for some leaflets he'd been meaning to give her for the parishioners. He looked up with a smile on his face while chewing on a mouthful of cheese and chutney expecting to see her return. It was not the vicar's wife.

'I'm glad I caught you on your own,' Mrs Bennett said as she sat down in front of him, placing her brown leather handbag on her lap. 'You may continue with your luncheon,' she said, but George had lost his appetite. Where was Audrey when she was needed?

'As I was saying . . .' Mrs Bennett interrupted his thoughts. 'I have proof the property next door is being run as a house of ill repute. I can call witnesses to prove this,' she said, glaring at George. 'Furthermore, Councillor Caselton, you are a frequent visitor to that house. What do you have to say for yourself?' She stared at him gimlet-eyed.

George was lost for words as his mouth opened and closed with not a word coming out.

'Your silence speaks a thousand words,' she spat at him. 'Well, Councillor Caselton, I will have you removed from office, so you are unable to influence the poor people of Erith any longer.' She leant from her seat towards the still open door intent on everyone waiting hearing her. 'Ladies of Erith, do not trust this man!' she bellowed.

'Now, look here,' George spluttered. 'I have no idea what you are playing at, but you have gone too far. The Carlisle family are good friends of mine, I will not stand by and see you besmirch their good name! Get out of here before I call the police!' He got to his feet and pointed towards the door. 'Be gone with you, woman!' he said, not caring who heard.

Mrs Bennett stood up, raising her hand to her forehead as if he had assaulted her. 'How dare you, sir.' She gave a loud sob as Audrey appeared. 'I can't believe what this man has just said to me,' she cried out, giving Audrey a despairing look.

'I heard every word, to be honest, Mrs Bennett, and if my husband wasn't a man of the cloth, I'd have been stronger with my words if you'd aimed them at me. I'll assist you to the door,' she said, taking her by the elbow.

Mrs Bennett glared at them both before glancing down to the desk where George had placed the leaflets ready to hand to Audrey promoting the Erith Players' Christmas pantomime. She spotted the name of Claudette Carlisle as well as that of Alan Gilbert. Her eyes glinted with anger. 'Don't think this is the last you will hear from me, councillor,' she spat before pulling away from Audrey's grasp and striding haughtily from the room.

'I don't know about you, but I need a glass of sherry after that,' Audrey grimaced as she went to a cupboard and took out a bottle and two glasses. 'There's no need to look so worried,' she said, giving him a sympathetic look. 'There's a Mrs Bennett in every parish and their threats rarely come to anything.'

George sighed as he raised his glass and thanked her. 'I fear I will hear a lot more from Mrs Bennett before the year is out.'

11

'Take a deep breath and pin a smile on your face – isn't that what you are always telling us?' Clemmie said to Betty, looping her arm through her stepmother's as they looked up at the tall building in Bond Street before going through the double doors of the London head office of F. W. Woolworths Ltd and entering the marble-floored reception area. The few times she had been there Betty hadn't been able to stop comparing the opulence to her little store in Erith.

'It is easier to give advice than to take it,' Betty said as she gave Clemmie's hand a squeeze. 'You look so smart in that suit; I'm pleased you are getting some wear out of your going-away outfit,' she said, thinking how grown-up her eldest daughter was, standing there in a navy blue two-piece suit over a white silk blouse.

'Jimmy likes me in it. He says it suits my colouring.'

'It does.' Betty looked at her fresh complexion and honey-coloured hair. Marriage seemed to suit her. 'I can't thank you enough for accompanying me. There was a time I took these things in my stride, but now . . .'

'Now you are fighting for the survival of the Erith store

and the jobs of all the staff. You've never had such a fight on your hands so no wonder you find it daunting. However, you have me to fight your corner and I've learnt from the best,' Clemmie replied, walking towards the reception desk. 'We wish to speak to someone in relation to the Erith store. This is the manager, Mrs Elizabeth Billington.'

Betty's stomach gave an alarming lurch. She'd not been called Elizabeth in many a long year. She managed to suppress her nerves and gave a nod of her head to confirm Clemmie's words.

'Please take a seat,' the receptionist said before picking up the telephone and turning away from Betty and Clemmie, who had decided to remain standing.

Betty looked around her at the wood-panelled walls and the plush armchairs. This all felt a world away from her store and the shop floor. In fact, she had to look closely to see any mention of the well-known company. She was so deep in thought she jumped when a woman spoke.

'If you will follow me, please.'

Betty and Clemmie fell in line behind a young fair-haired woman dressed in a sensible black skirt and crisp white blouse as they took the stairs to the first floor. The woman stopped at the second door in a long corridor and knocked before stepping inside. 'Mrs Billington and her assistant to see you, sir,' she said before ushering them inside and leaving the room.

A young man with unruly curly hair looked up from the paperwork strewn across his desk. 'Mrs Billington from . . .'

'Erith store number 397,' Betty replied, sitting in one of the two seats across the desk from him. 'I'm here to ask about the . . .'

He held his hand up to stop her speaking. 'And who is this pretty young lady?'

Betty looked sideways at Clemmie, who was too astonished to say anything. Below the desk Clemmie nudged Betty's knee to stop her berating him for being forward. 'I'm Clementine, one of the office staff at the Erith store. I'm so pleased to meet you. I've never visited head office before. It is quite an eye-opener after the office I work in,' she simpered back at him.

Betty had to fight hard not to grin. Clemmie was playing the man at his own game. If he preferred younger women, who was she to get in the way? It did no harm. She leant back in her seat to watch what happened next.

'I must show you around, perhaps another time when you visit London and have time to fit in lunch?'

Clemmie slipped her wedding ring from her finger and passed it to Betty. 'That would be delightful, but can we talk about the problem we have at our store – Erith 397? I'm so worried about my fellow staff I can't sleep at night and I do need my beauty sleep.'

'We can't have that, can we? Let me arrange afternoon tea for you both. I'll just be a minute,' he said, giving Clemmie a big smile before leaving the room.

'Oh, for heaven's sake . . .' Clemmie snorted with laughter while Betty begged her to be quiet in case he came back in.

Betty was worried. 'I don't like the way he is acting; it is so unprofessional. I wonder who he is as we haven't even been introduced.' She leant towards the desk to peer at his name plate. 'Hmm, Nathaniel Collins. I can't say I've come across him before, although there is a senior member on the board whose name is Sir Clarence Collins.'

'I'll see if I can find out while he is chatting to me, but first off we do need to know more about the future of our store.'

'Tea is on the way,' Nathaniel said as he returned rubbing his hands together. 'Any excuse for a cream bun, eh?'

'Delightful,' they both declared.

'Tell me, Nathaniel, are you by chance related to Sir Clarence?' Betty asked.

His face clouded over. 'Yes, he is my father.'

Betty gave him a motherly smile. 'You have big shoes to fill.'

He shrugged his shoulders. 'You could say that. I've not long been demobbed, and Father decided I should start at the bottom. I've only been in the job for two weeks.'

Clemmie gave him a sympathetic look. 'It can be hard having a parent as one's boss,' she said giving Betty a sideways glance. 'But, looking on the bright side, he could have started you at the very bottom by working in one of the stores.'

He ran a hand through his hair. 'Good grief, it doesn't bear thinking about.'

'Just awful,' Clemmie sympathized as a secretary appeared carrying a heavy tray. 'Here, let me help you,' she offered, taking the tray and laying it down on the desk. 'Shall I be mother?'

Betty refused a cream bun but took the tea gratefully.

'Strong and sweet, just as you like it, Mu . . .' She stopped herself from saying Mum as she felt it would be better for Nathaniel not to know they were related, and to believe she was simply a girl from the office at the Erith store. There were some things she'd not do for the store, but it wouldn't hurt for him to befriend her as they might find out more information about the store's fate than they would from an older person. She felt awful just thinking that way when Betty was one of the best managers Woolworths had ever had.

'Sugar, Mr Collins?' Clemmie asked as she paused with the sugar tongs over the sugar bowl, which certainly wasn't from Woolworths.

'Three, please,' he said before biting into his bun.

'Perhaps we could tell you why we are here?' Betty said before speaking as fast as she could, outlining what she knew about the demolition of Cross Street, and how rumours were rife about Pier Road and the High Street being victims of the wrecking ball. 'So, you see, we need to know if head office has been informed about any plans for us to lose the store?'

'Delicious,' he replied as he licked his fingers. 'As for your predicament, I'm afraid I have no idea. Yes, I should have, but as you already know I'm new to this job and haven't got up to speed with my workload. Are you sure you don't want your bun, Betty? They are rather tasty.'

Betty shook her head in exasperation, which he took to mean she didn't want her bun.

'Surely you could check? It would mean an awful lot to me if you could,' Clemmie begged, fluttering her eyelashes at him, although the action was lost due to a scattering of icing sugar across her top lip.

'I'll ask around, that's the best I can offer. I'm not entirely sure it's in my remit, not that I'm sure what my job is; I just potter about finding my feet,' he replied, brushing down his jacket. 'Ah, hello, Father,' he said as the door opened and an older, more rotund version of Nathaniel walked into the office.

'Mrs Billington, what a delightful surprise,' he said, giving Betty a firm handshake. 'Surely this can't be young Clementine? How is married life suiting you? I spotted the wedding announcement in *The New Bond*; what would we do without our staff magazine keeping us informed, eh?'

Clemmie assured him she was enjoying married life and looked towards Betty with a puzzled look on her face. How did this man know about her?

'Sir Clarence and I go back a long way,' she explained.

'It must be Ramsgate and God knows how many years ago.'

Betty nodded her head as she reflected on the happy time she spent at the rebuilt store from the end of the Great War. 'It was indeed, and you were already climbing the ladder of success to great things.' She smiled, thinking how Nathanial was so much like his father. 'Now you are here and I'm in Erith struggling to keep my store open,' she said, looking sad, but determined this man would give her answers. He owed it to her for old times' sake.

'Yes, I'd heard something about the possibility of them tearing down the store. It'll be a shame,' he said, not meeting her eyes. 'We will have to find you another store to run. Nothing too big of course, not at your time of life when you must be thinking of retirement.'

Betty bristled. 'I'm a long way off retirement and, if you don't mind, I'd rather stay in Erith. I just want to know if the store is to be part of the area due for demolition? News is so vague, and staff are beginning to worry with so many rumours flying about. Some have even resigned to find new employment. We're coping, just about, but if you could confirm the store will remain safe, I may be able to talk some of them into staying,' she said, getting impatient.

'Let them go if that's the way they feel,' he grunted. 'We prefer loyal employees, or have you forgotten that?'

Betty gave him a hard stare. The silly fool has lost his way, she thought. 'I'm as loyal as the day I was promoted to manageress for the first time and helped a young man who was on the brink of being given the sack. Now, what was that for? I'm not sure I can recall . . .' She tipped her head to one side as if she was thinking hard.

He raised his hand to stop her saying any more. 'It was a long time ago, a very long time indeed, and I don't know about you, but memories start to fade.'

'Mother has a very sharp mind and perfect recall,' Clemmie said as she slipped her ring back onto her finger. 'She is always telling me about when she started to work for this company, particularly her time living and working in Ramsgate.'

Sir Clarence, who by then had perched himself on the edge of his son's desk, stood up and walked to the window, looking out thoughtfully. 'Take yourself back to your store and I will see what can be done.'

Clemmie clapped her hands in delight while Betty frowned. 'You mean . . . ?'

'I mean, I will see what can be done,' he said, turning back to look at her. 'You know, I could give you a very good position here in head office.'

'My life is in Erith,' Betty said as she stood up. 'Come along, Clemmie. If we hurry, we can catch the next train out of Charing Cross.' She held her hand out to Sir

Clarence. 'It was a pleasure to see you after all these years. Please give my regards to your wife,' she said before turning to Nathaniel. 'Good luck with your career.'

Clemmie nodded her head to both the men as she hurried after Betty. Outside in the street she grabbed Betty's arm for her to slow down. 'What did all that mean?'

'It means we can only hope that before he does anything, he remembers about the past and his dalliance with one of the shop girls and how he almost lost his position and besmirched his family's reputation. It is time he repaid the favour he has owed me for so many years.'

Clemmie was aghast at what she'd seen and heard. 'What?'

'It was only when his son started to flirt with you that I recalled Sir Clarence was the same in his youth – it all came flooding back as if it were yesterday.'

'What can we do?' Clemmie asked, taking Betty's arm as they crossed the busy road after using a telephone box to inform Sarah they would be back at work earlier than expected.

'If I go to his boss and tell my tale, chances are I will be laughed out of the company, and we will both lose our jobs; men seem to stick together,' she sighed. 'We can only wait and see . . .'

The two women decided to forgo their planned meal at the Lyon's Corner House close to Charing Cross station and head back to Erith. On the train home they discussed how to cope with the staff who had handed in their notice.

Betty decided to put on a brave face. 'I'm going to call each one into my office and have a chat about their concerns. Just maybe I will be able to talk a few of them into staying with us. Several of the women have been with us a while, so I know it will be a wrench for them to leave their friends and our generally happy Woolies family. I'll remind them of that, and although I'll not beg, I will do my utmost to convince them to stay.'

'You could also suggest if the worst came to the worst and our store closes, we could arrange for most staff to be transferred to other branches, not that I'd relish working with my husband at his store, and I know Freda feels the same with her Tony being a manager at Dartford. We have to keep our home and work life apart.'

'That sounds sensible,' Betty said as she pushed open the double door to the busy store, and they headed to the door marked 'staff only'. 'Thank you for accompanying me; it worked out well. I never knew you were such an actress,' she said, joining in with Clemmie's laughter.

They'd reached the top of the staircase when Sarah came out of her office with a broad smile on her face. 'There are two ladies waiting to see you. I've put them in your office and given them tea.'

'Who are they?' Betty asked, removing her coat. 'I do hope they are enquiring about positions; we dearly need more staff,' she added, thinking that even if she managed to persuade the staff who had tendered their resignations to stay, it would still help to have several more staff on the shop floor.

'You'll soon find out,' Sarah said, not wishing to give the game away by showing her excitement as she returned to her own office, followed by Clemmie.

Betty entered her office and looked at the two middle-aged women who were sipping tea and chatting quietly.

They both looked up at her, causing Betty to step back in shock as she was transported back in time to when she was looking at the face of her first love, Charlie Sayers. 'It can't be . . .'

12

Betty couldn't believe her eyes. 'Olive? Peggy . . . ?'

The two women rushed to Betty and hugged her tight as the years rolled away and Betty imagined she was once more in her late fiancé's home with his two young sisters. 'Oh, my gosh, I am so pleased to see you both.' She stepped back and held the two women at arm's length. Olive, the older of the two sisters, was the most like Charlie with his warm eyes, brown hair flecked with grey and gentle smile. Peggy was darker with a cheekier grin that Charlie would have when he was joshing the girls and telling them a joke. 'Who'd have thought how grown up you are! Time has moved on so quickly.'

Olive laughed out loud. 'It certainly has as I am now a grandmother.'

'Surely you are not old enough?' Betty gasped.

'She certainly is,' Peggy replied, 'and my eldest is about to be married.'

Betty started to count on her fingers before shaking her head in disbelief. 'You are right! When I thought of you both, and that was often, I imagined you to be in your twenties. I just wish we'd managed to keep in touch,' she sighed.

Peggy shook her head in agreement. 'We tried to find you a few times and even wrote to Woolworths' head office but were told they could not give out their employees' private details. It was when we decided to move back to where we were born that we started our search afresh. Our biggest fear was that you had died in the war, but we never gave up. It was only recently when we took a day trip to Ramsgate that we visited the store there and asked about you.'

Olive took over. 'It was a bit of a long shot as it's been thirty years or so since our one visit to see you. We visited the house where you lived at that time, but it had taken a direct hit in the last war. At the store we struck lucky when a helpful lady, after listening to our story, made a telephone call to your head office and they said you were a manageress here.'

'So here we are,' they both chanted together.

'Thank goodness you never married, or we'd have not found you,' Olive said before clapping her hand to her mouth. 'I'm sorry, it wasn't meant to come out like that,' she said as her face turned beetroot red.

Betty raised her left hand to show her gold wedding band. 'Now it is my turn to surprise you. Not only am I married to the most wonderful man in the world, but I have four children and Douglas, my husband, was in the army with Charlie. He was injured when Charlie was killed. He'd heard so much about me that some years later he decided to seek me out.'

Peggy frowned. 'But your name . . . ?'

'Douglas is also a Billington, that's how the two men started to chat when they were on the troop ship going overseas. You will have to meet him as he would love to get to know Charlie's family,' Betty insisted. 'He took me to visit the battlefields a while ago to pay our respects. It was a most sobering occasion, but also comforting,' Betty said.

'It is something we should do,' Olive told her sister. 'Come with us, Betty. After all, you are like our sister.'

'I'd like that,' Betty smiled, thinking how her life was now complete as she was back in touch with Charlie's family. 'Now, if you'll excuse me for a minute, I have someone I need to have a few words with, which can't wait. I'll be back in two ticks.' She hurried from the office deep in thought until she bumped into a member of staff who was leaving the staff canteen.

'Watch where you're going,' an angry woman said before stopping dead on the spot. 'I was coming to see you as Maureen told me you wanted me for something.'

'Ah, just the person I wished to see,' she said, ignoring Gloria's sharp words. 'It will have to wait, Gloria, as I have people in my office. Give me twenty minutes.'

Gloria nodded her head and, giving Betty a surly look, turned to go back into the canteen.

Betty raised her eyebrows at the closed door, thinking how the woman seemed to have changed since she started work in the store. Returning to the office, her heart warmed at the thought of Charlie's younger sisters being back in her life. 'Now, tell me, how far do you have to travel home? Not that I want you to leave just yet!'

Olive and Peggy looked at each other before smiling back at Betty. 'It will take us exactly fifteen minutes to be back at the house we plan to share in West Street, but for tonight we have rooms at the Wheatley Hotel.'

'I don't understand. I know it was many years ago, but

you left the area to live with your aunt in the West Country. I assumed you had married down there and made a life for yourselves. It goes without saying I'm overjoyed to see you both, but why come back here?'

'I lost my husband in the war,' Olive started to explain.

Peggy shrugged her shoulders. 'And mine ran off with a woman he worked with – good riddance to the pair of them. We decided it was time to return to the area we grew up in, or not far from it. We came to the town today to look at the property and see the land agent. With luck we will be living here after Christmas.'

'We could do a lot worse than to share a home here now the kids are off our hands. We only need to find jobs and we will be set for life.' Olive gave Betty a wary look. 'It may sound cheeky, but we wondered if you would have any vacancies come the new year when we've settled in. We both have shop experience, although not in a store like Woolworths, but selling is selling, and we are always polite and keen to put in a hard day's graft.'

Betty couldn't believe her luck. Here were the two women she considered to be her family, not only back in her life, but enquiring about work when she was about to be short staffed. This was a gift from the gods. 'I'm going to hand you over to my good friend, Sarah, and she will sort out application forms and the right positions for you on the shop floor as we have to do things properly. It will be wonderful to have you back in my life again,' she said, feeling quite tearful.

'We'd love that,' Olive said as she kissed Betty's cheeks. 'It does feel rather strange us all being grown up as we two were only children when we last met.'

'I wasn't that old either. It seems such a long time ago and so much has happened.'

Peggy joined her sister and hugged Betty. 'Now we can make up for all the lost time. I still think of you as family,' she said as Betty led them from the room and they went to Sarah's office.

'Can I interrupt you?' she asked as she entered the office to see Sarah helping Clemmie to count the takings from the tills. 'This is Olive and Peggy Sayers, although they have married names these days,' she said proudly.

Sarah looked up with a frown on her face until the penny dropped. 'My God, are you Charlie's sisters? When you said you were Betty's family I had no idea; we've heard so much about you over the years I feel as though I know you!'

'Me too,' Clemmie said as she hurried over to give them both a hug. 'Mother never stops talking about the past and Daddy is just as bad. I'm Clemmie, the eldest Billington child, although I have another surname these days and live with my husband,' she grinned.

'I'll leave you to it as I have another person to speak to and it won't be as pleasant as our chat,' Betty said as she left the four girls to go to the canteen and ask Gloria to join her. She'd not walked a dozen steps when she heard a familiar voice.

'Hang on a minute,' a breathless Ruby called out to Betty. 'I need a word and it can't wait.'

Betty turned to see Ruby clinging to the hand rail at the top of the stairs. She hurried to her side as the older woman looked as though she would keel over at any minute. Taking her by the arm, she led her slowly to her office and helped her into a seat. 'Whatever is wrong, Ruby? I've never seen you so breathless. Did you run all the way here from your home?'

'Just about. I've been pondering over something I was told, and decided to catch you before I changed my mind and kept it to myself. I'm still wondering if I should keep my mouth shut . . .'

Betty raised her hand. 'Wait one moment, then you will have my undivided attention,' she said, hurrying from the room and heading down the corridor to the staff canteen where she found Maureen, Dora and Gloria cleaning up after the last tea break of the day.

'You're in luck, I've made a fresh pot for when we've finished clearing up,' Maureen said as she reached for a cup and saucer.

'Can you make that two strong ones, please? I have an unexpected visitor,' Betty asked as she reached for a tea tray; she heard Gloria give a snort. 'Gloria, please come in and see me after you've clocked in tomorrow morning. I'm sorry, but I've had rather a lot on this afternoon.' She waited until the scowling Gloria was at the other end of the canteen and busy with her broom before leaning close to Maureen. 'Ruby is in my office; she is rather het up about something. Once these two have gone home can you come in and join us?'

Maureen frowned. 'Ruby's not one for that. Don't worry, I'll be with you as soon as I can.'

Betty gave her a worried smile and carried the tray back to her office, where Ruby was fanning her face with her hand. Clearing her desk of files, Betty placed down the tray. 'It does get a bit stuffy in here late afternoon. I'll open a window.'

'There was no need to get tea for me. I was just a bit puffed after hurrying. Mind you, I won't say no,' Ruby said as she started to lay out the cups and saucers before lifting the lid on the stainless-steel teapot, giving the contents a rigorous stir.

'That's better,' Betty said as a cool breeze rustled papers on the side of her desk. 'I must say, I'm looking forward to a drink and a sit down; I have such wonderful news to tell you. But first you must tell me what brought you here in such a fluster, not that I'm not pleased to see you at any time,' she said, sitting down across the desk from Ruby, taking the tea she passed to her.

'It's that new girl who works with Maureen in the canteen. I have a feeling she's up to no good with her man friend. Well, I followed them the other day and bumped into young Bessie. The girl visited me yesterday to say she'd remembered where she'd seen him before. It was when she was knocking about with that lad who got her pregnant.' Ruby stopped speaking to sip her hot tea.

Betty sucked in her breath. What was it Ruby was trying to tell her? She waited with bated breath.

'He's one of the Unthank family who . . .'

Betty raised her hand to stop Ruby speaking. 'I know who the Unthank family are and what they tried to do. What I don't understand is what he is up to with Gloria and why you are so concerned?'

'I overheard her giving him details about our trip. I can't help thinking they are up to something, but for the life of me I don't know what it could be.'

'The girl's a minx and doesn't conform to what I'd consider to be a regular Woolworths employee. I wonder now what I was thinking employing her. I should have waited and let Sarah interview her. After all, that is her job.'

'You'd have had your reasons,' Ruby said as she sipped her tea.

'Maureen needed help in the canteen and that's all I was thinking about at the time. I'm unhappy that she has taken on working more hours after she'd cut her days back to spend more time with George and care for her grandchildren.'

'Don't you go worrying about our Maureen. Sarah will be off work soon to prepare for the birth of her baby and my George can look after himself; I taught him how to peel and boil potatoes, so he's not completely useless,' Ruby said with a chuckle.

'Who mentioned that Unthank family?' Maureen asked as she walked into Betty's office carrying her own cup of tea and sat down in the only spare chair left unoccupied. 'I couldn't wait any longer so packed the girls off home early. There's not much needs finishing before tomorrow morning's first break.'

Betty listened as Ruby told Maureen all she'd discovered about the new employee and her boyfriend until Maureen groaned out loud.

'You probably overheard a perfectly normal discussion,' Betty suggested.

'That'll be it,' Maureen said as she raised her eyebrows at Ruby while Betty turned away to close the window to save her paperwork from flying all over the place.

'You are right,' Ruby said, wondering what Maureen was getting at. 'I suppose I'd best be thinking about heading home as Bob will wonder where I've got to. Thanks for the tea, love,' she said, kissing Betty's cheek.

Maureen stood up to join her. 'I'll walk back through town with you. I think for now it would be a good idea if you kept her working with me so I can keep an eye on her,' she told Betty.

Betty bade them both goodbye and sat at her desk looking at the list of people who had added their names for the London trip. Against Gloria's name was 'and friend'.

'I wonder what you are up to, Gloria? I wouldn't have thought you'd wish to mix with fellow colleagues when you seem not to like working here,' she said out loud. 'However, it will be easy to watch the pair of you and nothing is going to spoil our trip.'

13
~

Maureen and Ruby had only just left the Woolworths store when they bumped into a tearful Claudette Carlisle, who was hurrying down the High Street towards Alan Gilbert's shop with her coat unbuttoned and her woolly hat in her hand.

'Whatever's the matter?' Maureen asked as the young girl fell into her arms sobbing her heart out. 'Why, you will catch your death of cold,' she exclaimed as she tried to button her up.

'Has something happened to your parents?' Ruby asked, fearing the worst as she started to stroke Claudette's back, coaxing the girl to calm herself.

'I've just come from the theatre. There was supposed to be a rehearsal for the pantomime. I'm to be Cinderella; it's to be my first starring role,' she explained, giving a small hiccup as she took a handkerchief from the pocket of her coat.

'Did it go wrong, lovie? You know you can't expect to be perfect to begin with,' Maureen consoled her. 'My Alan may know all his songs, but it takes him ages to learn his lines.'

Ruby nodded in agreement. Alan had come late to

performing with the local amateur dramatics group and took each role he was given extremely seriously. Her granddaughter, Sarah, had told her how she'd sat up late at night helping him until he was word perfect. 'There's plenty of time yet.'

Claudette looked at them both and shook her head as she cuffed the tears from her eyes. 'There probably won't be a pantomime, or any other performance come to that, as we are no longer allowed to use the theatre. There's nowhere else to perform it.'

Maureen was shocked. 'But why has this happened when the Erith Players always use the theatre?' she exclaimed, thinking of how much she enjoyed visiting the small theatre that backed onto the Thames close to the police station. 'That's such a shame,' she sighed. 'Would you like to come back to my house until you feel better? I can make you a hot chocolate drink. I do find it a soothing when I'm down in the dumps . . .'

Claudette kissed Maureen's cheek. 'It does sound tempting, but I have to see Alan and break the bad news before the gossip reaches his ears,' she said before waving goodbye and heading towards Alan's shop.

Maureen linked arms with Ruby. 'It's just not going to be Christmas without the pantomime, and with Woolworths possibly closing I could cry. What's to become of our little town? It won't be the same before long.'

Ruby could only agree. 'They say life goes on, but it's as though those who don't know the town and the people who live in it are hell-bent on ripping its heart out. No Woolies and no pantomime . . . Whatever is going to happen next?'

It was a subdued pair who parted ways in front of the Odeon, with Maureen walking towards the small bridge spanning the railway line and Ruby, pulling her scarf up over her mouth to ward off the chilly air, turning left towards Alexandra Road. Both were deep in thought, concerned about their beloved town.

When Maureen walked into her house, she found George sitting at his desk also deep in thought with a leaflet for the Erith Players' performances in his hand.

'A penny for them,' she said as she kissed his cheek. 'Your tea won't be long. I have a shepherd's pie ready to put into the oven.' She pulled the leaflet from between his fingers and dropped it into the waste-paper basket at the side of the desk. 'We won't be needing that,' she said before telling him of her encounter with Claudette. 'It is such a shame. I wish there was something we could do to help. So many people enjoy the performances.'

George removed the leaflet from the basket. 'I'll put my thinking cap on,' he said.

Maureen tutted. 'You can't solve every problem in Erith,' she said as she headed to the kitchen.

'I can try,' George muttered to himself as he picked up the telephone and placed a call through to the office of the local member of parliament, Norman Dodds, hoping he hadn't yet left for home. He waited as the phone continued to ring before being answered by his secretary. He asked to speak to Mr Dodds and gave his name. Tapping his fingers on his desk, he waited to be put through. 'Hello, yes, I need to speak to Norman in person,' he said when the secretary returned. 'I need information about the proposed demolition of Cross Street in Erith, and if it will

154

affect the shops and businesses in the town?' He waited again while she went away for a couple of minutes. He wasn't keen on telling a secretary what his business was . . . 'I beg your pardon?' he said before replacing the receiver and muttering, 'Margaret Roberts should have been elected.'

Maureen had moved closer to the living room door with a tea towel in her hand. She was perturbed by how upset George had become while on the telephone. 'Don't let them upset you,' she said, going to his side and placing her hand on his shoulder, surprised to find he was trembling.

'Maureen, every time I ring that man's office I can't get past his secretary. At this rate the whole bloody town will have been razed to the ground before I get to speak to him. I'm failing the local people. I know we are poles apart with our politics, but I thought the man cared.'

Maureen was just as surprised as she knew how he had helped the people living on the Belvedere Marshes after the big flood earlier in the year. 'You need to speak to him face to face and avoid his secretary.'

'Easier said than done as she seems to be glued to his office telephone on guard duty. It is almost as if she is trying to stop me speaking to him. To my knowledge, I've not upset the man.' He put his head into his hands. 'Time is ticking by, and the locals are expecting answers.'

'Betty feels the same. She went up to London this afternoon to ask the bosses at Woolworths' head office if they know anything about the store being shut down.'

George lifted his head and looked at his wife with hope in his eyes. 'And . . . ?'

'No news as such. Some big nob is going to write to her.'

'That sounds like she's been fobbed off. I wish her luck, but it doesn't sound good.'

Maureen patted his back. 'Why not put your mind to something else then tomorrow write Norman Dodds a letter? He can't ignore that, can he?'

George shrugged his shoulders. 'I suppose it depends if his secretary opens it.'

'Oh, come on, George, don't be so defeatist. Why not deliver it to his home? After all, you know where he lives.'

George stood up and held Maureen in his arms. 'Whatever would I do without you? It is you who should be a town councillor rather than me. However, there is something I can be doing to help the community,' he said, explaining about Bob's problem up at the allotments. 'I'll make a couple of telephone calls to drum up some help and then visit the allotments with Bob to see if we can catch the miscreant. I'll eat my dinner before I go as it could be a long night.'

Maureen wasn't so sure he should be taking the law into his own hands but knew when he had that determined look on his face there'd be no changing his mind. 'I'll make some sandwiches and a flask of cocoa. You must wrap up warm as the freezing fog is good for neither man nor beast. Take the car rug with you; you don't want to get piles sitting around up there. I'll check the shepherd's pie while you make your calls, then you can rest for a little while.'

George nodded his head in agreement, although he was thinking the bottles of brown ale he'd left in the boot of his car would go down a treat as well as Maureen's cocoa.

An hour later he was waved off by Maureen as he set out to pick up his two friends and then his stepfather, Bob.

He wasn't hopeful of catching anyone hanging about the allotments, but it would put Bob's mind at rest all the same.

Bob peered into the car as he walked from number thirteen, with Ruby's words telling him to wrap up warm echoing in his ears. 'I don't want the police involved at this stage,' he muttered, spotting his son. 'If it's just kids, we can scare them enough, so they don't do it again.'

'Good evening, Dad,' Sergeant Mike Jackson said with a grin. He was used to his father's ways and didn't take offence. 'You may not have noticed, but I'm not in uniform. I'm coming along for the ride to keep you company.'

Bob laughed out loud before greeting the fourth member of their little group. 'Nice to see you, James. How is Vera these days?'

James gave a belly laugh. 'My grandmother-in-law is getting along very nicely, thank you for asking. She has us all run ragged and if we aren't quick enough, she will have a bout of coughing to remind us she has been poorly. She certainly keeps us on our toes. We are thankful for Ruby visiting her, very thankful indeed. It won't be long before she's back on her feet, and out and about on her own, all being good.'

Only George heard Bob groan from where he was sitting in the front passenger seat. 'Does anyone have a plan for this evening?' he called above the sound of the engine as they set off away from Alexandra Road on the short journey to the allotments.

Mike started to sniff the air from where he sat in the back of the vehicle. 'I can smell fish,' he said.

'That's our alibi in the boot of the car, along with the fishing rods. We couldn't really tell the wives we were going off to catch a thief, could we?' Bob said. 'George picked up some fresh eels from the fish shop on his way home. Don't forget to take some with you when we finish up at the allotments.'

'I'm glad you never took up a life of crime as your alibi is a good one,' Mike said, thinking how he'd already told his wife, Gwyneth, what they were up to. 'I suggest we don't do anything rash. Let's hide ourselves away and observe. Where's the best place, Dad?'

Bob considered Mike's question before answering. 'We could tuck ourselves away in my potting shed, but it'll be cramped, and the likelihood is the thief will go there first if he is after stealing things, not that we have much worth stealing. I did wonder if he is dossing down there because he hasn't anywhere to live.'

'Whatever he is up to, he is going to freeze to death in this weather if he doesn't find somewhere to hide away; it's more than a little brisk,' Mike said, blowing on his hands and rubbing them together before pulling on his official police uniform gloves. 'Hopefully we will find some clues in what he has left behind. That's if he hasn't tidied up after himself,' he continued as the car pulled up as near as it could to the allotments situated close to the recreation ground. 'Let me go first in case someone is there,' he instructed the men.

'I'll walk with you,' James said, meaning the older men could safely follow behind. 'Be careful you don't slip.'

George was glad he'd invited the tall, well-built Caribbean man to join them. Apart from helping with the shared allotment patch, he would be a handy companion if the intruder became aggressive. 'That sounds like a plan.

Here, help me carry these,' he said, handing over the bottles of beer, plus the basket of food Maureen had provided.

Bob held up a bag he'd carried on his lap during the journey. 'Ruby thought we might starve,' he chuckled. 'I also brought this,' he added, waving the truncheon he'd carried for many years while he'd been in the police force. 'It has served me well in the past.'

James was impressed. 'The family profession I take it?'

'As was my father and I'm hoping my grandson, Robert, will follow in our footsteps,' Bob said proudly.

'We have a while to wait before that happens as he's still in primary school,' Mike said, thinking fondly of his son. 'I'll not pressure him to join the force. Now, let's keep our eyes and ears open and try not to make a sound. I hope we have time to hide ourselves away.'

'And enjoy George's beer,' Bob said as the other men warned him to be quiet.

They walked on in silence, following the frozen dirt track to the entrance of the allotments. There were twelve in total with Bob's one being closest to the footpath. George checked his watch. 'We'd best tuck ourselves away and be ready for our friend.'

'That's if he turns up again. He may have moved on,' James said.

'No, I think he will come back. Why else would anyone come here if not to hide away if he has nowhere to sleep? He thinks he is safer here . . .' Bob said thoughtfully as he pointed out where the person had broken the lock entering his shed and the tins where he kept his tea, sugar and biscuits were almost depleted.

'Not exactly the crime of the century,' Mike said as he

poked about among the paraphernalia Bob didn't take home in case he invoked the wrath of Ruby; the shed at home was already chock-a-block with his gardening essentials. 'Was anything else taken?'

'No, but my old gardening jumper and raincoat were on the floor along with empty sacks as if someone had made themselves a bed for the night and not bothered tidying up.'

'I can't help feeling sorry for the man,' James said. 'Who knows what he's been through?'

'There again, he could be kipping here while he's casing the big houses across the other side of the recreation ground ready to break in . . .' Bob suggested. 'That's where Maisie and Douglas live; perhaps we should warn them.'

'You've been reading too many American crime novels, Dad,' Mike snorted. 'Now, let's get settled and plan what to do if he should appear.'

Mike and George started to check out the allotment for suitable places to hide. 'Do you think we'll be seen from behind this compost heap?' George asked as he wrinkled his nose.

'Welcome to the world of crime fighting,' Mike laughed as they checked behind the huge pile. 'Dad prides himself on building a decent compost heap. This one will be shared by other allotments holders, so I reckon it'll be decent enough cover for us. Let's tell the others where we'll be. I reckon we deserve a bottle of that beer you brought along with you.'

They joined Bob and James, who had decided there was enough room behind the shed to hide, with James discretely informing Mike he would ensure Bob was protected in case there was an affray. Armed with sausage rolls and beer, they went to their hiding places and waited as the night grew older . . .

'I reckon we should give up and go home,' George yawned as he squinted at his watch by the light of the moon. 'It's almost two o'clock.'

'Let's give it ten more minutes,' Mike suggested. 'If we do decide to call it a day, then I'll go back to the car alone just in case he spots us as a group. We may scare him off for good.'

George wasn't so sure but bowed to Mike's expertise in catching criminals. 'I don't know what time you have to be at work, but I have a lot on tomorrow. For one thing, I must try to catch Norman Dodds before he leaves home.'

'Do you mind telling me why you need to do that when you can simply pick up the telephone and speak to him?'

'His secretary keeps fobbing me off with excuses as to why he isn't available. There was a time I could make a call and he would ring me back if he was in a meeting. These days it is nigh on impossible. You'd think he didn't care about what could happen to the town. We are soon off to London with the workers from Woolworths and they will be asking me what is going on.'

Mike nodded. 'Gwyneth is just as worried as she loves her part-time job in the Erith store, but you can't do everything. Why not tell them it is all in hand and when you know more so will they?'

'I don't like to give excuses when they want answers; so many people are affected by this. I have found out that most of the people living in Cross Street will be rehoused, but if they don't have jobs, I dread to think what could happen.'

Mike was considering how to answer when he heard footsteps on the gravel path and then the click of the gate. 'Shh, I do believe we have a visitor,' he whispered, getting to his feet and aiming his torch ready to switch it on when he reprimanded the thief, but he was too slow.

'Halt, who goes there?' Bob bellowed from beside the shed as James darted forward and grabbed hold of the person.

'So much for being quiet,' George said ruefully as he joined Mike, who hurried through the cabbage patch to assist James.

'Keep still, man, no one is going to hurt you,' James said as he held the struggling chap at arm's length.

Bob dragged an upturned box from the shed and insisted the man sat down and explained himself.

'I meant no harm,' he mumbled, looking up at the four men towering over him. 'Please don't hurt me.'

'We need some answers,' Bob grumbled, looking to Mike, who seemed to be studying the chap's face.

'I'm no thief, I just needed somewhere to kip while I look for a family member,' he said through pleading eyes.

Bob looked at the other men and shrugged his shoulders. 'I say we give him the benefit of the doubt. Let's sit down and have a chat. Pull up something to sit on,' he told the other three, who fetched a couple of boxes and old sacks to sit on. He shared out the rest of the food supplied by Maureen and Ruby while George retrieved the remaining bottles of beer. Handing out the bottles, he turned the bucket upside down and used it as a seat, trying to ignore the icy cold metal as Mike lit the kindling under a small fire and watched as the flames took hold.

'That's better,' he said, holding out his hands to warm them. 'God knows how you've lived outside in this weather,' he grimaced as the chap leant closer to the flames.

'Tell us your story,' George said after taking a swig from his bottle. 'You talk like a local, so I'm hard pressed to think why you are living rough round here.'

'Why not start by telling us your name?' Mike interjected as he stared at the man's face. He looked gaunt, two days' growth of a grey beard, unkempt hair, and his skin an unhealthy colour.

'I've been known as Daniel Carrington all my life. However, in the past year or so I've discovered I was adopted. For reasons I don't wish to share I couldn't return to my adopted family so wanted to contact my proper mother. I was told where she lived but haven't been able to speak to her on my own as she has people with her most of the day.'

Bob thought the man's excuse was genuine. 'Tell us what you know, and we'll see what we can do to help you,' he said with concern. 'No man should be separated from his family.'

Mike froze as he heard the man's story, forcing himself not to speak out.

'I'm looking for the woman who gave birth to me. I heard she was looking for me so thought I'd make contact. The only problem is, my suitcase and wallet were stolen and as I'd been planning to stay in a hotel while I made my search for her, I have been forced to live rough.'

'That is hard luck, just when you were about to find her.

I couldn't imagine not knowing my mother,' James said. 'What is her name?'

'Munro, Mrs Vera Munro.'

'I don't believe it,' James exclaimed as his companions glanced furtively at each other. 'That is my wife's grand-mother. I can take you home and introduce you to Vera,' James offered, oblivious to the silence that had fallen over his three friends. They had kept the news of Daniel from James in case Vera got wind of the situation and became involved when they had yet to sort out the situation.

'No, you can't do that,' Mike exclaimed as he stood up quickly, sending the wooden box he was sitting on flying towards the fire.

14

George had never lied to his wife before. Granted, there had been a few small fibs when he'd arranged surprises for her birthdays, but to bring a stranger into their home and not tell her he was most likely on the run was taking things a bit far. He had decided to work from home that day so that the man was at no time alone in the house, or with Maureen.

Not being able to explain to James as they'd sat around the fire that Mike's sudden outburst was because they knew Vera's son was a criminal, he'd quickly come to his friend's defence. 'You are forgetting Vera has been ill. The shock of James walking in with someone purporting to be her long-lost son could give her a heart attack. It is better he stays with one of us tonight so he doesn't sleep out in this freezing fog, or it will be the death of him.'

'That's very good of you,' Daniel said. 'I don't want to be an imposition to anyone. I was going to visit my mother before I moved on to a new position in Australia.'

Mike gritted his teeth. Carrington was falling back on a lie he had used before when he was stealing from local businesses. However, he could see where George was leading the conversation: if Carrington stayed with one of them tonight, he would be able to find out what was happening and why he was out of prison long before time. He also knew he couldn't have a possible escapee in his home with young children living there and he'd not want the man staying at number thirteen, possibly putting his dad or Ruby in danger at their time of life. 'You are the one with the guest bedroom,' he said. 'As much as I'd like to invite you back to my house, I'm afraid I don't have the room and neither does my dad.'

Before Bob could disagree, George jumped in. 'My pleasure and perhaps we could all get together to discuss how to break the news to Vera?' He hoped his friends had picked up on the way he had spoken. 'It is going to be a squeeze in my car, so I suggest I drop off Mike and Bob then come back for James and Daniel. It will give James time to tell him a little about Vera and her family. What do you all say?'

Thankfully, the men all agreed and in the short drive back to Alexandra Road with Mike and Bob, George was able to form some kind of plan for the day ahead with Mike promising to put James straight about the situation with Daniel Carrington.

At breakfast, Maureen appeared to fall for the story George told her about bumping into Daniel late last night when his train had arrived too late for him to book into the room he'd arranged at the Wheatley Hotel and, knowing George from way back, he'd been glad of a room. If she thought it strange, she would never be so rude as to say so in front of their guest. 'I'm sorry I won't be here for most of the day as I'm due in work. George will be here to keep you company. Now, can I get you anything more?' she asked, seeing he'd cleared his plate.

Daniel raised his hand to refuse her offer. 'I have been looked after royally,' he thanked her.

'Dad will be round later as he has offered to sort out the garden,' George told her.

'In that case can I show you what I would like done to the flower bed, so it isn't so bare until the spring?' Maureen said, indicating for him to follow her into the garden and closing the back door behind them. 'Now tell me the truth, George Caselton,' she said, keeping her back to the window in case Daniel was watching. 'You go out to help Bob with a possible intruder up at the allotments and come back with a visitor you put up for the night. You must think I'm daft if I'm going to fall for that one, especially as your first story was that you were going fishing. Of course I'll back you up with whatever is going on, but I first want you to tell me the truth.'

George took her by the arm, and they walked around the garden, stopping to look at the borders as if discussing what was to be done while he explained everything that had happened.

'Well, I never,' Maureen said as she bent to pull up a few weeds. 'Of course he can't stay with Ruby and Bob; it wouldn't be fair at their age. But how long is this going to go on? I mean, is he dangerous?'

'I don't think we are at risk of him attacking us, but we will know more later today when Mike has made a few enquiries. To begin with we aren't sure if he was let out of prison early or if he has escaped. There is one thing that perturbs me . . .'

Maureen knew her husband well enough to know what was playing on his mind. 'You think Vera should meet her son . . .'

'To be honest, I feel she should as it will give her closure after all the years she kept the story to herself.'

'But the man's a ne'er-do-well and could be on the run. It seems strange he is out of prison so soon after his arrest.'

George shook his head. 'I have no clear idea what has happened. I keep asking myself why he wants to see Vera at this time in his life. If he is as bad as we are led to believe, then he may well try to do Vera out of her house while she is weak from her illness.'

Maureen scoffed at his idea. 'You tell me he met James last night? I don't think anyone in their right mind is going to steal even a cup of sugar from that house; James is tall and muscular and would frighten even the devil.'

'And as soft and kind-hearted as a teddy bear,' George laughed. 'When Dad comes around later we plan to discuss it more then. We will be fine,' he added, seeing a concerned look cross her face. 'Mike will be able to fill us in on the state of the convict once he has made some telephone calls from the police station.' He smiled, trying to put her mind at ease.

Maureen misconstrued his smile. 'And you can wipe that smile off your face for starters. If you are going to be hanging about here today, you can make a start stripping the hall. It's looking shabby and I'd like it freshened up for Christmas. Get him to help you,' she said, nodding towards the window where Daniel was watching them.

'I must do some work first, but I promise I'll make a

start, depending on what Bob and Mike have to say when they arrive.'

Maureen left by the side gate still muttering about the house not being ready for Christmas 1954, let alone this Christmas.

'I'm sorry if I have caused a problem being here. Your wife didn't look pleased.'

George frowned. 'Maureen has a list as long as her arm for work she wants doing around the house before Christmas. She was reminding me I'd yet to get started,' he said, thinking how it was becoming easier for white lies to slip from his tongue. 'However, I do need to get some paperwork done this morning; I'm a local town councillor and have residents wanting me to perform miracles . . .'

Daniel looked worried. 'So, you know what goes on in Erith?'

George was cautious. He didn't want him to become aware he knew about his past. 'I know about bad landlords and people whose roofs are leaking, and I know people fundraising for local charities if that's what you mean,' he smiled. 'Soul destroying at times, and at other times I couldn't wish to be doing anything else.'

Daniel's face relaxed. 'I envy you, apart from having a nagging wife, that is. I wonder, could I help you? I could make a start on weeding the border your wife took you out to see?'

'I couldn't ask you to do that. For one thing, it's bloody cold out there, and the ground's rock hard.'

'I'm not afraid of hard work. If you have some old clothes, I could make a start now and leave you to get on with your work . . .'

George sorted out some old tweed trousers he kept for working around the house along with a Macintosh raincoat and a pair of wellington boots and showed him where the shed was that held the equipment he would need. 'I'll make a brew and give you a shout in an hour,' he called out as the man headed down the garden. To be on the safe side he decided to move the desk in his study so he could keep an eye on Daniel as he worked; he wasn't sure why as he was unlikely to abscond dressed as a tramp, and where would he go?

After taking a while to type a letter to Norman Dodds and propping it on the mantelpiece ready to hand deliver later, he made two decisions. The first was that he should consider hiring a part-time secretary as his typing skills were abysmal, and the second was to ring Mike Jackson at the police station on the off chance he had found out some information about Daniel, who was still busy sorting out his garden. He picked up the receiver and rang the Erith police station, waiting while someone called Mike to the telephone after he explained he was Councillor Caselton and needed to speak to Sergeant Jackson urgently.

'I'm glad you rang, councillor, as it has saved me a journey to see you,' Mike said, speaking as though he was not alone in the room. 'I have found out that the gentleman left hospital three days ago, which fits in with his hiding away in the allotments.'

'Hospital? Whatever for?' George blustered while checking through the window that Daniel was still in the garden.

'See you later, Cyril,' Mike called out as George heard

a muffled reply before a door slammed shut. 'Phew, I'm on my own. I thought he'd never go,' Mike said. 'I made the enquiry unofficially as I didn't want the desk sergeant to know just yet. I'm afraid I've dropped us in it as the prison now want to know why I enquired after Carrington. I've had to say we came across him but will have him back with them later today.'

'That does sound strange. I'd have thought they'd have arrived with all guns blazing to collect their escaped convict.'

'He's going to die, George. I think that's why he absconded from hospital. He's back in Erith to see his mum.'

George groaned. 'Oh god, you'd not wish that on your worst enemy. When can you get down here?'

'Give me an hour. I'm hoping we get some paperwork from the prison as all the information I have has come over the telephone. We don't even know what is wrong with him,' Mike said before saying goodbye.

'I was about to call you in for a cuppa. You must be frozen to the bone,' George said as he turned and saw Daniel standing there.

Daniel pulled off his coat and stood in his stockinged feet and didn't say a word, although he stared at George for a short while.

George went to the fire and lifted the coal scuttle, shaking more coal onto the fire. 'Sit yourself down in the armchair while I get the tea,' he said, trying to buy more time while he thought of what to say. He was just carrying a tea tray in when there was a thumping on the front door. Daniel jumped to his feet, looking startled.

'It'll be Bob,' he said, placing the tray down before going

to the door. Swinging it open, he was faced not just with Bob, but with Ruby too.

'Sorry, lad, I've never been able to keep anything from your mum. She can see right through me,' Bob said as she barged past them.

'Right, where's this blighter who is making life hell for our Vera? I'll give him what for,' she said, rubbing her hands together.

George grimaced at Bob. There was no arguing with his mother when she was in this mood.

'Sorry, she wheedled it out of me,' Bob said as he hurried to where Ruby was already berating Daniel, who was shying away from her with his arms over his face.

'I've never met the woman who gave birth to me,' he stammered.

Ruby shook her head. 'That doesn't make any difference to a woman who has been wanting to meet you since you were a nipper, and she gave you away. She's been very ill, and her last wish was to meet you before she meets her maker.'

He looked disappointed. 'You mean I'm too late?'

'No, she's getting better, but she's not giving up. Someone fed her a cock and bull story about you being a big businessman and off to some foreign country so as not to disappoint her when Vera was still poorly,' she said, wagging her finger at him while glaring towards Bob and George. 'All the time you were locked up in prison, and now you are here and no doubt going to give her grief. She doesn't need it at her age,' she said as she ran out of words and all but collapsed in the armchair opposite him.

'Mum, calm down, I'll make you a cup of tea,' George pleaded. 'There's more to this than you and Bob know.'

Bob frowned. 'I thought I knew it all . . .'

Ruby snorted in fury. 'There's too many secrets around here. Someone had better tell me what's happening or else . . .'

15

Betty sat in her office with her head in her hands. The future looked bleak for the store and with Christmas on the horizon she'd hoped to have good news for her staff. She picked up the letter emblazoned with the Woolworths emblem at the top. Scanning the words from Nathanial Collins, she couldn't believe that head office had decided that closing the store, regardless of the outcome of the plans to demolish Cross Street, was now their consideration unless the turnover for December increased by at least fifty per cent. She could have cried and likely would have done if Freda hadn't knocked on the door and walked in.

'Bad news, I'm afraid: the silver cake boards and decorations are missing from the delivery . . . Whatever is wrong? Has someone died?' she asked, seeing Betty's desperate look.

'It feels like it,' she replied, holding out the letter for Freda to read.

Freda, not taking her eyes from the letter, sat down at the other side of Betty's desk. 'I don't believe it. How can they say such a thing?'

'I fear it is my fault for bringing attention to the plight

of Erith when Clemmie and I went to head office to ask for their help when we were concerned Pier Road and the High Street would become part of the demolition of the town, along with Cross Street. Sir Clarence Collins' son has written this letter. It seems he now leads the team overseeing the future of the stores in Kent. If I hadn't gone in there with all guns blazing, he may not have noticed our little store in Erith,' she said, looking miserable. 'Now, I'm likely to have put everyone out of work and denied the people of Erith having a branch of Woolworths on their doorstep.' She covered her face with her hands and muttered, 'Whatever have I done?'

Freda watched as Betty crumbled under the strain of what lay ahead. Since the demolition of Cross Street had become public news, along with rumours that Pier Road and the High Street would follow soon after, staff levels at the store had started to drop. If it got out that head office planned to close the store, then even more staff would leave as they found new positions, and who could blame them? Freda had been thinking long and hard about her own position as she enjoyed the few days she was able to go out to work and would miss her friends. Already it felt different not seeing Sarah's happy face when she came to work, what with her being on maternity leave. She sighed as she thought of the days when she had worked alongside both Sarah and Maisie, who had carved out her thriving garment-making business. Perhaps she could ask Maisie for a part-time job? Not that she could thread a needle, let alone operate a sewing machine . . . But why was she thinking this way while Woolies was still open and serving the good people of Erith? Placing her hands on her hips, she cocked her head to one side, looking at Betty who seemed to have given in going by the desperate look on her face.

'Now, come on, Betty, the doors to the store aren't barred and bolted yet. We must do all we can to save our jobs.' She leant across the desk for Betty's trusty notebook and pencil. 'We need to make a plan and fight back.'

Betty shook her head, not believing Freda's words. 'Do you honestly think it will work? I've been lucky standing up to the powers-that-be on many occasions, but this time I fear it is too late. If we don't increase our turnover drastically by the end of this month, then the store will close. I don't know how we can do that as I can't think of a thing we can do.'

Freda put down the notebook. 'Now's not the time to discuss this as you need time to yourself to digest what is in that letter. I'm going to chase up the missing stock items and catch up on a few things. I'll speak to you later,' she said, getting to her feet. Reaching over, she squeezed Betty's arm. 'We're not beaten yet,' she said before leaving Betty to her thoughts.

As Freda walked back to the storeroom, she was deep in thought. She didn't mind stepping in to take on work other than her job as shop floor supervisor. In fact, she enjoyed the change to her routine. In another world without her beloved children, she would have considered training to work in management at Woolworths. The days had long gone when it was considered unacceptable for women to work in positions before only held by men. Perhaps later when the children aren't so young . . . she thought to herself as she started to check the fresh intake of stock before putting a call through to the office in charge of their branch's orders. In what she hoped was an assertive voice that she could use if she was in management, she insisted the missed items were with them first thing the next morning. She was surprised how her friendly but firm manner obtained results; she would adopt this attitude more in her work from now on, especially if it would help Betty to keep the store running in a professional manner. Checking her watch, she made a quick decision and called out to the one man still working in the storeroom. 'I'm popping out for ten minutes. It is on company business,' she added, seeing how he raised his eyebrows. Pulling off the brown overall she wore when doing this work and reaching for a thick cardigan she kept on her hook, she hurried out of the store and round the corner to where Alan Gilbert's shop was situated. As she'd hoped, Sarah was sitting by the counter deep in conversation with her husband.

'Why, Freda, this is a surprise,' Sarah beamed. 'Have you come to inspect the washing machines again?'

Freda glanced to where a row of white machines stood. She often went into the shop to admire them and keep abreast of the best one for her family's laundry. She thought of the tin she kept in her underwear drawer where she put away any extra money left over from her housekeeping each week, but with a growing family it was becoming harder to save much towards the longed-for appliance. Alan had offered her terms so she could have the machine now, but Freda wasn't one to buy things on tick. She would wait until she could pay cash; losing her job would be the end of her dream. 'Not this time. It's you I've come to see. There's a problem at Woolies.' She gave Alan an apologetic look. 'Can you spare Sarah for half an hour?'

Alan gave a sigh. 'Only if you don't tire her out; she should be resting. As it is she walked round here to talk to me about painting the box room ready for the baby when there's still plenty of time as he or she will sleep with us to begin with.'

Freda chuckled. She knew what Sarah had planned and that's how she knew she would be in Gilbert's at that time. 'I will treat her with kid gloves,' she promised as she helped Sarah from the chair and on with her coat.

They set off back towards Pier Road, only walking a dozen steps when a familiar voice hollered out to them. 'Oi, where are you two off to?'

Freda felt a surge of relief flow through her at the sight of Maisie. 'Just the person we needed to see. If you can spare ten minutes to save Woolies, follow me,' she said, using her new authoritative voice and beckoning them both to follow her to the store.

'What's this all about?' Maisie asked Sarah as she took her arm and helped her cross the road.

'I have no idea, but if she wants me to do a shift behind the counters, she's got another think coming. Mind you, I wouldn't mind helping on the broken biscuits or perhaps the confectionary counters for ten minutes,' Sarah said, licking her lips. 'Thank goodness sweet rationing is over as I've developed quite a fancy for sweet things.'

'I was always fancying savoury. In fact, when I had the last one it was coal. Do you remember how I carried a lump in my handbag in case I fancied a nibble?'

'Yes, and I've lost count of the number of times I had to point out that you had coal dust around your mouth.'

'I'd do the same for you,' Maisie sniggered as they walked into the store. 'Isn't that Ruby over by the haberdashery counter? She looks a bit flustered.'

'It seems to be the day for it,' Sarah said, nodding towards Freda, who had also spotted Ruby and was making a beeline for her.

'Nan, whatever is wrong? You look a little red in the face. Are you sickening for something?' Sarah asked before anyone else could get a word in.

'You could say that,' Ruby said as she rummaged through cards of elastic lined up on the top of the mahogany counter. 'I could have died of embarrassment. I was round George's in the middle of saying something important to . . . well, making a point, when I felt something go.'

Maisie started to giggle while Freda looked puzzled. 'What do you mean, Ruby?'

'The elastic's gone in my drawers. Luckily, I had a pin in my bag so I popped to the loo and pinned them to the waistband of my skirt. I knew I didn't have a bit of elastic back home so came straight here. Now, what width should I get?' she asked, looking towards Maisie, who was now pink-cheeked and trying not to laugh out loud.

'Get the wider sort as it'll wear longer. You don't want another accident, do you?'

Ruby made her purchase and turned back to the three girls. 'I don't often see the three of you together these days. What's going on?'

Maisie shrugged her shoulders. 'I've no idea. Freda dragged us here. There's something amiss and she needs our help.'

Ruby's eyes lit up. 'Then you'll need my help as well. I

can spare ten minutes before I get back to George's place. Lead on, Freda!'

Freda assumed Ruby would be able to help with her plan and pointed them towards the staircase that led to the offices. They'd just reached the top, waiting for Sarah and Ruby to catch their breath, when Maureen appeared. After greeting them all she started to look worried.

'I took a cup of tea into Betty, and she didn't look her usual self. Something is worrying her. Do you know what it is?' she asked Freda.

Freda thought for a moment. Around her she had a group of women who all cared for Betty and had known her for many years. 'You'd best come with us. I'll explain once we are in Betty's office. I take it she's alone?'

'She was three minutes ago,' Maureen said as she followed the other women to Betty's office, where Freda walked straight in without knocking.

Betty looked up at the women standing in front of her. The women who had been her closest friends since 1938 when Sarah, Freda and Maisie joined the company. Until then she had never had so many close female friends. Now looking up into their concerned faces, she prayed they could help her save the store for the people of Erith.

Freda quickly arranged seating, borrowing chairs from the canteen and calling Betty's daughter, Clemmie, into the office to join them. Once settled Freda quickly explained about the letter Betty had received that morning while Clemmie brought them up to speed with what had happened when she went to head office with Betty to find out if there was any news about the demolition of Cross Street and the shops.

'My George is at his wits' end trying to find out something from our MP, Norman Dodds,' said Maureen. 'When I left home this morning, he was writing a letter to hand deliver it to the man's home as he can't get past his secretary when he uses the telephone.'

'The way I see it, we need to make this store bring in more customers and increase the takings so we can prove to head office the store should remain open. What do you all think?' Freda asked, looking round the room.

'You've got less than a month; it's not long,' Ruby said.

Clemmie raised her hand to speak. 'I don't understand why this is happening as I've not seen a dip in sales since I've worked here. Do you think there's been a mistake?'

Betty listened carefully to each comment before getting up and going to a row of shelves at one side of the room. She pulled down a green leather-bound ledger and placed it on the desk, turning it towards Sarah. 'Sarah, you have helped me with the figures. Please tell me what you can see in here.'

Sarah pulled the ledger closer and checked back and forth between the neatly handwritten pages and started to frown. 'This can't be right.'

'Is it that bad?' Maisie said as she joined her and flicked between the pages, looking at the monthly turnover for the current year and the year before. 'I agree with you, it can't be right. Someone has made a mistake,' she exclaimed, slamming the ledger closed and looking at Betty.

'What do you mean?' Maureen and Ruby asked at the same time.

Betty was puzzled. 'Are the takings that bad? Head office have never queried the figures we send to them.'

Clemmie had a tremor in her voice. 'I hope I've not made a mistake when I enter the takings into the ledgers?'

'You haven't as I've always doubled checked them for you, and I believe Betty has done the same as you are still training.'

'Then what is wrong?' Ruby asked, looking confused.

Sarah looked triumphant. 'There's nothing wrong with the figures. In fact, month on month the takings are better than they were last year.'

'Ah, but we've had all the extra sales for the Queen's coronation this year, so that would have made a difference,' Betty said.

Sarah opened the ledger and was quiet for a minute or two as she checked back and forth. 'No, even if we deduct the sales for the coronation, we've improved on last year.'

'So, what are head office playing at?' Maisie asked. 'I can understand them closing the store if it is part of the area due for demolition, but we still have no idea what is happening, and I take it Woolies don't either. Is that right?' she said, looking at Betty.

'Going by this letter and the little Clemmie and I were told on our trip to London, I assume they have no idea. I fear my asking questions has made them decide the store must be closed . . .' She could say little more as tears fought to silence her. Her voice cracked with emotion as she uttered a few words. 'It is I who has destroyed the future of this store.'

'Nonsense,' Ruby exclaimed. 'You are overthinking this. Start fighting back, woman! I thought you were made of sterner stuff. We don't want the people of Erith thinking of this store with nostalgia once it has gone for good. If you don't do something now, it will be too late. Now, let's put our thinking caps on. We can show them,' she said, stabbing her finger on the letter from head office.

Freda, who had remained quiet while the women looked at the figures, raised her hand to silence the indignant comments. 'It seems obvious to me that we need first to find out once and for all if Woolworths and Pier Road are to be part of the council's demolition plans. Maureen, can we rely on you to get to the bottom of this? It would mean nagging George until you are blue in the face,' she said, looking towards Maureen to see how she felt about this. 'It's been a while since he said he would find out.'

'You can rely on me. George needs to be firmer to get the attention of Norman Dodds. So far, he's been stopped every time by his secretary who says he is busy or that she will pass on a message. It is obvious she hasn't been doing her job. When I left home this morning, he was planning to write a letter and hand deliver it to his home. I'll make sure he gets it done today.'

'I'll lend a hand with the nagging as well,' Ruby promised. 'What else can we do?'

Freda looked at Clemmie. 'From what you told us after your visit to head office, the man who wrote this letter had taken a shine to you?'

Clemmie nodded her head, eager to be able to help. 'He was under the impression I wasn't married as I'd slipped off my wedding ring so he thought I was single. It was the only way I could get his attention, although now he knows I'm a married woman. Please don't let this go any further as my Jimmy would be furious,' she explained. 'Do you want me to return to head office or use the telephone to sweet-talk him?'

'Use the telephone for now. Pretend you lost your glove and ask him if it is in his office,' Freda grinned. 'Just try to find out why he sent the letter to Betty.'

'Why, Freda Forsythe, you little minx,' Maisie laughed. 'I didn't know you had it in you.'

Freda blushed. 'I'll fight tooth and nail and whatever else it takes to save this store.'

Ruby patted her on the back. 'That's the spirit.'

'What else do you suggest?' Sarah asked. 'If it all boils down to head office thinking our turnover isn't good enough, they could still insist the store is closed.'

It was Ruby's turn to contribute. 'It's simple: you need to make sure the store brings in even more money in the run-up to Christmas.'

Betty shook her head. 'I'm not sure we can do it. Everyone shops here for their Christmas needs as it is; I doubt we could have them spend more money. Many people are still struggling since the war.'

The room fell silent as they thought what to do.

Maureen clapped her hands together as she came up with an idea. 'We intend to have a party for the old people and ex-employees; why don't we inform them we will keep the store open for their personal shopping and help them with their purchases? I remember we did this years ago when we had special parties for the old soldiers.'

Betty was thoughtful. 'That would help bring in a little more. It's a shame we can't have more than one special event for people to shop in the evenings by special invitation . . .'

'How about a cake baking demonstration? We could hold it in the staff canteen and sell our baking wares.'

'That's a jolly good idea,' Betty beamed. 'The ladies could bring along their undecorated Christmas cakes and you could show them how to finish them off in time for Christmas.'

Sarah too was enthusiastic. 'We could advertise the event and sell tickets.'

'And include some private shopping time,' Ruby added.

Freda became excited. 'I can ask my Tony to advertise it in his store as well to encourage new shoppers to Erith.'

Maisie, not wanting to be left out, suggested an evening for ladies who wanted sewing lessons. 'Again, we can keep the store open for the people to shop, and I can demonstrate some simple sewing techniques while the haberdashery counters sell patterns and everything to make a garment.'

'This all sounds very positive,' Betty grinned as she looked at a large calendar on the office wall. 'We will have to get cracking very soon or it will be Christmas Day before we know it.'

'Then let's start with the sewing evening,' Maisie suggested. 'We could call it "Make a Christmas pinny with Woolies". What do you think, Betty?'

'I think it's marvellous, but don't forget we have to work these events around the staff trip to London to see the Christmas lights and the show.'

'Why not have a knitting evening between Christmas and the New Year? Beginners and improvers welcome. I could run that,' Freda suggested.

Betty nodded enthusiastically. 'Even if we don't increase

the store turnover by much, at least we can show that our store is an essential part of Erith and should not be closed down.'

16

Sarah walked the short distance from Woolies round the corner to her husband, Alan's, electrical business. She knew she should be at home resting, but she needed to finish the conversation she'd been having with him before she joined her friends at Woolworths.

'I'm back,' she called into the empty shop before Alan's head bobbed up from behind the counter.

'Come and sit down,' he scolded her. 'You've been told by the doctor to rest up and all you do is rush about all over the place. Just look how your ankles have swollen,' he tutted as he helped her into a seat reserved for customers and eased off the sensible brogues, which were the only shoes that fitted these days apart from her slippers. 'Now, rest your feet up on this box and calm down. I'll get you a drink and then we can talk.'

'Nothing for me, thanks. I'm awash with tea as it is. Now, tell me more about your pantomime and what you are going to do now you don't have a venue. I couldn't keep up earlier after Claudette had called in to update you. I don't understand why you aren't able to put on the pantomime at Erith Theatre like your group have in the past.

It's all so confusing and such a shame after all your hard work.'

Alan shrugged his shoulders as he forced a cup of cold water into her hand. 'Claudette has been asking around to find out who it was that has stopped us from booking the theatre. From what we can work out, someone else is using the theatre.'

'Surely not over Christmas when you'd planned to run the show? That's ludicrous.'

Alan knelt to rub her ankles. 'I know that, and you know that, but someone at the theatre doesn't understand. So many people are going to be disappointed, as will the performers.'

'I'll speak to my dad. You never know, he may be able to pull a few strings. There's no point in having a parent who is a town councillor if you can't make use of him,' she laughed.

'I'm not sure that is how it works,' Alan said, getting to his feet and giving her a brief kiss as a customer walked into the shop. 'Now, when you are ready to leave, I'll close the shop and drive you home – no arguing,' he said as Sarah started to complain. 'Once you are home you are to stay there. If you want to speak to anyone, you are to use the telephone. Do you understand?'

Sarah agreed. It was nice being taken care of; she could get used to it. As she sat there a thought came to her . . .

*

Ruby and Maureen walked slowly from the town centre to where Maureen lived with Ruby's son, George. Ruby told her daughter-in-law more of what had happened before she had left the house a couple of hours earlier when she needed to make an emergency purchase of a card of elastic. 'I hope Sergeant Mike is there by now so he can get to the bottom of things.'

Maureen tutted. 'If it gets back to Vera that we've met her long-lost son and kept secrets from her, all hell will be let loose.'

'I'll be the first to feel her wrath as it was me she wanted to help find the baby she gave up for adoption. I should have known no good would come of it. Hey up, isn't that Mike coming up the road now?'

Both women waved as the sergeant hurried to catch up with them, looking warily between the pair.

'There's no need to look like that, we know who the man is,' Ruby said. She liked the police sergeant a lot and not only because he was her husband's only child. Mike was as honest as the day was long and could be relied upon in any situation. 'I hope you're not caught up in anything dodgy?' she asked.

'Come along in,' Maureen said as they reached the gate. 'I'll sort out a hot drink for us all as it's perishing out here, then you can tell us what this is all about and how we are going to explain to Vera.'

'I'll need to use your bedroom for a little while, so don't start without me.' Ruby discreetly nudged Maureen, who tried not to laugh.

Maureen was pleased to see the kitchen was tidy and any crockery the men had used had been washed, dried and put away in the cupboard. She pottered about making paste sandwiches until Ruby joined her. 'All secure?' she asked as Ruby gave her a grin.

'Yes, shipshape and Bristol fashion. It would have been

awful if they'd dropped around my ankles while we were grilling the prisoner.'

It was Maureen's turn to smile. 'Have you been reading Bob's crime novels he borrows from the library? I don't think we will be required to do any grilling. Let's leave all that to Mike, shall we?'

'All right, but to be on the safe side perhaps you should lock the back door in case he tries to escape. Do it now while the men are in the living room; I can hear them talking.'

'That is a good point,' Maureen agreed as she turned the key in the lock and placed it in the pocket of the apron she'd put on the moment she entered her kitchen. 'Don't worry, I'll do the same with the front door,' she said before lifting the tea tray. 'Come on, let's get this show on the road.'

George jumped up and cleared space on the coffee table in the middle of the room before helping Maureen to make sure everyone had a hot drink and a sandwich or two. 'Mike, would you like to go through everything you know so we have an idea what is going to happen next?'

A look of alarm crossed Daniel's face. 'No need to panic, son. Your real mother, Vera, is a good friend of mine and we all want what is best for her, and for you,' Ruby added, quickly trying to bury any anger she felt towards this man.

Mike cleared his throat, reaching into the inside pocket of his uniform jacket. 'I will read through my notes in order of what has happened. If anyone can add to them, would they wait until I have finished speaking?' he asked, looking towards Ruby who had perched herself on the edge of her seat as if she was ready to pounce. 'Mrs Vera Munro, while very ill, requested that her friend Mrs Ruby Jackson—'

'You can call me Ruby,' Ruby interrupted.

' . . . first requested that her friend, Ruby, help find the son she gave away as a baby. Vera thought she was about to pass away and wanted to meet the man and to make her apologies.' He looked around the room to see if anyone disagreed before continuing. 'For some reason Vera was under the impression Daniel had done well for himself. Councillor Jackson found this to be far from the truth and with some help from myself we discovered him to be wanted by the police for several offences. It was on the day of the coronation that he was discovered entering the country and charged for his offences, consequently being given a ten-year term, starting his sentence in Maidstone prison.'

'And you managed to escape and now you are here,' Ruby said, not being able to keep quiet a moment longer.

Bob and George groaned while James watched open-mouthed, not knowing much about what had happened in the past.

'Well, yes, that is right,' Mike replied, knowing it would be hard for Ruby not to speak. 'Perhaps Daniel can tell us why he felt the need to escape, which will have a detrimental effect on the time he has left to serve?'

Daniel looked around the room and took a deep breath. 'I don't have long left to live,' he said quietly. 'I told Sergeant Jackson in case anyone thinks I'm spinning a line. News got through to me that the woman who gave me away at birth wanted to meet me. The more I lay in hospital thinking about things, I thought that not only did I want to meet her out of curiosity, but also, if she was truly ill, I could make the old lady's last days a little happier. When it came down to it, once I'd escaped from the hospital, I became scared and hid away in your shed and that's where you found me,' he said, looking ashamed. 'I suppose now you are going to take me back to prison to live out the rest of my days?'

'Not to begin with,' George said as he moved seats to sit opposite the man. 'Look, I have an idea. We all want Vera to experience a happy outcome to this sorry business. She doesn't know you are a con man and believes you are a successful businessman working overseas. What we plan is to bring her here to meet you before you head to America to take up an important position in a major company. After that we will find a way for you to correspond once you are back as long as she never hears you led a life of crime. Let her go to her grave thinking she did the right thing by giving you away all those years before. Do you agree?'

Daniel looked around the room. 'My mother has very good friends, and if in some way I can make things up to her, I am willing to go along with your plans, even if it is only for a short while. When can I meet her?'

George looked to Maureen. 'Could we do it this evening, do you think?'

Maureen was flustered. 'I need time to cook; I cannot have guests in our home and not feed them.'

George smiled. It was typical of his wife that she had to feed people. 'We can have fish and chips. I'm sure Daniel would enjoy them?'

'I certainly would, but please don't go to any expense on my behalf.'

'We want this to be perfect for Vera. After all, we are creating a memory for her,' Ruby said, reaching for her handkerchief to blow her nose, fighting to hold herself together as she began to feel the emotion of the situation about to overwhelm her.

They all fell quiet, thinking of what lay ahead, while Maureen was thinking back to the meeting in Betty's office. She might not be able to do much about the situation with Vera and Daniel, but she could get cracking with her promise to guide her husband to do the right thing.

'George, would you help me carry the tray out to the kitchen, please?' Maureen asked once the sandwiches and tea had been consumed.

George understood the command to follow his wife as she undoubtedly wanted a quiet word with him. What had he done now? He pulled the door behind him after placing the tray on the table. 'I take it you have something to say to me?'

She threw a tea towel to him and started to explain what had happened in Betty's office a few hours earlier as he dried the crockery. 'So, my task is to encourage you to speak to our revered member of parliament and find out what part of the town is going to be demolished. I know you've tried, but do you think you could try harder?' she pleaded. 'So many jobs are at risk and I for one can't imagine us not having a Woolies in the town.'

George put down the tea towel and reached for his wife. As he held her in his arms, he promised he would do his utmost to pin the man down and get an answer. 'I've written a letter and meant to hand deliver it today, but with all that went on it was forgotten. I'll go tomorrow.'

'Why not go right now? I'll accompany you and we can pick up Vera on our way back. It will only add ten minutes to the journey.'

'Then get your coat and hat while I change into my shoes and fetch the letter.'

Maureen kissed the tip of his nose. 'You'd best wear a tie, my love. You've got to mean business,' she replied, thinking she would wear the hat she saved for Sundays and go to the MP's door with him.

The telephone started to ring as he watched her leave the room. He'd married a good one there, he thought as he reached for the receiver. 'Erith 412, George Caselton speaking. Hello, Sarah, love. There's nothing wrong, is there?' he asked as his heart beat a little faster. He worried about his daughter overdoing things when she was so close to delivering his third grandchild. 'Are you not well?'

'I'm fine, Dad. A little tired and as big as a barrage balloon, but I'm fine. I wondered if you could give me some advice if you aren't too busy?'

'If you are quick as I'm just off out.'

'Not to worry, it can wait,' she said quickly.

'Then I'll be worrying about you all evening. No, tell me now and I'll visit in the morning, and we can chat properly then.'

Sarah quickly explained about the Erith Players losing the venue for the pantomime and how she couldn't understand why. Furthermore, did George know of somewhere else they could put on the show?

George promised to do all he could and, hearing his wife coming downstairs, he quickly said goodbye.

Maureen hurried to get ready, leaving her hat on the

hall table and returning to the front room. 'I'm going with George to collect Vera and Sadie.'

Ruby said it wouldn't be a problem and told George not to drive too fast. Bob laughed at her words and was rewarded with a stern look.

George turned to Daniel. 'I've left a suit on your bed. I thought you could borrow it to meet your mother. We are about the same size, so it should fit.'

Daniel couldn't answer for a moment, appearing overcome by George's generosity. 'I don't deserve this after what I've done.'

Mike, who had unbuttoned his uniform jacket and loosened his tie now he was off duty, cleared his throat. He too was warmed by the caring thoughts of his friends. 'Daniel, we want to help all we can. Vera deserves this. She may be a grouch at times, but she's been through a lot over the years; it would be good to see her acquainted with her son.'

'Can you tell me more about her and the rest of her family?' Daniel asked, looking between James and Ruby. 'I would like to know about my family even . . . even if it won't be for long. I'd like to make it up to my real mother.'

'What about your adopted mother?' Ruby asked. 'Was she a good mother?'

Daniel smiled at the memory. 'I was very much wanted, but she was more concerned about education and making the right impression in front of people when sometimes I just wanted to be cuddled and loved – what young child doesn't?'

Ruby thought Vera wouldn't have been much different bringing up the lad although there wouldn't have been the money for private education and posh clothes. 'It's what's in here that counts,' she replied, tapping her chest close to her heart. 'James, why don't you tell him about how you came to Erith and met Sadie? That's Vera's granddaughter,' she informed Daniel, 'while I put the kettle on.'

'I'll give you a hand as I've heard this part of the story before,' Bob said as he followed her from the room, thinking how the amount of tea they'd drunk in the past few hours would mean him being up most of the night.

*

'Being a member of parliament must pay well,' Maureen said as she peered at the detached house while George parked their car. 'Perhaps you should think about standing for parliament? You could do better than this chap. At least you get things done,' she sniffed.

'There's a bit more to standing than just having your name added to the voting papers. My politics are the opposite to Norman Dodds' even though he stands for the same area. The working class like him.'

'They like you too,' she replied as he helped her from the car. She'd investigate what it took to become a member of parliament, she thought to herself as they started to walk along the path to the grand door. 'There's no need to be nervous,' she whispered as they heard footsteps approaching. 'Just remember, he has to go to the toilet just like you do.'

George just about managed to compose himself as the door opened.

17

The door was opened by a woman wearing a navy-blue cocktail dress, and a string of pearls around her slender neck. The full-skirted dress rustled around her legs, and she stopped and stared at George and Maureen. 'Oh, I thought you were someone else. They are rather late,' she said vaguely as she checked the time on a silver watch around her left wrist. In her right hand she held a delicate glass that Maureen thought contained champagne.

George held out his hand. 'I'm Councillor George Caselton and this is my wife, Maureen. We wondered if we could have a quick word with Norman? It's to do with something urgent that has cropped up in the town.'

'The town?'

'Erith. It is part of his constituency,' Maureen said waspishly. She'd taken an instant dislike to the woman. Who drank champagne at this time of the day? Why, most people hadn't even eaten their tea yet. Her stomach rumbled, reminding her of the fish and chips they would be collecting after picking up Vera.

'Darling, I wouldn't know. I'm just here for cocktails. I'll call his secretary, June. Step inside for a moment; you look untidy standing there,' she said, giving Maureen's hat a look of disdain.

They stepped into a hall that had double doors at one end leading on to a brightly lit room where they could hear a piano playing and people chatting.

'Mrs Dodds, if we could leave this letter for Norman,' Maureen said, nodding to George to hand it over. He reached inside his jacket and pulled out a letter marked 'urgent'.

'We will leave you to your party. I'm sorry we intruded,' he said.

The woman gave a shrill laugh. 'Good grief, I'm not his wife! I'm one of the footballers' wives.'

Maureen looked puzzled. 'I beg your pardon?'

'Norman is their patron,' George informed her. 'This must be a get-together for the players.'

'Oh, I see. May we speak with Mr Dodds?' she asked, looking around her.

'I'm afraid he has been held up at Parliament. June will help you; she is ever so efficient. I'm in awe of her,' the woman tittered, going to sip her drink and seeing the glass was empty. 'I'll leave you here while I fetch a refill and tell June she is wanted.'

They stood waiting . . . Maureen tapped her foot on the tiled floor as she grew impatient – where was the woman? 'Everyone back home will wonder where we are; they will be so hungry. Come on, let's go,' she said, taking George's arm to lead him to the front door.

'May I help you?' a tall thin woman asked as she appeared from a side room and stared at George, a frown wrinkling her high forehead. She could only have been in her early twenties, but she acted like a middle-aged woman with her dark hair swept up in a French pleat.

George took a double look as she was so familiar. 'I beg your pardon for asking but do we know each other?'

'It depends who you are?' she sniffed.

'Councillor George Caselton, and this is my wife, Maureen,' he said, holding out his hand.

'Miss June Bennett, and no, we haven't met before, but I recollect the name. I am Mr Dodds' secretary. I understand you have something you wish to leave with me?'

'I would prefer to see Norman, but if you could hand this to him, I will telephone tomorrow. What time is convenient?'

'It is rather inconvenient tomorrow; I will arrange a time later next week. He is a very busy man, you know.'

'I'm aware of that, but the people of Erith are worried about the demolition of the town they love. Would you perchance know the area that will be affected? I appreciate it hasn't gone before the planning committee, and much is hearsay, but when companies like Woolworths are planning to pull out of the town it won't be long before others follow. How will that look in Norman's constituency? He could lose votes if he isn't seen to be helping the common man. Tell him I'll ring tomorrow morning,' he said, taking Maureen's arm and going to the front door. As he lay his hand on the door handle, he turned. 'Out of interest, I was also going to ask Norman if he knew anything about Erith Theatre refusing to entertain the Erith Players' pantomime in a few weeks. He is still one of the trustees, isn't he? I know it is only an amateur production, but the members have put a lot of work into the panto, and they do raise a lot of money for local charities. Perhaps you could mention it to him, so he is able to answer me when I ring?'

Miss Bennett's face flushed with annoyance as she wished them good evening and closed the door sharply behind them.

'Blimey, what was that all about?' Maureen asked as she hurried after him. 'You certainly ruffled her feathers.'

George opened the car door and helped Maureen into her seat. 'Considering we have never met I can't help thinking she doesn't like me. Why would that be? The strange thing is, I recognize her from somewhere . . . Oh well, it'll come to me in time,' he said as he started the car engine and they set off back to Erith. 'Shall we pick Vera up first, or collect the fish and chips?'

'The food could go cold while we explain to Vera why she needs to come to our house,' Maureen said. 'It's best we go straight to her house and take it from there.'

'We should have brought Mum with us; she could have put Vera straight and had her out the door in record time.'

Maureen snorted at his suggestion. 'That would have meant taking her to Norman Dodds' house with us. As soon as she got a whiff of why we were going there she'd have really upset the secretary. Ruby means well but there are times she's less than tactful, bless her.'

'I don't know, Mum might have done better than I did. I feel as though I failed. I'm no further forward, and by the time I get to speak to Norman, Christmas will be over and Woolworths will be closing, not to mention all the other businesses. As it is, my open surgery is full of worried people who may be losing their homes. You should see the files on my desk. The landlords are sitting on their hands raking in rents and will leave it until the last minute to evicts their tenants.'

Maureen began to worry George wouldn't be able to help everyone in his constituency and could become depressed. 'What about if I came with you tomorrow and sorted out some of the files? You never know, I may be able to help you whittle down a few of the queries. I've got some jumble I want to drop off for the vicar's wife so I can kill two birds with one stone.'

George didn't think it would be that easy to whittle down his workload, but it would be nice to have Maureen there with him. 'I'd like that, love. It may also give me time to get through on the telephone to Norman Dodds,' he said as they pulled up in front of Vera's house just up the road from where he grew up at number thirteen Alexandra Road.

'Do you want me to go in?' Maureen asked with some trepidation.

'Let's both do it,' he replied, thinking it would be cowardly of him to allow his wife to face Vera alone; one never knew what kind of mood she would be in. Perhaps his mother would have done better, but it was too late to turn back to get her now as he'd seen the lace curtains twitch in the bay window. He'd hardly knocked on the front door when it was swung open by Vera.

'What's happened to Ruby? Don't tell me she's de . . . de . . . I can't even say it,' she said as a distressed expression crossed her lined face.

Maureen grabbed hold of her as she started to sway. 'Oh no, it's nothing like that,' she said, looking to George for help. Vera might have been of slight build, but she felt a dead weight as she started to crumple to the floor.

201

'Let's get you inside,' George said as he took command of the situation. 'You don't want people watching from their windows, do you?'

Vera snorted. 'Yes, help me inside; there are too many nosy buggers in this street.'

Maureen chewed on the inside of her cheek in case she laughed out loud. Vera was the nosiest of them all. Once they'd settled Vera in her armchair George knelt in front of her and took her hands. 'I have some news that may come as a shock . . .'

'It's Bob who's died. I thought he looked a bit ropey when I watched him walk up the road the other day,' she said, glancing to the bay window with the curtains hooked to one side from where she'd been watching George and Maureen get out of their car. 'Not that I was particularly watching, of course. Does Ruby want me to help lay him out?'

'You're getting your knickers in a twist,' Maureen butted in, knowing they'd be there all night if she didn't get a word in when Vera paused for breath. 'No one has died. In fact, we have a nice surprise for you at our house and came to collect you and Sadie so you could have a fish and chip supper and get to know him better – where is Sadie?' she asked, looking around her.

Vera frowned. 'She's gone to see Freda and took the kiddies so I can have a bit of peace and quiet. Not that I've had any yet. Who is it I'm supposed to meet? I've not got time to play silly games so tell me.'

George waited for Maureen to speak, but as she remained quiet, he had to bite the bullet. 'We have a guest . . .'

'I guessed that much. Now hurry up with the rest,' she snapped, causing him to flinch.

George had wanted to break the news gently, but she gave him no choice. 'Your son, Daniel, is staying with us, and we thought you'd like to meet him and have supper with us.'

Vera was silent for a while as she digested the news. 'I don't understand. Why didn't he come here rather than go to your house? You all know how I've wanted to see him for so long . . . Something isn't right.'

'He didn't want to give you a shock as you have been poorly. He's not been too great himself,' Maureen said, praying Vera wouldn't ask another question.

Vera's face softened. 'Bless him for thinking of his old mum,' she said, getting to her feet and reaching for her cardigan. 'Let's go.'

She'd reached the hall and was about to pull on her coat before George or Maureen had collected their thoughts. 'We need to wait for Sadie,' Maureen said, thinking the sensible young woman would be invaluable if things went downhill when Vera met her long-lost son. That did not go down well with Vera.

'I don't want to wait. She will meet him soon enough once he's moved in here.'

Maureen raised her eyebrows at George as they followed Vera out the door. Goodness knows what was going to happen once Vera eventually discovered the truth . . .

Vera took her place in the front passenger seat and said very little until they stopped opposite the Odeon cinema and Maureen jumped out to go into the fish and chip shop. 'I'll have rock and chips,' she called out the window before turning to George. 'What's he like? His dad was a handsome chap,' she said with a faraway look in her eye. 'He fair

203

swept me off my feet, but there was no future in it, what with me already being married. If only life had been different . . .'

George didn't know what to say. No doubt his mum or Maureen would have the right words. He felt hot under the collar and tried to clear his throat, all the time watching the steam-covered window of the chip shop and willing Maureen to hurry back.

'I've embarrassed you,' Vera cackled. 'Many women have fallen foul of men . . .'

He knew about his mother's past life, especially during the Great War, and if that was what Vera was alluding to, he wasn't going to be drawn into a conversation about it. 'That's their business,' he muttered before reaching for a cloth he kept under his seat and getting out of the car to clean the windscreen. That kept him busy until he saw Maureen and hurried over the road to carry her laden bag.

'Was it that bad?' she asked, knowing how Vera could get under people's skin.

'Worse, but I kept my temper and decided to polish the car. I had to remind myself she must be nervous about meeting her son after all these years.'

'You're a good man, George Caselton.'

'I'm a hungry man. Come on, let's get this food home before it goes cold.' He deposited the bag on the back seat and helped Maureen into the car. 'They smell good,' he said although the car would be sure to smell of vinegar for days afterwards.

'I hope you put salt and vinegar on mine; it always tastes better from the chip shop,' Vera said as he pulled away from the kerb and drove as fast as he could through the streets to his house.

'I'll take these straight through to the kitchen,' Maureen said as she hurried through the living room with Ruby following her, informing her of how she had put plates in the oven to warm and buttered the bread.

George took Vera's coat and led her to where Daniel was sitting. He stood up as Vera slowly approached him. 'You've got the look of your father about you,' she said as she reached up and stroked his cheek. 'You are as tall as him as well.'

Daniel held out his arms and Vera was soon being hugged so tight her face had turned pink. 'Hello, Mother. I've waited a long time to meet you,' he said as he led her to the sofa and sat down next to her. 'I understand you have been ill?'

Vera couldn't take her eyes from his face. 'It was nothing. I'm not one to complain,' she said in barely a whisper.

George nodded his head to James, Bob and Mike, and they slowly sidled from the room, closing the door behind them before joining the women in the kitchen.

'I'd not have believed that if I'd not seen it with my own eyes,' James said as he took two plates from Maureen and carried them through to the dining room, while Mike and George followed with cutlery and a laden tea tray.

'Whatever you heard, you are going to have to forget it and go back in there and tell them their food is ready,' Ruby said.

The men looked at each other but didn't move.

'Get out of the way, I'll go,' Ruby huffed before moving as quickly as she could to first listen at the door before knocking loudly and walking in. 'You'd best come and eat or it'll get cold.' She held the door open and watched as Daniel took his mother's arm and escorted her to the dining room, with Vera smiling sweetly as if she was being escorted by royalty.

The room was quiet as they all tucked into their food. 'I couldn't eat another chip,' James said as he sat back in his chair and gave a sigh. 'My Sadie will be sad to have missed meeting you,' he added, looking to where Daniel had put down his knife and fork having only eaten half his portion.

'She will meet him when he comes to stay with us,' Vera announced. 'I've been thinking about it, and you can have the front room as a bedroom; the single bed is still there from when I was poorly. We can pick up another bedstead and mattress from Hedley Mitchell's second-hand department – you can do that for me, can't you, James?'

James was puzzled and looked to Mike Jackson for help.

'Vera, Daniel is going away again later this evening. This is why we wanted the pair of you to meet tonight while there was still time.'

Vera's wrinkled face screwed up in concentration as she digested Mike's words. She turned to Daniel. 'Why did you want to meet me just to go away five minutes later? Anyone would think the police were after you.'

The friends sitting around the table all turned their attention to their plates rather than answer her.

She grabbed hold of his arm. 'Are you wanted by the police? Please tell me the truth.'

'I think you should put your cards on the table,' Ruby said to Daniel before giving Vera an apologetic look. 'It's a bit of a long story, my love. It all happened while you were ill, and we didn't want to worry you.'

'I was under the impression you were working overseas and had a very important job,' she said, shrinking away from him. 'Why was I lied to? Were you and Sadie in on this too?' she spat at James.

Ruby shook her head. Vera had woven so many stories in her mind about who her son was and how successful he had become that she had started to believe her own imagination. Where would this end?

George thought it was time to intervene. 'James had no idea about this until last night when we found Daniel hiding away at the allotment.'

'I was trying to find you, Mother,' he said, looking ashamed. 'I was fearful of what you would think of me but knew my time was coming to an end and couldn't go without apologizing face to face.'

Vera's bottom lip started to quiver as her heart thudded in her chest. 'Apologize? Whatever do you mean?'

Ruby gave a sigh. 'I'll put the kettle on while you all explain to Vera,' she said, nodding to Maureen to follow her. They collected up the crockery and hurried from the room.

'I'm not sure Vera is going to take the news very well,' Maureen said as she pulled on her pinny to start the washing-up.

'I blame myself. I shouldn't have held back from telling her he was a wrong 'un, then she'd have been prepared – that's if she'd ever met him.'

'Don't blame yourself. She was extremely poorly at the time, and we expected the worst. It would have been unkind to tell her he wasn't the golden child she believed him to be.'

Ruby picked up a tea towel to start drying the cups. 'I don't know about you but I'm full of tea. Shall we wait a while until everything has calmed down?'

'That's a good idea,' Maureen said, going to the pantry and returning a minute later with a bottle of sherry. 'Let's have one of these instead.'

'Are we interrupting?' Mike asked as he stepped into the kitchen followed by James to find the two women helping themselves to another glass of sherry.

Ruby gave her stepson a warm smile. 'We thought it best to let Daniel explain himself without too many people listening.'

'Besides, we know most of the story,' Maureen added. 'Can I make you a hot drink or would you prefer one of these?'

'No thank you, we've got to be off. I'm on duty shortly.'

'Sadie will be home soon and wonder where I am. I was supposed to be helping with the housework,' James said. 'I have a lot to tell her.'

'A man who helps with the housework! Whatever next?' Ruby said. 'Perhaps you can have a word with my Bob?' she chuckled. 'Here, take these back for Sadie. I bought an extra portion,' she said, handing him some fish and chips wrapped in newspaper. 'They only need a quick warm in the oven.'

'Thank you, she'll enjoy them, especially not having to cook.'

'Are Bob and George still in the dining room?' Ruby asked.

'No, they've gone into the living room. I heard them put

the television on. Dad's probably asleep by now,' Mike laughed as he kissed Ruby's cheek. 'I'll see you tomorrow to hear what happened.'

'Aren't you going to take Daniel back to prison?' Maureen asked.

'I'm coming back tomorrow for him and bringing a prison officer with me,' Mike said as he left. 'It'll give Vera time to talk to her son.'

'It's all very sad with them both just getting to know each other,' Maureen said as she peered through the slightly open door. 'They seem to be getting on like a house on fire. I've not seen Vera this happy in a long time. I wonder how long he's got?'

'Until tomorrow morning,' Ruby said, pouring them each another sherry. 'That's when he goes back to the hospital under guard.'

'No, I meant his illness; that was the reason he escaped to see his mum before . . . well, before he passes away.'

Both women looked at each other and frowned before rushing to the dining room. Daniel was still there talking to his mum.

'Thank goodness for that,' Ruby sighed.

'We shouldn't be so suspicious,' Maureen said, finishing her sherry in one gulp.

18
~

Bob opened the front door of number thirteen and took Ruby's arm, leading her into their front room.

'Why are we coming in here when we can sit in the living room? It's closer to the kitchen and the kettle,' she grumbled before giving a loud yawn. 'I'm more than ready for my bed after the day we've had.'

Bob went to the fireplace and struck a match, placing it against the kindling of the prepared fire. He rubbed his hands together as the fire took hold. 'That'll warm your cockles in no time. Now, let me take your coat and I'll make the cocoa,' he said, putting her slippers by the hearth to warm. 'Stick your feet up on the stool and make yourself comfortable.'

'You're a good one,' she smiled as the heat from the fire reached her chilled body. 'I'm glad Mike dropped us off so we didn't have to walk. I know it's not far, but it is cold enough to freeze my bones,' she said, pulling her cardigan around her shoulders. 'Hurry up with that cocoa.'

In the kitchen Bob filled the kettle and was deep in thought as he waited for it to boil. Something didn't seem right. They'd left while Vera was still deep in conversation with her long-lost son. She'd held on to his arm, hanging on to every word as he explained about his life as a young-ster and how he set out alone after his adopted mother passed way. There was little mention of the war years or perhaps he'd dozed off at that point; it had been hard to pretend to be sleeping while listening to their conversation in the next room. A newspaper strategically placed over his face had helped keep up his pretence. He'd needed to find out more about the man's terminal illness as there was little evidence he was poorly. Having been ill himself in recent months with some time spent in hospital and conva-lescing by the sea, he felt he could spot a sick person a mile off.

The whistling kettle startled him for a moment before he decided to do something about his concerns. Making their cocoa and carrying it through to the front room, he noticed Ruby was starting to fall asleep. 'Why don't I carry this upstairs for you? We can get you tucked up in bed. I'll make a hot water bottle or, better still, I'll light the fire up there.'

Ruby smiled at his concern. 'It's me who should be looking after you, Bob Jackson. You're not yet one hundred per cent better. I can get myself off to bed without you fussing, although a nice fire up there would be good. I'm starting to enjoy this one. It seems a waste to have lit this fire and then leave it,' she said as she watched the flames lick around the coals.

'I'll sit down here for a while. I want to read some more of my book, so the fire won't be wasted,' he said, not looking her in the eye. 'Now, let's get you up the wooden hill and tucked up in bed. You've had a long day and what with caring for the youngsters earlier today then helping

Maureen keep us fed and watered this evening, no wonder you are yawning your head off.'

'It is half past nine, so not that long before my usual bedtime. However, I'll go up and leave you to your book,' she smiled as she struggled to her feet and kissed his cheek. 'As I said before, you're a good one,' she said as she headed to the steep staircase just off the hall.

'I'm right behind you,' he said, picking up her cup.

After helping Ruby settle in bed and lighting a fire set in the fancy iron fireplace, he pulled the bedroom door closed and went downstairs. Taking a sip from his cup, he listened until it fell silent upstairs without even a squeak from the iron bedstead. He closed the door to the front room and went to the oak sideboard and picked up the telephone receiver. With luck Mike would still be in the police station down by the river if he hadn't been called out on police duties. He waited while the phone rang until it was picked up and a familiar voice answered.

'Erith police station, how may I help you?'

'Mike, it's your dad. Can you spare me a few minutes?'

'What's up, Dad?' Mike asked, sounding worried.

'I wanted to pick your brains about this business with Vera and her son. What's your opinion on the situation?'

There was a silence as Mike digested Bob's question. 'To be honest, there's something I don't like about the chap. I can't put my finger on it, but I know I'll be glad when he's back where he belongs behind bars. By rights I shouldn't have agreed for him to have tonight as a free man before we take him back to the hospital, but Vera pleaded with me to allow her more time with him, and George said it was fine for him to stay at his house for the night.'

Bob could hear how worried Mike was; he'd put his job on the line by allowing Vera to have a little more time with her son. But still he felt a growing sense of alarm.

'Mike, who told you he had a terminal illness? Was it the prison?'

'Come to think of it, they didn't. He absconded from the hospital when the prison guard turned his back. It was Daniel himself who said he was there because of his terminal illness. Dad, I have a feeling we've been conned by a conman.'

'It's not your fault, son. I have a feeling he has fooled us all. I do wonder if he made use of being in the hospital for whatever reason and after his escape he needed somewhere to hide out, and where better than the town where he was born?' He heard Mike groan on the other end of the line.

'And we fell for it hook, line and sinker. Do you think he has sweet-talked Vera into giving him much money?'

'I reckon she's sorting out what money she has to give him in the morning. I'm going to go up to her house now and see if I can have a few words with James. He may be able to put a stop to things his end . . .'

'Thanks, Dad. I can't leave the desk to go off on personal business. It's bad enough we know where he is and I've not had him arrested. This could cost me my job.'

'Don't talk like that, Mike. You've been sucked in as much as the rest of us. We all thought we were doing the right thing allowing him this one night of freedom as he is terminally ill and won't see his mum again. If we'd ignored that and had him carted off back to prison, we would have all looked heartless, let alone having Vera on our backs.

We did what we thought was right at the time, and now we must rectify that.'

'At least we know where to find him.'

It was Bob's turn to groan. 'If he's still there. Look, don't do a thing. I'll go up to Vera's house now and see what James knows. I'll be as quick as I can. Don't you do a thing, do you understand me?'

'Yes, Dad, I understand. Ring me as soon as you know something,' he pleaded.

Bob promised he would, before fetching his coat from the hall stand and stopping at the bottom of the stairs to listen for any sign Ruby was awake. Confident she was sound asleep, he slipped from the house, leaving the front door on the latch so as not to make a sound upon his return. The road was empty as he walked past the ten houses between his home and Vera's with not a soul to be seen, which was good as it meant no one would mention to Ruby that they'd seen him out late at night when most people were home in the warm. He blew on his hands before rubbing them together, wishing he'd not left his gloves behind. Approaching Vera's house, he was relieved to see a light behind the heavy curtains in the bay window. He gave a light tap on the door, hoping not to wake Sadie's children, and waited as he heard footsteps approaching on the lino floor, breathing a sigh of relief when James opened the door.

'Am I pleased to see you, Bob! I was beginning to wonder what to do,' he whispered as he took his coat. 'Vera is talking strangely, and I was wondering whether to call you and Ruby for help.'

'How do you mean?' Bob whispered back.

214

'She wants me to take her money over to George's house and give it to Daniel before he leaves. I'm going to do it now before he comes out in the cold night as they'd planned; she's worried about him being so ill.'

Bob was puzzled. 'I'd have thought what money she had was safe in the post office.'

James gave a wry laugh. 'She doesn't trust banks or the post office and keeps her money here. It's in different places around the house and she keeps moving it in case she is burgled; there's even some under her mattress. I found it when we moved her bed downstairs when she was ill last year.'

'At least she could wait until the morning.'

'I said the same, but she reckons he will be gone before then.'

Bob knew then that Vera was aware of what Daniel was up to. 'I'll have a word with her, if she's still up,' he said, pushing past James and not giving him time to protest. As it was, James was more than pleased to let Bob through and followed him into the front room.

'Hello, Bob, it's a bit on the late side for you to be visiting, isn't it?' Vera said, looking up from a small attaché case she held on her lap. She flicked down the lid and snapped the brass clasps closed, but not before he'd noticed what was inside.

'Counting the family fortune?' he grinned as he sat down on the overstuffed settee opposite where she was settled in her armchair.

Vera frowned, causing more lines to appear on her already wrinkled face. 'Not that it's any of your business, Bob Jackson, but I like to check that my house is in order in case anything should happen. There was a time not so long ago I was down on my uppers, and I don't want to be that way again. Neither do I want my family in the same situation,' she said defiantly.

'That's laudable, but it's a strange time of night to be doing it, don't you think?' he said, looking towards the door, expecting to see James standing there. He wasn't. Instead the stairs creaked as someone was walking upstairs. Bob was disappointed in James for not supporting him. Instead, he tried to continue a conversation with Vera. 'You must have been pleased to see your son after all these years?'

'It was a surprise, but a good one,' she smiled. 'I'd all but given up hope. You do know he's been poorly, don't you?'

Bob wasn't sure it would help if Vera was aware he suspected what he did about the man. 'He did mention it, but I wasn't able to talk with him for long due to him wanting to be with you. Did he have much to say?'

'We spoke about the past and I was able to reassure him that as much as I wanted to, I was not able to keep him after his birth.' A faraway look came into her eyes.

Bob shook his head. Vera could have such fanciful ideas at times. Ruby had told him the circumstances surrounding the conception of Vera's son out of wedlock and she was as much to blame as the young man who caught her eye while her husband was away in the army. She certainly viewed her past through rose-tinted glasses. There was no point arguing with her as she was set in her ways. However, he could stop her throwing her money away. 'Did he tell you about his current circumstance?'

Vera glared at him. 'Everyone seems keen to kick a poor man when he's down. He has been a successful businessman

216

and just because he is serving a sentence rather than the colleague who broke the law, it does not make him a bad man.'

'Don't you think it strange he escaped when taken to hospital from prison?'

Vera's eyes started to water. 'He was given a diagnosis that no man wants to hear, and his first thought was he would never see me. He took the opportunity to leave the hospital and seek me out.'

Bob fought hard to choke back a sharp retort. Daniel had certainly sucked her in, but then hadn't the same happened to him and the other men when he told his story up at the allotment? He was a slippery eel and no mistake. 'What happens now?' he asked, wondering what Vera had been told by her son.

'I'm going to help him escape,' she declared with a glint in her eye.

Bob couldn't believe what he was hearing but was stopped from answering as James entered the room, followed by Vera's granddaughter, Sadie.

'Nan, we couldn't find the envelope you asked James to fetch,' Sadie said with a nervous look on her face.

Bob noticed how she slipped her small hand into James's large one and he squeezed it to give her support. 'What have you lost?' he asked Vera.

'Nothing has been lost. I placed an envelope on top of my wardrobe for safe keeping. You couldn't have looked properly; go and try again,' she spat at James.

'I'll help you,' Bob nodded at James. 'I could kill for a hot drink, Sadie,' he added before following James out of the room. Sadie gave him a thankful look as this meant she wouldn't have to be alone with her nan while she had this bee in her bonnet.

'Now, James, what's this all about?' Bob asked as he followed him into Vera's bedroom that faced out over Alexandra Road. 'I've got an inkling but would rather hear what you know.'

James gave a grimace as he moved to where a large walnut wardrobe stood. 'As far as Vera is concerned, an envelope hidden on the top of a wardrobe is as safe as a bank, and money tucked away in a tea caddy is as good as a post office savings book. That's why she's got us finding where she's hidden coins and notes all over the house. Don't think it's a fortune, but it is all she has, and she is now handing it all over to that man. Sadie is so worried, just as I am. We don't want a penny from Vera; we are grateful for a roof over our heads, and we pay our own way. But to think she would give everything she has to someone she has built up in her imagination, and only met a couple of hours ago . . .' He sat down on the pink candlewick-covered bed and put his face in his hands. 'It beggars belief.'

Bob patted James's shoulder before sitting down beside him. 'I've known Vera a lot longer than you have, and she's always been a difficult woman. My Ruby reckons that deep down she's a good person, and when she was ill last year, she started to think about the baby she gave away to save her marriage. At her lowest she decided this baby had to be found so she could be forgiven for what she did, even though the poor mite had a better life than it would have done with its natural mother. From all accounts he had a good upbringing, but still turned out to be a wrong 'un. Now he's going to fleece Vera and disappear.'

James frowned. 'But he is going to die . . .'

'At some time, no doubt he will, but not now. My son, Mike, is checking the facts, but my gut is telling me he lied about that too.'

'I do tend to agree with you, but how can we stop Vera giving him all her money? He told her he will be here later tonight; he's going to slip out of George's house and be here around midnight. She's insisted he leaves town as soon as possible before he is re-arrested and has made him promise to keep in touch.'

Bob became angry. 'He has reeled her in hook, line and sinker. I could kick myself for thinking I was doing good leaving them to have a private chat this evening. I did try to listen in, but it was hard.'

'You can't blame yourself. We all thought Vera wanted some time alone to get to know her son. I did go into the dining room once and she sent me packing with a flea in my ear.'

George thought for a moment. 'I imagine the envelope is still up there on top of the wardrobe?'

'It is. Sadie and I were playing for time; we pushed it further back knowing she wouldn't be able to reach it if she stood on a chair and reached up.'

'Does she know how much is in the envelope?'

'To the penny. We did think of taking out some of the money and replacing it with newspaper cut to size, but she'd have spotted it straight away. She may be old, Bob, but she has still got all her marbles.'

Bob had to agree with him. 'Let's find that envelope and give it to Vera and I'll try to have a word with her to stop her giving her money away.'

James reached up to the top of the wardrobe and brought down a used envelope containing Vera's savings. He blew off the dust before handing it to Bob to check. 'I'd be grateful if you would, but how are we going to stop Daniel arriving and taking her for all she's got? I doubt she will listen to you.'

'In that case I'll make my views known to Vera and skedaddle back home and ring Mike. He will know what to do. Do your utmost to act as though we aren't planning anything.'

James agreed although he wasn't sure what they could do to stop Daniel taking Vera's savings.

Bob was soon walking back down Alexandra Road with Vera's sharp words ringing in his ears. Granted, perhaps he shouldn't have asked her why she was handing over her money to a stranger in such a forthright manner, but he couldn't think how to sugar-coat his words and hang around twiddling his thumbs while she extoled the virtues of Daniel. He also wanted to ring Mike to find out if he had any news on the miscreant. It was as he was approaching his house that he realized lights were blazing in his bedroom and the front room. Ruby must be up and waiting for him.

'I thought you'd have been dead to the world,' he said, ignoring Ruby's frown as she sat on the settee clutching a stone hot water bottle in her arms. 'Would you like me to refill that for you?'

'Next door's cat woke me up; it was sitting on my chest. If you are going to go out late in the evening, you should at least close the door behind you properly. You know what a nuisance it can be.'

Bob pulled off his overcoat and threw it over the back

of his armchair. 'I'll need it shortly,' he said, noticing her raised eyebrows. 'Let me make a telephone call and then I'll update you.'

He picked up the telephone from the sideboard, which smelt of lavender; Ruby did like to polish it in case a visitor wanted to use the instrument. He dialled the number for the police station and Mike answered immediately. 'You need to get here as soon as possible and bring someone with you. Daniel is due at Vera's at midnight.'

Ruby started to throw questions at him, causing him to place a finger in his ear so he could hear what Mike was saying. 'Tell me when you get here. I'll keep an eye out the front in case he arrives early. Shall we contact George and Maureen?'

He held the phone from his ear as Mike shouted, 'No!'

After placing the telephone receiver down, he turned to Ruby to find she was on her feet and heading towards the door.

'I'll be back down in two ticks. I need to put some clothes on so I can help you,' she said, hurrying from the room.

Bob looked at the large wooden clock sitting proudly on the sideboard. He hated it, but as it had been a wedding present, he would never suggest to Ruby that they move it somewhere more discreet. It was twenty minutes to midnight. If Mike was walking from the police station, he could well bump into Daniel. If he used his bicycle, it would save a couple of minutes, but he would still be spotted. Would the man scarper, or would the lure of Vera's money be too enticing? The beat of his heart thumped fast in his chest as he went to peer from behind the heavy curtains hanging at the bay window. The road was empty.

221

'Don't do that,' Ruby snapped as she came back into the room still doing up the buttons on the front of her dress while slipping her bare feet into her shoes. 'Only people like Vera are curtain twitchers. Come on, let's hide in the garden,' she said, holding out her hand to him.

'There's nowhere to hide out there apart from behind the front wall and as it's not four feet high we will be caught out very quickly and look like a couple of darned fools. Better to be a curtain twitcher than a fool,' he said, turning out the light and pulling back the curtain enough for them both to peer out.

'There's a car coming up the road. I don't recognize it,' Ruby, who knew every car owned by neighbours, said as her breath cast a misty cloud on the glass.

Bob peered over her shoulder. 'That's Mike in the passenger seat and one of the constables is driving.'

'How exciting,' Ruby declared, grabbing his hand. 'Come on, let's go outside and see what's happening.'

'There's no need. He will come here first as he said he'll update me on what he has found out.'

Ruby went to put the kettle on as Bob opened the door. 'He won't have time for a drink,' he called over his shoulder before opening the front door. 'Hello, son, isn't your constable coming in?'

'No, I've left him on watch in case Daniel comes down the road.'

'I take it you've found out more about him? Can you do something before he gets to Vera's house and takes her money?'

Ruby appeared holding Bob's truncheon he'd used when he was in the police force. 'The little she has, that is.'

'The thing is, the chap we all helped and who is now after Vera's money isn't her long-lost son; he passed away in hospital last week. The man who is purporting to be Daniel Carrington, or Gerald Munro as Vera prefers to call him, is, in fact, a professional criminal who had shared a cell with Daniel. After Daniel died in prison he pretended to be ill with a stomach disorder, and was taken to hospital where it was easier to escape when officers weren't so observant. He used what he'd learnt about Daniel to come to Erith and . . . well, you know the rest.'

'Then it is time we went and caught the blighter,' Ruby declared, leaving the house before Bob and Mike could stop her.

19

'We've got to head her off,' Mike said. 'She could ruin any chance we have of arresting Daniel, or whoever he is, and getting him back to prison.'

'Worse still, he could get away with Vera's money. All hell will let loose if she finds out Ruby was to blame,' Bob said, breaking out in a cold sweat as he pulled on his overcoat for the umpteenth time that evening.

'I've got an idea,' Mike said as he stood at the open front door and waved to the constable still seated in the unmarked car out the front of number thirteen.

'You wanted me, sir,' the fresh-faced constable said as he hurried up to where Bob had joined Mike on the doorstep.

'Ted, you're in the force's athletics team, I believe?'

'I am, sir. We recently won the inter-division relay race,' he said proudly, beaming from ear to ear.

'Then get your skates on and catch up with Mrs Jackson before she reaches number twenty-five. Tell her she is wanted for interfering with our investigations. Escort her down the alley and into her house by the back door. Once she is inside you are to join us out here where we are hoping to apprehend the man. Do you understand?'

'Yes, sir,' the constable said before racing up Alexandra Road and taking Ruby by the arm to lead her down the side alley between the terraced houses.

'There was a time I could run like that,' Bob said as they both watched the young man.

'Me too,' Mike grinned, 'but why exert ourselves when there are younger men in the force who can do the job – and faster? Now, we need to tuck ourselves out of the way and wait to catch the man pretending to be Daniel. I reckon we can hide behind that large bush two doors up from Vera's house.'

'What do we do once we've caught him?' Bob asked, thinking how he wasn't as fit as he used to be. 'I doubt I can help you walk him back to the station. Ruby will have something to say about that,' he added, rubbing his chin thoughtfully.

'We don't have to. There's a police van up on Britannia Bridge waiting to hear my whistle. They will soon have him carted off. Come on, let's get cracking before he finds us nattering on your doorstep.'

'Sir, where do you want me?' a red-faced Constable Ted asked as he appeared at the front door.

'Stay in there and make sure Mrs Jackson doesn't compli-cate the arrest. Ask her to make you a cup of tea. That'll keep her out of trouble,' Mike grinned to Bob before they headed off to hide until Daniel appeared and they could make their arrest.

They waited patiently until they heard footsteps approaching.

'Excuse me,' Mike said, stepping out from behind the hedge as the man appeared. 'May I have a word?'

Daniel was startled and looked behind him to see if they were alone; they appeared to be so. 'Hello, old chap, I was popping in to see my mother before . . . well, you know I'm being, er, being collected tomorrow.'

If this had really been Vera Munro's long-lost son, then he would have been torn over arresting the man, but as it was, this man was simply an escaped prisoner called Jim Mayhew who was about to fleece a family friend. 'I'm afraid I'm going to have to ask you to accompany me to the police station, Mr Mayhew.'

'I-I have no idea what you mean and who is this person you mention?' he stammered. His sharp eyes were scanning around, looking for a place to run.

'Don't even think about it,' Mike said as he raised his police whistle to his lips and gave several high-pitched whistles. 'Be a good chap and stay where you are,' he added, reaching for his handcuffs.

Mayhew's eyes widened before he turned and ran back down the road with Mike in hot pursuit. Bob, who had been watching from between the branches, started to follow, but knew it was fruitless as he'd not catch them up. With the sound of running footsteps behind him he stepped back against the wall as three officers rushed past him. 'Hello, Syd,' he called out to one of the officers. 'See you down the Prince of Wales on Friday night.'

Syd raised his thumb in agreement but kept running.

Bob was about to follow them at a sedate pace when James came out and joined him. 'I've been watching from our bedroom window. Do you think they will catch him?' he asked.

'Let's hope so. He deserves to be back behind bars . . .'

He stopped speaking as a cry pierced the air from close to number thirteen. He heard Ruby bellow out loud.

'That'll teach you . . . you swine!'

James and Bob looked at each other and hurried down the road to find Mayhew out cold on the pavement with Ruby holding Bob's old truncheon over her shoulder, looking red-faced and angry.

Mike pulled a handkerchief from his pocket to wipe his hot face while Constable Ted gently took the truncheon from Ruby before leading her into the house, as the other officers dragged a befuddled Jim Mayhew into the police van that had just arrived from where it was tucked away by Britannia Bridge.

'Perhaps we should let Vera know what's been happening out here? She must have heard the commotion,' James said.

'I know just the person to tell her,' Bob said as he called out to Ruby to join them. Ruby was the one who'd first agreed to help Vera when she decided last year to search for her son, so it was only right that Ruby tied up the loose ends. Perhaps she could also advise Vera on a better place to keep her money safe.

'I'll accompany Ruby back to Vera's. She's bound to be distraught when she knows her son is dead,' James said. 'I have no idea how she will cope with this news.'

*

The next morning, Claudette walked into the kitchen and collapsed into a vacant seat at the table.

'You look as though you've lost a shilling and found a tanner,' Maisie said, noticing her daughter's glum face.

'Mum, if we don't do something, there's not going to be a pantomime this Christmas. Think how disappointed the people who purchased tickets are going to be, and I can't even start to think about the children who are looking forward to the show. We'd planned a special one for the children's home and the old folk and now we will let them all down. The worst thing is we can't afford to give everyone their money back as the group have invested in staging and costumes.' Her voice cracked with emotion as she whispered, 'I don't know what we can do.'

Maisie was thoughtful as she put boiled eggs and toasted soldiers in front of Claudette. 'Don't worry about the money, your dad and I will cover that side of things. Eat up your breakfast and let's put our thinking caps on. If we can come up with some ideas, you can go to the other performers and see what they think. In fact, why not invite them all here next Sunday afternoon for tea? You can use my workroom for your meeting, and I'll help out where I can.'

Claudette looked up at Maisie with tears in her eyes. 'Thank you, Mum, you are one in a million.'

Maisie flung her arms around Claudette and hugged her tight. 'I don't know about that, but I do know I'd move heaven and earth for my children. Now eat up your breakfast before it gets cold.'

A small laugh bubbled from Claudette's throat. 'I know I will always be one of your children, but boiled eggs and soldiers?'

Maisie ruffled her hair. 'You will always be a baby to me, and I will continue to make toasted soldiers and eggs, so eat up. I'm going into Woolies today to see Betty as they have problems as well. You never know, you may be able to help each other.'

'I swear you've got something up your sleeve,' Claudette grinned as she tapped the shell of her egg with a teaspoon.

'Let's just say a few ideas are starting to bubble. What are you working on today?'

'I was going to finish off Cinderella's ballgown and work on some sketches for the spring collection. Now I don't need to finish the ballgown, was there something else you wanted me to do?'

Maisie gave her a stern look. 'First you finish Cinders' ballgown or she won't be able to go to the ball, and the panto won't go ahead without the correct outfits. Don't give up that easily. Please promise me you won't, or I'll be forced to finish the gown myself and you know I'll add too many pink bows and frills.'

Claudette raised her hands in mock horror. 'No, please not that!' she shrieked. 'I'll get on with the job once I've finished my breakfast. Don't forget to tell Betty I'll help where I can although I have a million or so sequins to add to the top layer of Bessie's ballroom dancing gown. There's only one week before the competition.'

'I can help you with that,' Mrs Ince said as she entered the kitchen to clear the table.

Maisie kissed the woman's cheek, declaring her to be a treasure, and left Claudette to her breakfast. If only all problems could be settled so easily, she thought as she picked up her handbag and let herself out the front door. As she walked down the short drive to the pavement, she spotted Mrs Bennett at her window and gave her a smile and a small wave. The woman turned away, looking as though she had a nasty smell under her nose. Her gut told her the woman was up to something and when she found out, there would be hell to pay. She just needed to find out what it was, and why she hated Maisie and her family so much.

Heading down Avenue Road and into the town, Maisie's thoughts turned to her beloved Woolworths. However successful she became as a businesswoman her first love would always be the Erith store with all its memories of meeting her friends and finding happiness. She was prepared to fight tooth and nail to keep the place open, but what if it were true that the town was to be bulldozed flat? She gripped the handles of her leather bag even tighter, aware that the next few weeks would tell what was to become of them all. She would find time today to see George Caselton and ask if he had heard anything from their member of parliament. Confident she could fit all that in, she walked even faster until she reached Woolies and marched through the double doors, pinning a smile to her face just as Betty had taught them to do.

'Maisie!' Freda called out from where she was training a new counter assistant. 'I'll be upstairs in fifteen minutes. Don't start without me.'

'We won't,' Maisie promised as she took the staff staircase up to Betty's office. As she was early, she thought she'd visit the staff room, say hello to Maureen.

'She's not here,' a sullen-faced woman said as Maisie enquired after Maureen.

This must be the woman who Maureen didn't like. Maisie had to admit her first impressions were not favourable. Why would anyone want to work in a staff canteen when they were as obviously grumpy as this woman? 'Not to worry. May I have a tea tray for four with biscuits, please? It's for Mrs Billington's office.'

'You'll have to pay. We can't have every Tom, Dick and Harry saying they are picking up tea for the management.'

'That's not a problem,' Maisie said, pulling out her purse from her handbag; she wasn't going to kick up a fuss over a few shillings. 'Can you arrange for someone to bring it through to the office when it's ready?'

If looks could kill, Maisie thought, she'd be six foot under. She was about to open her mouth to say not to bother when Dora spoke out from where she was elbow-deep in washing-up. 'I'll take it to Mrs Billington's office, Maisie.'

'Thank you, Dora,' Maisie said, blowing the girl a kiss, which seemed to infuriate Gloria even more. Maisie chose to ignore her and left the canteen, calling out hello to the people she knew. Betty's door was ajar as Maisie approached and, not seeing anyone with her, she walked straight in. 'Blimey, Betty, you look as though you've not slept in weeks,' she said as she removed her blue woollen coat trimmed in velvet and hung it alongside Betty's brown tweed jacket.

'It feels as though it's been months. When I finally drop off to sleep, I dream of watching a wrecking ball crash into the store front even though I'm screaming for them to stop. Douglas has bruises on his arms where I've been throwing my arms about and yelling at the council officers who are about to ruin the town for ever.'

'Oh, Betty,' Maisie said as she left her handbag on the seat opposite her friend and hurried round the desk to give her a big hug. 'We will do all we can to fight to keep the store open. But we need you to be fighting fit. Make an appointment to see your doctor and explain to him about your sleeping problem. He will be able to give you some tablets that will help; just don't take too many or you will sleep for ever,' she grinned as she went back to her seat and took out a leather-bound notebook and pen. 'I've been making notes just like you,' she said. 'Oh, and I've ordered tea and biscuits to help us think.'

Dora pushed open the door with her backside, carrying in a large tea tray laden with crockery and a steaming teapot. 'I found some of Mrs Caselton's cake hidden in the pantry,' she beamed. 'I'm sure she made it for you, Mrs Billington.'

'Bless you,' Maisie said, thanking the girl as she returned to the canteen.

'She's a nice girl,' Betty said as she unloaded the tray.

'Unlike the other one who acts as though she doesn't want to be here.'

'I know. Maureen isn't pleased with her, and I did promise to move her to another department, but with everything that's been going on it slipped my mind. I'll make a note right now to have her in the office and talk to her. Maureen doesn't deserve the miserable girl making her life hell, although I can't sack her when we have staff leaving now they think they will be out of work with the store possibly closing.' Her hands trembled as she wrote herself a reminder to speak to Gloria. With all her other worries she found some of her duties were slipping.

'I'm here,' Freda announced as she entered the room followed by Clemmie. 'Sarah told me to keep her updated on all our plans and she will do what she can from home.'

'Then apart from Maureen and Ruby we have a full compliment.'

'Speak for yourself,' Ruby said as she entered the room. 'It looks to me as though we are a cup short.'

Freda turned and hugged Ruby. 'How are you after last night's hoo-ha? I hope you had a good night's sleep. I was surprised to look out my window and see so many police in the road.'

'My goodness, whatever happened?' Betty asked, looking concerned, while Maisie frowned.

'What's been going on, and how come I don't know about this?'

'My Tony went over to find out what was going on and Bob gave him the bare bones. Who knew these things could happen in a quiet road in Erith?'

Ruby shrugged off their concerns. She sat in the seat she was offered and explained from beginning to end how the man who had fooled them into believing he was Vera's long-lost son was now safely back behind bars.

'My goodness,' Betty exclaimed as she took a cup of tea from Clemmie, who'd remained silent during Ruby's news, although her eyes had opened wide in surprise.

'Can we get started?' Freda asked. 'I don't want to get in trouble for not being on the shop floor.'

Betty laughed. 'I'm the manager and if I've summoned you to a meeting, then no one can complain.'

Freda grimaced. 'You try walking into the canteen and see the looks on certain faces. You would think I was the chosen one.'

'Freda's right,' Clemmie agreed. 'I've overheard a few comments about only having my job because I'm your daughter.'

Betty almost blew her top. 'Why, that's ridiculous as

everyone knows you attended college and learnt about bookkeeping and accounts work and are perfect for the job! Whoever is saying such things?'

Clemmie and Freda looked at each other, not wishing to cause trouble for any member of staff.

'There's no need to say another word,' Maisie said. 'It's that nasty girl who works in the canteen. I had a taste of her sharp tongue this morning. She rubbed me right up the wrong way and I don't work here. Honestly, Betty, if you don't sort her out before too long, she is going to undermine your authority.'

'I am due to have a word with her about her prospects. I'd best see her when we've finished here and not put it off any longer. Now, I see our first after-hours event is going to be a sewing lesson from Maisie and her girls along with tea and a slice of cake. How are ticket sales going?'

Maisie looked at her notes. 'We decided to make a festive apron with my business donating the fabric. We are bringing along six sewing machines that will be set up in the canteen, and me, Claudette and Bessie will help people sew their aprons together and we hope to have someone with us who will help the women embroider their name on their work. Currently we've sold twenty tickets through my shops.'

'We've sold another thirty-five here,' Freda beamed. I plan to man the haberdashery counter and Sarah said she will help me, but I will make her sit at the till to keep her off her feet. She really shouldn't be coming into work, but she won't listen . . . Oh, and I have nine volunteers to work on the counters so all the ticket holders will be able to do their Christmas shopping in between sewing. I also intend to try to learn how to sew,' she chuckled.

Ruby interjected. 'I'll be on duty helping Maureen. It will be good practice for when Maureen has her baking evening; I've heard tickets are selling well for that too.'

'My goodness,' Betty said, lost for words. 'I'll help you with the takings and paperwork,' she told Clemmie, who immediately disagreed.

'No, Mother, you will be busy talking to the mayor and Councillor Caselton who will be our guests. I also have you down to speak to members of the press.'

'The press?' Betty exclaimed.

'It's the *Erith Observer*, and they are sending along a photographer as well,' Clemmie beamed. 'We want to make it clear we are against any development that affects local traders. Hopefully by next week we will have more information about the proposed demolition.'

'We should have our member of parliament here as well,' Freda said.

'I'm popping in to see George at his surgery when I leave here. I'll ask him for an update,' Maisie added. 'There is something else . . . would you like some entertainment during the evening? We have the Erith Players who could sing songs from their pantomime now there isn't going to be one,' she said, updating her friends on what had happened.

'We would love them to come along and sing,' Betty said. 'I do wonder why they have lost the use of the theatre as there has been a pantomime performed there for as long as I can recall. It is such a shame as I know Claudette, as well as Sarah's Alan, have put so many hours into the rehearsals.'

'I'll let them know,' Maisie beamed. 'Now, as much as I'd love to sit here nattering, I must get a move on, or I'll be so far behind by the end of the day. Keep me posted on what's happening. Even if Woolies is doomed, we can at least give it a good send-off,' she added.

'I'll walk down with you,' Freda said as she took a final gulp of tea. 'Overseeing the seasonal counters is keeping me on my toes.'

As Maisie and Freda walked side by side downstairs Maisie gave a big sigh. 'It's this time of the year that I miss working here the most.'

'You can always come back and work a few days,' Freda joshed, knowing Maisie worked seven days a week building her own business. 'I may have a new assistant starting today, but she's part time and, to be honest, if we weren't so short staffed, I doubt we'd have taken her on. It's as if Betty has lowered her standards just to keep the store afloat. Even Sarah offered to come back to help out.'

Maisie was horrified. 'That would never do! Why, I was worried when she said she was coming to our special evening, and I told her that she was not to move all evening and I'd glue her to her seat to make sure she didn't. That baby is due just after Christmas.'

'She will do as she is told or she'll have Ruby and Alan to answer to,' Freda said as she stopped at the bottom of the stairs with her hand on the door handle. 'To be honest, it is Betty I'm worried about most. We need to take special care of her until all this ghastly business is over and done with.'

'We can do that and be here to support her. If I could have one wish for Christmas, it would be that the store was still open in 1954 and the worry of closure was all in the past.'

'As Ruby would say, I'll raise my cup to that,' Freda said, giving her friend a kiss on the cheek before they both got on with their day.

20

Betty carried the laden tea tray back to the staff canteen despite Clemmie insisting she could manage. 'I have someone I need to speak to,' she said. Clemmie went back to the cashier's office and got on with her work. She entered the canteen, and silence fell as she went to the counter and put down the tray. 'Gloria, I would like a word with you in my office now,' she said, noting how staff started to whisper. Gloria didn't seem to be at all popular and she had become the topic of conversation.

Betty returned to her desk and tidied away paperwork before prying eyes saw anything. From all she'd heard about Gloria, she didn't trust her not to notice something on her desk, and start telling tales to whoever would listen to her. She was poisonous, but Betty didn't understand why she was like this. If she didn't like working for the store, why did she not leave rather than cause so much misery? It followed her like a black cloud.

'You wanted to speak to me?' she asked, walking straight into the office without knocking.

Betty sucked in her breath; she'd ignore the girl's rudeness for now and get straight down to business. 'Take a

238

seat, please,' she said, sitting down opposite her and opening a file labelled with Gloria's name. 'I thought we'd take a look at how you are getting on since starting work here,' she said, looking through the couple of pages of notes. She frowned, noticing there were no up-to-date references; she would have to chase those. It was remiss of her not to be on the ball, but she recalled that Sarah, her personnel manager, had been off work that day and Betty herself had employed the woman on a day when she was particularly rushed off her feet. There was a paragraph from Maureen on Gloria's progress, and it didn't make for good reading. Looking up from the file, she saw how the woman was slouched in her chair and had adopted an air of insolence. 'Are you not happy working here?'

Gloria looked her square in the eye. 'It'll do me for now,' she shrugged.

'I wonder how you see your future with F. W. Woolworths?'

'It's a job and, like I said, it will do me for now. Why are you asking? It's not as if you are putting me up for promotion to management, is it? You seem to have your favourites who get all the good jobs,' she laughed.

Betty smarted. 'I like to think I get along with all my staff and if they have problems, they can come to me. I award hard workers with promotion rather than promote my friends, as you seem to infer.' Inwardly she was telling herself not to let the girl rile her, but it was easier said than done as she was getting under her skin. 'Tell me, where in the store would you prefer to work?'

'On the counters, when I'm ready,' she added quickly,

knowing she'd told Betty before that she preferred a behind-the-scenes job. 'But not the vegetable one as that's too much like hard work and messy.'

Betty nodded her head thoughtfully. When she had discussed the girl with Maureen they had agreed they couldn't afford to sack her until more staff had been hired. She still had the problem of employees leaving, so couldn't be too hasty in dismissing this woman who, according to Ruby and Maureen, was associating with someone whose family were not as squeaky clean as they could be, and furthermore seemed not to want to do her best in her employment. 'The reports I've received about your work haven't given me any encouragement to move you from your current job.' Betty raised her hand to silence her as she started to object. 'However, I'm prepared to give you the benefit of the doubt and if you knuckle down and work harder for the next three months, I will reconsider moving you to work on one of the counters.'

'But this store won't be here in three months, going by the rumours . . .' she pouted at Betty.

'We don't listen to rumours here, and we definitely don't start them or discuss them with fellow employees – do you understand?'

Gloria stared back at her. 'I don't gossip, if that's what you mean. I do listen to facts, though.'

'Then I request you bring the facts you hear to me. Now, I suggest you get back to work.'

Gloria stood up to leave then stopped. 'Isn't there a vacancy in the warehouse? I'm not afraid of hard graft.'

Betty winced at her words. They weren't exactly ladylike and up to now she'd not seen evidence of her hard work.

However, it would give Maureen some relief from constantly having to watch her. 'There is, but other staff are covering the work until I advertise the position. However, I'm prepared to allow you to split your shifts between the canteen and the storeroom, if you don't shirk.'

'Fair enough,' Gloria said with a glint in her eye. 'Who will be my boss there?'

'Mrs Forsythe and you are to do as she says without question,' Betty said, silently apologizing to Freda for adding the overseeing of this girl to her workload.

'Very well,' she replied, heading towards the door. 'Is there anything else you want to speak to me about or can I get back? With Maureen off work, we are busy.'

'I'm sure you can cope,' Betty smiled sweetly. 'Get back to your work. I'll give you your new schedule by the end of the day. Oh, by the way, are you joining us on the coach trip to London?'

'I'd not miss it for the world,' Gloria said with a sly grin.

*

'Thank you for coming in to help me, love. There are never enough hours in the day to do the filing and keep my desk tidy,' George said as he kissed Maureen's cheek.

Maureen was standing hands on hips looking at the piles of paperwork. 'However did you cope when you had a full-time job working for Vickers?'

'I had an assistant and a secretary,' George said, looking shamefaced. 'It is only now I appreciate how hard they worked since I have to look after my own paperwork in my study.'

Maureen started to roll up her sleeves. 'I don't know much about office work, but if you tell me what to do, I can at least start to tidy things away. It is very good of the church to lend you this room for your constituency work, so you really ought to keep it tidier,' she scolded him.

George sighed. 'I know, its finding the time . . .'

'Perhaps we should find you a secretary, but for now I'll step in and help when I can. Let me start with this pile of papers,' she said, picking up various notes and letters that were about to topple off the desk. 'I'll tuck myself out of the way and keep as quiet as possible while you undertake your interviews. Do you think people will mind if I'm in here while they share personal details? Perhaps you could cough or make a noise as a signal, then I'll go outside?'

George laughed. 'I doubt we will need secret signals, but if we do, I will ask you to fetch some papers from my car.'

Maureen preferred her suggestion, especially considering that they'd walked to the church hall as it was close to their home. 'Let's play it by ear,' she said as she took the pile of papers to the side of the room, placing them on a side table before starting to go through them. 'I shall know a lot more about your work by the time I've been through this lot,' she said as Audrey, the vicar's wife, arrived with a tray holding tea and slices of seed cake. 'This is a treat,' Maureen said as she thanked the woman.

'There are three people waiting to see you,' Audrey said after asking after Maureen and the family. 'Shall I show the first one in?'

'Please do,' George said as he helped himself to sugar and stirred his tea.

Maureen placed a new notepad and a sharpened pencil

in front of him. 'I shall sit quietly and get on with my work,' she grinned at Audrey before returning to her filing.

Maureen slipped from the room to return the used crockery to Audrey. She found her working in the kitchen attached to the church hall.

'You didn't need to do that,' Audrey said as she wiped her hands on her apron and took the tray from Maureen. 'How are you getting on?' she asked as the door to the hall opened and an elderly couple entered, looking around to see where they should go to see Councillor Caselton. Audrey quickly took their names and showed them to a row of seats before returning to Maureen, who'd picked up a tea towel and was drying items left on the draining board. 'There was no need to do that, but thank you all the same,' she said as she checked the teapot. 'I can squeeze two cups out of this,' she said, nodding to chairs set around a scrubbed wooden table at the end of the large kitchen. 'Take the weight off your feet.'

Maureen thanked her. 'The cold isn't doing my gammy leg any good. It's my war wound,' she explained as Audrey gave an enquiring look. 'I was caught in a raid, but I'm lucky to be here so can't complain.'

'And you've been on your feet for hours. I think we can find you somewhere better to work and a little more private, if you don't mind me wandering about. This table isn't used much, and you can sit down while you work. It's handy for the kettle as well,' she grinned before looking serious. 'Of course, if your work isn't too private to be done in here while I'm popping in and out?'

'That would be wonderful,' Maureen said. 'It is such a

warm and cosy room and so much better than where I work at Woolworths. I'm on the go most of the time.'

'Ah, yes, George mentioned you work at Woolies. That must be so satisfying to be able to feed the workers and keep them happy. I have happy memories of being a counter assistant before I married my Cedric and became a vicar's wife. I had thought now my children have flown the nest I may have time for myself, but sadly life is just the same. I seem to do even more work for the parish now, not that I'm not happy to do so,' she said quickly. 'Keeping the diary for the hall and liaising with renters takes a lot of my time. Then come the special church festivals and I can be doing all kinds of things to support Cedric and the church.'

'It must be so fulfilling,' Maureen said as they heard the door to George's office open and him bid farewell to the constituent. 'Stay where you are, I'll show in the next couple.'

'Thank you, Maureen. There's a diary on the table where I add details of the people who see George, if you wouldn't mind updating it?'

'Will do,' Maureen said as she went out to the hall just as a woman entered. 'If you would like to take a seat, my husband will see you shortly.' She smiled politely, thinking she had seen the woman somewhere. Most likely it was at Woolworths as she often went down to the shop floor and stopped to talk to customers. 'May I take your name and address?' she asked, picking up the diary.

The woman looked down her nose at Maureen. 'I hope Mr Caselton won't be long as I am very busy. I am Mrs Bennett from Avenue Road. It is an ongoing problem with my neighbours.'

Maureen froze. That was where she remembered this woman. It was Maisie's troublesome neighbour . . .

'You look troubled,' Audrey said when Maureen returned to the kitchen. 'Can I help?'

'Oh, it's nothing, just some snooty woman wanting to see George.'

'I heard her. Mrs Bennett can be a little difficult at times; she likes the sound of her own voice. I tend to hide away from her when we attend the same club or committee,' she tittered. 'Is that bad of me, what with being a vicar's wife?'

'I don't blame you for one minute,' Maureen laughed. 'I think I'll stay here until she has finished speaking with George.'

'Then drink your tea and tell me about your job at Woolworths,' Audrey said as she pushed a plate of biscuits in front of her.

They chatted for a while about this and that until the sound of George's door opening brought them to a halt. 'I'll see her out,' Audrey said, to which Maureen responded with a thankful sigh.

'Ah, just the person I wanted to see,' Mrs Bennett said as Audrey joined her in the church hall. 'I'm not happy with this Councillor Caselton and have decided to stand for election against him. We can't have someone who visits unsavoury women representing the decent people of Erith. I want the vicar to back me . . .'

Audrey looked over her shoulder before speaking, hoping Maureen had not overheard. 'Now is not the time or the place,' she hissed, 'and my husband is not the person to be involved in your political endeavours.'

'I take it you are casting aspersions on my husband's good character?' Maureen said as she joined Audrey.

'And I and my daughters are not the scarlet women you are painting us to be,' Maisie said as she walked into the hall. 'I reckon you have too much time on your hands and are making up stories to ruin people's reputations. You need to find yourself a job. I could find you one, if you wish?'

Mrs Bennett's mouth opened and closed, with not one word making an appearance before her face turned deep puce. She pulled herself up to her full height and marched from the room. At the door she turned back. 'Don't think this is the last you will hear from me,' she sniffed before slamming the door closed behind her.

Maisie swore loudly before apologizing to Audrey.

'No need to apologize to me, my dear. That woman brings out the worst in all of us. Now, did you wish to see the councillor or is there something else we can help you with?'

'I would like to have a word with George if he can spare me a few minutes. However, I can always chat to Maureen, and she can relay my query if that's all right with you?' she said, looking between the two women.

Audrey checked the diary. 'There are three people who have booked appointments, but we may be able to squeeze you in before they arrive,' she said as her pen hovered over the page.

'I must remind George he has an urgent telephone call to make before he forgets; it is very important,' Maureen said, apologizing to Maisie.

'Then you come into the kitchen with me as I would

like your advice on having a dress made for the spring,' Audrey said, taking Maisie's arm and leading her away.

'And I must beg a favour from you,' Maisie replied as she reached into her handbag for the leaflets advertising the special events to be held in the Woolworths store leading up to Christmas.

Maureen entered George's office just as he slammed down the telephone receiver in frustration.

'Don't tell me, you weren't able to speak to our venerable member of parliament?' She sighed, looking at his haggard face; his hair needed a trim, and his tie was askew. 'You look tired, my love.'

'I could do without this extra hassle,' he said, running a hand through his hair. 'How can I get to speak to Norman when his secretary blocks my every move? It is almost as if she has her own agenda for me not speaking to her boss.'

Maureen was thoughtful as she went to his side to straighten his tie. 'Perhaps we ought to look at this from a different angle,' she said, reaching for the telephone. 'Is this the right number?' she asked, pointing to where George had scribbled a telephone number on the blotter in front of him.

'It is, but—'

Maureen put a finger to her lips to silence him as a ringing tone could be heard. 'Good afternoon, I wish to speak to Norman. It is very urgent, a matter of life and death you might say.'

George frowned. Whatever was she up to?

'I'm afraid I can't say, my dear, as it is a private family matter. I'm a relative with bad news.'

George sucked in his breath and tried to take the receiver from Maureen. She was going too far.

Maureen stepped away from the desk and turned her back on George. 'I don't think I recognize your voice; I take it you aren't family? Oh, you are Miss Bennett, his secretary,' she replied as a frown crossed her face. 'Not one of the Erith Bennetts, I suppose?'

George, who had leant over to tap Maureen on the back and get the receiver from her, froze. 'What?' he said out loud as Maureen flapped her hand at him to be quiet.

'Such a coincidence, I was only speaking to your aunt a little while ago . . . I so agree, it must be a terrible problem . . . I'd love to chat more, but I desperately need to speak to our Norman . . . Thank you, my dear . . .'

Maureen turned to wink at George. 'Mr Dodds? I have Councillor Caselton for you,' she said, passing the receiver to George and leaving the room.

21

'You look as though you lost a tanner and found a shilling,' Maisie said as Maureen joined her and Audrey around the kitchen table.

'You could say that,' Maureen said as she sat down and winced as a pain shot through her knee. 'Ouch, it catches me sometimes,' she explained, rubbing her injured leg as Audrey looked concerned.

'Come and sit by the boiler. It's much warmer there and they do say a bit of warmth helps old bones.'

Maureen ignored the comment about her age as it was said in a thoughtful way and moved closer to the boiler; it certainly helped. 'I managed to get our member of parliament on the telephone and have left George talking with him.'

'Well done,' Maisie cheered. 'He's been rather hard to get hold of and we are hoping he can explain more about the streets in the town that are due to be demolished. Everything seems to be so hush-hush,' she explained to Audrey. 'If I'd been you, I'd have hung about to hear what was said,' she grinned at Maureen.

'We will hear shortly, but I've discovered something that will delight your ears,' Maureen said, reaching for a pile of papers she'd brought with her from George's office. 'I've been going through this paperwork trying to put it in some kind of order. George makes notes about his meetings with residents and I came across these,' she said, holding them out to Maisie, who read the pages while Audrey looked over her shoulder.

'Why, the old . . .' Maisie muttered before again apologizing for her language.

'I'd have said stronger. That Mrs Bennett is always causing problems. She is such a bitter woman, but to say what she does about the goings-on in your house is going a bit too far. She seems to think she and her husband are the upper class of Erith.'

'And me and my crowd moving in next door to her hasn't gone down too well,' Maisie sighed. 'I can take care of myself, but it's my children I worry about. They shouldn't have to live next door to someone who is watching their every move.'

'And calling your home a house of ill repute,' Audrey said, pointing to a few lines written at the bottom of one of the pages. 'If I was you, I'd be banging on her front door and waving this in her face.'

Maureen and Maisie couldn't help giggling at the thought of the vicar's wife up in arms marching up the avenue to confront Mrs Bennett.

'However does your husband deal with her?'

'It seems he has also received the sharp end of her tongue. He's written something here,' Maureen said, oblivious to the thought she was sharing her husband's private notes. 'She accused him of visiting your house of ill repute as one of your customers . . .'

Maisie guffawed. 'In a way he is one of my customers as he asked me to run up that red frock for you as a surprise. Do you remember?'

'Bless him,' Maureen said. 'He knows how to treat a woman.'

The three women were deep in thought at the kindness of George until Maisie broke their silence. 'All this is no more than what we already knew, or thought may be the root of the woman's hatred of my family. I came here to speak to George about my Claudette's problem with there not being a home for the Christmas pantomime since the theatre cancelled their booking. I thought he may have a contact who had a hall where the show could be put on.'

'That's what I was about to explain,' Maureen sighed. 'When I spoke to Norman Dodds' secretary just now it turns out she is the niece of the Bennetts and is aware of her troublesome neighbours . . . I reckon she's been able to pull strings and have a word in certain ears to cause you as much distress as possible. She's bound to have seen the leaflets for the pantomime, and don't forget some of the cast have been rehearsing in your house.'

'And garden when it's been fine. Mrs B. shouted over the wall that Claudette and Alan were disturbing her peace when they were practising one of the big numbers. I wouldn't mind but it was a beautiful song, and both Claudette and Alan's performance was worthy of being in a West End show,' she sighed. 'I'm beginning to think we should never have moved into that house.'

Maureen leant over and patted Maisie's hand. 'Don't say that, love, you've worked hard to be able to live in such a lovely house.'

'An MP's secretary would be able to do a lot of damage without her boss even hearing about it. Perhaps something should be said to him?' Audrey suggested.

'Let's leave that to George, eh?' Maisie said, although she knew whose front door she'd be banging on within the next hour. After what her family had been through it would give her great delight to be able to put her neighbour in her place.

'It may not feel like it now, but you have made inroads into the problem. Let's have a hot drink and a slice of cake to celebrate,' Audrey said as she scooped up the paperwork and handed it to Maureen before going to the sink to fill up the large enamel kettle.

George walked into the kitchen rubbing his hands together. He went over to Maureen and enveloped her in his arms before giving her a sound kiss on the lips.

'You seem glad to see your wife,' Maisie grinned.

'She is a star,' he answered before helping himself to a slice of cake. 'I've had a very satisfying conversation with our venerable member of parliament who has managed to put my mind at peace on several matters.'

'And . . . ?' Maureen prompted him as he concentrated on eating his cake.

'It is good news for many people living in Erith, as well as businesses. The demolition is only in the Cross Street area, and not the High Street or Pier Road as we've been led to believe.'

'Why the hell have they kept us in the dark for so long?' Maureen exploded. 'People have been so worried.'

Maisie was nodding her head at Maureen's comments. 'Betty has been so worried and has had many sleepless nights over this. It will ease her stress,' she said, not mentioning that Betty was still unsure of Woolworths' head office plans for the store.

They all sat down to enjoy fresh tea, all the time keeping an ear open in case someone else arrived requesting Councillor Caselton's advice. Audrey was thoughtful as she watched the joy on George's face. 'Excuse me for one moment,' she said as she left the room, coming back ten minutes later with several theatre programmes. 'These hold the missing link,' she said, passing the programmes to Maisie.

'These are shows put on at the theatre last year. I went to see *Blithe Spirit* with my husband; it was a good performance, although not as good as when it was performed in the West End.' Maisie flicked through the pages, not sure what she was looking for until Audrey took one from her and opened the page that showed the history of the theatre, along with a list of trustees. She stabbed her finger at two names near the top of the page.

'Well, I'll be blowed,' Maisie exclaimed as she passed the programme to Maureen and George to read.

'Mr G. Bennett and Miss June Bennett,' Maureen read out loud. 'So that's who must have put a halt to the Erith Players using the theatre for their panto. Considering the group put on shows for their love of performing and raising money for charity, the Bennetts have a bloody nerve,' she fumed. 'Who the hell do they think they are? I've never seen such spiteful people in all my years on this earth.'

Audrey took a deep breath before speaking. 'What are you going to do about this, George? We can't have people running roughshod over the townspeople of Erith.'

Maureen passed him the notes she'd found in among his paperwork. 'These will help you prove what a trouble-maker Mrs Bennett has been and I'm sure Maisie can write a few words about the hell the woman has put her family through.'

George was thoughtful. 'She can deny all of this. In fact, Mrs Bennett could very well say she never came to see me.'

'I have proof she was here on quite a few occasions,' Audrey said as she reached for the large desk diary on the table. 'I also recorded why she wanted to see the councillor.' She pointed to her neat handwriting where she'd recorded the time of the appointment along with why she wished to speak with him.

Maisie gave a wry smile. 'That's all well and good, but Mrs B. could say you made this up.'

Audrey shook her head. 'No one would doubt the word of a vicar's wife.'

*

Maisie could hardly contain her excitement as she walked the short distance from Christ Church hall to her home. The weather was cold and crisp although the last of the fallen leaves were soggy on the ground. She looked along the tree-lined avenue and grass-covered verges. Where she lived now was a far cry from her childhood home in the East End of London. She thought herself truly lucky. Even though her family were facing a few problems they would face them together. First she would let Claudette know who had scuppered her drama group's plans to put on a pantomime and see if they could find a way ahead for Cinderella to still go to the ball. She must find time to have a chat with Bessie, who'd seemed so glum of late even though she had the ballroom competition approaching. There was something amiss with her eldest and Maisie knew she must find time to have a mother and daughter chat to get to the bottom of her woes. She also needed to place a telephone call to her husband, David, and Betty at Woolies and give them the news about the proposed demolition of the town. So many of her business-owning friends would be thrilled to hear the news. Perhaps she should throw a small party to celebrate? Deep in thought, she approached the short driveway to her house before spotting the curtains twitching in the window of the Bennetts' house. There was something she needed to do before she spoke to her family and friends.

Marching past her own home, she hurried up the pathway to the Bennetts' property and banged loudly on the black-painted door with an imposing door knocker in the shape of a lion's head. The sound echoed through the house, but no one answered. She tried again and still silence. Pushing the flap of the letter box, she shouted, 'I know you are in there, Mrs Bennett, as you were watching me from behind your lace curtains just a minute ago. I'm going to stand here and keep calling out even if every neighbour in the street comes out to hear what I have to say to you . . .'

She waited and listened until she heard footsteps approaching the door. Straightening the lapel of her warm woollen coat, she pulled herself up to her full height ready to face Mrs Bennett and give her a piece of her mind. The door slowly opened, and she found herself face to face with the woman who had made her life hell since she'd moved up the avenue – something she'd dreamt of for ages.

'Why are you making such a rumpus on my doorstep?' Mrs Bennett asked, looking down her long thin nose at Maisie before checking to see if anyone close by was watching.

'I'm not 'ere to answer your questions,' Maisie retorted, realizing her years of trying to talk nicely had slipped in her anger. That would please the old cow. 'I'm here to warn you to stop causing trouble for my family. I know what you've been up to and I'm telling you it has got to stop right now, or I'll take action. You wouldn't like your name in the local paper, would you?'

'I have no idea what you are talking about,' she sniffed.

Maisie wagged her finger at the woman. 'I'm not playing your games. Where I come from, we call a spade a spade and right now your spade is blooming grubby. I know your niece is conspiring with you and using her position working for a member of parliament . . .'

Mrs Bennett's face turned pale although she kept up the pretence. 'I still have no idea—'

'You can say what you want, but we both know you are a meddling old cow. Stop right now or I will take this further, and through the proper channels. I'll bid you good day,' she said, feeling her work there had been done – for now.

The door of her own house opened wide just as Maisie was rummaging for her door key and Bessie stood there wide-eyed. 'Mum, what the heck is going on? I could hear you bellowing from indoors,' she asked as she closed the door behind Maisie and helped her off with her coat. 'Dad's home, but I don't think he heard you as we turned up the wireless and started talking to disguise what was going on.'

Maisie kissed her cheek. 'Bless you, love, I was just putting her next door straight. Let's go into the kitchen and get warm; it's perishing cold out there.'

'Do you think we'll have snow for Christmas?' Bessie asked as she followed her mum. 'The kids will love it and we can build a snowman in the garden.'

'I don't mind a bit of snow for a few days, but more than that can give us problems getting to the factory and delivering orders to our shops. It could affect takings.'

'Gosh, I never thought of that. There's a lot to think about when you run a business, isn't there?'

'Nothing for you to worry about,' Maisie said, not wanting to have her children under pressure at such a young age. 'Thanks for keeping an eye on the little ones while I was out. I didn't like to ask Mrs Ince to do extra hours when she was off to visit her sister. What would we do without her, eh?'

The girls both agreed that Mrs Ince was a treasure. 'I couldn't do my job if she didn't look after Jenny,' Bessie said.

'You couldn't spare so much time for dancing lessons with Nella either,' Claudette added.

Maisie noticed how a cloud passed over Bessie's face. Something was most definitely on the girl's mind. 'I must go upstairs and make a call to Betty. Would you bring a drink up to me, Bessie? Once I've finished, I have a lot to tell you so perhaps we could have an early dinner with your dad and I can tell you all at the same time,' she said, giving them a broad smile before disappearing upstairs to her small office. Sinking into a leather armchair, she reached for the telephone on a side table and dialled the number she knew off by heart for the Erith branch of Woolworths.

'Store 397, Mrs Billington speaking, how may I help you?' Betty's clipped tone answered after three rings.

'Betty, it's Maisie. I have some news of the business closures in the town.'

Betty's voice faltered for a moment. 'Tell me the worst,' she begged.

'It's good news – at least it is good news for the business owners. The demolition is just for Cross Street and not the shops and businesses in Pier Road and the High Street. I've not told my David yet as I wanted to catch you before you lock up for the day. There is lots more to tell you. Perhaps we could meet for lunch tomorrow along with Freda and Clemmie so we can compare notes? Do you think Sarah will be able to join us?'

'I'll do my best to encourage her depending on how she is feeling. With less than a month to go she is under her doctor's orders to relax and not get excited. One of us can collect her so she doesn't have to walk. Thank you for letting me know,' Betty said before bidding Maisie goodbye.

*

Betty gazed out of the window of her first-floor office at the darkening sky before heading downstairs to inspect the shop floor and talk with her supervisors. As heavy-hearted as she felt, the sight of the counters festooned with Christmas decorations lifted her spirits and she could see it did the same for the plethora of customers making final purchases before the doors closed for the day. She stopped to inform Freda about Gloria being transferred part time to the stockroom, and to give her the news from Maisie. Freda was delighted and jumped up and down in glee, which made the younger staff giggle.

The seasonal Christmas counter sat under a canopy of silver tinsel and bright paper chains. Betty's favourite decorations were the colourful Chinese lanterns; she'd chosen a selection for her own home and looked forward to hanging them from the ceiling of her living room at the weekend. The counter was full of Christmas tree baubles, while Christmas cards and calendars were stacked high and selling fast. She smiled as she spotted counter staff wearing tinsel in their hair or pinned to their lapels; not exactly the strict uniform code she insisted her staff followed, but she was prepared to overlook it at this time of the year. Betty loved this season in the store but knew that, although they might have won one small battle, the Erith 397 branch still had to show the powers-that-be that the store was viable and should not be closed, or this could be the last year Woolworths ever celebrated Christmas in Erith.

22

Maisie was deep in thought after replacing the telephone receiver. She couldn't help thinking that although Betty had been pleased about the news she was still not as exuberant as Maisie would have expected.

'Knock, knock,' Bessie said as she entered the room with Maisie's drink. 'I made cocoa as a treat,' she added, placing it beside the telephone before sitting on a rug at her mum's feet. 'I couldn't help overhearing you talking to Betty as I came upstairs. Does this mean the town is safe and we won't lose Maisie's Modes, and Dad's business is safe?'

Maisie stretched her long legs, kicking off her shoes. 'It sounds like it, thanks to George and Maureen digging out the information, but even more importantly, we have got to the bottom of our unfriendly neighbour's behaviour,' she said, going on to explain to Bessie all that had happened during the afternoon.

Bessie looked downcast. 'It doesn't mean it's all over, though, does it?'

'If only life were that simple,' Maisie sighed, stroking her eldest daughter's hair. 'At least we know who is at the root of the nastiness and we can either avoid or confront the unpleasant people.'

Bessie grinned. 'You certainly did that. I'd hate to get on the wrong side of you!'

Maisie chuckled. 'You know your old mum very well. Now, I want to know what has been making you look so glum these past days. Are you having problems learning your dances for the competition?'

'The dancing is hard, but it is fun, and Nella is a very good teacher. I'm so glad she came to us for her wedding gown as I feel as though I've made a friend for life.'

'She's a lovely girl,' Maisie said, thinking back to the day she was fitted for her dress. 'So, what is the problem?'

'It's Jeremy. He is such a nice person and so generous with his comments when I get the steps wrong and I've done that quite a few times,' she said, giving a wry smile. 'I am getting better, though.'

Maisie, who had accompanied her daughter several times to her dancing classes, had to agree. 'You make the perfect couple. So why the long face?'

Bessie looked away, chewing her lip as she tried to find the right words. 'It's the other people who attend the dance sessions where Jeremy teaches. Some of the boys who attend have refused to have him teach them. They make such nasty comments as well and call after him outside the dance studios.'

'Oh dear, I did wonder if this would happen,' Maisie sighed. 'I've seen a few of the people who attend be rude to him. I told off one of the older girls for her spitefulness. You do know why this is happening?'

'I do as I had a word with Nanny Ruby, who told me about a good friend of hers from the old days . . .'

Maisie grimaced more about Bessie using the words 'old days' than the content of her comment. Time really was passing by at quite a pace; there were times she felt quite old. 'I really don't know what to say that can help other than it takes all sorts to make the world go round. From what I've seen of the lad he is pleasant enough, and on top of that you're a good judge of character, so concentrate on your dancing and don't let the other kids upset you too much.'

Bessie shrugged her shoulders. 'I'll try not to worry, but as for me being a good judge of character I'm not so sure you're right there. Look at the trouble I got into hanging about with Jenny's father . . .'

'But that's all over and done with now and we have the joy of Jenny in our lives. You may have made me a granny, but I couldn't be more thankful for that little girl. We should look to the future and not dwell on what happened in the past.'

'You are right,' Bessie said, getting to her feet. 'I'll say goodnight as I'm off for another rehearsal.'

'What about your dinner?'

'Mrs Ince made me a sandwich to take with me. If I'm hungry, I'll have something when I get back.'

'All right, but remember you need to keep your strength up – and don't forget to wrap up warm, it is really cold out there and the night air isn't good for your chest so wear a scarf,' she called after Bessie while thinking perhaps she was starting to act like an older woman. Next she'd be making the children wear liberty bodices. What Bessie had told her was worrying. Why was the dance studio allowing this to happen? Jeremy was a wonderful dancer with a bright future as a teacher, but he was a sensitive lad and didn't need a few louts and their hangers-on taunting him because he was different. It wasn't as if the police would step in if anything happened to him. She decided to drive down to the dance studio and offer to take Jeremy and Bessie home after their lesson; she could say she thought Bessie had forgotten her scarf and gloves. Bessie would scoff and see straight through her, but Maisie would sleep sounder knowing nothing had happened. Perhaps she could catch Nella and have a word about the situation. If Jeremy was being picked on, who was to say they wouldn't start on other students and that would be detrimental to her business.

*

Bessie hurried down Avenue Road towards the town centre. The clock on the wall of the Royal Arsenal Co-operative Society showed she had only ten minutes before her lesson started. Nella had been generous in not charging for the professional lessons as she was keen to have Erith Dance Studios win trophies to promote the business. It was approaching seven o'clock and most of the shops in the town had closed apart from the pubs and cinema. Turning left past the Prince of Wales pub, she could see Burton's the tailor's up ahead and breathed a sigh of relief. The dance studios had two floors above Burton's, and she could see lights shining from the tall windows. Jeremy had said he would wait for her at the corner as the side road that led down to the docks was dark and a little creepy in the evenings even though the High Street was brightly lit. She looked about but couldn't see him; perhaps he was fed up waiting out in the cold and had gone in ahead of her. But then she spotted a dark figure lighting a cigarette and hurried on towards him. 'I'm sorry I'm late . . .' she started to say until she realized it wasn't Jeremy. She apologized and tried to step around him as he reached out and grabbed her arm.

'Please, I'm trying to get past,' Bessie said as she pulled away from him, causing her to step into the road.

A car screeched to a halt, barely missing Bessie, who froze in shock.

'I'll see you later, darling,' the man said as he disappeared into the shadows.

'Bessie? Are you all right? I thought I'd hit you,' Nella said as she climbed from her vehicle. 'What was going on?'

Bessie took a deep breath and held on to the door of the car to steady herself. 'It was that man . . . h-he tried to grab me,' she stammered. 'I pulled away from him and didn't think there could be a car coming down the road. I hope I didn't startle you,' she added, thinking of the baby Nella was carrying.

Nella peered around her. 'I'm fine, but where has the man gone who grabbed you?'

Bessie shivered. 'I don't know and don't care. I just want to get out of this dark street and feel safe.'

'Cross over the road and I'll keep my headlamps on to light the way. Will you wait for me while I park the car? I confess to being a little jittery myself now.'

'Of course I will,' Bessie replied as she hurried over the road and stood under a lamp post in front of the stairs that led up to the studio from the small entrance corridor, vowing that in future she'd carry a torch and be more aware of her surroundings.

'Bessie!' Jeremy called as he ran down the road. 'I'm sorry to be late. I missed my bus. Have you been waiting long?'

'No, I've just arrived. Let's wait for Nella and we can go up together,' she said as Nella appeared carrying an armful of records. Jeremy relieved her of her burden, and they climbed the stairs together.

'Let's not say anything to your students. I'd hate to scare them away from attending,' Bessie whispered as they removed their coats.

'That's kind of you to say so, but I don't want anyone else being frightened like you were. I'll arrange for someone to stand outside in future. We have an extra session this evening so there will be quite a few people arriving in the next half hour. Now, if you are ready, let's get ourselves up to the top floor and work on your competition pieces. It might be a good idea to take your coat with you as it's rather chilly up there.'

'Perhaps we should start with a quickstep to warm us up,' Jeremy said as they headed up the stairs.

The dance studio on the top floor of the building was identical to the one below apart from the lack of a cafe bar in one corner. Instead, a coat rack and a gramophone player sat beside an armchair. The downstairs studio also had seats set around the walls that seemed to make the room smaller. Here dancers had full use of the floor apart from two pillars in the middle of it. Bessie walked over to one of the tall windows and stared down over the High Street. She could see Maisie's Modes as well as her father's funeral parlour while further up the High Street stood Alan Gilbert's electrical business. She felt proud that her family and close friends had made their mark on the town. To the left of the dance studios was the end of Pier Road and by craning her neck she could see Woolworths, which at this time of night was closed. But what was that? She strained her eyes against the dark night to where a pool of light outlined a couple close to the double front door into Woolworths. To begin with she thought they were a courting couple, but then what appeared to be the male of the pair cupped his hands to his eyes and was peering into the store. Bessie remembered from working there part time that a light was left on at the back of the shop that let off enough light to illuminate the rest of the shop floor. Was it enough for a burglar to see into the store? For she believed that was who this man was.

'Come here,' she called out to Jeremy. 'I think that couple are about to break into Woolworths. Look,' she pointed as he joined her.

'I'm not so sure; I think they are just canoodling,' he said, taking off his spectacles to polish them before putting them back on and looking through the window.

Bessie held back a laugh. 'No one would canoodle on the main steps leading into Woolies as they'd be interrupted by anyone walking past. That kind of thing is done in private.'

He shrugged his shoulders. 'I'd not know,' he said, looking away. 'Why don't we telephone the police to be on the safe side?'

Nella, who'd been standing behind them, agreed. 'I'll go downstairs and ring them right now.'

Jeremy went back to the gramophone to sort out the records for their dance practice while Bessie stood watching the couple. While the female of the pair stood on the bottom step keeping watch the male could just be seen putting his shoulder to one of the double doors. In exasperation he turned to the woman who reached into her bag and handed him something that turned out to be a brick. Who kept a brick on their person if it wasn't to do something illegal? Within seconds he'd smashed the door and Bessie could see him climbing into the shop. She had to stop them as it was too soon for the police to arrive even though the station was close by. She pushed up the sash window and leant out, bellowing as loud as she could and pointing towards the Woolworths store. 'Stop, thief, stop!'

The girl turned and ran up Pier Road while the man looked out through the broken door and ran in the opposite direction. As he approached the junction of the High Street and Pier Road, he looked up and spotted Bessie and Jeremy, who had just joined her. He stopped for a moment and raised a cheeky hand to her before cutting down an alley out of sight.

'He recognized us,' Jeremy gasped. 'This could have repercussions for us,' he almost whimpered.

She didn't tell him that this was the man hanging about outside the dance studio not fifteen minutes ago. The girl wasn't with him then; perhaps he had been waiting for her. But Bessie couldn't shake off the thought she should know her. She was about to scold him for being pathetic when she spotted a police car pulling up; it was Sergeant Mike Jackson and a constable. Bessie leant out of the window. 'The man has gone down the alleyway behind the Odeon cinema,' she shouted, ignoring Jeremy's pleas for her to come in and close the window. 'That's it, just down there,' she called after Mike.

'Oh, for heaven's sake,' Jeremy exclaimed. 'Let the police do their job.'

Bessie decided she couldn't stand there doing nothing and raced downstairs, with Jeremy following her trying to remind her she was there to practise their dances.

She ignored him and continued down the stairs, pushing past people who were there for the open dance lessons.

'Bessie, what's wrong?' a familiar voice asked as he grabbed her arm.

'Oh, Jake, please let go of me. I have to get out there and help the police. They are after a chap who was breaking into Woolworths. I spotted it from the upstairs window.'

'Then I'll come with you,' he said, releasing her arm and taking her hand, leading her through the crowd of dancers climbing the stairs.

Bessie felt awkward as she'd not spoken to Jake since they'd had their falling-out.

'I witnessed the attempted robbery and Nella called the police,' she said, not liking the silence between them as they hurried along the pavement towards the cinema. Jake looked back at her as she started to lag.

'Why, you're not wearing a coat and look at your feet,' he said in an annoyed voice. 'This freezing cold will be the death of you. Here, take my jacket,' he added, pulling the tweed jacket around her trembling shoulders. 'I'm not sure what we can do about your shoes,' he said as they both looked down at the white satin slippers that were now soaked in muck from the wet pavements.

'We can't do much about that now. Come on, let's catch

up with Sergeant Mike and I can tell him all I know about the break-in.'

They started to walk faster, despite her flimsy footwear. 'Didn't your boyfriend want to come with us? I thought he'd have wanted to protect you?' he said knowingly.

Bessie snorted with laughter. 'You've got the wrong end of the stick as usual,' she said, thinking back to when she caught him listening to Mrs Bennett's tall tales over the garden wall he'd been building. 'Jeremy isn't interested in me apart from my dancing skills, and they are debatable.' She looked down at her feet as they stopped to cross the road. 'He won't be impressed with my twinkle toes at the moment. Thank goodness I have another pair of shoes in my bag, that'll keep him happy.'

Jake frowned. 'If he cared about you, he wouldn't be bothered if your shoes were mucky.'

Bessie couldn't help but giggle. 'Believe me, he is not interested in me. We have what could be called a professional partnership. His world is dancing and nothing more.'

'Then the man's an idiot,' Jake said gruffly.

Bessie felt a tingle run up her spine. Was this Jake's way of apologizing to her? Did he really like her after all? She was about to ask him when there was a shout up ahead.

'Stay where you are, police!'

Bessie froze. 'That was Sergeant Mike Jackson's voice. Has he caught the burglar?'

'No, it looks as though the films are over and everyone is leaving the cinema. He is telling everyone to stand still,' Jake said, as light from the foyer spread out over the darkened street.

Bessie ran over to where Mike was standing scratching

his head. 'I know what he looks like,' she said, quickly explaining what had happened to her earlier.

'Do you think you would recognize him again?' Mike asked, looking to the hundreds of people who had just enjoyed watching *The Titfield Thunderbolt*.

'I'll do my best,' she said as she started to peer at the men as they passed her. It didn't help that the side emergency exit doors opened, and the crowd spilt out from the other side of the building as well as the main doors.

Jake joined her and stood watching as she looked from left to right. 'Were there any distinguishing marks and what was he wearing?'

'I only remember a dark jacket, the kind the workers on the docks wear. He had a pockmarked face with a small scar on his left cheek. I'd say he was in his mid-twenties . . . Oh, this is futile.'

'Keep looking.' He patted her shoulder before going over to give the information to Mike Jackson and his constable.

Gradually the crowd drifted away. Even those watching to see why the police were in attendance became bored and headed to the fish and chip shop across the road.

Bessie shivered even though she was wearing Jake's jacket. Pulling it up around her ears, she could smell shaving soap and a faint aroma of cigarettes. She closed her eyes for a moment and inhaled deeply.

'You must be cold,' he said as he re-joined her. 'Come on, I'll take you back to your dancing lesson. Not that much of the hour is left,' he said, looking up at the clock on the outside of the Royal Arsenal Co-op building. 'The police sergeant reckons the chap must have slipped away

270

in among the crowd coming out of the building. Pretty rotten luck, eh?'

'Yes, it was, but I'd know him if I ever saw him again,' she said with a shiver as they started to walk back towards the dance studio.

Jake slipped his arm around her shoulder, and she leant into him as they walked in silence until turning the corner with the studio coming into sight. 'Promise me you won't do anything daft if you do spot him,' he begged as she turned towards him and slipped the jacket from her shoulders.

'I promise,' she said as he leant into her to kiss her lips. Bessie closed her eyes and waited . . .

'Bessie, there you are! We've been worried sick,' Jeremy said as he hurried to her side, followed by Maisie and Nella.

'Not worried enough to follow her,' Jake muttered just loud enough for Jeremy to hear.

'I say, old chap, that was uncalled for.'

Bessie, sensing an argument was about to erupt, stepped in. 'Jake kindly accompanied me while I helped Sergeant Mike. I'd seen the man trying to break into Woolworths and followed when he ran away.'

Maisie pulled Bessie to her and hugged her tight. 'Thank goodness I decided to drive down to collect you. I had a feeling something was going to happen; call it a mother's instinct,' she said, looking towards Nella and thinking she would soon understand this. 'Why, you are freezing cold.'

'And your dancing shoes are ruined,' Jeremy added, glaring at Jake as if he were to blame.

'I'll be fine. Jake gave me his jacket to wear; I've only just returned it,' she said, noticing he had yet to put it back on. 'Don't get cold,' she smiled at him.

'I wonder, would you like to join me at the dance session? I can't guarantee I can dance as well as a semi-professional, but it may warm us up a little,' Jake asked, looking at Maisie for encouragement while avoiding Jeremy's glare.

Jeremy turned to Nella. 'Can't we continue our lesson?'

'I'm afraid not. In fact, I must get back inside as Tina and Tommy Wright will be waiting for me. They too are entering the dancing competition,' she explained to Maisie.

Maisie was surprised how dedicated the dancers were. 'Do you want to stay?' she asked Bessie. 'I can come back later to collect you, and drop anyone else off who would like a lift?'

'There's no need, Mrs Carlisle, I have my vehicle and can bring Bessie home safely. I won't let her come to harm.'

Maisie raised her eyebrows, noticing how Bessie's face shone. 'Well, if you are sure, but you must come in for a hot drink before you drive home.'

'I'll do that, thank you, Mrs Carlisle,' Jake replied as he led Bessie towards the steps up to the dance studio, closely followed by Jeremy.

'I'd best be on my way,' Maisie said as she gave Nella a hug. On the way home, she started to wonder what the future would hold for her daughter.

*

Bessie quickly changed into her dry shoes and pulled on a cardigan she'd left with her coat before joining Jake, who had found two seats where they could sit and watch the dancing. He'd also purchased hot coffee, which Bessie sipped gratefully, feeling the warmth seep through her body.

'Would you care to dance?' Jake asked after they'd

watched a demonstration by one of Nella's colleagues. 'I can't promise to be as good as Jeremy, but I'll enjoy dancing with you,' he said as he stood and held out a hand to her.

'I'd love to, and please don't feel you have to be a perfect dancer. It is enough to enjoy the experience,' she said, placing her hand in his as they walked to the middle of the room to join the other beginners.

They moved around the room slowly to the strains of the Percy Faith Orchestra playing a song from the film *Moulin Rouge*. Bessie couldn't have felt happier in Jake's arms. They stumbled several times over the steps, but quickly corrected themselves until the record came to an end and they stopped to clap the other couples who'd successfully followed the instructions.

'That was fun, thank you,' Bessie said as they returned to their seats. 'I love the waltz. You were very good.'

'I had the right partner,' he said nervously. 'Usually, I'm treading on my partner's toes all the time. You must be keen to dance with someone who knows what he is doing?'

'Don't put yourself down. I much prefer to dance with you than be shouted at all the time. I'm not very good at competition dancing. If it wasn't for letting people down, I'd give it up as it's not much fun any more.'

'That's a shame,' he said as Jeremy approached them. 'I have a feeling someone is going to invite you to dance.'

Bessie frowned. 'I . . .'

'Go ahead, I can wait for a quickstep. I'm a man of many talents,' he grinned before giving Jeremy a stony look.

'Bessie, we should practise,' Jeremy said, holding out his

273

hand. 'The situation isn't ideal, but we can show these beginners how a foxtrot should be done.' He waved his hand dramatically around him.

She looked between Jake and Jeremy and gave a shrug of her shoulders. 'I'm sorry, I promised this dance to Jake.'

Jeremy scowled and turned to walk away.

'Hang on a minute,' Jake said. 'I have someone who would love to dance with you.' He ushered Jeremy over to where a row of wallflowers sat at the side of the dance floor. 'Rosemary, Jeremy would love to dance with you,' he said, introducing the tall pale-looking girl. Returning to Bessie, he led her to the dance floor as the strands of a foxtrot started to play.

'What have you done? He will be livid.' Bessie tried not to laugh as he took her in hold.

'I wouldn't be so unkind just because I want you to myself,' he whispered into her hair. 'Rosemary is a very good dancer.'

Bessie turned her head to look at where Jeremy was steering Rosemary through the now crowded dance floor, a look of amazement on his face as the shy young woman followed his every move. 'She can really dance. You know, she could be a better partner for Jeremy than I am . . .'

'Would you be disappointed to give up your place dancing with him?'

'Not at all. I don't think I'm really cut out to dance in competitions. I rather enjoy social dancing.'

'In that case would you accompany me to a dance at the British Oil and Cake Mills next weekend? It's their staff Christmas bash; my brother works there and has tickets.'

Bessie had heard of the large factory down near the river

partway to Belvedere and their active social club. Her parents had been there for an event. 'I'd love to come with you,' she smiled, thinking how this Christmas could be very special indeed.

23

Maisie was early meeting her friends for lunch and decided to go into the Woolworths store to see Betty. As it was, she didn't have to enter the store as Betty was supervising the repair work to the double doors that had been damaged in the previous night's attempted burglary.

'It is amazing what damage a brick can do,' Maisie said as she watched the handyman adding putty around the newly inserted glass panel.

'It could have been much worse if the police hadn't been alerted so quickly. I can't thank Bessie enough, although I do have one fear,' Betty said, looking worried. 'What if the man knows it was her who alerted them?'

'That thought had crossed my mind too and that's why David and I have decided she is never to be left alone. It helps that she has a new boyfriend – at least he appears to be her boyfriend – and from the little I know of him he adores her.'

'A boyfriend? That is such good news! She deserves some happiness after that lad that led her astray. Ah, here's Clemmie. Let's head over to Mitchell's tea room and you can tell us all about it.'

Maisie would normally not allow anyone to say anything negative about her children, as any mother, but Betty was a good friend, they'd been through thick and thin together and that meant she could speak her mind and Maisie valued her opinion. 'I'm starving! I missed breakfast due to trying to get ahead of myself with paperwork.'

Clemmie stepped between the two older women and linked arms. 'And knowing the pair of you, you will chatter non-stop and forget to eat. I'll make it my mission to feed you both,' she chuckled. 'Besides, I have news to impart that you may or may not be happy about,' she continued as they said hello to a few customers they passed, making their way down the steps of the store and across the road to Erith's one department store. 'Don't look so excited, Mother. I am not about to make you a grandmother just yet . . . I have enough on my hands with my stepchildren and a home to look after; a baby would mean I could no longer work even part time in Woolworths. I'm young and there is plenty of time for babies. I enjoy my life too much for major changes like that.'

'Babies come along when you least expect them,' Maisie said. 'Like you I had two nippers I'd not given birth to before my own arrived.'

'It was different for you, though, as they were your brother's children even though Bessie and Claudette had different mothers,' Betty sympathized. 'It was such a sad time for all concerned.'

'The least said about my late brother, the better,' Maisie sniffed as they arrived outside Mitchell's tea room. 'Oh, look, here come Freda and Sarah.' She waved enthusiastically to her friends.

'We planned that well,' Sarah said as she kissed her friends and hugged them even though it had only been days since they last saw each other. She glanced across the road to where the handyman was clearing up after repairing the double doors. 'I'm all agog to hear about the break-in. Come on, let's get inside. This foggy weather is playing havoc with my chest.'

'You sound like an old lady,' Maisie laughed.

'Believe me, I feel like one,' Sarah said as she held her back. 'This baby is ready to arrive and my back aches from carrying him.'

'Oh, it's a boy, is it?' Freda giggled. 'Joking aside, wouldn't it be nice to know if they were boys or girls before they arrived,' she said, holding the door open for her friends.

'I don't know, I quite like the surprise when they arrive,' Betty said.

Freda wrinkled her nose. 'It would be nice to know so we could plan what colours to knit, and in my case, it would have distinguished which twin was which.'

'My twins soon made it clear who they were, and I didn't need different coloured outfits,' Maisie said as they entered the tea room where they were guided to a large table in a snug corner of the dining room. Their coats were taken by one waitress, while another presented them with menus. Once orders had been placed, including one for sherry for everyone, apart from Sarah who chose lemonade, Betty reached into her bag to pull out pages of notes. 'Shall I start? I took the liberty of making an agenda just so we don't forget what we must discuss.'

'Blimey, this is more like a boardroom meeting rather

than mates meeting for lunch,' Maisie said as she toasted them all with her sherry. 'Cheers to you all!'

The others raised their glasses before Betty cleared her throat. 'I had hoped Maureen would be joining us as she has news from George. As it is, she is busy making food for tomorrow night's special event. I take it everything is under control at your end, Maisie?'

'Everything is tickety-boo,' Maisie replied, thinking as she spoke that she should check in with Claudette and Bessie to see if everything was in fact tickety-boo.

'Thank goodness for that. I must say, I'm looking forward to having a sewing lesson. Douglas offered to treat me to a sewing machine as a Christmas present, but I'd not go as far as to say I'd be good enough a sewer to have my own machine.'

'I'll give you lessons and even lend you some patterns to make your own haute couture clothing,' Maisie enthused.

Clemmie's eyes lit up. 'Mum, that's got to be worth considering. I'd love to make my own clothes, and some for the children. Think of the savings.'

Betty nodded her head, wondering if Clemmie should be given a sewing machine for Christmas. 'Now, George made some notes after his telephone conversation with our member of parliament, Norman Dodds. I'll pass them round for you all to read, but what he has been told is that the homes and businesses in Pier Road and the High Street are not affected by the demolition of Cross Street.'

A sigh of relief rippled around the table.

'The idea is that those still living in the houses will be found homes and he says that no one will be indisposed.'

'Tell that to the old folk who have lived in those houses

since the last century,' Sarah said. 'Nan knows some of them and they are distraught at the thought of leaving their homes.'

'I was very happy when I lived in my little house there,' Betty sighed. 'I have such happy memories.'

'Me too from when I lodged with you,' Freda said. 'It seems an age ago now. But some of those terraced houses suffered dreadfully during the bombing and the sanitation is awful. In the long run it will be better all round when they have gone. Do we know what will be put there?'

'I've no idea but it will open up the vista over the river,' Betty said as she handed round George's notes. 'There is to be a public meeting in the new year so locals can ask questions of the housing department and Mr Dodds. I'm just relieved our store will remain standing.' She gave a sigh of relief.

It was Clemmie's turn to cough for attention, staring down at her lap. 'The building may remain standing, but it probably won't be a Woolworths store.'

Sarah frowned. 'Is this a passing comment or do you know something we don't?'

'At our last meeting I was asked to keep up a dialogue with Nathaniel at head office in the hope he will tell me what is happening with their plans for our store. Out of the mouths of babes and all that . . .'

'Even though I have the official response, our Clemmie kept to her assigned task,' Betty said, again delving into her bag for the letter she'd received from head office and passing it around the table for them to read just as their food arrived.

'I've rather gone off my food,' Sarah said as she poked

at the liver, bacon and onion with no enthusiasm. 'Why can't head office see what a good job you are doing down here? It is almost as if someone has a vendetta against us,' she sighed, piercing a piece of liver before putting it into her mouth with a grimace.

'You know, Sarah could have something there,' Maisie said with a glint in her eye. 'Do you suppose it could be my next-door neighbour up to her tricks?'

'Oh, come on,' Betty scoffed. 'I know your neighbour is an obnoxious woman, but how could she coerce Woolworths' head office into closing down the store just because you once worked there?'

They all agreed and continued eating in silence until Freda spoke. 'Clemmie, what was the outcome of your chats with Sir Clarence's son?'

'He reckoned his hands were tied.'

Freda pushed Clemmie to say more. 'Did he happen to say why?'

'No, and as much as I tried to wheedle the information out of him, he clammed up. I do feel he knows something and whatever it is, we must find out, even if it is that the store will close down as I feel someone is doing the dirty on us,' she said, pushing her plate away from her.

'Why not invite him to our special evening?' Sarah suggested. 'We could delegate you to take care of him and show him around . . .'

'Honestly, Sarah, I'm a married woman! Whatever would my husband think? Besides, he may even be there to give us support. I must admit, his head is easily turned, though – and I mean Nathaniel Collins and not my husband,' she grinned as Maisie's eyes lit up.

'Please do invite him,' Betty said. 'I'll make sure he is shown around by several different staff members, young and old. We will have his head turned so much it will start to spin. Now, who would like a pudding? I rather fancy jam roly-poly and custard; I've given up trying to control my expanding girth.'

As Betty called the waitress over and placed their order, also asking for a tray of tea, Maisie explained to the others how Bessie had spotted the break-in and helped Sergeant Mike try to catch the burglar.

'It can't be anyone who knows the store as they would be aware there's no money in the tills once we close at night. Sergeant Mike said there were two of them, but he had no idea where the other one went and, not having any idea what she looked like, they are none the wiser.'

'Crikey, you mean the other one was a woman?' Sarah said. 'Whatever next!'

Maisie nodded thoughtfully. 'Bessie thought she may have been the lookout as she was standing on the bottom step of the entrance to the store rather than helping the other one break in. She's kicking herself for not taking more notice of the woman, but once the glass shattered everything happened at once, then the girl ran away up Pier Road.'

Freda had been listening intently. 'It sounds like an opportunist burglary rather than a planned one; they were probably after some of our stock they could sell to make money. They call it a smash and grab.'

Maisie laughed. 'You've been watching too many crime films! If it was a smash and grab, they'd have broken one of the shop windows rather than the main entrance. You have so much stock displayed in the window it was a burglar's paradise.'

'You must admit it's rather strange,' Sarah said. 'I just hope it was a chance burglary and they won't be back as, if they are local, they may well recognize the person who witnessed the attempted break-in. Our Bessie could be in danger,' she added, feeling a shiver run down her spine.

*

Betty felt as though she could burst with pride as she gazed around the store. 'You've all pulled together and made such a wonderful effort, thank you! I've never seen the Erith branch of Woolworths look so beautiful. What time do the ticket holders arrive?' she asked Sarah, who had been forced to sit on a comfortable chair beside the till on the specially set up counter.

'About fifteen minutes. We have two people on the door to take tickets and another two staff directing them to the canteen to leave their coats and have drinks before Maisie's talk starts. I went to see what they'd done up there and it looks wonderful. Two thirds of the room's been set up with sewing machines on the tables and the other part is for refreshments. It's going to be wonderful,' she sighed. 'I hope Nathaniel Collins is going to turn up just to see how important the store is to the people of Erith and what we can do to promote Woolworths. I've told the girls on the door to let us know when he appears. Has the reporter and photographer from the *Erith Observer* arrived?'

Clemmie joined them and answered Sarah's question. 'They are upstairs eating mince pies. I'm going to escort them through what we are doing so they cover everything.

They've promised us some photographs to send to *The New Bond*, our staff magazine.'

'I wonder if we should invite them to our outing up to London the day after tomorrow? I do have a couple of spare tickets for the show,' Betty said. 'It would be good to have them on our side to cover everything we are doing up to Christmas.'

'That's a lovely idea,' Freda said as she turned towards the front doors. 'Stand by your beds, ladies. The troops have arrived. Before I forget, I've put Gloria on duty in the storeroom so we are on top of stocking up the counters if there is a rush. She's not that happy about it, but at least it keeps her dour expression out of view. That one would curdle the cream on Maureen's trifle.'

Sarah giggled. 'That's a terrible thing to say although you are right. Perhaps you could allow her up to the canteen for a break during the evening or she'll be even more miserable than usual? Oh, look, there's Dad and he has brought along a guest,' Sarah said, getting off her chair and taking Betty by the arm. 'Come along and meet his companion.'

Betty frowned. Whoever could it be?

George looked smart in his best suit as he stepped forward to first kiss his daughter before greeting Betty. 'Mrs Billington, I'd like you to meet our member of parliament, Mr Norman Dodds. Betty is the much-esteemed manager of this store,' he informed the MP before the three walked away with Betty explaining what would be happening that evening to help the women of Erith.

'Gosh, Nan's going to enjoy meeting Mr Dodds when he gets upstairs. I just hope she doesn't curtsey.'

Freda chuckled as she helped Sarah back onto her seat by the till. 'Hopefully Maureen has tipped her off otherwise Ruby may be overwhelmed, bless her. When I was upstairs just now, she was very much in charge of the teapot while Maureen served. She is as much a part of Woolies as the rest of us even though she's never been on the payroll.'

'That won't stop Nan. I just hope she doesn't tire herself as it is going to be a busy evening.'

'Maureen will take care of her and once you go upstairs you can do the same. No buts,' she said as Sarah started to object. 'I have someone who is going to take over here after one hour so you can relax in the canteen. I'll not have Alan after me if you are taken poorly. Besides, you want to enjoy the coach trip to London the day after tomorrow and you can't do that if you are tired.'

Sarah reluctantly agreed, leaving Freda to head to the stockroom to check on Gloria. Freda didn't mind for one moment helping in the stockroom, although the brown coats the staff wore were a little on the large side, she thought as she pulled one on and rolled up the sleeves. She'd have to take it home to make some adjustments. 'Where are you?' she called out, not being able to spot Gloria, although she could smell cigarettes and noticed smoke coming from a side door that led on to an alleyway behind the store.

'I was getting a breath of fresh air; it's too stuffy in here,' Gloria said as she appeared from behind some shelving.

'It wouldn't be so stuffy if you didn't smoke. You know you aren't allowed to smoke in the store,' Freda sniffed as she went to check the door was locked. 'As I thought, you'd not bolted the door properly. Honestly, isn't it bad enough we had an attempted burglary yesterday without you leaving doors unlocked so another ne'er-do-well can steal from this store?'

Gloria laughed in Freda's face and turned away. 'You're overreacting. It's just a bloody shop.'

Freda reached out and grabbed the girl's arm, pulling her round to face her. 'This is our livelihood and a place that the people of Erith love. It is more than just a shop,' she almost snarled. 'What's wrong with you?' she asked as the girl whimpered.

Gloria pulled away and held her arm close to her body as blood dripped to the floor from under her warehouse coat. 'It's nothing.'

'Surely I didn't do that to you?' Freda asked, looking concerned.

'I said it's nothing.'

Freda looked closer at the girl. 'You are rather pale. Here, let me check your arm. You've obviously hurt it and, as stubborn as you are, you need help. Sit down before you fall down,' she said, almost dragging her towards an old wooden chair that had seen better days. Freda pulled the girl's arm out of the warehouse coat and rolled back the sleeve of her blouse. It was caked in dried blood, and there was also fresh blood dripping slowly to the floor. She sucked in her breath at what she saw. 'How the hell did you do this?' she asked as Gloria slumped into a dead faint.

Freda took a clean handkerchief from her pocket and reached over to the small sink nearby, running cold water to drench the fabric while trying not to let go of Gloria in case she slid from the seat. She ran the wet handkerchief over the girl's face, begging her to wake up until she came to and pushed Freda's hand away.

'What happened . . . ? I feel awful.'

'You passed out. Put your head between your knees while I go and get the first aid tin from the manager's office. I won't be long.'

Gloria reached out to grab at Freda but failed. 'No . . . you mustn't tell anyone.'

'Everyone is too busy to ask me what I'm doing. I'll only be a couple of ticks. We can talk after I sort out this mess,' she said, looking to where drops of blood had dripped to the floor before hurrying from the room. On the shop floor the event was well under way with a group from Claudette's amateur dramatics group singing Christmas songs while ticket holders for Maisie's sewing demonstration were being directed upstairs to the staff canteen. Freda found it easy to weave among the groups of women until she reached Betty's office. Thankfully the door was unlocked, and she slipped inside and collected the ornate biscuit tin containing first aid items from the top drawer of a filing cabinet. Tucking it under her arm, she started back along the corridor to go downstairs when she heard her name being called out.

'Freda, have you got a moment?' Ruby was calling from the doorway of the canteen.

Freda froze. For some reason, and she did not know why, she was loathe to explain to anyone why Gloria was in the stockroom with a wound to her arm. Perhaps it was that she didn't want anything to happen to spoil this special event that they'd all worked hard to bring to fruition. On the other hand, she didn't want to lie to a single soul, let alone Ruby.

'Hello, Ruby, how are you getting on in there?' she asked, walking over to her and giving a grin.

'It's all going to plan, and the room looks a treat. It's so festive with the decorations and tablecloths up our end. Why not come in? Maisie's about to start her talk; I was looking out for latecomers.'

'I need to drop something downstairs but will be there soon,' she called, rushing off before Ruby asked about the tin under her arm.

Freda burst into the stockroom. 'I have the first aid tin, now let's sort you out . . .' She came face to face with Bessie, who was looking at Gloria with a puzzled expression.

'What's happening here?' she asked as Gloria slumped in her seat holding her injured arm.

'I went to get the first aid tin from Betty's office as Gloria has cut her arm,' Freda explained, busying herself removing bandages and checking they were the correct size. 'I've not had cause to practise my first aid since the war, so I hope I've not forgotten anything. I'd hate your arm to drop off,' she laughed, aware there was tension in the room, but not knowing why. 'Was there a reason you came to see me? Not that I don't like you visiting me.'

'Mum sent me to ask if we could have some reels of red thread upstairs for the demonstration as we are short of that colour?'

'Of course,' Freda said, going to a metal rack and pulling out a box of threads.

Bessie thanked her and left the room, giving a backward glance and a frown as Freda returned to the task of cleaning Gloria's wound and dressing it.

As Freda cleaned away the dried blood on the girl's arm

and added a gauze dressing to the two-inch wound, she was thoughtful. 'Tell me, did you and Bessie have words before I came into the room?'

Gloria looked secretive. 'No, she'd not long come in when you arrived. She asked me where you were, and I said you'd be back shortly. Why do you ask?'

Freda shrugged her shoulders before starting to roll a bandage around her arm. 'No reason, I just felt there was an atmosphere, that's all.'

'I didn't notice it, but then I'm not feeling well. Do you think I could go home and rest? I don't want to miss the outing.'

Freda pursed her lips; she didn't feel Gloria had her priorities right. But in fairness she didn't look well and, being young, a treat to visit London would be more important than working in the Woolworths stockroom. 'Of course you can go home and rest, but be here bright and early tomorrow as we have a lot of work to get through. First, sit here for a while until you don't feel so light-headed. There is one thing, if you don't mind me asking. How did you hurt your arm?'

A shadow crossed Gloria's face before she answered. 'You aren't to let this go any further . . . My father can be violent when he's had a drink and he pushed me as I tried to help him upstairs to his bed and I fell down.'

Freda was quiet for a moment. The injury she'd just dressed wasn't bruised or grazed; it was a clean cut rather like one would get from something sharp. However, Gloria's injury was her own business. 'I'll not say anything but promise you will let me check your wound tomorrow and, if it looks worse, you will visit your doctor or go to the cottage hospital to have it treated? Now, can you stay there while I go out to the shop floor and ask someone to take over your duties?'

Gloria nodded. As soon as Freda left the room, she hurried back to the outside door to finish what she had started earlier.

24

Freda was thrilled when Sergeant Mike Jackson's wife Gwyneth turned up to help her in the stockroom. 'I never seem to see you at work these days,' she said, giving the affable Welshwoman a hug. 'And considering we only live a few doors apart I've not seen you in ages.'

'It is because we are busy working mums. My own family are horrified that I work,' she laughed as she helped Freda unpack a case full of boxes of glittering Christmas tree baubles. 'They think my Mike must be earning very little not to be able to keep his wife and family in comfort,' she laughed.

Freda sighed. 'So many people look down on mothers who want to work, and it isn't always about bringing money into the home, although I must admit my contribution to the kitty is welcome. For me, it is about being Freda, rather than a wife or mother.'

'I'm thankful my Mike is so understanding, although I'm not sure he is keen when he is left to change nappies,' she smiled. 'Bless him, he does try.'

Freda straightened up from bending over the packing case as the door opened and Betty appeared, followed by an entourage of suited men. A smile flickered over Betty's face as she turned to the men.

'This is our stockroom, which is currently being managed by our shop floor supervisor, Mrs Freda Forsythe, who is ably assisted this evening by Mrs Gwyneth Jackson, who is another of our long-term reliable cashiers.'

Gwyneth said afterwards how she felt as though she should curtsey and that it had been a wink from her father-in-law, George, that had put her at ease.

Freda showed them the layout of the stockroom.

'What about the foodstuffs? Where are the broken biscuits?' a rotund man wearing a gold mayoral chain around his neck asked as he looked around him.

'Any perishable items go straight to the counters apart from boxed and tinned sweets.' Freda pointed to the top shelves of the racks.

Betty sucked in her breath as Mr Dodds spoke. 'I understand there was an attempted burglary recently?'

Freda noticed that a young man standing towards the back of the group looked alarmed and raised his hand to ask a question. If Betty noticed, she didn't say anything, instead shepherding the group out of the room. 'If you follow me, I will take you upstairs to where we have a demonstration on sewing skills along with a delightful array of refreshments.' As the men filed past, Betty turned to the two girls. 'You can lock up here and go upstairs if you'd like to watch the demonstration. I'm sure Maisie could do with your support.'

'What about Sarah? I was going to stand in for her so she could attend,' Gwyneth asked.

'I've found someone to take her place. It should be very

busy after the demonstrations with customers wishing to purchase haberdashery items.'

'We can both help on the counter. Just tell staff to call me if they require anything from the stockroom,' Freda said before Betty hurried to catch up with the VIP guests.

Gwyneth finished tidying away the packing case and turned to Freda. 'Let's get rid of these awful warehouse coats and tidy ourselves up before we head to the party. I do hope I can learn something as it would be nice to make more clothes for the children.'

'I agree with you, but when will we find time being wives and working women?' Freda laughed good-naturedly.

When they were ready, they headed upstairs, following the laughter and happy voices in the canteen. Freda spent a few minutes talking to colleagues and customers she recognized before Claudette came up to her looking officious with a clipboard in her hand.

'Aunty Freda, we have put you, Aunty Sarah, Clemmie and Aunty Gwyneth on table six along with two of our customers. We've put seats around the table and there are three sewing machines for you to share.'

A feeling of panic washed over Freda. 'Will someone show us how to use the sewing machines? The little I've done has resulted in mutilated fabric. I'm all fingers and thumbs, but keen to learn.'

'Don't worry, Aunty Freda, either me or Bessie will be sitting with you and the joy of this project is that you only have to sew in straight lines.'

'It's that hard?' Freda grimaced as Claudette laughed at her. 'Oh, and Claudette, there's no need to call me aunty; you are grown up now.'

Claudette gave Freda a hug. 'You will always be an aunty to me.'

'Even though we aren't related?'

'Yes, even though we are not related,' she grinned as she went to direct more keen dressmakers to their seats.

'Gosh, this is scary,' Freda said, joining the group on her table. Sarah was looking at the bundles of fabric neatly rolled and tied with red ribbon.

'There's a bundle for each of us and the machine's already threaded with red cotton. I must say, it looks as festive as the rest of the room.'

'At least the red thread won't show the blood when I stitch my fingers to the fabric,' Freda joshed.

'For goodness' sake, you act as if you've never made anything before! Why, your knitting and crochet is wonderful and so much better than mine,' Sarah scoffed as she wriggled in her seat to get comfortable on the wooden chair. 'Would someone mind fetching the cushion in my office?' she asked, looking at her friends.

'I'll go,' Clemmie said. 'I put it away in the filing cabinet in case someone pinched it while you were off work. Don't start without me.'

'Fat chance of that. Clemmie is the only one not frightened of these machines. If Betty isn't careful, Maisie will be pinching her to work at the factory where she makes the clothes for her shops,' Gwyneth chuckled.

The girls had just settled Sarah on her cushion when Betty clapped her hands for silence. 'Ladies . . . and gentleman,' she said, smiling at the one man who was sitting by his wife looking uncomfortable. 'Welcome to the first of our Woolworths special Christmas events. For anyone who doesn't know me, I am Betty Billington, the manageress of this store. I have worked for Woolworths for more years than I care to recall. Another long-serving member of staff here this evening is our wonderful canteen manageress, Maureen Jackson, who, along with our friend Ruby, is serving all our refreshments.'

Applause rippled through the room as Maureen and Ruby took a bow.

'How long have you worked here?' Ruby whispered to her daughter in-law.

'I've lost count. It must be twenty years, apart from when I did some war work on the railway for a short while. Shh, listen, Maisie's about to start her lesson.'

Betty looked around the room full of pride for what her friends and staff had organized. 'Now, it is time to introduce Maisie Carlisle. She is the owner of Maisie's Modes as well as an ex-employee of F. W. Woolworths, and she, along with her daughters, Bessie and Claudette, will be running this evening's sewing lesson. Thank you, Maisie,' she said, holding out her arm for Maisie and her girls to step forward. Amid loud cheers Maisie took to the floor while Betty left the room and joined Nathaniel Collins from head office, who was sitting in her office.

'We are here to have fun and to make a pretty apron each for Christmas. I'm not a strict teacher and I don't want anyone to be afraid of the sewing machines,' Maisie said, glancing towards the table where Freda was sitting. 'Members of my staff from Maisie's Modes will be seated at each table and if you don't understand something, please ask them.

'Now, my Bessie is going to tell you more about the project before you all start to create magic.'

Bessie gave a shy smile but spoke out clearly. 'In front of each of you there is a fabric bundle. If you untie the ribbon securing the bundle, you will find three different lengths of fabric. The largest piece is the main part of your apron; you will be shown how to gather it together. The long piece is the waistband that will be attached to the apron, so it ties around your waist. The final piece will be the pocket.' She waited while the audience viewed their pieces of fabric. 'The sewing machines are all threaded up so that is one less thing to think about this evening. In the basket on each table there is a selection of ric rac braid, lace and other decorations for you to personalize your aprons . . .' She stopped speaking as Claudette stepped forward.

'I just wanted to say that we have bundles on sale here at the front of the room. Some are for aprons like the ones you will be making this evening, while others are cut out ready to sew items of children's clothing, along with instructions. We at Maisie's Modes have donated all the fabric for this evening's event and any money raised from the sale of these bundles will go to the Hainault Maternity Hospital to help the less fortunate mothers in our community clothe their new-born babies.' She looked back to her sister to continue.

'Are we ready to sew?' Bessie called out.

'Yes!' came the reply from all present.

Bessie joined the table where Freda sat and gave them all a warm smile. She first asked everyone's names so those who weren't colleagues at Woolworths got to know each other. 'I'm going to put you in pairs at the three machines. Freda, would you sit with Clemmie and Gwyneth, and

Sarah, would you sit with Doris and Annie who are two of our customers? I will show you how to turn in the edges to the main part of the apron; this will be done on the sewing machine once we have pinned and tacked the three edges. After that we will use large tacking stitches across the top of the apron to create a gather; this will be done by hand so you can all use the sewing machines while others tack. Is that clear?'

Most of them nodded in agreement while Freda sat looking petrified. 'Don't worry, I'll help you,' Clemmie whispered. 'I did something like this when I had sewing lessons at school.'

Bessie sat at one of the sewing machines and after quickly pinning and hand tacking a sample apron, she showed them how to use the sewing machine. 'Turn the handle slowly and you can't go wrong,' she said confidently. 'I'm going to check on the other table and I'll be back shortly.'

'I have an idea,' Clemmie said once Bessie had gone. 'Why don't we set up a production line with some of us pinning and others tacking the edges? We can all personalize our own aprons afterwards.'

'That's a good idea. I nominate you to man our sewing machine,' Freda said, giving it a fearful look.

Sarah looked across the table and laughed. 'Don't let her fool you, Clemmie, our Freda can strip down a motorbike engine and put it back together again so handling a sewing machine shouldn't bother her at all.'

*

In her office Betty sat across from Nathaniel Collins waiting to hear what he had to say. She was hoping he was impressed by the way staff had pulled together for this evening's event but wasn't so sure going by the look on his face. 'Thank you for joining us at such short notice,' she said.

'I'm glad I did, considering what I've heard about the store being broken into. Can you tell me if this has been reported to head office?'

Betty's back stiffened. So this was his game. 'It will be in my weekly report. Nothing was stolen as the person didn't get any further than the main door to the store. Our regular handyman repaired the damage to the glazed door, and I paid him out of petty cash. Would you like to see his invoice?'

He raised his hand to stop her getting to her feet to go to the safe. 'That won't be necessary. I spoke to one of your staff, who informed me it would have been an opportunist trying his luck. They explained you get a lot of undesirable people hanging around the town at night from the docks and the public houses.'

Betty frowned. He seemed to be painting an untrue impression of the town. 'I can assure you that is not the case. This is a respectable town, and we have a very good police force on patrol. If you check our store records, you will find very little evidence of crime.'

'I'm sure I would, especially if you tend to pay for repairs through petty cash and don't file reports.'

For a moment Betty was lost for words. What was he up to? 'As I said, I have a report to file along with the police report. Nothing has been hidden from you. You can see from your visit this evening that this store is thriving. I'm at a loss to know why we are being told to increase our turnover or we close, when business is brisk and figures are good. Perhaps you could explain?'

Nathaniel Collins stood up, reaching for his overcoat and hat. 'A few women making merry will not sway me. Nothing has changed,' he said, walking from the room.

Betty couldn't move from her seat. Why, oh why was this happening? Perhaps she was to blame in some way. After all, she was getting on in age and there were so many young men running the stores these days. Times seemed to be changing. She would never forgive herself if she was to blame for her staff losing their jobs and the town losing its Woolworths store.

25

'Thank goodness it's time for a break,' Freda said as she accepted a cup of cocoa from Ruby before helping herself to a homemade mince pie. 'I can't eat enough of these,' she said, licking her lips, 'and no, I'm definitely not expecting again,' she added as Maureen raised her eyebrows. 'Can't a person fancy food without being pregnant?'

'Pregnant? Who is pregnant?' Bessie asked as she joined them at the serving counter. 'Have I missed something?'

'Shh, you haven't missed a thing. It's just these two pulling my leg. If you aren't careful, big ears will start her gossiping – not that she's here,' Freda said, remembering she'd sent her home.

Ruby looked around her. 'Where is the little madam? Shouldn't she have been working with you this evening?'

'I sent her home earlier. She had a nasty cut on her arm and looked quite faint.'

'Any excuse not to work,' Maureen tutted, turning to serve some of the guests.

'No, it was a very nasty cut. She wouldn't say much, but

intimated it was a family matter. I believe she comes from a violent home.'

Ruby was pensive as she thought back to the day she had followed the girl home. 'Do you think it was a knife wound?' she asked.

'Possibly. Either that or glass as it was a neat cut. Perhaps something was thrown at her. Either way, she was reluctant to show it to anyone but did let me clean and dress it.'

'She possibly was up to no good when she cut herself,' Bessie mused, thinking of the female figure she spotted running away from Woolworths the previous evening.

'What makes you say that?' Maureen asked.

Bessie shrugged her shoulders, not wanting to speak out of turn but feeling troubled all the same. She spotted Ruby watching her and felt as though she was reading her mind.

'Oh, well, it is no use standing here chatting, we'd best get on with the show,' Ruby said as she finished her tea, refusing another mince pie.

'Come along, ladies, back to your sewing machines,' Bessie said, clapping her hands together. 'We are so close to completing your projects and don't forget we have lots of bundles on the table left to sell for charity and downstairs in the store there are counters full of haberdashery items.'

'And you can shop at any of the counters downstairs. We have staff waiting to serve you,' Sarah announced from her table.

'Where is Mum?' Clemmie asked as she started to help Freda, who had broken the thread in the machine she'd just started to use.

'She went to her office to speak with Mr Collins, but that was before the tea break.'

Ruby collected a small tray and poured two cups of tea; she would sit and have a chat with Betty as she'd seen the worried look on the woman's face. It must be hard to run a busy store like this and know that the survival of so many people's jobs relied on her alone. Yes, she had her friends, and very good friends they were too, but sometimes only an older shoulder to cry on would do.

'Betty, love, I've brought you a hot drink,' she said, entering the half-opened door and placing the tray on the desk to give Betty time to collect herself. It was obvious to Ruby that the poor woman had been weeping.

'Are you going to tell me what has upset you?' she asked as she shut the door against any prying eyes.

Betty looked at her through red-rimmed eyes. 'Oh, Ruby, I've failed everyone. I think we've lost the store for good. I'm just too old to carry on; the store needs someone younger like Freda or Clemmie to take control. They will make excellent store manageresses.'

'Take a sip of your tea and tell me what has gone wrong,' insisted Ruby as she stood with her arms folded, not taking no for an answer. 'Who is this young chap and why has he the power to close this store and make you all unemployed?'

'I thought when he appeared he would see how much work we'd put into making the store as good as it could be, but he didn't seem to understand. As far as he was concerned the store would be closing in January.' She started to shake uncontrollably, so much so that Ruby hugged her until she had calmed down. 'Thank you,' she said after taking a deep breath. 'You won't . . .'

'If you are going to ask if I'll tell anyone I caught you sobbing your heart out, I promise I won't. It will be our

302

little secret. A good cry doesn't hurt anyone. In fact, it often sets us up to face our problems. Now, tell me more about this young man.'

Betty took a sip of tea to calm herself. 'I have no knowledge of him apart from him being the only son of Sir Clarence Collins. Nathanial has only just joined the company and when I visited him at head office with Clemmie to try to sort out this sorry business, he said he had no idea what his role in the company was to be.'

'It sounds very much like jobs for the boys and I'm not in favour of that,' Ruby sniffed.

'Neither am I, but it seems the son has his feet under the table. He was born just as lucky as his father. If only I'd not helped Clarence many years ago . . .'

'Tell me more,' Ruby asked, settling down to listen as Betty explained about her early years at the Ramsgate store not long after the end of the First World War and the spot of bother he'd found himself in that could have lost him his job and his reputation.

'I wish sometimes I didn't have such a good memory when the past comes back to haunt me.'

'It is good to have memories of the past; I'd not have it any other way,' Ruby said, thinking of her late husband and her family and friends who had passed on. 'Never forget the past, Betty.'

'I'll do my best,' Betty said, forcing a smile. 'What do you suggest I do?'

'I suggest you powder your nose, put on some fresh lipstick and go and mingle with your guests. From what I've seen the evening is a great success and the tills haven't stopped ringing. As for the rest, let's wait and see for a few days. The day after tomorrow we are off on our trip to London so we will enjoy ourselves. If I spot you looking miserable, I will have something to say. Even Betty Billington is allowed to be free from worry for the day.'

Betty blew her nose and reached for her handbag. 'You are right, as always. I can't thank you enough for your advice. I wish you were one of my staff as I'd sit you on my shoulder to guide me when I had doubts. I'm not sure we can beat this, but I'll give it a damn good try.'

'That's my girl,' Ruby said, patting her on the shoulder before leaving the room, only stopping to glance at the staff rota. Back in the canteen she nabbed Maureen and pulled her to one side. 'Dig out your best bib and tucker as we are on a mission tomorrow morning.'

'That sounds intriguing,' Maureen replied. 'Where are we off to?'

'London, but don't tell a soul.' Ruby winked. 'Do you have a pencil and paper I could borrow?'

Maureen reached into the pocket of her pinny generously given to them both by Maisie. 'Here you go,' she said, handing over the stub end of a pencil along with a dog-eared notebook.

Ruby perched herself on one of the stools by the counter and licked the blunt lead of the pencil before starting to write.

*

'Will I do?' Maureen asked as she gave a twirl while standing on the doorstep of number thirteen.

'You look a million dollars! What do you think of my outfit?' Ruby asked as she stepped out into the winter sunshine. 'The suit is years old from when Sarah and Alan

304

were married and the hat I picked up more recently from Maisie's second-hand department.'

'Purple suits you,' Maureen smiled. 'I wore mine when we were invited for tea at the House of Lords last summer; I was that worried about letting George down, so he treated me to a new outfit. I feel I need to get the wear out of it. I don't look overdressed, do I? Considering I have no idea where we are going,' she added, waiting for an answer – she never got one as Ruby walked to where George was standing by his car.

'Are you our chauffeur to the station?' she asked as he gave her a kiss.

'Step this way, ladies,' he laughed, opening the car doors and helping them both in.

'I told him we are going shopping up town,' Maureen whispered as she sorted herself out after shuffling along the seat beside Ruby.

'I said as much to Bob,' Ruby replied, waving to him as the car pulled away.

'When are you going to tell me where we are off to?'

'Once the train has pulled out of the station and we are on the way to London, and you can't turn back.'

'As long as we aren't off to rob a bank as I can't run far in my best shoes,' Maureen said, wondering what her mother-in-law had dropped her into.

Ruby didn't say a word and looked ahead as George drove through the town and dropped them at the railway station. 'Two returns to Charing Cross,' she asked, waving away Maureen's offer to buy her own ticket.

'You got ten minutes,' the ticket seller told them, causing the pair to hurry over the bridge to the up line, where they stood trying to catch their breath before the train arrived.

A porter helped them into their carriage. 'Now will you tell me where we are going?' Maureen asked as she opened her handbag and took out two boiled sweets, passing one to Ruby.

'We are going to Woolworths.'

'Why would we go to London to do our shopping in Woolworths when we have a perfectly good branch in Erith? And we wouldn't need to get dressed up either,' she huffed.

'This is the Woolworths' head office in Bond Street. I intend to find out what is happening and why they have upset our Betty so much.'

Maureen frowned. 'Won't they sack us for poking our noses in?'

'They can't sack me as I don't work for them, and as you are always saying you plan to give up work before too long, they can't do anything to upset you. Besides, in our best clothes they won't recognize us. As the saying goes, clothes maketh the man, so they can damn well maketh us as well,' she said with a nod as she crunched on her sweet. 'We will make them sit up and notice us.'

Maureen wasn't so sure, but knowing Ruby, she would go into head office with all guns blazing. The trip would be interesting.

They spent the rest of the train journey discussing Maureen's upcoming cake decorating evening in the staff canteen. 'It won't be as spectacular as Maisie's sewing evening, but we've sold lots of tickets and intend to sell as much baking equipment as we possibly can. It'll help the sales figures and with the *Erith Observer* covering it we will be able to show the people at head office who are ready to shut us down that we intend to fight them to the death.'

'We will do our best,' Ruby agreed as the train pulled into Belvedere station and several people got into their carriage.

*

Ruby paid the taxi driver as Maureen looked up at the building. It was hard to think that the people in this building controlled the lives of her fellow colleagues at the Erith store. She knew the company started in America, but as that was somewhere she would never know she deleted it from her thoughts. Rubbing her hands together, she turned to Ruby. 'Right, let's get this show on the road.'

Ruby marched up to the reception desk and cleared her throat to get the attention of the man standing behind the desk. 'I'm here to see to Sir Clarence Collins, please,' she said in her best authoritative voice.

He started to run his finger down an appointment book.

'Why are you checking? Do you not believe me?' she huffed. 'Perhaps you could point the way to his office?' She turned to Maureen. 'Honestly, doesn't he know who I am?'

Maureen held back a laugh. How could he know who Ruby was when she'd not given her name?

Ruby started to walk towards the lift and the young man hurried after her. 'You will find him on the fourth floor,' he said, almost bowing as the two women stepped into the lift.

'What a twit,' Ruby murmured as she waved him goodbye.

They were soon on the fourth floor and, stepping from the lift, the pair found themselves in a carpeted reception area.

Ruby took a deep breath, hoping she could talk her way to Sir Clarence's office. Walking up to a desk, she found no one there. She looked about, spotting two doors off a short corridor. One was labelled with Sir Clarence's name. 'Keep your fingers crossed,' she said to Maureen as she headed towards the door, almost jumping out of her skin when it opened and out walked a red-cheeked portly gentleman with a full beard.

'Ah, who do we have here?' he asked, looking between the two women.

'We were told to come up to see you, that's if you are Sir Clarence? It is important,' Ruby said, thinking how much he looked like Father Christmas. She just hoped he would be as jovial and generous.

'Come along in,' he said, stepping back to allow them into his sumptuous office. 'Make yourselves comfortable,' he said, pulling two chairs closer to his oak partners' desk.

Both Maureen and Ruby sat clutching their handbags on their laps as he took a seat opposite. 'How can I help you both?'

Ruby had expected to be turned away and for a moment was at a loss to know what to say. She looked at Maureen for help while Sir Clarence gave a small cough. 'We've come to ask you not to close down the Erith store,' she said as the words tumbled out.

Maureen felt she should back up Ruby's plea. 'The store is taking more money than it did last year, and we have arranged events for customers. Last night it was a sewing evening and next week we are decorating cakes. Customers have purchased so many items that we ran out ... We know for a fact none of the stores local to us have done so well . . .' She stopped speaking as her heart thumped in her chest and she gasped for air.

Sir Clarence leant back in his chair observing Ruby and Maureen thoughtfully while rubbing his whiskered chin. 'I take it you two ladies work in the branch?'

'Oh, no, I'm retired although I pop in and help Maureen when they have special events running. Maureen is my daughter-in-law and her husband, my son, is a town councillor,' she said proudly, adding, 'He knows the MP Norman Dodds,' for good measure.

'Norman is a good chap; I know him and his staff very well. In fact, my son is walking out with one of his staff,' Sir Clarence nodded. 'But tell me, what makes you think we are going to close the Erith branch? Now there is no threat of that part of Erith being demolished I can't see why you should think as you do? In fact, this full report sent by your manager, Mrs Billington, just last week showed me how valued the store is. I said as much to my son when the report arrived, and he told me he planned to visit the store.' He opened a leather-bound diary and ran his finger down a full page. 'Yes, he was there yesterday; I have yet to hear from him. If you would excuse me for a moment, I will ask him to join us,' he said, leaving the office.

'None of this makes sense,' Ruby said. 'Look at the state Betty was in after his son had that meeting with her last night. The reason we've come today is to sort this out.'

Maureen did wonder if Ruby had poked her nose in too far, but she would stick by her nonetheless.

They both looked up as Sir Clarence returned with his son, Nathanial, in tow. Nathanial lurked at the back of the

309

room until Sir Clarence indicated he should sit down beside him as they both faced the women.

'Nathanial, perhaps you would inform these good ladies what you discovered when you visited the Erith store?'

Nathanial looked nervous. 'As you know, sir, I have yet to hand in my report. However, I was disturbed at what I found and, to make matters worse, there were local dignitaries and a member of parliament in attendance. I did my utmost to not let on that I was a member of the senior staff in head office in case anyone thought I was checking up on the event.'

Maureen was ruffled. 'Was one of these dignitaries the town councillor, Mr Caselton, by any chance?'

Sir Clarence looked between Ruby and Maureen as a small smile crossed his face.

Nathaniel's head bobbed up and down as he agreed, 'Yes, and he looked none too impressed either.'

Maureen did her best to hold back her temper. 'Councillor Caselton happens to be my husband.'

'And he is my son,' Ruby chipped in.

Nathaniel's Adam's apple bounced up and down as he gulped. 'The councillor is highly unlikely to discuss important business with the female members of his family,' he explained, giving them a benign smile.

'Don't you be so sure, my lad. You and your father may keep Lady Collins in the dark as to what you get up to, but in my family the women rule the roost. Isn't that right, Sir Clarence?'

It was Sir Clarence's turn to gulp. 'Are you very friendly with Betty Billington?' he asked Ruby as he looked worried.

'She's like a daughter to me and we have no secrets,'

Ruby said pointedly. 'Now, can we discuss your findings, please, as I have a feeling they differ from what's really been happening in the store?' she asked Nathanial before facing Sir Clarence. 'Sir, have you compared the turnover from last year with this year's? My granddaughter works in this area within the store and has said they are having a very good year . . .'

Sir Clarence picked up the telephone and dialled a short number. 'Miss Jones, please bring in the trading accounts for this year and last for Erith store 397. We would also like tea for three as well,' he said, smiling at Ruby and Betty. 'My son will not be staying as he has work to be getting on with.'

26

By the time Maureen reached home in the late afternoon she was bursting to give George her news. She almost stopped at a telephone box on Charing Cross station but as their train was due to go, she had to wait. Dare she tell Ruby what she thought, or keep it to herself? In the end she'd kept quiet in case Ruby spoke out of turn without realizing what she was saying. If what Maureen believed she had pieced together was true, it would be the answer to all their prayers.

When they reached Erith station Maureen rang George, who drove down to collect them. 'I don't see any shopping bags,' he said, looking puzzled.

'We had better things to do than shop,' his mum said from where she was sitting in the back of the car. 'I wanted to give that chap at Woolworths' head office a piece of my mind.'

George gave Maureen a strange look.

'Don't ask,' she mouthed and changed the subject to chat about the trip to London to see *The King and I* with the rest of the staff. 'We ought to have a whip round and buy something nice for Betty as she's treated all of us to tickets for the show; perhaps pay for her and Douglas's meal in the Corner House?'

'It doesn't seem a lot after all she's done,' George said as he pulled up in front of Ruby's house and got out to help her onto the pavement. 'We shall have to put our thinking caps on. Now, I'll see you at the front of the store tomorrow. Are you excited?'

'Oh, get away with you, George, I'm not a child. Although I must admit to looking forward to watching the show. Bob took me to see the film, but to see it performed live will be . . . well, yes, it will be exciting,' she grinned at him. 'I'll see you tomorrow. Goodbye, Maureen.' She bent down slightly to wave into the car. 'Don't forget to speak to Betty in the morning.'

'I won't,' Maureen called back.

'What was that all about?' George asked as soon as the car was moving out of Alexandra Road. 'I was under the impression you'd gone Christmas shopping and you've come back empty-handed, which is unusual.'

'We didn't go shopping. I had no idea what Ruby was up to until we were on the train. She took me to Woolworths' head office to speak with Sir Clarence Collins. I couldn't believe how she brazenly wheedled her way into his office. Your mother is dangerous when she has a bee in her bonnet,' Maureen laughed.

George groaned. 'My mother will be the death of me. Let's get home and you can tell me everything that happened. Have you eaten?'

'No, after what we heard, we couldn't face food and came straight home. I was all for going to Woolworths and

313

letting Betty know, but time was getting on so we decided she could be told in the morning.'

'That makes sense. Now, what shall we have for our tea while you tell me everything you've learnt today?'

Maureen roared with laughter. 'You and your stomach! I've got a steak and kidney pie in the pantry; we can have some mashed potato and cabbage with it. Perhaps you'd like to peel the spuds while I change out of my best clothes?'

George agreed and within the hour they were sitting down to eat, Maureen having told him everything that happened with their trip to Woolworths' head office.

George was thoughtful as he tucked into his meal. 'It seems to me young Nathaniel Collins isn't working to the rule book. You could say he has his own agenda.'

'He seems to like the young ladies from what Clemmie told us when she went to see him with Betty. Betty may as well not have been in the room.'

'It is one lady in particular I'm interested in. The Bennett family seem to have their fingers in a lot of pies.'

'I didn't take to her when we dropped off that letter for Norman Dodds. Do you honestly think June Bennett is behind the attempt to close the Erith store?' Maureen asked.

'My thoughts, for what they are worth, are that Miss Bennett has caused mischief on several levels. First, she has helped her aunt's mission to be rid of the Carlisle family simply because she sees them as inferior and thinks they should not be living in Avenue Road. I also believe she is behind the amateur dramatics group losing their venue for the Christmas pantomime.'

Maureen fumed. 'When you think of all the people who get such delight watching those shows, not forgetting the money that is raised for charity – why, I could scream with anger,' she said, stabbing the pie crust with her fork so forcefully segments flew across the table. 'How does the woman sleep at night?'

'Along with her aunt, their troublemaking could have caused ripples that affected many honest people's lives. The Carlisles can stand up for themselves, but along the way their businesses would have been affected by the gossip, as would my political career. After all, I was accused of visiting a brothel,' he chuckled.

'I don't think it's a laughing matter, George.'

'Thankfully no one would believe it.'

'Don't you be so sure. It won't be that long before you are considered for the town mayor position and mud sticks.

'Hmm, perhaps you are right,' he said before forking cabbage into his mouth.

'How do you feel Miss Bennett has been involved?' Maureen asked.

'Influencing Nathaniel Collins to cause problems at the Erith store. I believe he fell into the job after being demobbed, when his father found him a position thinking he was doing the right thing, but the lad was more intent on enjoying himself and not concentrating on the job. The old man's getting on and took his eye off what was going on. That's only my opinion, mind you, so don't go telling my mother . . .'

'I wouldn't dare, or she will be carting me back to head office so she can put another flea in their ear. Seriously, you need to do something. Poor Betty is beside herself with worry and I don't like what the Bennetts have done to my friends. You must ring Betty in the morning and discuss the subject of Collins Junior with her, perhaps ask her about the father as there is some kind of history there. He seemed alarmed when Ruby told him she knows Betty very well . . .'

'I'll ring her first thing before I make my other calls,' he promised.

*

'Why are we having to attend the dance studio this evening when we have a busy day tomorrow going to London?' Claudette sighed as she climbed into the back of Jake's van.

Bessie smiled at Jake as he started the van; she'd lost count of the number of times she'd explained this to her younger sister. 'It's because I feel bad about leaving Jeremy in the lurch. I want to be able to talk him into inviting Rosemary to be his partner for the competition. Giving her the ballroom gown I'd have worn will encourage her to say yes, and it will ease my conscience.'

'As long as I don't have to sew any more sequins on the dress,' she sulked. 'Are you staying to dance?'

'Yes, and so are you if you want a lift home,' Jake called over his shoulder. 'Your mum doesn't want either of you walking home on your own until that bloke is caught.'

Claudette gave a shiver. 'It doesn't bear thinking about.'

All three fell silent until Jake parked the van outside the dance studio and went to the back of the vehicle to help Claudette out, along with the large bag containing the gown. 'Shall I carry that?' he asked after passing a small case to Bessie.

'Please do as Claudette is bound to drag it on the ground,' she grinned at her sister, reminding her how she almost muddied the hem of Nella's bridal gown when they delivered it to her home.

'Please don't remind me. I still cringe to think what her mother would have said. With the wedding in just three days' time there'd have been no time to have it cleaned. Let's get this dress upstairs before any harm comes to it.'

At the top of the staircase that led to the first-floor dance studio Bessie stopped to ask if Nella was around.

She was given a strange look by one of the two girls who was to be Nella's bridesmaid. 'I take it you don't know?'

'Please don't say something has happened to her baby or that the wedding has been called off?'

'The wedding is still going ahead,' the girl said, reaching below the counter and pulling out an envelope with Bessie and Claudette's names written on the front.

Bessie quickly scanned the words and turned to Claudette for her to read the letter. 'I just knew it was getting too much for her,' she sighed.

'What's wrong?' Jake asked.

'The strain of her mother organizing the wedding got too much. They've run away to Gretna Green. Bless her, she says she intends to wear her gown and will have a party when they return in the new year just to get the wear out of the dress. I think that was a joke,' Bessie said sadly.

'Oh no, it's true,' the girl behind the counter said. 'We are planning the party for St Valentine's Day. We will all get to wear our finery.'

'Thank goodness it all worked out for the best. I do hope she has a photograph taken when she weds as I'd love to see her in her dress,' Claudette sighed.

'I'm sure she will,' Bessie smiled. 'Now, let's find Rosemary and Jeremy and hand over the frock.'

'Did I hear my name mentioned?' Jeremy said, entering the room behind them as they stood talking at the counter.

Bessie took a deep breath. 'Jeremy, I know I have disappointed you by deciding competition dancing isn't for me, but I truly believe Rosemary will be your perfect winning partner.'

'We have a dress for her,' Claudette announced, pulling the froth of lemon covered in sparkling sequins from the bag that Jake still held. 'I have my sewing kit with me if it needs altering . . .'

Rosemary walked over to join them, mesmerized by the dress that Bessie had shaken out so it could be seen in all its glory. 'Oh, it's wonderful,' she sighed, reaching out to touch the satin top.

'It's yours if you agree to dance with Jeremy in the competition. I can lend you my dance shoes,' Bessie said, knowing she would agree.

'I can help with pinning up your hair,' Claudette said, admiring Rosemary's thick lustrous dark curls.

'Would you really?'

'I think you have a dance partner,' Jake grinned at Jeremy.

'And so do you.' Bessie nudged Claudette as a lad approached them and asked her sister to join him in a foxtrot.

'Shall we?' Jake asked as Bessie melted into his arms.

Bessie peered over his shoulder to where shy Rosemary had come alive as Jeremy danced with her. 'They seem to be getting along very well,' Bessie said as she nodded for Jake to observe the couple. 'I was rather worried they wouldn't like us interfering, but it looks as though everything is going well,' she sighed happily.

The evening flew by with Claudette dancing with three different lads.

'I've never been so popular,' she declared when she joined Bessie in a refreshment break. 'I don't understand it, when I've longed for boys to dance with me for so long.'

'I know the answer,' Jake said as he joined them. 'You are more relaxed and acting natural and the lads like that. No one likes a pushy girl.'

Bessie frowned while Claudette looked sad and asked him what he meant.

'I'm sorry, I'm not trying to be rude or anything. It is just that because you were busy talking about the dress for Rosemary and chatting about the competition you weren't thinking about if a lad likes you enough to ask you to dance, whereas normally you would become nervous.'

'That sounds so simple, but I wonder, now that you've explained . . .'

Jake laughed and before Claudette could argue he took her glass of lemonade from her and passed it to Bessie and led her to the dance floor for a quickstep, stopping halfway round to talk to a mate. Before Claudette knew what had happened the lad had swept her away and all she could do was laugh and enjoy being led around the floor.

'That was a good thing you did,' Bessie said as she snuggled up to him when he returned to his seat.

'She only needed some confidence around the lads,' he smiled before kissing the tip of her nose. 'You wouldn't believe it, but I used to be the same. If a girl as much as looked at me, I'd run a mile.'

'Are you saying that now you chase the girls?'

'Not exactly. Besides, my chasing days have gone.'

Bessie chuckled. 'I'm glad to hear it. You're still free for tomorrow, aren't you? It will be a glorious day going up to London then seeing a show and I want to share it with you,' she said, tucking her arm through his.

'I wouldn't miss it for the world. Remind me, what time are we meeting?'

'Although Mum has booked a coach for her staff, we will be travelling on one of the two coaches booked by Betty, so be outside the store for two o'clock. I would have met you somewhere beforehand, but Claudette is working at the store in the morning, and I said I would meet her and help her get ready.'

'That's fine by me as I have something to do before I meet you.'

*

Maureen knocked on the door of George's study before entering. 'I'm going up, love, it's been a long day.'

George turned from where he was sitting at his desk and held out his hand to take hers. 'I'm nearly done. It's been a very successful evening. I managed to speak to Norman Dodds without being put off by his secretary, and even Sir Clarence was at home.'

'But Betty? Did you manage to speak to Betty?'

'I did and she was almost speechless. At first, she didn't believe me and thought I was pulling her leg. I told her I'm not in the habit of ringing married women in the evening to pull their legs,' he chuckled.

'She must have been over the moon,' Maureen beamed.

'I've never heard her happier. Now, I have one more person to ring and then I'll join you upstairs.'

Maureen let go of his hand. 'I may be a little late going to bed.'

George was confused. 'But you told me you were going up, that's why you came in just now?'

'That's before I knew I would have to bake a cake; in the morning there will just be time to ice *Congratulations Betty* across the top before I leave for work.'

27

There was excited chatter as staff arrived at work the next day. With it being half-day closing, many of them would be heading off on the trip to London straight from work. Betty had allowed the female staff to hang their clothes in the canteen, Maureen only laying on cold food for the morning break so the clothes would not pick up the smell of bacon and hot sausage rolls. George had helped her by carrying a large box that she seemed to be guarding with her life. On a table in the middle of the canteen she had laid out napkins and a knife with the box in the centre of the table. She had instructed Betty's friends to be in the canteen as soon as the bell rang for the first tea break of the day. As the time approached, there were a few other guests there too. George arrived first, quickly followed by Ruby and Bob, who were with Alan and Sarah Gilbert. The bell had just started to ring as Maisie and David dashed in.

'We haven't missed it, have we?' Maisie asked, quite red in the face from hurrying from over the road where David had told her he wanted a word.

'Freda, would you go and fetch Betty, please?' Maureen said as everyone started to pour into the canteen. 'Gloria and

Dora, I will leave you in charge of the teas and refreshments.' Dora started laying out cups and saucers whereas Gloria scowled and carried on pottering away in her own time.

Maureen just shook her head; nothing was going to spoil her day today. 'Here she comes. George, get ready with your speech.'

Betty walked into the canteen with Clemmie by her side. She looked confused to see so many people in there, including her friends. 'What's this? Have we started getting ready for the trip early?'

George stepped into the middle of the room and cleared his throat. 'Betty, I wanted to make an announcement in front of your staff and your friends who have been so helpful over these last weeks. Although I informed you last night that there would be no plans to close the store . . .' He had to stop speaking as a cheer rippled through the room. 'As I was saying, there are no plans to close the store. However, I have a letter here that came by special delivery this morning from Sir Clarence Collins that I am to hand to you personally with his profound apologies for the way you and your staff have suffered during this turbulent time.'

Betty stepped forward and took the envelope from George before giving him a hug and turning to speak to everyone in the room. 'I can't begin to thank you all for your loyalty and hard work at a time when we've had a dark cloud hanging over this store. Starting today we can look forward to a bright future where hopefully nothing will go wrong that can spoil our Christmas.'

Maureen uncovered the cake that she'd been up late baking and Betty cut the first slice. 'This is just like being a bride at her wedding,' she laughed.

David Carlisle slipped an arm around his wife's shoulder and whispered in her ear, 'We will have to commission Maureen to bake our Bessie's engagement cake.'

Maisie spun round to face him. 'Is that what Jake wanted to speak to you about?'

'Yes, it was all very formal. He told me of his intentions towards our daughter, and I asked him if he would be able to care for her and our granddaughter in the manner to which they are accustomed. I was worried about it being rushed as they've only been courting a few weeks, but you've only got to look at them to know they are as much in love as we are. However, I've insisted on a long engagement to be on the safe side.'

Maisie agreed with his decision before a sudden thought came to her. 'Oh, my gawd,' Maisie shrieked, 'I'm going to be a mother of the bride.'

'Don't inform the world, the poor lad hasn't proposed to Bessie yet.'

'When is he going to do it?'

'From all accounts while we are on the trip later today. I imagine he will pick a nice spot somewhere in London.'

'Oh no, she needs a nice frock to wear if she's going to be proposed to. I'd best dash home and bring back something prettier than what she planned to change into here.'

Maisie went over to where Betty was chatting with George. 'I've got to shoot home for a little while. I'll explain later,' she said, ready to hurry away.

'Not so fast,' George said. 'There's something I need to tell you. Come with me and Betty to the office. You too, Alan and Claudette.'

'What's this all about?' Alan asked as he followed them into Betty's office. 'I must get back to the shop.'

'And I'm expected downstairs on the Christmas counter,' Claudette said, looking a little worried. 'My tea break is over; this is a bit of a tight fit with us all in here together.'

'It won't take long. You will want to know what it is George has to say.' Betty smiled as she thought how today felt like a very special day for the store and her friends.

'I know we all feel like celebrating as our branch of Woolies isn't going to close. It was a misunderstanding at head office,' George said, remembering the disappointment in Sir Clarence's voice when he realized his son, coerced by his lady friend, a Miss June Bennett who worked for Erith's member of parliament, had been up to all kinds of tricks. He would find Nathaniel a commission in the army, pull a few strings with his old chums – that would keep the family name safe.

Alan was sympathetic but looked up at the clock on the wall of the office thinking of all the jobs he had to clear before he could get on the coach to London that afternoon. 'All very interesting, but what has it got to do with me?'

'June Bennett is behind the reason your amateur dramatics group lost out on the chance to perform at the riverside theatre this Christmas; her aunt is none other than Mrs Daphne Bennett who lives next door to you,' he said, turning to Claudette, whose mouth dropped open in shock. Thoughts ran through her mind as the jigsaw of events pieced itself together. She sat down suddenly as her legs started to shake.

'Do you mean to say all of this that's happened to the Woolworths branch and the cancellation of our pantomime is because I turned a hosepipe on Mrs Bennett?' she whispered. 'I do apologize,' she said, looking first at Betty and then Alan. 'I shouldn't have been so childish, but the woman has made life hell for my parents since we moved up the avenue. Sorry, Mum,' she sniffed.

George was shocked. Never for one moment did he think Maisie and David's children were to blame. 'No, Claudette, you are wrong. Mrs Bennett is just a vindictive woman who has ideas of grandeur. Your family simply became victims of her deluded mind. I'm not sure what can be done about her,' he consoled Claudette, although he had decided he would be asking his own solicitor to write a letter to the woman pointing out the errors of her ways, and how close she had come to him taking out a private prosecution over her name-calling and insinuations.

'She's just a nasty old woman and when I see her, I will give her a piece of my mind,' Maisie fumed.

Betty was thoughtful. 'I do wonder if she will keep her head down after this. Think of the embarrassment this is going to cause her.'

'I've had quite a few telephone conversations since Maureen returned from visiting Woolworths' head office, along with my mother,' he said, noticing Betty's raised eyebrows. 'I was able to prove to Norman Dodds how his secretary was involved in discrediting and upsetting some of the community that he represented. Miss Bennett will no longer be a problem as the last I heard she was seeking new employment away from Erith.'

'That soon . . . ?' Betty murmured.

Claudette brightened up. 'Does this mean our pantomime can go ahead?'

Alan shook his head. 'That boat has sailed, I'm afraid. I've heard a play is being put on in what would have been our slot.'

'So, Cinders won't go to the ball,' Claudette sighed.

'She will,' George was quick to say. 'I have found you another venue. It will be just the two performances, on Christmas Eve and the day before. The Prince of Wales pub has given us use of the hall for those two days. There is a lot to do in the days ahead, but with all hands to the pump the show will go on,' he smiled at the happy faces.

*

Maisie hurried up Pier Road; the good news that morning had put a spring in her step. She was so pleased for her daughter and just knew that Jake would make a good husband. They might have only been courting for a few weeks, but it was obvious to all that the pair were soulmates. She agreed with David's suggestion for a long engagement. David liked the lad, and he cared as much as she did for their daughter's future. She would leave well alone and just enjoy her daughter's happiness.

Approaching her front door, she stopped for a moment. Was that someone calling out? There it was again.

'Help me! Please, help me!'

She walked back out to the pavement. 'Hello,' she called, looking up and down the road. There it was again, a little feebler but just as desperate.

'Please, I've hurt myself . . .'

She walked a little way past her home to the Bennetts' drive and turned to see Mrs Bennett crumpled in a heap on her doorstep.

28

Maisie hurried up the drive to where Mrs Bennett lay
groaning on the doorstep. She was in two minds whether
to turn away and leave her there. Let her suffer for a few
hours as it would be nothing to the pain the woman had
caused her family since the summer. Then she felt ashamed
of her thoughts. What had the world come to if she could
not help a person in distress? She knelt beside the woman
and took her hand. It was freezing cold, what with the fog
that was curling around the trees and bushes in Avenue
Road, and the woman was only in a skirt and cotton blouse
with thin indoor slippers on her feet. How long had she
been there? 'Whatever have you done?' she asked kindly,
trying to put the woman's mind at rest that she wasn't there
to harangue her.

'I stepped out to my porch to look . . . to check if the
newspaper lad had left the *Erith Observer*, and slipped on
some wet leaves that had blown in. I've been here several
hours calling out, but no one came . . .'

Maisie did wonder how many people had ignored her
calls, not realizing the woman had hurt herself. 'Don't you
worry yourself as I'm here now. Where does it hurt?' she

asked, looking over her body and seeing one leg was at a strange angle.

'My leg hurts . . . and my shoulder . . .' she mumbled. 'That's why I couldn't pull myself up or wave to anyone.'

'Well, you are not to worry. I'm going to make you more comfortable and then I'll call for an ambulance.'

'Thank you,' she mumbled before closing her eyes and giving a deep sigh.

Maisie was worried. The elderly woman looked paler than she usually did, and her hands were so cold. She shrugged off her thick woollen coat and tucked it around Mrs Bennett. Her head looked uncomfortable on the tiled porch floor. Maisie pulled off the matching Cossack-style hat and placed it under the side of her head that was closest to the floor.

'That smells nice,' Mrs Bennett murmured as a smile flitted across her face.

'Only the best,' Maisie told her as she got to her feet to climb over the woman to get to the telephone she could see on a hall table; thankfully the door hadn't closed during the time Mrs Bennett lay there. 'That's my Chanel Number 5 you can smell. Now, I'll be just behind you while I telephone for help. Don't you move a hair,' she said as she attempted to place her feet without stepping on the woman.

Picking up the telephone receiver, she dialled 999 and asked for an ambulance before explaining how Mrs Bennett might have been in her uncomfortable position on the floor for several hours and that she felt cold to the touch and was extremely drowsy. With instructions to try to keep her awake Maisie replaced the receiver.

'They won't be long, Mrs Bennett,' she said as she sat

next to her neighbour. The tiled flooring in the porch that jutted out from the front of the house was certainly very cold. Maisie couldn't help thinking of Ruby who was always saying they would get piles if they sat on the cold ground. That's all I need, she thought. She leant closer as Mrs Bennett mumbled something. 'Sorry, love, I didn't catch that.'

'Call me Daphne,' she whispered.

'I'd be honoured to, my love,' she replied, patting her hand before starting to chat about her family and her business and how clever her older two girls were just to keep Daphne awake.

The ambulance took no time at all to get to the house and before Maisie could say Bob's yer uncle they were putting her neighbour into the ambulance to take her to the cottage hospital.

'Is there anyone I can let know about your accident? What about Mr Bennett?' she asked, leaning in close as Daphne's voice was quite hoarse.

'He is helping my niece move from her flat; her number is in the book by the telephone. I would be grateful if you would let him know.'

'I'll do that right away. Is there anything else?'

'Yes.' She reached out and clutched Maisie's arm. 'Thank you. I don't deserve your kindness. I'm sorry for any unpleasantness I have caused,' she added through watery eyes.

'Think nothing of it. I'll pop up and see you in the hospital tomorrow. Take care,' she said, kissing her cold cheek.

As she watched the ambulance drive away Maisie had

mixed feelings. Should she have been so nice to the woman who had caused hell for her family? There again she couldn't have lived with herself if she'd not done something and also put the injured woman's mind at ease. She planned to live in Avenue Road for many years and someone had to put a stop to the animosity; it might as well be her.

*

'Save the back seat for me,' Vera called out as the first of the coaches arrived outside the Woolworths store. 'Are you sure it is safe for you to drive in this weather, driver?' she went on as James and Sadie helped haul her up the steep steps into the coach. 'Come and sit with us, Ruby.' Ruby and Bob were standing by the open door on the pavement, but Bob chose to ignore her.

'Let's sit in the other coach with Sarah and Alan so we can help Sarah get in and out without struggling. We don't want the baby born on one of Margot's couches,' he laughed, hoping Ruby couldn't hear Vera calling out.

When they reached the second Woolworths coach Sarah and Alan were sitting with Maureen and George. The coach had left the outskirts of the town before George had updated Ruby and Bob on everything that had gone on since the night before.

'Fancy Maisie helping that awful woman after all she's done?' Bob said.

Ruby couldn't have been prouder if Maisie had been her own child. 'That's Maisie all over; she would help the devil if he was in distress.'

'Women are made of harder stuff than us men,' Bob said. 'Look at the way Vera bounced back after hearing her long-lost son had passed away.'

'Don't be surprised if she is holding it all inside ready to burst out sometime in the future,' Ruby admonished him.

In the Maisie's Modes coach Maisie was leaning back with her eyes closed, oblivious to the world while she caught thirty winks.

'Your mum looks shattered while you look amazing,' Jake said to Bessie as he held her hand.

'Thank you. I think Mum is amazing. Imagine if she hadn't gone to fetch me another dress after spotting a mark on the one I was going to wear. Why, she would never have found Mrs Bennett, and she could have died in this fog,' she said, staring out of the window. 'Is it my imagination or is it getting thicker?'

He peered past where she was sitting in the window seat looking worried. 'Yes, it is. I hope it doesn't mean we will miss the show.'

'The drivers wouldn't have set off if they thought that would happen,' she said, squeezing his hand.

The three coaches remained one behind the other all the way to London, where they were dropped off only half an hour late outside the Marble Arch branch of Lyon's Corner House with strict instructions to be outside again, on time, although the drivers weren't sure if the lights of the department stores would be seen through the fog.

'If push comes to shove, we will have to walk to the theatre and hope the fog thins by the time the show ends,' Bob said, rubbing his hands at the thought of the posh afternoon tea.

'I'm not sure I should be walking far,' Sarah whispered to Alan. 'I'd hate to go into labour and have the baby in a

London hospital rather than the Hainault Maternity Hospital. It would almost make our baby a foreigner.' She shuddered.

'Don't worry, love, I won't let that happen. I'll find you a ride even if it's on a costermonger's barrow.'

Sarah giggled; Alan could always make her laugh. 'And wouldn't that be a sight for sore eyes?'

Throughout their meal of fancy sandwiches, cakes, jelly and fruit, there were many eyes looking towards the windows of the Corner House with Bob keeping a running commentary on whether the fog was thicker or possibly clearing. In the end Ruby spoke.

'Stand up and swap seats with me,' she snapped. 'You are putting everyone on edge with your constant weather reports. I want to enjoy this meal. It's not often I get to eat in London in a Lyon's Corner House sitting underneath crystal chandeliers. This is more upmarket than Headley Mitchell's tea room.'

Bob did as he was told, getting sympathetic looks from the men in the family. No one liked to get the sharp edge of Ruby's tongue.

On a nearby table, Maisie was jittery. 'When do you think he will ask her?' she whispered to her husband.

David, who was enjoying an iced fondant fancy, shrugged his shoulders. 'He didn't say. In fact, perhaps he won't do it today. I'm sure when the time comes you will be told. You won't miss it.'

Maisie sighed and chewed on a corner of a sandwich, thinking she would not settle until she heard her daughter say, 'I will.'

There was a commotion at the main door of the Corner House as one of the coach drivers came in looking for

Betty. She waved to get his attention. Around her the Woolies staff held their breath.

'Miss, if you've finished your tea, we – that is, the other drivers as well as me – thought we should take you straight to the theatre. If this fog lifts, we could take you past the Christmas lights on your way home.'

'That's jolly good of you,' Douglas Billington said, reaching inside his jacket for his wallet. 'Here, take this to buy yourselves some warm food while we are in the theatre.'

'That's mighty kind of you, sir. Thank you very much. We will be waiting outside when you are ready.' He tapped the edge of his cap and went outside.

Betty sent Clemmie and her younger stepdaughter, Dorothy, to share the news with people seated at the other tables and soon everyone was pulling on their coats and hats and heading on to the next part of the day's trip.

Outside the theatre, Betty and Maisie distributed the seat tickets. 'I have two over,' she said, looking to where Freda was ticking names off a list.

'It is Gloria and her friend,' Freda said, looking around her. 'Come to think of it, I've not seen her all afternoon.'

'There were two spare seats on our coach and in the Corner House,' Maureen said. 'I did wonder who was missing.'

Freda was about to share her thoughts with Betty when there was a shout and a cheer from the steps leading up to the theatre. 'What's going on?' she asked, forgetting about checking names on her clipboard as she pushed through the crowd alongside her friends, all keen to see what the noise was about. Perhaps there was an actor from the show outside the theatre? 'Why is Maisie crying? Has something happened?' she asked one of her colleagues.

Vera, who was hanging on to Ruby's arm trying to stand on tiptoe to watch, turned to Freda. 'That young lad is down on one knee. He'll ruin his trousers.'

Freda could see Betty had a better view and shuffled between the people crowding on the pavement in front of the steps to the theatre. 'Will someone tell me what is happening?'

'Oh my,' Betty said with her hand against her heart as Jake could be seen on one knee proposing to Bessie. 'That is so romantic.'

29

As everyone gathered around Bessie and Jake to congrat-
ulate them, one of the front of house staff appeared and
spoke privately with the happy couple.

'Mum,' Bessie said to Maisie with sparkling eyes. 'The
theatre has offered us special seats. I can't believe it! I'm
so happy I could cry. You don't mind that Jake and I have
only known each other since he came to start on the garden
work, do you? I promise we won't rush into a wedding or
produce any more babies until we have a home of our own
and are settled.'

'Too true you won't,' Maisie said, doing her utmost to
appear strict. 'Besides, you have a part to play in Maisie's
Modes, so I can't lose you just yet.'

'You will never lose either of us,' Jake said, stepping
forward to hug Maisie. 'Thank you for trusting me to care
for your daughter.'

'I'm a blubbering mess,' Maisie said, reaching for her
handkerchief. 'Now, go off and enjoy the performance and
we will see you outside afterwards,' she sniffed.

Claudette enjoyed the musical even more than she
expected to. The costumes, the songs, the theatre in all

its Victorian glory of red velvet drapes and plush carpeting were out of this world, especially as she spotted Bessie and Jake sitting in one of the special boxes that looked out over the stage. She scribbled in her notebook, taking notes of colours and costume designs, intent on copying some of them for future performances of the Erith amateur dramatics group and, more importantly, for Maisie's Modes Bridal Wear. In the intermission her dad went to buy ice creams and came back with a glossy programme for Claudette to add to her collection of reference material. Maisie peered over her shoulder as she flicked through the programme and pointed to the photographs of the ornate gold-coloured cherubs and mouldings that adorned the theatre. 'I could do with some of that in my bridal wear shop,' she said. 'It would make the place look so posh.'

Along with every other woman in their party, Claudette sobbed her heart out at the sad finale and felt quite exhausted as they left the theatre, making their way back to the coaches parked in a side road, chuckling when their drivers kept calling out 'Woolies' to attract their attention as they clung together in the swirling fog.

'Are you sad we didn't get to see the bright lights of London?' Maisie asked as she put an arm around Claudette.

'We can come another time. The important thing is that Jake proposed to our Bessie.'

'And they lived happily ever after,' her dad said as he linked arms with the pair.

'No, Dad, that's just in pantomimes,' she replied seriously. 'Speaking of which, we have just a week to get the show on the road.'

'You just need to find a barn and you have your show,' David chuckled.

'Oh, for goodness' sake, Dad,' Claudette sighed light-heartedly. 'You are getting confused with American movies, although it would have been lovely to put on a show in a barn,' she chuckled, seeing his face drop before he realized she was joking.

The journey back to Erith was slow as the fog swept in and out the closer they got to the Thames. At one point the coaches crept along close to the kerbs with the men getting out to walk in front in case of danger. As they entered the town and the fog cleared a little Alan Gilbert gave out a cry. 'Look at our shops! Some bastard has smashed the windows!'

As the coaches slowed down the friends looked through the windows at the glass strewn across the pavements in front of the Gilberts' shop as well as David Carlisle and Douglas Billington's funeral business.

Maisie cried out in shock as she spotted Maisie's Modes had also been attacked.

'Is it every shop?' Bob called out.

Vera stood up to get a better look. 'No, the butcher's and Hedley Mitchell's have all their windows intact.'

The coaches stopped to allow the Gilberts and the Carlisles to alight and look at the damage before moving on to park in front of Woolworths in Pier Road.

'Oh no,' Betty groaned. 'We've been targeted as well,' she all but sobbed as she viewed the store front. 'Why would anyone do this?'

*

Even though he was off duty enjoying a night out in London with his family and friends Sergeant Mike Jackson was at once in charge. 'No one's to enter the properties in case you disturb someone, or interfere with evidence,' he said before going to a nearby police box to call for back-up from the police station. 'Maureen and Gwyneth, would you take the ladies back to Ruby's house while the men stay here to help me?'

'I'm staying here as my business is one of the ones that has been under attack from God knows who,' Maisie said, red-faced and angry. 'Jake, can you take the girls back home as Mrs Ince will be expecting us and she will want to go home to her bed?'

'I'll do that and drive her home then come back here. I have my tools in the van, and they may be needed to board up any broken windows. I can let my dad know. That's if you want wood and stuff?'

'Thanks, Jake,' David Carlisle said, thinking what a decent and reliable lad he was.

'I'll go back home with Nan and everyone else to help with the children. I'll see you later,' Sadie said, standing on tiptoes to kiss James on the cheek. 'Please don't do anything daft,' she said with fear in her eyes.

'I'm going to find Betty,' Freda said, worrying about what she would find.

'I thought I'd stay and watch,' Vera said before being led off protesting by Sadie and Ruby.

The men started peering through the windows of the shops to see if they could tell what damage had been done. 'There's just a mess in the funeral parlour and the florist next door, but no substantial damage.'

'It's worse in Maisie's Modes,' George said as he returned with Bob and a distraught Maisie after looking through the windows of her shop. 'The clothes in the window display have been destroyed by broken glass, and it looks as though with so many empty racks inside that your stock has been stolen.'

They walked along to Alan's shop to see him in deep conversation with James. 'Nothing stolen here,' Alan said, 'but they've taken an axe to all the stock in my shop . . .'

Freda and her husband, Tony, ran up the road to the Woolworths store, with Freda fearing the worst, to find all the lights on in the shop and the police arriving at the same time.

'Come in this way,' Betty called out, opening one of the main front doors as she spotted the couple.

'This has got to have been a gang as they have attacked Maisie's shop, Alan's place as well as Douglas and David's business.'

Betty shook her head in disbelief as they looked around the mess in the store. 'They entered through the side door in the stockroom. I can see stock has gone, but not as much as I'd have thought burglars would have taken. There seems to have been more damage than theft. The Christmas counter has been wrecked as well, which I felt was quite vicious.'

'Have you been upstairs?' Tony asked.

'No, I wanted to remain here in case I disturbed anyone. Do you think they are still in the building?' she said, looking fearful.

'I'll go up there as I know the layout of that floor,' Tony said to the police officer as he introduced himself as another Woolworths store manager.

Freda linked arms with Betty as they observed the damage. 'Someone has a mighty grievance against this store,' she said. 'Can I look at the damage done in the stockroom, as I was one of the last working in there this morning?'

'Don't touch anything, madam,' the police officer said.

Betty reached for two pairs of woollen gloves from a nearby counter. 'We will wear these,' she told him.

'I feel daft wearing mittens but if it makes it easier to look for fingerprints, then I can put up with it.'

'I wonder if it was the same person who tried to break in the other day?'

'If they dusted for fingerprints, they may be able to tell,' Freda said.

'I take it you learnt that from a Clive Danvers film?'

Freda grimaced as they made their way to the door that led into the stockroom. All those visits to the cinema had been worthwhile.

They looked around at the mess left by the intruders. 'They must have had a key . . .' Betty said thoughtfully as Freda walked closer to the door before going to where spare keys were left hanging on a wall close to the telephone.

'The spare is still here, and I have my one in my bag as I was coming in at seven o'clock for an early delivery in the morning.'

'Curiouser and curiouser,' Betty said as the telephone rang. 'Erith store,' she replied before falling quiet. 'We will be there shortly.' Turning to Freda, she said, 'Once the police have finished with their investigation we are to go to Ruby's house. She reckons she knows who did this.'

*

It was not far off midnight as Freda, Tony and Betty arrived at number thirteen.

'Come along in,' Ruby said as she ushered them into the front room where Bob was handing out cups of cocoa along with cheese sandwiches.

'Gosh, this is very good of you, Ruby,' Betty said as she went to the fire to warm herself. 'There have been so many doors open in the store tonight that I am beyond frozen.'

'What is the state of the store?' Alan asked as he gave her his armchair and sat on the floor.

Betty explained what state they'd found it in in between nibbling on a sandwich and sipping hot cocoa.

Between them the men and Maisie also updated Betty on what they'd seen.

Ruby joined them, wiping her hands on a tea towel. 'I have a theory, and don't look at me like that, Bob Jackson. Don't think I've not heard you calling me Miss Marple,' she sniffed.

'What do you know, Ruby?' Maisie asked. She was keen to get home to her children and her bed and wasn't in the mood for fairy stories.

'The Unthank family are behind this,' Ruby said, looking around her.

'You may well be right, Mum, but we need proof before Mike can do anything,' George said, running his hand through what hair was left on his head.

'Let's piece together what we do know. First, that Gloria who started in the canteen at Woolworths – she is part of this and so is the chap she met outside the store.'

'Just because she's an unpleasant woman—' Betty started to say, before Ruby raised her hand for silence.

342

'I followed them, and they live together up the prefabs at the top of the road.'

Everyone started to speak at once. 'Mum, you shouldn't have done that; you could have been harmed.'

'Let me finish, please. I spoke to Bessie, and she knows them from somewhere. When she remembered, she said it was when she used to go down West Street to meet that chap who is Jenny's father. The penny dropped and she then knew he was the same bloke who also tried to break into Woolworths that night and had a girl with him . . .'

Freda jumped to her feet in excitement. 'Gloria has a nasty cut on her arm that could have come from that evening. It was a clean cut as if it had been caused by a knife, or perhaps a shard of glass. She gave me some cock and bull story about a family conflict, but I wasn't so sure she was telling the truth. She also knew where the outside door key to the stockroom was kept and could have slipped in at any time.'

Ruby nodded her head in agreement. 'When I was following the couple, I overheard them talking about Woolworths and the details of today's trip. It can't all be a big coincidence.'

'But why would they do it?' David Carlisle asked.

'Because all of us were there on the day our Freda and Tony were married and several of the Unthanks died in the riverboat accident,' Maureen said, shaking her head.

'And that was after the father had been arrested and he has since died in prison . . .' Alan said.

David shook his head, horrified at what he was hearing. 'Would they do that?'

'They hate us all and wanted to cause us as much trouble

343

as possible. Next time it could be worse,' Alan said, causing them to gasp in horror.

'I thought the same,' Ruby agreed. 'We need to hand this information over to Mike and let him do what he can to bring them down otherwise we will be looking over our shoulders for a very long time.'

'Bugger,' Maisie exclaimed.

30

On Christmas Eve, Mike Jackson walked into the public bar of the Prince of Wales pub. For once he wasn't on duty; he'd drawn the lucky straw this year. Spotting David Carlisle, he walked over and wished him a happy Christmas. 'How did the pantomime go this afternoon?'

David laughed. 'Pure mayhem, but the children loved it. The stars of the show were Alan and Claudette. The pair of them should seriously consider turning professional.'

Mike smiled at the suggestion. 'I must say, it was a good idea to have a performance just for the children to watch as they'd have been far too excited to concentrate for long this evening. Our kids went out like a light as soon as their heads hit the pillows. Ruby's sitting with them, but I doubt they will wake before we get home.'

'Lucky you. Our younger kids were still full of energy when we came out. I shall have to give Mrs Ince double pay just to keep them under control. Who'd have children, eh?'

'I don't know, I'd rather look after mine than a cell full of Unthanks,' he said, giving David a wink before looking around him to make sure he wasn't being overheard. 'We rounded them all up yesterday afternoon.'

David shook his hand. 'That's a job well done. You must be pleased?'

'I am. It's a feather in the cap for Erith nick. My one concern is that they will target our family and friends in years to come, but we will face that when and if it happens.'

David waved to the barmaid to fill their glasses. 'What I don't understand is why they did it?'

Mike gave a wry smile. 'Frederick Nigel Unthank, aka Freddie, was the youngest child in the family and bitter that his father had been taken from him. His attitude when we nicked him was as if no one had ever lost a parent before.'

'I've seen this when we have family come to arrange a funeral. Grief affects people in so many ways. What about Gloria?'

'She was also an Unthank by marriage, although these days she is a young widow.'

'Don't tell me she was the wife of one of the brothers who perished in the Thames the day of Freda and Tony's wedding?'

'Spot on and now she seems to have hooked up with Freddie. Perhaps once locked up for a while they will contemplate who was truly to blame for those deaths.'

'We can only hope so. Can I tell the family?'

'Be my guest, but for now we'd best go into the hall as it sounds like the pantomime is about to begin.'

*

'Are you comfortable, dear?' Maureen asked as Sarah wriggled on her seat. 'I could try to find you a cushion. This hall is fine to sit in for wedding receptions when we can get up and stretch our limbs, but a couple of hours is going to be testing for many of us,' she said as she looked around the room that held memories of many happy and some sad events in their lives. The small stage at one end of the room was where she'd sat at a piano and entertained family singing alongside her son at weddings. The dark wood and cream-painted walls needed refreshing, but no one cared about that as they were happy the show would go ahead.

'I'll be fine, thank you. I just want to hear my Alan sing then I may go home,' Sarah winced.

Maureen reached out to hold her hand as the lights went down and Cinders appeared on the stage in her ragged dress. On the other side of her, George was oblivious to the fact his third grandchild was on the way.

The audience laughed at the interaction between Cinderella and Buttons and all the time Sarah stared ahead biting her lip. Maureen knew that Buttons' solo song was further on in the panto; would Sarah be able to hang on to hear him? Maureen doubted it and leant closer to her to speak. 'My dear, I reckon we should take you up to the Hainault. There was talk of another performance in the new year, so you can hear Alan sing then. I'll leave a message for him to be told when he comes off stage.'

'No!' Sarah said out loud, causing those close by to look at her for a moment before turning back to the stage as the Ugly Sisters appeared. 'Don't tell him or he will want to come with me and that will be the end of the performance – there's no understudy.'

Maureen felt she had no choice and helped Sarah ease herself from her seat. She had to nudge George to follow them as he was busy guffawing at the antics of young children dressed as mice. Thankfully they were sitting at the end of a row and in the darkness weren't observed by the other members of the family.

They took the side door and once in the cold night Sarah took a big gulp of air. 'It is definitely on its way,' she said calmly. 'Sorry you are going to miss the show, Dad.'

George led the women to the car that was parked nearby, and they were soon on their way, the Hainault Maternity Hospital being only a five-minute drive away.

Maureen hurried in to warn the staff, while George held his daughter's arm as she walked slowly towards the entrance until a porter arrived with a wheelchair and whisked her away. Her last words to George were to ask him to collect her small suitcase from home and not to tell Alan until the show was over.

When George returned, he met Maureen in the waiting room. The Hainault, as it was affectionately known, was once a grand Victorian private residence before being purchased by the local council and turned into a place where local mothers could have their children. The room was sparsely furnished with a few Bentwood chairs, two armchairs that has seen better days and a table scattered with magazines and pamphlets for expectant families. George rubbed his hands together to try to warm them, wishing the iron fireplace hadn't been boarded up. 'How is it going?'

'I've just spoken to a midwife. She is quite a way gone and the baby will be here shortly.'

'That quick?'

'It's her third birth so the baby won't hang about if there isn't anything wrong. I'd not want her to go through what she did when she had Buster as that was touch and go.'

George gulped. 'But our Georgie came quick, didn't she, and she was Sarah's first?'

'Darling, she was born in an Anderson shelter in your mum's back garden during an air raid. She knew she was in labour before that raid but didn't want to make a fuss. This time I'd like to have had a Christmas Day grandchild, but a Christmas Eve one is just as precious, apart from poor Sarah having to miss Christmas at home.'

'I've heard it can be very nice here and in the cottage hospital at Christmas,' he said, ignoring the few paper chains hanging from the ceiling until he saw Maureen's waspish glare. 'What do you want me to do?'

'Let's just sit patiently and wait. Give it another half an hour in case the show has run over then you can drive down to the Prince of Wales and let Alan know. You can tell him that Sarah so wanted to hear him sing but couldn't hold on another moment longer.'

George agreed and settled down to read his newspaper, jumping each time he heard footsteps. 'Thank goodness I only went through this once,' he said, wiping sweat from his brow. 'That was bad enough.'

Maureen shook her head and said nothing.

The minutes clicked by until the door swung open, and a masked midwife appeared. She pulled the mask from her face and smiled. 'Mr Gilbert?'

'My son isn't here yet, he is performing in a pantomime. We are the grandparents,' Maureen explained. 'How is Sarah?'

'Sarah did very well. She is tired but happy now her daughter is with us.'

Maureen wiped her eyes while George jumped from his seat and kissed Maureen. 'Can I go and collect Alan?'

'Yes, you can, but drive carefully or you will be spending Christmas in the cottage hospital,' she told him. 'Nurse, may I see Sarah?'

'You can peep in, but she is likely sleeping, so try not to disturb her. She is just being taken to the ward and I don't want the other mother disturbed.'

'Another Christmas Eve baby?'

'Yes, and this one is a first-time mother, and she is exhausted and needs her sleep.' She checked her watch pinned to her uniform. 'It is long past visiting hours so perhaps Father could visit tomorrow?'

'Alan will be disappointed, but you are right. I'll just peep around the door so I can tell him all is well,' she said as she followed the nurse down a corridor carrying Sarah's small case; she would be grateful for her own things in the morning. The nurse pushed open the door and Maureen caught her breath. There was Sarah looking pink-cheeked, but perfectly happy. She lifted a hand to wave to Maureen. Maureen blew a kiss back.

Thanking the nurse and handing her Sarah's case, she walked outside into the clear night air. Looking up, she felt that Sarah's late mother, Irene, was very close. 'Your girl did well, Irene,' she whispered as George's car pulled up in front of the doors and Alan jumped out still in his elaborate costume complete with lace ruffs and a satin jacket from the final scene, his face heavily made up.

'How is she?' he asked, looking towards the doors. 'I should have been here. I'll never forgive myself.'

Maureen caught hold of her son and hugged him close before letting him go. 'You would only have been able to sit in the waiting room, so it was best for you to be entertaining the audience and making people happy. You will see them both tomorrow, and tomorrow will be here soon enough. Time to go home and get some sleep,' she said, taking his arm to lead him to the car. 'You know, she held on as long as possible as she wanted to hear you sing.'

Alan bowed his head, looking ashamed. 'I don't sing to her very often these days. I'm always too busy.'

'There will be other days and many songs to sing to Sarah and your three children.'

Alan smiled. 'Three children . . . That's something to be proud of. Georgina, Alan and Carol.'

'Carol is such a sweet name and so festive,' George said, shaking his hand.

Alan turned to his mum. 'I can't go home until I've sung to her. Where is her window?'

She pointed. 'Down the side of the building on the left.'

Alan looked up at the two-storey building before running to where Maureen had pointed and taking a deep breath. '*Drink, drink drink! To eyes that are bright as stars when they're shining on me . . .*'

George looked to Maureen. 'We have to stop him before someone complains,' he said, backing away towards his car that was parked in front of large double doors before Maureen grabbed his sleeve.

'*Here's a hope that those bright eyes will shine. Lovingly, longingly, soon into mine . . .!*'

'He will wake up all the babies,' George hissed, wiping his sweating brow as he looked around in panic.

'There's only Sarah and one other mum in there. Let him be,' Maureen urged him as she looked at her son singing his heart out in front of the grand house.

351

'*May those lips that are red and sweet tonight with joy my own lips meet . . . !*'

Maureen was openly sobbing as Alan finished the sweet words of Sarah's favourite song just as a round of applause could be heard from inside the maternity home and the church bells rang in Christmas Day.

George cuffed away his own tears and hugged Maureen. 'A Christmas baby. Nothing could be more perfect.'

Acknowledgements

We often hear that writing is a solitary career as we labour away at our keyboards – or, as I like to think, huddled over a single candle in our attics! However, neither perception could be further from the truth. When we step into the professional fiction writing world, we are enveloped with love from fellow writers and the many associations we join. My thanks go out to my writing friends, as well as to the board/committees of the Society of Women Writers and Journalists and the Romantic Novelists' Association. The support and companionship from these organizations are legendary.

I feel rather like the Pied Piper of Hamelin when I mention the followers of my books and writing. Be it on Facebook, through my newsletters or in person at my talks, I value your support so much; you wouldn't believe how one kind message can boost my spirits. Thank you all, from the bottom of my heart.

A special thank you to my literary agent, Caroline Sheldon, who has buoyed me and kept me focused when the going gets tough and I go into meltdown. Thank you, Caroline.

The team at Pan Macmillan deserve a special thank you for producing my books and getting them onto shelves, especially when there are so many wonderful books competing for space.

I must mention the lovely Wayne Brookes, who was my editor until recently. Good luck for your future endeavours, Wayne.

I cannot sign off without paying respect to our wonderful librarians who not only support authors, but also bring books to readers who may not be able to purchase their own copies. For me, the Central Library in Bexleyheath, Kent, shines, as they always wave the flag for my books and organize events for me to meet and chat with readers in the area where most of my books are set.

Last, but by no means least, a big thank you to my husband, Michael, for always supporting me. Also, our dog, Henry, our constant companion. What would I do without you both?

Thank you all!

A Letter from Elaine

Dear readers,

How are you? Did you enjoy reading my latest book about the girls from Woolworths? To think we first met them in 1938 and they are still with us fifteen years later; so much has changed in their lives during that time.

What was special for me in this book was that we reached Christmas 1953, when I was born at the very same hospital mentioned, the Hainault Maternity Home in Erith, on Christmas Eve. Yes, that was my mum in the final chapter of the book . . .

Within my close family and circle of friends, there has been too much illness since I last wrote to you. I'm sending love to them all (naming no names) and I hope that if you or your loved ones are poorly you will soon see brighter days.

As I write this letter, I am working on a new Woolworths story for 2025. Although it is a departure from the Erith store, rest assured that some of the usual girls will make an appearance. It has been an interesting book to write and it came about after I attended a guided talk through Hall Place in Crayford, Kent, when we were told of the American soldiers who were involved in top secret work connected to Bletchley. I was shown a bridal gown, belonging to a local girl who married one of these soldiers, and at once a story started to weave through my head. I said to my husband that if I could link it to Woolworths then it would be written. I could – so please look out for *Far Horizons for the Woolworths Girls*.

Wishing you a very peaceful Christmas.

With love,

Elaine xx

Keep in Touch

I love to hear from readers and there are many ways you can follow me and contact me to chat, as well as enter competitions.

X (formerly Twitter):
Find me @ElaineEverest

Facebook author page:
Come and chat and hear my news on Facebook.
www.facebook.com/ElaineEverestAuthor

Instagram:
I have an account on Instagram, so why not find me and say hello?
www.instagram.com/elaine.everest

Website:
This is where you can not only read about me and all my books, but also read my blog posts, where I write about my life and everything to do with my books.
Go to www.elaineeverest.com

My newsletter:
Sign up to receive a copy of my monthly newsletter, where I give you the latest news about my books and also run some fab competitions. In the past, there have been competitions to win a sewing machine, a leather handbag, hampers, jewellery and signed copies of my books. You will find the link to sign up on my website:
www.elaineeverest.com